Barefoot Billionaire

Sue Langford

To my friends, my family,
my cheering squad and my inspiration

"There are few things as powerful as the joy of someone who got a second chance and found their purpose."

Kim Reynolds

Sue Langford

Chapter 1

"Are you still talking to him or not?"

"He messaged me Emerson." Lily got up and walked out of the main ensuite and walked downstairs. She got her laptop and walked outside, sitting down on the chaise. She opened her laptop and when she saw a shadow over her head, she shook her head.

"We're talking," Emerson said.

"I'm good," Lily replied.

He closed her laptop and slid it onto the table. "Tell me what's going on."

"Emerson, he's been texting since last night."

He took her phone and walked in the house, putting it on the counter of his security guy's desk. "No more calls from him."

He walked outside and saw Lily walking in the water. He walked down to her and Lily shook her head, walking the other way. She made her way down the shoreline, trying to avoid the conversation that Emerson was determined to have.

"Lily."

She kept walking, making her way past that author's beach house and saw nobody.

"Would you stop ignoring me and walking off?" She kept walking. "Lily, at least talk to me." She shook her head and turned and walked the opposite way. "Lily."

"Are you seriously gonna tell me who I can and can't talk to? Really Emerson?"

He walked closer to her and she walked off. "Lily." She shook her head and kept going. He followed her and tried his best to get her to come closer but she walked out deeper.

"Lily, you're being ridiculous."

"I got the house."

"Lily," he said almost nervous.

"I wanted my own place Emerson. Now I can."

He walked out to her and picked her up. "You're not leaving Lily."

"Says who? You? Tell me what the truth is. Tell me why you would even think to do what you did."

"Lily."

"Three?"

He kissed her and pulled her tight to him. "It took a lifetime to find what I always wanted you and I to have Lily. Life started over when we saw each other on the beach."

"I bet it did for you." She managed to get him to let go as her feet splashed back into the water. She walked off and he stood there completely stunned.

Lily got back to the house, got her laptop, and walked into the security office. "Where's my phone?"

"He asked…"

"Did you," Lily asked.

"I was about to."

Lily took the phone back and walked upstairs, throwing her things in the bag when she heard the door close and lock behind her.

"You aren't leaving."

"Really? Why?"

"Because you aren't." He came up behind her and turned her to face him.

"What do you want?" He kissed her.

"What do you want," Lily asked again.

"You aren't leaving Lily. Not because of a stupid text message from him." She broke out of his arms and went to walk out when he stopped her. "Not happening."

"Emerson, if you're playing a damn game then I give up. You win. Happy now?" She pulled away and walked out to the balcony, trying to get air before she cried.

"Baby, please. You know that I wouldn't ever do that to you. This whole thing is just him starting a damn problem. We both know that. He's been starting problems since we got together."

"Emerson."

He shook his head leaning against the frame of the door to the balcony. "What?"

"I can't do this."

"Lily, the more he pushes and tries to throw you off of what we have, the more he wins. He's not a good person. Never has been. Just come inside." She shook her head, brushing tears away. "Lily, I promised you a long time ago that you were the only one. You are. I promise you that you are. I don't want anyone else. Since the day I kissed you that first time, there wasn't anyone else. There still isn't." Lily shook her head. She was almost worried that he was just saying it. "I haven't left your side since we saw each other again. Not unless you made me go to work in the office. Come here." She shook her head again.

"Emerson, I got the house. I'm fine with that. I can get..."

He walked over to her and turned her to face him as he saw the tears in her eyes. "You're not leaving me."

"I'm going and staying at my own house. We can date or something," she said as he shook his head.

One finger of his slid to her chin, raising her gaze to meet his. "We're engaged Lily. I don't want to date. I just want you. That's it. Just you. I love you Lily. Why are you so dang worried that his stupid texts could be right?"

"Because I don't want to have any worries that they are. I just want to trust something Emerson. Anything. I need to know that it's not gonna blow up in my face."

He kissed her, devouring her lips. He picked her up and carried her back into the bedroom, leaning her onto the bed. "Why are you so dang convinced that I'm not gonna be honest with you?"

"Because I don't think you are."

He shook his head and kissed her again. "Lily, look at me and tell me that you don't trust me." When she looked up at him, she shook her head. "You can't even look me in the eye and say it. You know that the crap he said was just a big ole lie to get your attention right?"

Lily shook her head. She tried to slip out of his arms and he wouldn't let her go. "Tell me what you want me to say Lily. Just say it."

She shook her head and tried again to slide out of his arms. "Emerson, just stop."

He kissed her. She broke out of his arms and walked back outside. She sat down on the chair and relaxed. "Tell me what I have to do then."

"Let go."

He shook his head. "I can't do that." Lily shook her head and went to leave the room. "Lily, please."

"Emerson, did you actually think that someone would believe that you didn't date three women at once?"

"I didn't. One date isn't dating. Let them think what they want to. I didn't do any of that." Lily looked at him with a look that told him that she didn't believe a single word he said. "The question is, why do you believe that lying conniving idiot over your own fiancée."

Lily shook her head. "I need to go."

"No."

"Emerson, I wasn't asking."

"You aren't leaving." She shook her head again and looked at him. "Answer me."

"Because I don't know who to believe. I don't want to be…"

He kissed her. "Be what?"

"Be in a position to lose everything. I can't just marry you knowing that you aren't to be trusted."

Emerson shook his head. "The truth? I dated. I didn't exactly see a future with anyone. When I saw you, I wanted one. I knew the minute I kissed you. There is nobody else Lily. There's nobody else that I even care that much about. I'd pass up the stupid parties with my mom's snooty friends in a heartbeat. I just want you in my life. That's why I proposed. That's what that ring means. It means forever."

She shook her head. "I need to go."

"No."

"Emerson, you aren't gonna keep me locked up in this room. I have work to do."

"So do I. I'm not gonna stand here and watch you leave."

She unlocked the door and walked downstairs. She grabbed her laptop, walked outside, and put it on the table. She peeled her shorts and tank off and walked out to the water, diving in, or at least what felt like diving.

At least she could relax in the water. It was peaceful. It was stress-free. It was warm. When she saw dolphins jump not 5 feet away, she smirked. She heard splashing a few minutes later and felt arms slide around her waist. When she turned, she was face to face with Emerson. "Can't give me five dang minutes alone."

"Lily, did you not see how far out you are?"

When she looked, she shook her head. "And?"

"Are you attempting to swim to Sullivan's Island or something?"

She dunked him and made her way back to shallower water. When she got back to the sand, she grabbed a towel that he'd brought out and sat on the sand.

"Seriously? Dunking me in the ocean?"

Lily shook her head. "I said leave me alone."

"And I said that I wasn't doing that." He went and got another towel, laid it out beside hers and handed Lily her laptop.

"Emerson, leave me alone."

"No. Lily, we're getting married. We're engaged. Nothing is gonna change that right now."

"And if I handed you back..."

"Don't even go there. If you're that convinced that he's right, what can I say that will fix this?"

Lily shook her head, got up, grabbed her laptop, and went back into the beach house. She put her things together and went and got dressed. She slid into her sundress, got her bag, handed it to his security and walked downstairs. "Babe, did you want to sit outside for lunch," Emerson asked. Lily made sure she had everything and left with his security.

"Where are we headed Miss Lily," his driver asked.

"The house. I don't want a word to him either."

Lily got 10 minutes down the road and her phone went off. She ignored the call from Emerson. Not 5 minutes later, she got a call from Zack. She ignored that one too and opened the window, feeling the breeze. She needed space. A lot of it. She got to the house and had barely any time to make sense of anything. She walked upstairs, grabbed some more clothes, grabbing her other suitcase and put a few things in it. When she heard the front door close and footsteps getting closer, she shook her head.

"Lily," Emerson said as he saw her.

"What," she asked.

"Where are you going?"

"I need to clear my head. Away from you." He came up behind her and slid his arms around her waist.

"Babe."

"Don't babe me Emerson."

He shook his head. "Tell me what you need me to do."

"Emerson, leave it alone."

"I dated. There were no promises and definitely no proposals. I don't know what you want me to say Lily."

"I need to clear my head alone Emerson. Not just for an hour or two. Just let me go."

"I can't do that."

"Emerson."

He knew that if he left her at the beach house, Zack would show. If she went to a hotel, she wasn't safe. No matter what way it worked, he would lose her all over again.

"What if I go and stay at the beach house and you can stay here on your own for a few days. You tell me when you want me to come back here."

"Emerson."

He kissed her neck. "Please."

"Emerson, I need to know. I need to know deep down that you wouldn't even think of doing that to me. I can't just marry…"

He kissed her shoulder and turned her to face him. "I want you and me. I want to forget the stupid past. What's wrong with that?"

"Emerson, tell me that you weren't doing that. Tell me that there weren't three women at a dang time."

"Lily, I dated. I never found the right one. I didn't until I saw you on the beach. Please don't leave."

She shook her head. "I can't make a damn decision without 3 people contradicting everything I think. You, Zack, Addy. I need to go and be away from all of it."

"Baby."

"Emerson, just stop."

He kissed her. "I love you Lily. You want to get a house, fine. You want to get space, fine. Just please don't leave." She shook her head. He hugged her, holding on for dear life. "Please," he asked.

"I can't…"

He kissed her. They touched foreheads and he saw the tears welling in her eyes. "Baby, please. I get it. He's put doubt in your head. All I want is a chance to make this right. I just want you my love. You." She shook her head and he kissed her again. "Baby."

Lily shook her head. "Emerson, I can't."

"I love you. I always will. Please love."

Lily shook her head and he kissed her again. "What do you want me to say Emerson? Pretend that I didn't hear it?"

"Trust me. The one and only thing I could ever want is for you to actually trust me for once."

"Emerson."

He kissed her. "Don't go. I can stay at the beach. I just want you to be alright."

"Emerson, I need space."

"Tell me what you want me to do. I'll do anything."

"Breathe. I can't do anything right now."

He kissed her. "Tell me where you want me to be Lily. I want to be here with you. Anywhere. Baby, please," he asked.

"All I see is you with..."

He kissed her, picked her up and leaned her onto the bed, curling up with her.

"Emerson."

He kissed her again. "What," he asked.

"I can't do this. I can't be in the middle of a fight between the two of you."

He kissed her again, devouring her lips. "All you have to do is tell me what you want me to do. If I have to kick his backside into a pile of pythons I will. Just tell me."

She shook her head. "I need space."

"Then we go somewhere."

"Emerson." He kissed her again and devoured her lips.

"I'll handle it. Stay here. Do whatever you want. Stay in bed, come out to the beach. Just don't leave." He kissed her again and snuggled her to him as they curled up together on the bed.

"Tell me what he said."

Lily shook her head. "Emerson, I can't."

"Say it." He kissed her. She told him all of it. She knew the more she told him, the more he'd be irritated. The more he'd want to whoop Zack into a pile of sharks.

"Emerson."

He kissed her. "I love you. I've loved you since I first met you."

"Emerson."

"Yes I want to kick his butt. No, I won't do it with you watching either."

"Emerson, don't."

He kissed her. "I want us to have the wedding. It'll finish all of the drama. There won't be any more worrying or second-guessing. What do you think," he asked.

"Emerson."

"Right after Valentine's Day."

"You're talking crazy. You know that right?" He kissed her again.

By the time it got to dinner, they were curled up together in bed and the housekeeper was making fresh seafood for them.

"Emerson."

He kissed her. "Come. We can have our seafood then we can figure all of this stuff out."

"Emerson."

He kissed her again. "No more stress. I promise you."

They came downstairs and it's like everyone had vanished. "Where is everyone?"

"I wanted alone time. I want you happy. Your favorite seafood, then you can decide where you want to go. I'll stay at the other house if that's what you want. All you have to do is say it," Emerson said.

"Emerson, it has nothing to do with that. I need to be away from it. I get that you're irritated with him, but he's at least being…"

"Don't even say it. He isn't. He's not being honest."

"Really? This coming from the guy who was with three…"

He kissed her. "Nope. I told you."

Lily shook her head. "Whatever you say."

"What would it take to prove it?"

Lily almost rolled her eyes. He didn't get it at all. They finished dinner and Lily went to clear the dishes when his housekeeper came and got them, refilling their wine. "Lily."

"Don't." Lily took her wine and sat down, sliding her shoes off and slipping her feet into the cool saltwater of the pool.

"Lily." She shook her head.

"Don't start Emerson. Just don't. I get it. You want to go whoop his butt because he ruined what we've done. He ruined the chance. That's not gonna fix anything and you know it."

"Me punting him all the way to the moon would be a ball of fun," he said sarcastically as he sipped his wine. "Lily, you have to see it from my point of view. We're finally alright and he shows up and ruins everything all over again. Babe, the man is incapable of doing anything good. He's threatened both of us to get his way. When he gets the deal we made changed, then he comes after you. How is that supposed to be right?"

Lily had her wine. She wasn't going to say anything. She just needed to breathe. She needed more wine, and she needed space. He refilled her glass. "Thank you."

"Baby."

She shook her head. "You two go ahead and throw punches and do whatever you want. I'm still making my own decision."

He kissed her shoulder. "I just want you. We can have the wedding in the spring. Whenever you want to. I just want you to be happy. I want to have a family with you. He's determined to ruin everything. He's probably just jealous." Lily shook her head and sipped on her wine. "Baby, say something."

"I'm not playing the game Emerson. Do whatever you want. I'm not planning a wedding. I'm not ready to. Not after..."

He kissed her. "Come here for a sec," he said as he smirked.

"Emerson, cut…" He kissed her again and slid her into his lap. "Emerson, stop." She grabbed her glass and got up.

"Lily."

"Why are you so dang determined to get me in bed when I said I was upset?"

"Because I don't think he deserves any more of our time," Emerson said.

Lily shook her head and walked inside, getting another glass of wine. She walked upstairs, went into the bedroom, and slid into her satin nightgown and slid her hoodie overtop. She grabbed her laptop and sat down in the chair to get more writing in and a little editing. She sipped on her wine and when she heard him coming up the steps, she shook her head.

When he saw her, he smirked. He went and got changed, getting freshened up and ready for bed. When he walked back into the bedroom, she was sitting on the balcony. He walked out there and saw her on the chair. "Baby, come in here."

"No."

She kept going and he closed her laptop, putting it on the counter, then picked her up and brought her in, sitting her on the bed. "Emerson, stop treating me like a child."

"Talk to me."

"What part of alone didn't you get?"

He kissed her. "The part where I don't want us to be apart."

"Then let me go to the beach house on my own."

"Not when he pulled that."

Lily shook her head. "You realize that I can handle..."

He kissed her. "I know you could. I also know you could toss him into the dang ocean if you wanted to. I love you baby. I can't just pretend that he will go away and not start more problems."

"Emerson, I'm an adult."

He kissed her. "I know. I trust you with everything I have and with my heart, but I don't trust him. I know you don't want security either. I don't want him near you."

Lily shook her head. "I know Emerson. Just let me have some space."

He nodded. "You gonna let me sleep with you tonight," he teased.

"Same bed, fine. I just need space to breathe."

He kissed her neck and sat down beside her. "Tell me what you need."

"Space. Alone."

He nodded. "If you come out to the beach house, will you let me stay at night with you," he asked.

"No. Emerson, I need time to think."

"A week."

She shook her head. "If I decide to come back to the house, you'll know. Does that work?"

"Too long."

She shook her head and he linked their hands. "A couple days?"

"Emerson." He kissed her.

He was petrified that he'd lose her. More than petrified. If Zack had his way, he'd lose Lily altogether all over again. He couldn't let that happen. Not now. He made a decision right then and there. He was finding the perfect place for them to have their wedding.

"What," Lily said as she looked at him.

"You have space. I'll prove that his story was bull. Then we can plan out a wedding."

"Emerson, you're being ridiculous." He kissed her again and stood up, taking her hand.

"What are you doing?" He kissed her and flipped music on. "Emerson." He kissed her again and they danced in the bedroom.

"What?"

He kissed her again and snuggled her close to him as they danced to all of the ballads that he loved.

"Emerson."

He kissed her forehead. "Fiancée." He looked at her. "Forever and ever," he replied.

"I know. I just need time. That's all."

He kissed her. "I know," he said. "Doesn't make it any easier."

Lily looked at him. "I'm not losing you baby. I don't care how long it takes."

"I know. Emerson, it's just space. It's not separating or anything."

He kissed her, devouring her lips. "Good, because I don't think that I could handle it if we were. I'd be a driveling mess."

She shook her head. "Emerson, I love you, but I need to know that it's not actually real. That what he said wasn't the truth. You can say whatever you want to, but it doesn't change what happened."

He kissed her again. "Tell me what you want me to do. Do you want me to get them to talk to you?"

Lily looked at him. "I need to know for myself."

He kissed her again. "Then I'll get it done so you can talk to them yourself." He picked her up, sliding her legs around his hips and leaned her onto the bed, hitching up the hem of her nightgown. He slid the hoodie off, throwing it to the chair and devoured her lips. He didn't want to let go for even a split second.

He made love to her. That feeling that he'd had the first time they were together felt like a pile of ash compared to how hot things were at that exact moment. He curled her up with him among the blankets and when they managed to come up for air, he curled his arms around her and snuggled her to him.

"Emerson, promise me something."

"What? Anything."

"Were there really three?"

"A date or two. Nothing else. I didn't sleep with them. I just couldn't. I knew it wasn't what I wanted. I dated since high school, but I couldn't get serious with anyone. Not when I knew that you were the only woman I wanted."

"And if I'd said no?"

"I would've kept asking until you said yes." He kissed her forehead. "I just want you happy baby. That's all I could ever want." She rested her head on his chest and nodded off in his arms. "I love you Lily."

"Love you more."

He smirked and snuggled in closer. When his security knocked quietly, he motioned for them to come in as one of them went and closed the balcony door.

"What's up," Emerson asked quietly so she wouldn't wake up.

"That text happened again and there's someone at the door."

He shook his head. "I'm not getting up."

"I appreciate that, but she's not leaving."

Emerson shook his head. "10 minutes."

They nodded, quietly exiting the room, and Emerson went to get up.

"Where are you going?"

"Just grabbing something from downstairs. I'll be right back up."

Lily shook her head. She got up, slid her robe on and asked him what he needed. "Lily."

"Truth."

"One of the three showed. I'll handle it."

She shook her head. "If I'm getting the truth, it…"

He kissed her. "Not tonight you aren't." He kissed her again and went and slid his jeans and a hoodie on. When she went to head down the steps, he tried to grab her hand and she kept walking.

He ran down the steps, took her hand and walked with her into the den. "Samantha, what did you need," Emerson asked as he sat down and took Lily's hand.

The bleach blonde was gorgeous and looked like she'd got a ton of frequent flier points to a plastic surgeon. Lily could see how Emerson would love being with her. She was completely his type even if he'd never admit it to her.

"So, this is her," Samantha said looking Lily up and down and not being impressed, looking down on her and almost laughing at her.

"My fiancée thank you," he replied.

"Why couldn't you just give what we had a chance?"

"Two dates and you were starting to google my net worth, and don't bother denying it," he said.

"I just don't understand," Samantha said.

"We broke up over a month ago. You showed at the party because you heard I was coming with someone. Did you think that running to Zack to try and break Lily and I up was a good idea," Emerson asked.

"I miss you."

He could feel Lily trying to pull away and he held on tighter. "I'm not changing my mind. This woman right here is the one I've loved since I was a teen. I love her. I always will. I'm not letting her go because you're lonely. Find someone else."

"Emerson."

"Go," he replied.

"You sure? I mean, handling you on her own might be a little much," Samantha said.

Emerson could feel Lily about ready to clock her. "i'm good. That's where the ring comes in. Superpowers," Lily replied sarcastically as Samantha looked at her and saw the ring. The ring that was almost too much, but he thought was just enough. The emerald cut, the halo, the heart side diamonds, the platinum band. Samantha was past jealous.

"I can't change your mind," Samantha asked.

Emerson shook his head. "Not in a billion years," he said.

Samantha finally left and Lily headed upstairs with the satin robe flowing behind her. She went into the bedroom, slid on one of his t-shirts and slid into bed, flipping the light off. She was livid. When he came in the bedroom, he kicked his jeans off, closed the bedroom door. And pulled the hoodie off, throwing it on the chair with hers, and slid into bed. "Baby, come here." She wouldn't move. He slid his arm around her and she pushed him away. "Lily."

He kissed her shoulder. "Come curl back up with me."

"No."

He shook his head and slid an arm around her waist, sliding her closer to him. "Lily, come here. Please." She pushed him away and went back to sleep on her side of the bed. He kissed her shoulder and curled up behind her.

When Emerson woke up the next morning, a note was in her place:

> *I'm going to the beach house alone. Security is determined to follow me. Just leave me be for a couple days. When you claimed you were getting a drink is when I knew. You lied to me even then.*

He shook his head, got up and saw her bags gone, half of her clothes gone and all of her toiletries missing from the counter. He pulled his workout shorts on and walked downstairs. "Good morning," his housekeeper said.

"Who's with her at the beach house?"

"Carlisle. I sent over some fresh seafood and steaks. I thought I could go over and get her dinner together for her until she's back here or you're out there."

"She's mad."

"I noticed this morning. You slept in."

Emerson nodded, still mad. "I'm going to get a workout in before I have to start trying to think of what to do."

"I did make one small purchase," his housekeeper said.

"Which was?"

"Extra wine that we had here and red roses. The roses will be delivered this morning around 11," his housekeeper said.

"Thank you. I don't know that they'll help, but it's worth a try." He finished his workout and came back upstairs, shaking his head and stared at her side of the bed. She'd left in what felt like the middle of the night. He wanted to call, but he also knew that he would be pushing.

Lily pulled into the beach house and security pulled in behind her. She put her truck into the garage and went inside. "Miss Lily, there's only one request that I have. If you're gonna go out, please let me know where you're going. You want to go for a walk on the beach, just please stay away from Zack's area."

Lily nodded. "Alright," she said.

He walked her inside and she saw that everything was still pristine. "I'll take your things upstairs," his security said as Lily grabbed her laptop and sat outside on the deck. She opened it and looked out at the view. It wasn't hot outside yet, so it was perfect to get writing done.

She wrote and when she turned to get a drink, a pitcher of sweet tea was beside her with a glass. She shook her head, got a glass, and sat on the bottom step, sliding her feet into the warm sand. When she heard her cell phone, she grabbed it from her pocket and saw Emerson's name.

"Hey handsome," Lily said.

"What time did you leave," he asked.

"6:30. I did a quick workout then headed out. You were out cold. I didn't want to wake you."

"Thank you for the note at least baby. You have everything you need?"

"Emerson."

"I can come have lunch with you if you want. Just say it."

"I got writing done all morning so far. Honestly, I know you wanted me to be home with you, but I needed this."

"Lily, I get it. I just hate that we're not in the same house."

"Emerson, I get it. It's a few days. I'm not going over to his place. I'm just hanging here and getting some air and some space. That's it. I just need it to see straight."

"If you want company for a night, tell me?"

"I'll miss you too. Go get some work done," she teased determined to get away from everything.

"Fine, but I still want you."

"Back at ya fiancée," Lily said with a fake smile as she heard the smile on his face.

"I'll see you on the weekend?"

"Yep," Lily replied sarcastically as she hung up and put her phone down.

She got up and walked down to the water, letting the warm salty sea water run between her toes. She needed it. She walked a little, feeling the waves roll in and out, feeling the sand swirl around her feet and ground her into the ocean. If only she could bury that worry out there with her feet. The previous night hadn't helped anything. She had too many things swimming around her mind.

"Miss Lily," his security said.

"What's up," she replied as she came back in.

"A package arrived for you," he said. Lily grabbed her sweet tea and came inside to see 3 dozen red roses.

"What in the world," Lily said letting the sweet scent of the roses hit her. He handed Lily the card that came with them:

>   *You always have been my forever. You always will be. I love you even if you're there without me.*

Lily shook her head and sent Emerson a text:

>   *Had to go all out didn't you?*

She sent a photo of the flowers and a big thank you. She went back outside and had some more sweet tea when her phone went off again. One look and she ignored the call. Talking to Zack wasn't happening. She wrote a little more and got a text:

I need to talk to you. Where can we meet? – Zack

Chapter 2

Lily ignored him, deleting the text. She went inside with her laptop and saw Emerson's housekeeper. "I thought you'd be at the house," Lily said.

"I wanted to make sure that you had lunch. I got fresh lobster for some lobster rolls and for some lobster salad. Which would you like," she asked.

"Your choice so long as you come eat with me."

"I brought it for you. I have to get back to the house and put dinner on."

Lily shook her head. "Fine," Lily replied as she went upstairs and curled up on the chaise on the upper balcony. She curled up and relaxed, editing and writing. She had lunch and relaxed in the sunshine. Around 4, she got a text from Emerson:

> *I have a question. Do you want to put all of the stupid Zack rumors to rest? Emmie called and wanted to talk and I'm not doing it without you there. It's up to you. I love you.*

Lily looked at the text, re-reading it more than once. When her phone rang, she looked and took a deep breath.

"Hi," Lily said.

"What do you think," he asked.

"Emerson, I don't..."

"Babe."

"I don't want them near me or you for that matter."

"I know. I just want all of this stupid stuff put into a dumpster where it belongs."

"Fine. I'm not coming to the house. Somewhere that isn't here and isn't the house."

"Neutral turf?"

"Emerson, I don't want that idiot coming down the beach and getting the wrong idea. I also don't want to be in that house with another idiot woman that you used to date."

"What if we went…"

"Emerson."

"Choose wherever you want. Name it."

"I don't want her in the house Emerson."

"Back patio."

"She'd have to go through the house." Lily thought about it.

"What if we just went to the beach. Kiawah."

"Are you willing to come?"

"Emerson."

"This mean I get to take you out after?"

"This means I'm coming back here."

"We're going there together."

"Alright handsome."

"I'll see you in an hour then?"

"Fine," she said sarcastically. She hung up with him and went and slid into her sundress, slid her heels on and came downstairs to see the other security person there waiting on her.

"Fine," Lily said as she threw her keys, phone, wallet, pocketknife, and cash into her purse. She slid it over her shoulder and they headed off to get Emerson.

When they pulled back up the long driveway, Lily shook her head. They got to the front door and his security opened the door for her, helping her out of the SUV. "Why am I getting out," she asked.

He walked her into the house and Lily saw Emerson going through paperwork. "What happened," Lily asked.

"She said she was coming here or nothing."

Lily shook her head. "Outside." He nodded and took her hand. "What?"

"Follow me," he replied as he walked her upstairs. She shook her head and he walked her into the bedroom, closing the door.

"Emerson."

He kissed her and slid his arms around her. "I missed you."

"I know. It's been a long day."

He kissed her again, cradling her face in his hands. "I love you," he said.

"I love you too. Can we just get this stupid discussion with her overwith?"

He kissed her again and nodded. "Nice dress by the way."

"What?"

"First time you let me take you on an actual date."

"Emerson."

"I know. I just want you included so it's not behind your back or I'm doing this without you."

"I get it. I just need time to process it."

He slid his arms around her and kissed her shoulder, then her neck. His cologne was intoxicating. He was almost too sexy. He was in beat up jeans and a dress shirt. The one that she'd worn a million times when she went outside to get air when he was sleeping.

"What," he asked.

"Nothin," Lily said as she shook her head and went to walk downstairs. He pulled her back into his arms and kissed her.

"What's wrong?"

"You know what," Lily said.

He picked her up and kissed her.

"I want you to stay, but I know you're going to the beach house."

"Emerson, put me down." He kissed her again, devouring her lips until he heard the buzz of the gate. She slid to her feet and brushed her lipstick from his lips.

"I love you. Don't forget that."

"Emerson, what is she gonna say that you're that worried about?" He kissed her and snuggled her to him.

"Promise me that you won't take off."

Lily shook her head.

She went to walk out of the bedroom. "Babe."

She shook her head, went and touched up her lipstick and they walked downstairs. He got Lily a glass of wine, handing it to her when Lily shook her head. He poured another for himself and sat down beside her, sliding an arm around her.

The last time they'd had a conversation like this, she'd wanted to leave. She was even more determined to stay away at that moment. She had a sip of the wine and he kissed her shoulder. "I love you. You know that right?"

Lily nodded. She was too quiet. Way too quiet for his liking. When Emmie walked in, Lily was pissed. She was the equivalent of a dang runway model.

"Emmie," Emerson said. When Emmie went to give Emerson a hug, Lily got up.

"Oh."

"Whatever you need to say, just say it. This is my fiancée, Lily," he said.

"Hi," Emmie said as Lily sat down and had a sip of her wine.

His arm slid around Lily's waist. "Go ahead," Emerson said.

"I thought we were gonna be together. We had two perfect dates and..."

"I told you then, and I can say it again. I didn't want a relationship with you. After two dates, I knew you wanted the attention and the notoriety. You didn't want me. You wanted the house and the plane and the cars. I wanted someone who loved me for me. That wasn't you. It never was gonna be you. Lily was the one I wanted. Hell, I even told you about her when we went on that second date when I called it off," Emerson said as Lily had another gulp of wine.

"I just thought that we could try and make it work," Emmie said.

"It wasn't worth fighting to hold onto," Emerson said.

"Did you talk to Zack Fairchild about Emerson," Lily asked.

"He's my boyfriend," Emmie replied.

"Then keep Emerson's name out of your mouth from now on. Understood," Lily asked as coldly as possible. Emmie nodded. Lily was mad. Way past mad.

"You need to leave it be Emmie. Just go and get on with your life," Emerson said. Emmie nodded and left a few minutes later.

As soon as Emmie was out the door, Lily finished her wine, got up and put the glass in the sink and went to leave. "Lily."

"I'm going."

"Babe, please." He grabbed her hand and she pulled away.

"Emerson, I'm going back to the beach house."

"Dinner."

"I'll get something," Lily said as she went to walk out. He stopped her and picked her up, carrying her upstairs to their bedroom. "Emerson, put me down." He walked into the bedroom and closed the door, sitting her on the bed.

"Please."

"Emerson, I'm so over…" He kissed her. "Emerson."

He kissed her again, leaned to his knees and wrapped his arms around her waist. "Please don't leave."

"Emerson, I told you that once this was over, I was going back to the beach house. I still am."

He kissed her. "Stay and have dinner."

She shook her head. "Emerson, I need to breathe."

He kissed her again, devouring her lips. "Please." He looked at her.

"I need to go," Lily said.

He shook his head. "I can't lose you."

She went to get up and he picked her up, leaning her back onto the bed. "What do you want me to do Emerson? I told you that once we…"

He kissed her again. "Dinner."

"Then I'm going back on my own."

"I'll come with you and we can have dinner there." She shook her head.

"I'm going back and having dinner on my own. I get that you're determined to hold on with both hands, but I need sleep and space."

"Babe, I love you. Just dinner."

She wanted more than anything to say that she'd had enough after that conversation with Emmie, but she also knew he wouldn't let her leave that easily. "Please."

"After dinner, you're staying here on your own. No more trying to talk me into letting you stay." He nodded and kissed her as he slid his dress shirt off.

"Emerson."

He kissed her again and slid her sundress off. "We aren't doing this."

He kissed her again. "Lily."

She went to get up as he kissed down her torso. "Emerson…"

He kissed her. "Lily."

She shook her head. "Enough."

"Babe."

"Don't babe me." She got up and grabbed her jeans and a shirt from the closet and was about to get changed when he came up behind her. "I know what you're doing Emerson."

His arms slid around her and he kissed her shoulder. "I love you. You know I love you."

"I get it. I love you too Emerson, but…"

He kissed her. "Tell me what you want me to do."

"Let me get dressed. I get that you want me to jump into bed with you, but I can't. Not after that."

He hugged her and kissed her forehead. "I love you. All I was trying to say was that I was telling you the truth. I wouldn't want him starting more trouble baby. That's all."

"He already tried to," Lily said as she got dressed.

"What?"

"He texted and attempted to call but I declined it. I don't need him causing any more drama than he already has," Lily said.

Emerson went and grabbed a shirt from his closet and came back in to see her sitting on the bench in the closet in tears. "Baby." He walked over to her and slid his arms around her, snuggling her to his chest. "What's wrong?"

"The same feeling. Why would I think that you and I would be any different than they are?"

"Baby."

"Emerson, I'm serious."

He kissed her. "Come here," he said as he walked her into the bedroom. He sat her down on the edge of the bed. "Babe, I wouldn't walk away from what we have for anything in the world. This, you and me, this is what I wanted. This is what I always wanted. Baby, I don't want to go through life without you. I don't want to go a night without you. Don't even think what you are thinking. You're my world Lily."

"I can't let it go. I can't try to brush it off Emerson. I can't sit there and go through..."

He kissed her. "No more," he said.

"I just need..."

He hugged her. "Come on beautiful. I'll take you to the beach house."

"Emerson." He kissed her and they got up and walked back downstairs, then headed out to the beach. When they got there, Emerson and Lily went inside and the security guys went and got the takeout order that Emerson had ordered for them.

"What did you order?"

"Crab and lobster pasta with the olive oil sauce stuff. The one you always get."

She shook her head. "Wine," she asked. He smirked and kissed her. He went and got the wine, pouring two large glasses, and handed one to her.

Lily walked outside and sat down on the chaise. When she felt Emerson slide onto the chaise behind her, she shook her head. "I love you," he said as he kissed her neck.

"Emerson, I..." He kissed her neck, kissed her shoulder then snuggled her closer to him. "Just stop."

"Babe, you're the only woman I ever loved. What other proof do you need?"

"I need to stop my head from wondering."

"Then we get married. Babe, I didn't feel this way about anyone else. Never. Asking you was the only time in my life that I ever proposed to anyone. Don't you see that?"

"As long as I don't have to hear any more from women you used to date, and you don't get messages, I can live with it Emerson. How many of them have contacted you?"

When he went silent, she got up and went and sat in the chair. "Lily."

"What's the answer?"

"5. People heard we were engaged and a few people I dated once or twice said congrats. That's it."

Lily shook her head. "Emerson."

He got up and walked over to her, kissing her. "I even got work emails from employees saying congrats babe. I get that it's irritating and you're worried that someone isn't gonna have good intentions, but you have to trust me. You need to know that I'm not gonna lie to you."

She put her hand out. "What?"

"Cell phone." He took a deep breath, unlocked it, and handed it to Lily. If that was the only thing that would make her believe him, that's what he had to do.

He went and re-filled the wine glasses and she saw the texts from ex-girlfriends. There had to be 10 in his text messages. Emails were nothing out of the norm, and always 100% professional, until she found one message that wasn't:

> I miss you. Honestly, I still don't know why you chose her over being with me. If you start getting bored, this will give you a little distraction so sleeping with her won't be quite so bad. Just take a look before you sleep with her.

The woman had attached a photo that was practically porn. When she handed the phone back to him with the photo and email up on the screen, she went to walk back into the house and he grabbed her hand.

"What do you want Emerson?" When he pulled up his reply to the email, he showed it to whoever the sender was:

> She's the love of my life and has been since I was 15. I choose her over anything and anyone. Take the photo and show it to someone else. You never were my type. Don't contact me or my soon to be fiancée ever again.

"And?"

"Babe, breathe."

Lily pulled away and walked inside to see his security guys coming in with the food. Emerson walked in the sliding door, handed her the phone, and deleted the email and blocked the email address of that sender. He plated their dinners, walked outside, and put the plates and cutlery on the table, then came in and took her hand, walking her back outside. He closed the door and sat down with her. "What else," he asked.

Lily shook her head and ate. "Lily, tell me what else you need me to do." She shook her head.

"All I want is to not have any doubts. That's it. Right now, that email and the..." He got up and walked over to her and kissed her.

"Lily, it was an old email. It was the day that I proposed and I don't even know how she found out."

"Was she at your mom's party?" He nodded.

Lily shook her head and finished her dinner, trying to just breathe. She needed him to leave. She needed to be away from him to clear her mind. As soon as they were done, he took the dishes inside and came outside to see her walking down to the beach. He kicked his shoes off, rolling his jeans up and walked down to the water. He made his way down to her and slid his hand in hers.

"Emerson."

He linked their fingers. "Walk with me."

"Why can't you just leave me alone?"

"Because I love you. I always have and I always will even if you're mad."

She shook her head, walked through the waves, and tried her best to untangle their fingers. "Babe, please just stop. I get that you're mad. I get that she irritated both of us. The fact is, I wouldn't hurt you like that, and I'm not about to cheat on you either."

She kept walking, noticing the waves getting a little higher then moved closer to shore. She was about to keep walking when he looked up and noticed the clouds. "Babe, I know you're mad at me and want to whoop my butt right now, but we're gonna get soaked if we don't head back," he said.

Lily shook her head and walked a little more, then heard thunder. She turned and looked at him.

"What? Tell me what I have to do to get you to stop looking at me like I'm the damn devil."

"I can't do this. I can't pretend that this doesn't kill me Emerson. Every woman that pops up and shows or texts or emails is starting to feel intentional. Whether it's your mom or Zack or someone getting back at you, I can't keep doing this."

He walked over to her. "You shouldn't have to. Babe, I get cold feet, but you have to know that I'm not losing you."

She shook her head and went to walk away when he stopped her, picked her up and wrapped her legs around him, devouring her lips. "You're my forever Lily. The forever that will never ever end. I don't want any other woman. I don't care about any other woman. I just...want...you." He devoured her lips again and the rain started falling, drenching them both.

He didn't care about the rain. He didn't care if he froze out there. He just wanted her back in his arms. Back where she had always belonged. He fell to the sand and didn't let go.

"Don't leave me."

"You would never let me Emerson." He kissed her again. "Emerson, it's too cold out here."

"Tell me that you won't leave." She shook her head. "Tell me."

"Fine." She got up and he got to his feet, and they ran back to the house, running up the steps. They came inside and he picked her up and carried her up the steps to the bedroom. It's like everyone had vanished. Like they were alone in the house, even though she knew they were there.

He walked into the bedroom, kicked the door closed and peeled his shirt off as she slid to her feet. She went to walk into the bathroom and he pulled her back to him, devouring her lips. He followed her, walking her backwards to the counter of the massive bathroom and he peeled her shirt off, still kissing her. He picked her up and sat her on the counter, undoing her jeans and pulling them off along with the lace panties underneath.

"Emerson." He kissed her and pulled the bra off then undid his jeans, kicking them to the floor. He kissed her again and went and flipped the hot water on in the shower and picked her up, walking her in and leaned her against the wall.

"What are you doing," Lily asked.

He kissed her and they had sex. Hot, passed legal sex that had both of them throbbing and hearts racing. "I'm reminding you who loves you. Who wants you," he said as her legs tightened around him. They kept going until his body wouldn't let him continue. They crumbled to the floor and he kissed her again as they attempted to catch their breaths. "I'm not leaving you Lily. I'm not looking at other women, I'm not talking to other women. I just want you. Only you. Forever you." She looked at him and he could see the tears welling in her eyes. "I'm not leaving you," he said.

Lily shook her head and got up, sitting on the bench in the shower. The tile was warm and the steam warmed her from the outside in.

"Lily."

"I don't know why I doubt what you say. I don't. I just can't keep doing this. If I have doubts, I can't plan a wedding Emerson. I can't."

He looked at her. "Tell me what I have to do then."

She shook her head. "I don't know."

He managed to get up, walked over and sat down beside her. "I love you. I get that you are scared and worried, but you can't keep doubting everything."

"I want a guarantee."

"Of what?"

"That you'll never cheat."

He kissed her. "Then we go and write the contract."

"Emerson, this isn't a joke."

"I didn't say it was. You want a guarantee, I'll write it. Hell. I'll get security to witness it."

Lily brushed tears away and he kissed her, pulling her into his lap. "I want babies with you. I want to be 98 years old and curled up on a porch swing with you. I don't want to be with anyone else. Ever." She looked at him and he kissed her again. "You warm?"

She nodded and he stepped out of the shower, flipping the water off and grabbed a towel from the warmer, wrapping her up in one of them and grabbed the second, wrapping it around his waist. "Are you okay," he asked. Lily nodded and went to leave the bathroom when he slid his hand in hers. "Babe."

"Promise me."

He nodded and kissed her. She went into her closet, sliding a hoodie and joggers on to try and warm up.

When he came into the bedroom, he grabbed his joggers, slid them on and walked over to her. "What," Lily asked.

He leaned over and kissed her. "I love you."

"I love you too."

One more kiss and he grabbed his laptop. "What are you doing?"

"You want it in writing, it'll be in writing." He sat down on the chair beside hers, wrote it out and showed it to her:

> *I promise to remain completely faithful to Lily for the rest of my life. If I cheat on her in any way, emotionally or physically, not only will she be given all of my money, but all of my vehicles, homes, and investments as well. I have made this agreement without duress or demand.*

"What do you think?"

"Emerson."

He kissed her, devouring her lips. "I'll get the lawyer to file it."

"Emerson, you didn't need to go that far."

He sent it off to his lawyer and slid the laptop onto the table. "I meant every word. I'm not losing you. If that's what it's gonna take, you'll have it." He took her hand and walked her to the bed.

"What?"

"Come curl up on the bed with me." She sat down and he slid his arms around her. "No more fighting. No more worrying. I love you too much." She hugged him and he curled up on the bed with her. When there was a knock at the bedroom door, Emerson told them to come in.

"I wanted to check in and see how you two were before I headed out," his security said.

"I'm staying out here with Lily." He nodded and closed the door.

"You don't need to stay out here."

He kissed her forehead. "I'm staying until you're ready to come back to the house with me."

"And if I'm not?"

"Then we stay out here." Lily curled up with him and they snuggled on the bed. They talked and within the next hour or two, they were both out cold under the blankets.

Lily woke up at 8am the next morning to the scent of coffee. "I knew that would wake you up," Emerson said as he kissed her.

"Vanilla?"

He nodded. "Made it in the kitchen. How are you feeling beautiful fiancée of mine?"

"Tired. Exhausted. I need to know I'm not just another woman in your life. I don't want to have another fight about this. Never again. Ever."

He kissed her again and slid the coffee from her hand, sitting it on the counter beside her and leaned into her arms. "There's never gonna be another one. I love you baby. I will for as long as I live."

"Promise me something."

He kissed her. "Anything."

"That if someone starts trying to contact you again, I know when it happens." He nodded. He devoured her lips and slid her hoodie off.

"Emerson." He kissed her and slid back under the blankets with her, kicking his joggers off.

"I'm yours Lily. All yours. Head to toe. All I want is you." He peeled her joggers off and slid her legs around him. Just as he was leaning in to kiss her, his phone buzzed. She smirked.

"Get it."

"Nope."

"Emerson." He grabbed his phone and saw a message from his lawyer, that Lily noticed:

> *If you're serious about what you wrote, we need to discuss.*

He threw the phone onto the chair and kissed Lily.

"What," she asked.

He kissed her again. "We're fine."

"Emerson." He kissed her and pulled her legs around him and they had sex. Neither of them managed to come up for air until their bodies were both completely spent. He leaned onto his back and curled her to him.

"You okay," he asked.

Lily nodded and kissed him. He snuggled her to him and she went and got up. "Where are you goin Lily?"

"Food."

"Lily."

She slid her robe on and headed downstairs to see the housekeeper making Eggs Benedict.

"What's all of this," Lily asked.

"I was going to bring it upstairs for you. Good morning."

"Morning. Thank you for this," Lily said.

His housekeeper nodded and Lily got herself some juice then felt someone kissing her neck. She turned and Emerson slid his arms around her waist.

"Do you want to eat outside," he asked.

Lily shook her head. "I have a feeling that it's still gonna be wet out there after that storm." His housekeeper almost giggled. She plated their breakfast and Lily and Emerson curled up together at the table and ate.

"What did you want to do today," Emerson asked.

"I don't know. Write maybe."

He kissed her. "I love that you think that's what is gonna happen."

Lily shook her head. "I'm writing. I'm finishing the end of the book so I can get going on the editing and get it done."

He smirked. "Then I can get some work done."

Lily nodded. She finished breakfast and as she was about to get up, Emerson got the plates and cleaned them off, putting them into the washer. She finished her juice and he kissed her.

"Are you coming upstairs," he asked. Lily nodded.

She headed upstairs and saw Emerson flipping the water on in the shower. Just as he did, she saw his phone light up. She looked at it and saw a text:

> *I miss you too. Let me know when you're home.*

She walked into the bathroom, put the phone on the counter and went and slid into her bikini. She grabbed a beach towel and walked downstairs.

"Miss Lily," the security officer said.

"Going swimming."

She walked down the back deck, walked out to the beach and within a matter of 5 minutes, was in the water. She hadn't even looked at who the text was from, but she needed to stop thinking that he'd talked to another woman.

She swam and relaxed, clearing her mind in the beautiful salt water. When she started to swim back in, she saw Emerson on shore. He was shaking his head. Lily headed in closer and she saw Emerson jump into the water and swim towards her.

"What," Lily asked.

"Swimming alone?"

"I wanted to swim."

He shook his head and kissed her. "You sure you're okay?"

"Depends."

"Mom said to come by when we're back from the beach." Lily shook her head, slid under the water, and swam past him as he caught up and pulled her back to him as he stood on the bottom with his tiptoes.

"What," Lily asked as she surfaced.

He kissed her, devouring her lips. "Still second-guessing?"

"I wanted you to have your phone in case you needed it."

He kissed her again. "You swimming or coming in with me?"

"Swimming then maybe coming in."

He shook his head. "You sure?"

She nodded and slid back under the water, swimming past the waves. When she turned to come back in, Emerson was on the beach, on a beach blanket with his laptop, and had hers on the towel. She made it to shore and Emerson handed Lily a towel and she sat down with him.

"Are you seriously working out here?"

He nodded. "I thought you'd rather see me on the shore instead of security." She shook her head.

When she heard her phone ringing, he handed it to her.

"Lily," her doctor said.

"Hi. How are you?"

"Good. I wanted to book your check-up. Are you available this afternoon?"

"I could. We're out in Isle of Palms."

"1pm?"

"Okay," Lily said.

"See you then," her doctor said as they hung up.

"What's at 1," Emerson asked.

"Doctor check-up. It won't take me long. You hang and get work done."

"Nope. I'll come with you," he said. Lily shook her head. She knew there was no point in fighting him on it. "Come sit," Emerson said. "I was thinking. Now that all of that worry is over, would you want to come up with some ideas for what we want for the wedding?"

"Emerson."

"April 20th."

"Why?"

"Because. It's spring. The lilacs are in bloom, it's actually nice weather. What do you think?"

"Are you seriously planning?"

He nodded. "I have a couple options for locations too."

"Which would be?"

"The house, my mom's, the church downtown that I know you love."

"Emerson, how many people are you inviting to this tiny just us wedding?"

He smirked. "Maybe 40 each."

Lily shook her head. "I don't even know that many people."

"30 each."

"Why don't we come up with a list first."

He nodded. "Then you'd kinda have to go dress shopping," he teased.

"Emerson, I am so not in the mood to dress shop."

"I thought you might say that. Addy can come with you. You tell me when you're ready and I'll arrange it. Has to be in the next two weeks though." Lily shook her head.

"From having a long engagement to this," Lily asked.

He kissed her. "If you want to have a wedding, yeah," he said.

Lily looked at him. "I thought women were the ones who were supposed to be excited about planning out a wedding," Lily teased.

"You aren't."

"I wanted to wait. Take our time. Have something with just a few people."

He kissed her, devouring her lips. "Run away to the islands and get married with our toes in the sand?"

"Or wherever," Lily teased. He shook his head and snuggled her to him.

Lily went to get up and he shook his head. "What," she asked.

"Nope. Come and relax," he said.

"I have to get changed so I can go to the appointment."

He shook his head. "It's 10am. We have time beautiful wife to be."

Lily shook her head. "Emerson, I love you, but I still want to wait."

"What's the harm in finding a dress then?"

Lily shook her head. "When I actually finish the edits, we can talk about it."

He kissed her. "Then get to editing."

Lily shook her head and set her alarm for 11:30 am. She edited and Emerson put sunscreen on her back, arms and shoulders.

"What?"

"Making sure my bride doesn't get sunburned."

Lily smirked. "Thank you handsome." He kissed her again. She got the first 5 chapters done within the hour and got up.

"Where are we goin," Emerson asked.

"I'm getting showered and ready to go."

He got up, got the towels, and Lily grabbed the laptops. They headed inside and came upstairs. Just as Lily was sliding into the shower, Emerson slid in behind her. "I thought you already showered," Lily teased.

He kissed her and leaned her under the stream of hot water.

"Mm." He kissed down her neck.

"Emerson." He slid the shampoo into her hair, running his fingers through it and taunting her. "I know what you're doing," Lily said.

"So the doctor has something to check," he teased. Lily shook her head and he rinsed out the shampoo and then picked her up, sitting her on the bench, running the conditioner through her hair.

"Emerson."

He kissed her, devouring her lips. "What?"

"Are you up to something?"

He smirked. "Nope. Just happy that we can wake up together for once." He kissed her again.

"In other words, you're just happy that we aren't waking up in separate houses?"

He nodded and sat down beside her, curling her into his arms and onto his lap so she was straddling him.

"I know what you're doing."

He kissed her. "And?"

"We have to leave by quarter after."

He kissed her and smirked. "We have time." She smirked and he snuggled her to him. "All mine," he said.

"We still have to go."

He nodded and pulled her to him so they were having sex all over again in the shower. He was hot, bothered and beyond ready when they collapsed onto the bench together.

"Mine," he whispered as they both laughed. She got up and rinsed the conditioner out then walked over and kissed him. "Am I allowed to say that you are way past sexy right now," he teased as Lily kissed him again.

"Full of compliments," Lily joked. He nodded and devoured her lips.

"Come on handsome. We have somewhere to go," she teased as she flipped the water off. She stepped out, handing him a warm towel as he picked her up and sat her on the countertop.

"Emerson."

He devoured her lips again. "Now, are you gonna ask him to do another test?"

"Since you're so convinced?"

He nodded. Lily freshened up and slid off the countertop then went and got dressed, intentionally putting on a sundress. When she came out, sliding on her bracelet, he kissed her.

"I love the dress," he teased with a smirk ear to ear.

"I bet you do." She sat down on the bed and put her lotion on her legs while Emerson watched and almost drooled.

"I'm seriously taking that lotion away from you," he said.

"Too tempting?" He nodded. "Must remember. Legs and lotion works for you." He shook his head and Lily got up, sliding her sandals on.

He got up and took her hand. "You keep doing that, you're gonna end up pregnant before we get there," he teased.

They made their way into Charleston and he smirked. "What," Lily asked.

"Nothin. Would you be pissed if I made an appointment for you to look at dresses while you're in there?"

"Up to you, but I can handle it," Lily said.

"You sure? I came up with an alternative. If you don't want to go in somewhere, you can do it at the house. I'll get them to bring dresses to you."

"You sure," Lily asked.

He nodded and kissed her. "Whichever one that you want is yours. No price tags."

"Emerson."

He kissed her. "As long as you feel amazing. I don't care what you wear. I just want you."

She kissed him. "I love that you are so convinced."

He kissed her again and snuggled her to him, wrapping an arm around her shoulders. When they pulled into the doctor, Lily shook her head.

"You coming," Lily asked. He nodded and hopped out, grabbing her hand, and walked in with her.

They came into the exam room 10 minutes later and the nurse did a little blood work then handed her the fated cup. "We do a pregnancy test when you come just to know for sure," the nurse said.

Emerson smirked and Lily shook her head. She got what they needed and came and sat down.

"Lily," he said.

"What?"

"You sure you aren't?"

"I don't know," Lily said.

"Good answer. What are you gonna do if we are?"

"You get your way about having the wedding soon."

He smirked and Lily shook her head. "What would you think if we had it at the house? The reception part."

"You sure you want people in the house?"

"We can set up the pool house so people can come and use that," he said.

"You sure," Lily asked.

"We can just have the important people instead of all of the business friends and family."

"Better," Lily said. He kissed her hand and the doctor came in.

Chapter 3

"Well," Lily said.

"Well," the doctor said.

"And," Emerson said.

"Are you worried that you are," the doctor asked.

"Just say it."

"Yes," the doctor said.

Lily looked at her. "What?"

"The test was positive."

"There's no way," Lily replied.

Emerson got a smirk ear to ear. The doctor checked her over and when she was totally healthy, Emerson got a grin.

"Now, you have to follow-up with the OB, but I can send her out to wherever you need her to go."

"Thank you for that," Emerson said.

"Most welcome. Here's the prescription for the pre-natal vitamins, and I included something in case your nauseous. All natural and won't have any effects with the baby. Just eat as healthy as you can. Lower the stress."

Lily almost laughed. "Okay," Lily teased.

They got in the SUV and Emerson had a grin ear to ear.

"Cut it out Emerson."

"So, we're gonna go get a dress."

"Emerson, leave it."

"I'll get them sent to the house. You can look at them with Addy."

Lily shook her head. "Emerson, I want to wait."

He shook his head. "Babe."

"I'm not doing it until I'm ready."

He kissed her. "We can talk about it later. Still think that you need to go find a dress."

Lily shook her head. "And we can't just run off and do it just us right?"

"That's up to you, but you'd still need a dress."

She shook her head and he kissed her as they made their way back to the beach house. "Not a word," Lily said.

"Babe."

She shook her head. "Nothing. My friends always told me that you wait until you're past the 3-month mark. Like I said, not a word not even your mom."

"Especially her."

Lily shook her head. They got back and went inside.

Emerson walked her upstairs and closed the bedroom door. "Am I allowed to be excited?"

"It's your fault," Lily teased.

"True, but are you happy," he asked.

"Petrified."

He shook his head. "You're gonna be an amazing mom."

"There's still a problem."

"What?"

"You know what."

"Babe, there aren't any more issues. We ironed them out. We both know they were. Nobody is getting that close to either of us. The only one allowed in that house other than us is Addy. Does that feel any better?"

"Emerson."

He kissed her. "Tell me what you're worried about."

"9-months pregnant."

"I wouldn't in a million years. I know what you're thinking Lily. If we make it that far with this peanut, I'm not leaving your side. I wouldn't ever even think about it. You'd have to force me to go to the office."

"You know what I'm talking about."

He kissed her. "Not leaving your side. I just want us to go wherever you want and have whatever kind of wedding. Even if it's 20 people."

"Maybe."

He shook his head and devoured her lips. "I want my wife. I'm yours forever."

"Emerson, we can't have a wedding in a week or two. We need time."

"Wanna make a bet?"

"Emerson."

He kissed her. "I'll get them to send the dresses to the house. You go look. All we have to do is come up with a day and it'll be arranged."

Lily shook her head. "What happened to waiting until after the premiere?"

He kissed her. "Christmas." She shook her head. "Babe."

"I don't want to rush all of this."

He looked at her. "Would you be happier with you and me on a beach or something?"

"At church. You, me, my folks, and yours. Addy and whoever. That's all that matters."

He kissed her and hugged her. "I'll organize it. It'll be beautiful. Babe, I know what you love. Pick a random day. Any day. Even in the middle of the week."

"I want to be away from prying eyes." He nodded. "No drama."

He smirked and kissed her. "And no stress for you. Especially now," Emerson replied.

"Then we need to call Addy."

He kissed her, sat down on the sofa, and pulled her into his lap, opting to FaceTime Addy.

"I never thought I'd see that name on my call display. How are you," Addy asked.

"Well, what are you doing October 25th," Emerson asked.

"It's August. Probably complaining about the cooler weather. Why," Addy asked.

"Well, we're having the wedding. I want you there," Lily said.

"We don't even have your dress yet," Addy replied.

"Are you around today," Emerson asked.

"Why?"

"I'll get my driver to come get you. I'm getting dresses sent over to the house for Lily to try on."

"What's the rush," Addy asked looking at Lily on the screen.

"Because I can't wait any longer. Lily doesn't want to either."

"Alright. I can drive over. I'm over at Kiawah."

"Alright. I guess I'll see you around 3," Lily said. Addy smirked and hung up.

"How are you getting the dresses over there this fast Emerson?"

"Sorta already had it set. Just needed a time," Emerson said.

"And what are you gonna do while I'm trying on dresses?"

He kissed her, devouring her lips. "Missing you and getting dinner. Do you want to come back out here?" Lily nodded. He snuggled her. "Are you sure you're okay with all of this," he asked.

"I have 9 months to get used to it," Lily teased.

By the time Addy and Lily got to the house, there were two vans coming in with 5 racks of dresses. "Seriously," Addy asked as they came in.

"Miss Lily. I got you sparkling grapefruit juice in a champagne glass. Miss Addison, would you care for one," the housekeeper said.

"Sure. Are you on a no-drinking thing," Addy asked.

"Yep. Doesn't do me any good at all."

"You and Emerson made up?."

"Addy, it has nothing to do with it," Lily said as the bridal consultant Sarah showed them the dresses.

Lily saw a few she liked, but nothing really jumped out at her. "What about this," Addy asked as Lily walked over to her.

"It's okay," Lily said.

"Pick 6 that are okay. Try them on. Some look much better on," the consultant said.

Just as Lily was about to hand her some, she saw two that she liked. One was a satin dress with a draped back that was elegant and simple, another that had sleeves that were simple but romantic.

"Alright. Go try them," Addy said as the housekeeper came over and put some champagne in Addy's glass.

Lily turned down two of the dresses then slid on the silky dress. When she came out and showed Addy, her jaw was on the floor.

"Dang," Addy said.

"Too simple," Lily asked.

Addy shook her head. "I love it." The consultant slid a veil on with it and Addy smirked. "It's simple but I like," Addy said.

Lily thought about the baby bump that she'd have if she managed to hold onto the pregnancy and shook her head, walking back into the change room. They put it in the maybe pile and slid on two others. One was too big of a dress for what they wanted, one was not gonna work if she was showing. They were down to 3 last dresses. Lily slid into one and came out to show Addy. It really wasn't right. Even Addy knew it.

"It's too in your face. Not your style," Addy said.

"Agreed," Lily said.

She slid on the second and didn't like it. When she put that last one on, she felt the satin, the chiffon, the little touch of sparkle in just the right spot. She came out and showed Addy the dress.

It had a little train, a little lace with sparkle along the base of the back, a little in the lowest part of the neckline and just a little sparkle.

"Okay. Hear me out. This one for the wedding, the other one for the reception," Addy said.

Lily smirked. "Well, this one also has a cape if you wanted to try it," the consultant said.

Lily nodded and she slid it on. "Well damn," Lily said.

"What do you think," Addy asked as she came up to Lily and the housekeeper came and looked.

"I love it," Lily said.

"And do you want to do the other one too," Addy asked.

"Can we make the train a little longer on this one," Lily asked. The consultant nodded. "Then both," Addy asked.

"We can add the train on the cape part, then you don't need two," the consultant suggested.

"Okay, I'm trying the other one on," Lily said as she went and slid back into it.

"Well," Addy asked.

Lily nodded. "If it's over 10, I'm not doing two," Lily replied.

"Way under. They're both from a relatively new designer. I have no idea how, but you picked two that were the least expensive out of all of them."

"And," Addy asked.

"Less than 5," the consultant said.

"Good," Lily teased.

"I just have to pin them."

"What do you mean pin them," Addy asked.

"Off the rack. We can get started on the alterations," the consultant said.

"I'll be back in 10," Lily said as she went back into the other room to change.

"Did you talk to Emerson?"

The consultant nodded. "Both dresses have a little stretch just in case. I'm just going to pin the straps and two spots across your back. To be honest, you're almost a perfect fit of both."

"Good," Lily replied.

They finished with the dresses and Lily came out to sit with Addy.

"I can't believe you with those dresses. You look like an angel."

"Good. That was my plan," Lily teased.

"I have to ask something. Don't get all mad or anything," Addy said.

"What?"

"I thought y'all were having a long engagement." Lily took Addy's hand and walked her upstairs, closing the door to the bedroom. "What," Addy asked.

"It's not a guarantee yet, and I don't even know if it'll stick."

Addy looked at her. "Lily."

"Not a word."

"How far?"

"No idea. Like I said, not a word. He literally pulled all of this together after the doctor appointment today."

"Is that why it's in October?"

Lily nodded. "It'd be 3 months."

"I still think that y'all could just wait."

"I said the same thing. I just don't want Zack hearing about it."

Addy hugged her. "What's going on with him anyway?" Lily told her the story and she shook her head. "Am I ever glad that I told Sam to screw off," Addy said.

"I doubt he's gonna back off if he's anything like Zack."

"He started dating someone else Lily. She looks like a blow-up doll from what I saw. I did meet a new guy though."

"Addy."

"He's kinda sexy. He's the opposite of Zack and Sam. He's a sweetie."

"And what does Mr. Handsome do?"

"He's a chef." Lily smirked.

"How long?"

"Since you vanished into Emerson land." Lily smirked. Just as Lily was about to tell her about the insanity that had been going on, her phone buzzed.

"Yes handsome," Lily said.

"What did you find," he asked.

"Two. All ready to go whenever."

"Good. I was just getting a little work finished. Did you want to come back out here or should I head back," he asked.

"I'm coming. Someone's here that wanted to talk to you," Lily teased.

"I know, but I didn't think that it could talk yet."

"Emerson." Lily handed Addy the phone and went and grabbed two more bikinis.

"She doing okay," Emerson asked.

"For now. What else do you need me to do?"

"There's a dress in there for you."

"Who's the best man?"

"My dad I think. If not, then Carter Sams."

"As in the same Carter that you were best friends with in high school? I haven't seen him in I don't know how long," Addy said.

"Either have I to be honest."

"Emerson, it's supposed to be someone who means a lot."

"There's only one other person, but it's not the smartest move."

"Meaning," Addy asked.

"Parker Callum."

"Why do I know that name?"

"He was out with me when I saw Lily talking to Zack at that bar."

"Hold on. Parker is a musician isn't he?"

"And yes, he's single."

"Has he even met Lily?"

"He's the one that asked why I wasn't going and interrupting her talking to Zack."

"Okay."

"Do me a favor though."

"What would that be Emerson?"

"Keep an eye on her and make sure she's alright."

"She's grabbing bikinis."

"Remind her there are a bunch here."

"Hey Emerson."

"What friend of mine?"

"I'm glad it's you."

"Me too." Addy hung up with Emerson and looked at Lily.

"He said to tell you there are a bunch of other bikinis at the beach house."

"Have a nice chat," Lily asked as Addy handed Lily her phone.

"Am I allowed to say that I'm glad you two found each other again?"

"Do you want to come have dinner with us?"

Addy shook her head. "I'm going to see my chef."

Lily gave her a hug and walked downstairs with her. "Miss Lily, I got the food together for both of you for dinner. Are you ready to head over," the housekeeper asked as Emerson's security came out of his office. Lily nodded and walked Addy outside, giving her a hug. Within 10 minutes of Addy leaving, Lily headed back to the beach house.

When they got back, Emerson was sitting on the chaise outside on the phone. Lily slid her shoes off and walked down to the sand. Within 10 minutes, Emerson walked down the steps and sat on the bottom step, looking out at Lily. When she turned, he motioned for her to come closer. She walked over to him and he stood up. "Everything okay," he asked.

"Just thinking."

He slid his arms around her and hugged her. "What's wrong," he asked.

"I still think it's rushing."

"You really want to wait?"

"Next summer."

"Babe."

"I know, but if it doesn't stick, then what," Lily asked.

He kissed her. "Then we have each other for life. Nobody goes anywhere. That was the agreement. I wouldn't move a muscle even if you asked me to."

"Are you sure you want to do this now?"

He nodded. "I wanted to the day I bumped into you on the beach. I would've if I could've." He kissed her again.

"You're sure you want me?"

He kissed her, picking her up and wrapping her legs around his waist. "More than I ever wanted anything in the entire world. I wouldn't change that for anything baby. Nothing." He kissed her and hugged her. "Swim?" She shook her head. He slid her to her feet and walked her inside to the scent of lobster tails and steak. "Yum," Emerson said.

"I also have the claws. I used the rest of it for lobster bisque for tomorrow," his housekeeper said.

"Thank you," Emerson said as he saw Lily heading upstairs.

He followed her and saw her walk into the bedroom. "Babe, are you okay," Emerson asked.

"Just needed some quiet time." She sat down on the bed and Emerson shook his head. They curled up together for a while. "Do I get a hint about the dress?"

"Dresses."

"Hint?"

"White with a little sparkle. Soft and flowy."

He smirked. "Do they make you happy?"

Lily nodded. "And they're comfy."

"Danceable?"

She smirked. "Yes."

"Good. That's all that matters."

"And did you talk to the church?"

He nodded. "They said that they will have the date put aside. I talked to a pastry chef friend and he's doing the cake."

"Emerson."

"White and silver with white magnolias." Lily looked at him.

"How?"

"Silk flowers."

She shook her head. "Where would we even have the reception?"

"We have options. The resort at the marina that you seemed to love. The fancy one downtown."

"Belmond Charleston?" He nodded. "That might work."

"They have the date put aside just in case."

"White and Silver?"

"Silver sparkle. I didn't know if you wanted any other colors."

"Red."

He smirked. "Ever the Falcons fan." Lily smirked.

They relaxed, talking through a million and one ideas they both had about the wedding. "So, no red roses?"

"Emerson."

"It's just so simple."

"I know."

He shook his head. "You sure you don't want lavender or pale pink or something?"

"Then silver and white."

He nodded. "I can live with that."

She shook her head. He kissed her forehead. "I love you," Emerson said.

"I love you too. I still think you're nuts, but..." He kissed her.

They both nodded off and when Emerson woke up, his phone was buzzing quietly in his pocket. "Yep," Emerson said.

"I saw her today. That's what you chose over me?"

It was a voice he knew well. "In a heartbeat," he replied as he realized that it was his ex, Liz.

"I heard that y'all were getting married."

"Yep."

"You sure I can't talk you out of it," she said.

"Nope. I'm marrying the woman I've loved since we were in high school. The most amazing woman I know."

"Can we meet up for a drink before you do it?"

"Nope."

"Locked down?"

"Voluntarily."

"Alright then. Congrats. If you change your mind, I can always pop over for a quickie."

Emerson hung up and kissed Lily's shoulder not knowing that she'd heard what the woman had said. "Another ex-girlfriend?"

"She said congrats."

Lily shook her head. She got up and he grabbed her hand. "Lily." She shook her head, pulled away, grabbed her laptop, and went and sat down on the chaise outside on the balcony.

She got writing done, finished another chapter of edits and Emerson walked outside, sitting down on the chaise behind her. "Lily."

"I don't want to talk about it."

"Babe, I told her I wasn't leaving your side and that you're all I ever wanted. She took the hint."

Lily shook her head. "Not the point."

He kissed her shoulder and snuggled her to him. "Tell me what you want me to do."

"I know it's pointless...but wait. Next summer. Later. Not rushing and doing it in October."

"Babe, it's gonna happen anyway. Why wait?"

She shook her head. He rubbed her shoulders and her neck. "Tell me what you need me to do Lily."

"What did your lawyer say?"

"It's almost like a prenup. It can be drawn up. He's working on it now."

"Emerson."

He kissed her neck. "What?"

"Promise me that if you change your mind, you say something."

He kissed her shoulder. "Like I said, I'm not going anywhere."

By the time they came downstairs, dinner was ready and smelling amazing. The salad, the food and the dessert that came after was amazing. When they finished, Lily took her sweet tea outside and walked down to the beach. Emerson saw her sit down on the sand. He took a deep breath and came out there with his wine in hand and sat down beside her.

"What you up to out here," he asked.

"It's relaxing."

"I know. How are you feeling?"

"Tired. I just wanted to relax a little."

"Do you want me to go inside?"

Lily shook her head. "Walk with me?"

He nodded, kissed her, and got up, helping her to her feet. He put the glasses on the steps and walked with her as they talked all the wedding plans through.

"I still think we should wait," Lily said.

"Babe, if you are, I don't want to wait. I want us married before the baby comes. What's wrong with that," Emerson asked.

"I don't know if I'm ready."

He kissed her. "Babe, I get it. It's a lot. We just found out about the baby stuff then all of this. I understand. There's no point in waiting."

"There is if I'm not ready to. I get that you want to rush it all and have your way with everything. I get that you want to have a massive wedding with all the bells and whistles. I get that you want the damn world Emerson. I just want to be happy. That's it."

"And you aren't?"

Lily looked at him. "I just want us to take our dang time. We had world war three and you just brush it off. We almost break it off altogether and you still push. I can't do this."

He kissed her. "Lily, I'm not doing it because I don't want to lose you. I just want to be with you and start our forever now. I don't want to wait anymore. I waited since we were 15 Lily. I lost you once. I can't do it again. Not when I finally got you back."

Lily shook her head and walked down to the water.

"What are you doing?"

"Getting space." She walked through the water and Emerson shook his head.

"Lily, just come here."

She shook her head. She walked and kept going, walking towards the one spot he didn't want her to go. "Lily, please."

"I know what you're anxious about Emerson."

He shook his head. "Lily."

"You gonna tell me that he has nothing to do with it?"

He rolled his jeans up and walked out to her, picking her up and carried her back to the sand.

"We're not going there Lily. Not now, not tomorrow and not next week."

She shook her head. "You sit there and try to convince yourself that his stupid antics had nothing to do with rushing everything. We both know that they did. It was his move showing up here that pushed all of this into overdrive," Lily said.

"And? It showed me one dang thing. One. I'm not losing you to him or anyone else. I'm not losing you period. Not now, not tomorrow, not ever," Emerson said.

"And it has nothing to do with the doubts he tried to plant?"

He shook his head. "All it did was make me realize that I could lose you."

Lily shook her head. "Is that why you're so dang worried?" Lily looked at him.

"Partly." He kissed her. "Stop worrying about all of this. Stop wondering if it's too much. Stop worrying about everything else. Do you love me," he asked.

"Emerson." He kissed her.

"Yes or no?"

Lily nodded. "Then why are you worried?"

"Because I don't want to make another massive mistake. I don't want to do something that's gonna backfire."

He kissed her. "Nothing is gonna backfire Lily. Nothing. Whether we end up with a peanut or not, I just want to have you. That's just a dang bonus. Don't doubt all of this. I'm here. You're here. We're getting married. We're not running to the dang electric chair."

"I want a life Emerson. I want a choice. I want to have the wedding of our dreams, not the most rushed one. It's too much too fast."

"When it gets to the day, we'll either be 3 months or we'll be baby-less. Either way, I want to marry you. I want us to have Christmas as a married couple. I want us to start the new year and be married."

"And I say wait until after Valentine's Day like we talked about."

He kissed her. "Compromise?"

"No."

He shook his head and sat down, realizing that they weren't far from Jaxon's beach house.

"Lily, you can't keep putting everything on hold. I get that you're worried. I get that you're petrified that things will backfire, but you can't just put your life on hold. You have to take a chance. A leap of faith." Lily shook her head. He pulled her onto his lap. "Babe, I get being worried. I do. Just trust me."

Lily took a deep breath. "I'll think about it."

He kissed her. "Come walk back with me?"

"That worried about walking near his place?"

"Avoiding the inevitable."

He kissed her and they got up and Emerson started walking her back towards the house.

"You sure you don't want to wait until after Valentine's Day?"

He kissed her forehead. "I don't want to wait for one more second. I'd do it tomorrow if you wouldn't complain."

"Emerson."

He kissed her. "I would. You and me at the house, Addy, my parents and yours. That's it. I'd be perfectly fine with that."

"Then why aren't we doing that?"

He looked at her. "That's what you'd want?"

Lily nodded. "Everything else could wait. We can have the big hoopla in March or April. Why do we have to rush into a big thing now?"

He looked at her. "Lily."

"What?"

"Are you saying that you'd do it sooner?"

"When we know if it sticks, we discuss it. We can do it at home." He looked at her. He shook his head, kissed her forehead and they made their way back.

When they got to the beach house, Lily's phone was ringing. "Hello," Lily said.

"It's Doc Marshall. I wanted to book you an ultrasound to check and see how baby is in a month or so. That alright," the doctor asked.

"Just let me know the date. We'll be there," Lily said.

"Alright. I'll send over the appointment information."

"Thank you," Lily said.

"If you need anything just let me know."

They hung up and Emerson looked at her. "She's sending the appointment info over," Lily replied.

Emerson kissed her. "Then what," he asked.

"Then we'll know. If we aren't, no more rushing."

"If we aren't what," the housekeeper asked as she came in.

"Nothing," Emerson said. Emerson took Lily's hand and walked her upstairs.

"And," Emerson asked.

"I'm not doing this Emerson. I have the dress for whenever we do it. We take our time. I'd rather have the tiny just us wedding and have a big one with everyone else later."

"Lily."

"The wedding is for us Emerson. You and me. Those are the only two people that matter. What do you think," Lily asked.

He looked at her. "Are you being honest about it? You're seriously okay with just us and Addy and my friend?"

Lily nodded. "We need to slow down Emerson. We jumped into living together, then you proposed. All of it's a little much."

"I get it."

"If we aren't, then we need to just take our time. Promise me."

"If we are, I want us to be married before we have the baby," he said.

"We can talk about it after we have the ultrasound. There's no guarantee. If we lost it, we're waiting."

He looked at her. "Are you sure?"

"I'm not making any decisions Emerson. None."

He kissed her. "If we are and we make it to the 3-month mark, then what," he asked. He wanted more than anything to just marry her. It didn't matter who was there, it didn't matter where they were. All that mattered was the two of them together. Him never losing her for even a split second was what mattered. He was petrified that she'd walk away like she had in high school. He didn't want to lose her for even a split second.

"Then we have something small, just us and Addy and your friend and maybe parents, if your mom doesn't start world war three." That was part of her being hesitant. She knew exactly how his mom felt about her. Everyone was a gold-digger to her. Her getting up in the middle of a massive wedding with an objection was the big fear, and the biggest worry that Lily had. Second was the two of them not working in a stronger relationship. In a longer relationship. In one that would be an example to the peanut that she had growing. She wanted it to work, but was it worth the leap of faith?

"What's the real worry," Emerson asked.

She looked at him. "You know what it is."

He shook his head and took a deep breath. "I'll fix that," he said.

"Emerson."

"Right now." He grabbed his phone and called his mom, putting her on speakerphone and closing the bedroom door.

"My baby boy. How are you doing," his mom asked.

"Well, there's a little issue," Emerson replied.

"Which would be?"

"I need you to apologize to Lily."

Lily went and got up, getting changed into pajamas. "Emerson."

"She's not a gold-digger mom. I can promise you that. She's the polar opposite."

"We'll see when you two get married."

"Well, I did tell you that I proposed right?"

"Still say you two need a prenup."

"All there is gonna be, is a document that says that if I ever cheat, she gets everything. She's not a cheater and she never will be mom."

"Baby, I get that's how you feel now, but that document is a mistake."

"She loves me mom. She always has. I've loved her since I was 15."

"She's not the kind of woman you should be with. I told you that then, and I meant it." Lily shook her head and went downstairs. She didn't need to hear more.

Lily curled up on the sofa, grabbing the blanket off the back of the sofa and pulling it over her. She flipped her laptop open and saw a message from Addy:

CALL ME ASAP

Lily grabbed her phone and called Addy. "What's up," Lily asked.

"So, I went out with a friend and you wouldn't believe who I bumped into?"

"If you say Carter Sams, I will fall off this sofa."

"First off, why are you on the sofa? Second, stop being a psychic."

"Emerson's talking to his mom."

"Great. Queenie. How did you know that I bumped into Carter?"

"He's friends with Emerson." Addy shook her head. Something was up and Lily could smell it a mile off.

"That's just creepy. Anyway, he asked me if I wanted to go to dinner. Should I go?"

"What happened to the chef?"

"Long story. I saw a text from another woman. Seemed to duplicate overnight," Addy replied.

"Girl, we had that same fight remember?" Lily talked to her and when Carter called Addy, they hopped off the phone and Lily got edits in.

When Emerson came downstairs, Lily's laptop was on the table and she was asleep on the sofa. He smirked, walked over to her, and kissed her forehead. When she didn't move a muscle, he slid his arms under her gently and carried her upstairs. He leaned her onto the bed, tucked her into the blankets and got changed for bed. He came out a few minutes later and she was still curled up on the bed. He flipped the light off, closed the shutters and slid into bed beside her, leaning over so he was as close to her as possible. When Lily somehow instinctually curled up with him, he got a grin ear to ear. "I love you," he whispered as he nodded off.

When he woke up the next morning, Lily wasn't there. He looked over and she wasn't in the bedroom. He walked downstairs and saw her curled up on the sofa working on edits. "Babe, what are you doing down here?"

"Editing. How did the rest of the..."

He kissed her. "I'm not talking about her. End of discussion."

"Okay then."

"Do you want to come do a workout?" Lily shook her head. "Babe."

"Don't."

He took a deep breath and sat down with her. "Babe, I love you. I don't care what stupid crap she says." Lily almost rolled her eyes and he kissed her again. "Beautiful fiancée of mine. Stop worrying about my mom. I love you."

"Still doesn't make me feel better hearing all the negative crap she said."

"Babe, I promise you. She's handled. My mom has no say in our lives or our wedding or our marriage for that matter."

"Emerson."

He kissed her. "Babe, I promise you. She isn't getting in the middle and if she opens her mouth during it, she's being removed."

"I don't want to risk that Emerson. I get it. She's your mom. We have enough stress with the wedding and the baby situation. I don't want to add even more. It's supposed to be a memorable day. It's supposed to be happy."

He slid his arms around her and kissed her. "Babe, I'll talk to her again when we make the wedding decision. See where her head is at. We can go from there," he said. Lily nodded and he kissed her shoulder.

"How are you feeling," he asked.

"I'm not nauseous if that's what you're asking. I'm just trying to lower my stress as much as I can. I need to finish the editing."

He kissed her neck. "Come with me for a few," he asked.

"Why?"

He got up and took her hand, helping her to her feet. "Come," he said as he walked her upstairs.

"Emerson." He walked her into the bedroom, slid her laptop out of her hands and put it on the bedroom counter, walking her towards the bed.

"Come curl up with me. Lowers your stress," he teased.

Lily shook her head. "I have…"

He kissed her, picked her up and sat her on the bed, sliding on the bed beside her. "You need to rest. You said it yourself."

Lily smirked. "Still need…"

"Laptop can sit for a while. Just relax. I'll even get you breakfast in bed," he teased.

Lily shook her head and he kissed her. "I'll be right back," he said as he kissed her again and got up. He plugged her laptop in and headed downstairs. Just as he made it to the bottom step, he heard her cell going off. He shook his head, knowing that either it was Addy or it was Zack starting another war. He wanted more than anything to walk down the beach and kick his backside to another solar system, but he wasn't leaving Lily in the beach house alone. He got breakfast, carried it upstairs and saw her asleep. Her phone was still on the sofa. He shook his head, walked over to the bed, and put the breakfast on the footboard.

"Hey," Lily said when she saw him.

"You didn't answer?"

She shook her head. "Do you want…"

"No," Lily replied. He shook his head, grabbed it and saw the text from Zack:

> *I'm coming down. Are you still at the beach?*

He opened it and replied:

> *I'm with her. Leave my soon to be wife alone. You start this, the business deal is over.*

He deleted the entire thread of texts, seeing the million and one messages that Zack had sent. He was getting more and more irritated but seeing that she hadn't replied to a single one other than telling Zack to leave her alone. He slid her phone in his pocket, handed Lily her juice and breakfast and curled up on the bed with her, having his breakfast.

"Are you giving me my cell?"

He shook his head. "Nope. Not when he's texting you."

"Emerson."

He kissed her. "Eat," he said as he kissed her neck.

"Emerson, give me the phone."

He shook his head. "Eat then you can have your phone," he said. Lily shook her head. They had breakfast in peace and quiet. He snuggled her when she finished eating. She had her juice and Emerson finished off his coffee.

"Phone please," Lily said.

He kissed her. "Nope." He slid the phone from his pocket and put it on the charger on the side table.

"What," Lily asked. He kissed her again, slid the juice out of her hand, put it on the side table and put the dishes on the footboard.

When he came back up to the top of the bed, he slid into her arms, pulling her legs around his hips. "What," Lily asked.

"Mine," he teased.

Lily shook her head. "You are just so convinced that I'm just gonna do whatever..."

He kissed her again. "Yep."

"Emerson, don't you have work to do or something?" He shook his head and devoured her lips, kicking his joggers to the floor. "Emerson."

He kissed her again. "Yes fiancée."

"I think we need to get up."

He shook his head and leaned her into the pillows and snuggled up with her. "Nope. Mine. All mine," he teased as he snuggled her close to him.

"And what else did you want to do today?"

"Stay in bed and pretend the world doesn't exist," he replied.

"Nice try. Don't you seriously have work to do?"

"I could, but my woman is more important," he teased as he kissed her.

He smirked, propping himself up on one arm with her legs still wrapped around him. "You realize that you're way too dressed to be in this bed right," he teased.

"And you're way too undressed," Lily teased.

"You sure you're okay?"

Lily nodded. "I'm fine Emerson. Just relaxing."

He kissed her. "Okay. I have a question. How would you feel about getting away for a weekend?"

"Depends on where we're going."

"What if we went to Charlotte or went out to the outer banks or something?"

"You really want to go out there?"

"Partially, yes."

"And it's not because Zack just texted something stupid?"

"If I'm going to be honest, yes."

Chapter 4

Lily shook her head. "Emerson, you're the man I'm marrying. Get it through your crazy mind. I'm not gonna be swayed by him."

He kissed her. "I know, but..."

Lily kissed him. "Regardless of his ridiculous texts, I'm not going anywhere. If anything, I'm going back to the house. That's it. If you really want to vanish into the middle of nowhere in North Carolina, okay. I'd say go into the mountains."

"I'd say the Biltmore estate, but it's not where I want us to be."

"And where is it? On a beach that we have all to ourselves?"

He nodded. "If I could do that here, I would," he teased.

Lily shook her head and he kissed her. "Because you want me in a bikini or because you don't want to worry that he's watching?"

"Both."

Lily shook her head. "Then plan what you want to do for a honeymoon. It'll get the beach stuff out of your mind," Lily replied as he kissed her again.

"Think so do you?" Lily nodded and he slid closer and devoured her lips. "

You in a little bikini isn't getting wiped from my mind for anything in the world."

Lily shook her head. "Emerson."

He kissed her again and kissed down her torso. "What are you up to," Lily asked.

"Seducing my fiancée." He kissed her and was about to start peeling her clothes off when his phone went off. "You gonna answer that?"

Emerson shook his head and his hands slid to her backside. "Not a chance."

"Emerson."

He shook his head and peeled her shirt off, throwing it to the floor. He devoured her lips, peeling what was left of her clothes off and throwing them to the floor. He smirked and slid her legs tight around his hips.

"What if it's work?"

"They can wait." He kissed her again and made love to her. It was passionate, love-filled, and body humming sex.

When they curled up together again, his phone went off for a third time. Lily went to try and grab it, and he pulled her to the middle of the bed and devoured her lips. "Mine," he teased.

"You do know that I'm not property right," Lily teased back.

"And I also know that I'm all yours for the rest of your life." Lily smirked and he devoured her lips. They curled up together on the bed and his phone went off again.

"Emerson."

He shook his head, kissed her, and grabbed his phone.

"Yep," Emerson said.

"There has been a request Sir. Zack is requesting to talk to you."

"Pass," Emerson said.

"Sir, he said that if you didn't agree to it that the deal was off."

"Right. Like he has any choice in the matter. I'd rather remove him from the company."

"What would you like me to put in the contract then," his VP asked.

"Nothing. He has the choice between those two. Either he stays and has no contact with me or my fiancée, or he loses his business and his job and most of his money."

Emerson hung up with his VP and Lily got out of bed. She slid her robe on and went into the bathroom, closing the door. She went and hopped into the shower on her own.

She washed her hair, slid her conditioner in and was just washing up when Emerson slid in behind her.

"Hey beautiful," he said as his arms slid around her.

"Hey yourself. Are you going in to work?"

"Probably have to after that. I don't exactly want to," he replied.

Lily shook her head and kissed him. "I'm just relaxing and editing. It's fine."

"I don't want you here alone."

She smirked. "Emerson, I'm not gonna swim off into the sunset. I'm editing and relaxing. I can't exactly leave security behind since they won't leave me alone."

"Just promise me something."

"What?"

"Don't have the lobster rolls until tonight."

She smirked. "I can't promise, but I'll try," Lily teased.

He kissed her again, devouring her lips as he slid her under the stream of water, watching it slide down her skin.

"What," Lily asked as she noticed him almost drooling.

"Nothin. Just realizing how sexy my woman is."

Lily shook her head. "Are you showering or just here to watch," she joked.

"Both," he teased as he pulled her to him and devoured her lips. She slid him under the water and he shook his head, handing her the sea sponge. She put some of her body wash on it and washed his back for him as he shook his head. If he hadn't needed to go into work, he would've stayed in bed with her all day. She handed him the sea sponge, kissed him and stepped out, grabbing one of the two warm towels and wrapped it around her. She was just running a comb through her hair when he stepped out. He slid his arms around her, kissing her neck.

"Emerson."

"Fiancée of mine."

"Are you going to work," she teased.

"Trying to delay it as much as possible." He kissed her shoulder and turned her to face him.

"Yes handsome."

He kissed her, devouring her lips and picked her up sitting her on the countertop.

"I need you to do something for me."

"What?"

He kissed her. "If he calls, block him. If he shows up, let security deal with him. Is that doable?"

Lily nodded. "That's what my plan was anyway."

"Babe."

"I know. After that phone call, I get it. I'd prefer him to not be near us at all. It's fine."

"And if you need anything, tell me. Something happens, tell me. I don't care what it is."

"And what are you thinking is gonna happen?"

He kissed her. "You know what." She shook her head and he picked her up, walking her into the bedroom and leaning her onto the bed.

"Go get dressed handsome. You have work," she said.

He nodded, kissed her, and got up. Lily went and slid her robe on while she found something comfy to wear. She slid into shorts and a cozy shirt. She got herself a big ice water and when Emerson came down the steps, he smirked.

"My sexy fiancée and you're seriously walking around in that," he teased.

Lily looked at him. "And? What about it," Lily teased.

He motioned for her to come closer. She shook her head and walked over to him. "What," Lily asked.

He kissed her, devouring her lips. He picked her up and walked into his office, sitting her on the desk. "You have work remember," Lily said.

He shook his head and kissed her again. "It can wait," he said as he slid her shirt off.

"Emerson."

He kissed her again and within a matter of minutes, they were having sex on the desk.

"What has got into you," Lily said as he kissed down her neck.

"You," he replied. He kissed her again and then picked her up and carried her to the sofa, taking full advantage of the quiet and soundproof office. When he curled her into his arms, he shook his head.

"Emerson, you're supposed..."

He kissed her again. "I don't want to leave you here."

"Emerson, it's not like you're vanishing for a month. You're going to work. It's maybe 20 minutes from here."

He kissed her again. "Still too far away." She shook her head and he snuggled her to him. "You sure that I can't talk you into coming with me?"

"You're going to work. I'm sitting here and editing Emerson. It's not like I'm disappearing with the waves." He kissed her again.

"Promise me one thing."

"Depends on what it is handsome."

"Marry me. September. Two months."

"When?"

"12th."

She looked at him. "I thought we were gonna discuss this when we knew."

He kissed her. "Please."

She shook her head. "Fine, but don't go insane alright?"

"Meaning?"

"Just us, my folks and yours if your mom can stop causing a problem. Addy has to be there."

He kissed her. "And my buddy will come. Beyond that, nothing. Nobody else?"

"Just close family."

"Okay."

"We can do the other one later."

He kissed her. "Alright beautiful. I love you."

"Go get cleaned up. I can come down for lunch, but since it's kind of almost 10, you should probably just go in and I'll see you tonight."

He nodded. "Come at 1."

She smirked. "Emerson."

"Come at 1. Come to the office."

"We'll see how much I get done." He kissed her again, devouring her lips.

When he finally managed to get out the door to work, it was almost 10:30. Lily went upstairs, cleaned up a little, slid her sundress on and went and sat down on the balcony, working on edits. A half hour later, her phone buzzed and she saw yet another text from Zack:

We need to talk. Can you come over?

Lily deleted the text before she read any more of it and shook her head. She kept going with edits and when her phone rang a half hour later, she shook her head. Zack hadn't got the hint. She ignored the call and kept going.

"Lily, come down," Zack said as he spotted her on the balcony.

She shook her head, went inside, let security know that Zack was at the house and went back up to the bedroom, sitting in the chair by the window.

She got another few pages edited when she heard her phone again. "Hello fiancée," Lily said as she answered and got a big ole grin ear to ear.

"Hey yourself gorgeous. How was the rest of the morning?"

"Quiet. One little interruption, but beyond that nothing. How's work?"

"I ordered us chicken souvlaki. That stuff you love. Are you coming to hang with me," he asked.

"I mean, I could tear myself away, but not for long. You have work to get done."

"Oh I know. I still think that you need to come," he said.

"Alright handsome. I'll head up there in a few minutes."

"See you soon gorgeous."

They hung up and Lily headed downstairs, sliding her laptop onto the charger. "Miss Lily," Emerson's security said.

"He wants me to come over for lunch. You alright if I drive myself?"

"I'll take you Miss Lily."

"I can drive myself."

"Understood, but I'll drive. Gives you time to concentrate on other things," his security said as he went outside and got the SUV.

Lily shook her head. All the security was not what she was used to, and she didn't want to ever get used to it. "Whatever happened with that visitor," Lily asked as she got in the SUV.

"We suggested that he went home. That you weren't up to talking to him and probably never would be."

"I can only imagine what his answer was."

"He wasn't happy about it and did try to push his way through and into the house to talk to you."

Lily shook her head, determined not to think about what his security had just said. They went over the bridge as Lily watched the boats go by like she always did. "Is everything alright," his security asked.

Lily nodded. "Just thinking."

"We handled that gentleman. He said he needed to talk to you, but we pointed out that you didn't want any contact."

Lily almost rolled her eyes. She could've handled it on her own, but Emerson would've hit the roof. When they pulled up to Emerson's office building, they headed in and his door was locked. The blinds had been drawn. When she knocked and there was no answer, Lily texted that they were coming up the elevator. When she saw someone leave his office, she shook her head. She walked back down to the elevator, made her way out of the building, and went for a walk alone. He must've called 10 times after she left.

She got down to the Belmond Charleston Place hotel and went and had lunch alone. She was far enough away from windows and prying eyes that she could have a little quiet.

"What can I get you," the waitress asked.

"Sweet tea and the soup and a salad," Lily said.

The waitress left her side and Lily's heart felt like it had been ripped in half. When her phone went off again, quietly, she looked and saw Addy's name and answered.

"Yep."

"He's called me 5 times. What's going on," Addy asked.

"Nothing," Lily replied.

"Since I know you're full of it, what is really going on?"

"Addy, leave it."

"Café at the fancy horse fountain place," Addy asked.

"I'm eating alone. Not a word."

"I'm already in the hotel. I went to Soma," Addy said.

"I don't want…"

"I'm not saying a word to him. See you in 2."

When Addy came in, she walked over and sat down in the quiet booth with Lily. "He called when I was walking in."

"And?"

"I told him that I was meeting my man. Then he said if I saw you to let him know. What's going on Lily?"

Lily shook her head and the waitress brought over the food, got Addy's order, and headed off. "What'd he do now," Addy asked.

Lily shook her head. "I'm not talking about it."

"He said he was meeting with the wedding planner today."

"Hope he had a good time with that," Lily said sarcastically as she felt chest pains.

"What's wrong," Addy asked.

"Nothing."

Addy shook her head. "Lily."

"I don't want to talk about it."

When Lily's phone went off again, she ignored it and turned her phone off. "Talk," Addy said. Lily shook her head. "That man is about to lose everything isn't he?"

"Addy, talk about something else." When Addy's phone went off, Lily shook her head.

"Yes Emerson."

"Where's my wife?"

"You two aren't married yet. I can't even reach her. What happened?"

"Nothing. If you see her, let me know so I can talk to her."

"Whatever you did, you must've really screwed up."

"Addy, it's none of your business. Tell me that you know where she is."

"I don't. I'm just heading back to my car. If I hear from her, I'll let you know," Addy said.

He hung up on her and Lily finished her salad and soup. "Not a word," Addy asked. Lily shook her head.

When they finished lunch, Lily went out the back way and went to turn her phone back on. "What are you doing?"

"Going anywhere but the beach," Lily said.

"Tell me what happened." Lily shook her head again. She didn't need Addy in the middle of it too. "All of your stuff is at the beach house."

"All I need is my laptop and my bag from the closet."

"Fine. Where do you want me to bring it to?"

"Message me."

Addy nodded.

Addy dropped Lily off at her place, knowing that Emerson would never show up there, went over to the beach house and went up to the main bedroom. "Miss Li...oh. Miss Addison. What are you doing," his security asked.

"I needed something out of Lily's laptop. I might be able to figure out where she went. Emerson's been calling me for hours."

"Miss Addison."

She looked at security. One look and she knew that getting that laptop out of the house wasn't gonna work.

"At least tell me that she's safe."

"She is. I was asked to bring the laptop over to her mom and dad's."

His security nodded, Addy packed her stuff up, seeing the prenatal vitamins, grabbed them and her chargers and headed out before Emerson came to the house.

When she pulled out of the driveway, she saw Emerson coming up the street. "Did you find her," Emerson asked as he opened the back window.

"She told me to bring her laptop to her mom's. That's all I know."

"I talked to her mom. She's not there."

"That's all I know Emerson," Addy said.

"If you hear from her, call me." Addy nodded and headed off, getting as far from Emerson as she could, making sure that nobody was following. She pulled off to get gas, made sure that there weren't any trackers or anything on her laptop or anything and topped up the gas tank, heading back towards her place.

She got there, brought Lily's stuff in, and saw Lily running for the bathroom. "Girl, are you okay," Addy asked as she locked the door behind her. When she heard something thump, she got into the bathroom and saw Lily on the floor.

"Lily."

When Lily didn't respond, Addy sat down and got a cool towel, putting it on Lily's head. When she saw Lily grab her stomach, she shook her head. "Are you alright," Addy asked.

"No."

"Lily."

"Ow."

"Lily, talk to me." Lily shook her head. "What's going on?" Lily shook her head again. "Doctor? Hospital? What?"

"Jack," Lily replied as Addy saw her eyes welling up with tears.

"Girl, you can't have Jack and you know that." Lily shook her head.

"I don't care Addy."

She shook her head and helped Lily up. "Come lay down."

"I'm dizzy alright?"

Addison helped her to the sofa, put the cool towel on her neck and got her an ice water. "What happened," Addison asked.

"It has nothing to do…"

Just as Lily was about to say it, Addy's phone went off. "Yes Emerson."

"She's not at her mom and dad's. Where is my wife?"

"Fiancée," Addy said.

"Where," Emerson asked.

"I don't know. I told you that if I knew I'd call and let you know."

"And I know you didn't go to her mom's. Where's Lily?"

"Whatever you did that has you going this insane has to be bad. What did you do," Addy asked.

"None of your business. I'm coming over there."

"No, you aren't Emerson. You don't run the damn world. This is my property."

"And I know that my wife is there."

"Fiancée." Addy hung up and Lily went into the guestroom.

Not 10 minutes later, there was a knock at the door. "What," Addy asked.

"Open," Emerson said.

"No."

"Addison, I need my fiancée. Now."

"I told you that I didn't know where she was. Go home Emerson."

"Open the door." Addy shook her head and opened it. "I've been trying to find her myself. She's not here."

"I need to find her."

"Then go find her. She isn't here."

Emerson shook his head. "Addison."

"What did you do that had her vanishing?"

"Doesn't matter."

"Emerson, just say it."

"I was trying to plan the wedding with the planner. I had the door locked so there wouldn't be any interruptions. When Lily showed, she saw her heading out and then she vanished."

"Whatever lie you need to tell yourself," Addy said.

Emerson shook his head and looked, seeing the blanket on the sofa. "She's here isn't she," Emerson asked.

"No."

"Blanket and an ice water with pink lipstick. Right. I bought her that lipstick. Where is she?"

Addison looked at him. "Leave."

"Where," Emerson said.

"Wherever she went, she has a damn good reason. Go home. Wherever she is, when she cools off you'll know."

Emerson shook his head. "Lily, come out here." When he heard nothing, he walked past Addison, seeing the guest room door locked. "Why is it locked?"

"Because we have storage stuff in there. Emerson, just go home."

"Lily, I know you're in there. Please baby. Please just come out."

When he heard nothing, he shook his head. "Baby, please. It's not what you think. I just needed privacy to plan it. Please just come out." Still no noise. He couldn't hear her crying. He couldn't hear her curling into the fetal position. He couldn't hear her heart crumbling into a million pieces. "Baby, please. Yell at me. Tell me off. Kick my backside to the moon. Something. Anything. Please."

"Emerson, she's not here."

"And that's why her laptop cord is on the sofa right?" "Babe, please just unlock the door."

"Go away," Lily said.

He took a deep breath and exhaled. "Please Lily."

Addison walked over and stood between the door and Emerson. "Leave her alone. Go home. Just go Emerson."

"No. Baby, please just come out here and talk to me."

"No," Lily replied.

Emerson glared at Addy. "Like I said, go home," Addy said.

Emerson shook his head. "Lily, at least tell me that you're alright."

"Go away," Lily replied.

Emerson took a deep breath. "Fine, when you're ready to come back, let me know. We need to talk baby." Addison pushed him and his security out the door.

She double locked the door and knocked on the guest room door. "He's gone," Addy said.

When Lily started sobbing, Addison shook her head. She got the key to the room and unlocked the door, walking in to see Lily curled into the fetal position and sobbing. "What do you want me to do," Addy asked.

"He's not gonna back off."

"I know. You knew that. Tell me what you want."

"What if I went to..."

"He'd find you regardless. Lily, what did you see?"

"A woman buttoning up her shirt and running out of the office."

Addy's fists started to clench. "What do you want me to do?"

"Make him go away."

Addy sat down beside her and gave her a big hug.

"Ow."

"Lily, what are you ow-ing about?"

"My stomach keeps cramping," Lily said.

Addy shook her head. "Bad cramping or..."

"Ow."

Addy looked out the window and saw that Emerson had actually left. "We're getting up. I'm taking you to the hospital."

"No."

"Lily, if you are losing..."

"No," Lily said.

"Lily, you need to." She shook her head. "Are you bleeding?"

"Addy, I'm not."

She shook her head. "You're still going. Either I take you or the EMT takes you," Addy said. Lily got up and Addy saw two little red spots. Two. Two too many.

They got to the hospital and the doctor rushed Lily into the exam room. "Lily, I need to do the ultrasound. Are you alright," her doctor asked.

"Pain. Chest pain too," Lily said.

Addison paced the hall and when the doctor came out and ran for the ultrasound machine, Addy came in. "Are you okay," Addy asked.

"I don't want him here. Not here," Lily said.

"Luckily I grabbed your stuff when we were leaving."

Lily shook her head. When the doctor came in, they did a quick ultrasound. "Alright. Baby is still comfy in there. It's probably just stress. Your blood pressure is a little high too. Are you okay," the doctor asked as she closed the door.

"No. Not even close," Lily said.

"I gather there was a high-stress situation?"

Lily nodded.

She shook her head. "Alright. You can stay here. We're gonna get you an IV. Lower the stress. Calm yourself down. I'll be back in a few minutes."

"I don't want him knowing," Lily said.

The doctor nodded. Addy grabbed the chair and sat down beside her. "Lily, I get it, but you need to tell him." Lily shook her head. "I can't do this. I can't just not tell him that you're in the hospital."

"Addy, leave it. He doesn't need to know and I don't want him here. Let him go do whatever with the fake wedding planner." When she saw Lily welling up again she agreed and held her hand.

By the time that Lily was allowed to go, it was almost 10pm. Addy went to get the truck and saw Emerson.

"What are you doing here," Addy asked.

"She's here isn't she?"

"She was told to lower stress. If she doesn't, she's gonna lose it. That means you backing off. Leave her alone."

"That's..."

"My best friend. Go home."

Emerson shook his head and pushed past her. He made his way down the hallway and found Lily.

"Baby."

"No," Lily said.

"Why didn't you tell me you were here," he said.

"Go away," Lily said.

Just as he went to sit down, her doctor came in. "You're gonna have to leave," the doctor said.

"She's my fiancée."

"I don't care if Lily is your sister. Her blood pressure just shot up. She needs it low. Either leave or I'll have you removed," the doctor said.

"I'm not leaving my fiancée."

"Then be silent and leave her alone. She needs to lower the blood pressure or she'll be here overnight."

Emerson tried to hold her hand and she pulled away from him. His security stood outside the door and when Addy tried to come back in, they stopped her.

"Either you two get out of my way or I'm kicking your kneecaps in," she said as she went into Lily's room.

"Baby, please just talk to me," Emerson asked. When Lily pulled her hand away from Emerson, Addy shook her head.

"Do you need me to do anything," Addy asked.

Lily motioned to get rid of Emerson.

"Lily, please just talk to me," Emerson said.

Addy gave her a hug. "Emerson, leave her be. I'll let you know when she's allowed..."

"No. I am staying with her."

"Go home Emerson."

"I'm not leaving until you talk to me." Lily shook her head and Addy walked over to Emerson.

"If you don't go, she could lose it. You want that on your hands, fine. She's peeved, she's stressed and she was having freaking chest pains. Next time you try to lie, try not to have whatever woman that was in that room not run out doing up her shirt," Addy said as she pointed towards the door. "Go Emerson."

"It's not what..."

"Go," Addy said. He tried to go and kiss Lily's forehead at the least and she shook her head, pushing him away.

"Lily."

She shook her head. "I'm sitting in the hall until you are allowed to leave. Please baby."

Addy shook her head. "I'll keep you posted."

Emerson nodded, looking at Lily again, and went into the hallway. She could hear him going from mad, to irritated, to crying and back again. When Lily calmed, and finally the pain stopped, the doctor came in.

"Alright. Much better," the doctor said.

"And," Lily asked.

"I'm gonna redo the ultrasound and see how you're doing. That stress can't happen Lily. Not now."

Lily nodded and the doctor did the ultrasound. "Alright. You're good. Baby is good. Keep the stress down. You see one drop of blood, you tell me."

Lily nodded and the doctor went to leave. "Is there anything that she can take to calm down?"

"Unfortunately, no. Just stay calm. I get that you can be under stress, but you need to take a deep breath and breathe through it. You'll be okay so long as the stress doesn't escalate like that again."

"Thank you," Lily replied.

"So, what are you gonna do now," Addy asked.

"I don't know. If he's screwing around, I can't be there in that house. Not now."

"Lily, if he's pushing too far, then all the more reason to move into that house."

"I already signed the papers on it. Closes end of August," Lily said.

"He's not gonna leave that hallway. You know that right?"

Lily nodded.

"Do you want to talk to him?"

"If he can stay calm."

Addy gave her a hug and walked into the hallway.

"Is she okay," Emerson asked.

"Sit," Addy said.

"What?"

"She told me. The doctor said that she needs to keep the stress down. Low. No raised voices, no drama, and no aggravation. No crying either or she'll lose it." Emerson got up. "I mean it," Addy said. He nodded and went into the room to see Lily asleep on the hospital bed. He sat down beside her and tried to hold her hand.

"What do you want," Lily asked.

"I want my fiancée. Babe, I know that you are mad. I get that you saw something you didn't need to. I love you. Please just let me take you home."

She shook her head. "No."

"Babe, you need to be somewhere safe and calming."

"I said no Emerson."

He looked at her. "Then tell me where and we'll go."

"Go home. I'll go stay with Addy."

"No."

Lily shook her head. "You were with someone else Emerson. I saw her buttoning her shirt. That doesn't happen unless it was unbuttoned for some reason. I'm not playing this game anymore. Go home. I'll go back to the house with..."

"No."

"Emerson, it's either that or you stay at the beach."

"I need to be with you."

"And I need to be away from you after that."

"I promise you, nothing happened."

Lily shook her head. "Emerson, don't lie to me. It's not a good idea."

"Babe." Lily shook her head again and took a deep breath. "She..."

"What?"

"She hit on me. I told her that you were on the way there and..."

"Emerson, stop. I don't believe you alright?" Lily got up and the nurse came in. She undid the IV and helped Lily up.

"No stress," the nurse said. Lily nodded and grabbed her bag, slid off the bed and went to leave behind the nurse when Emerson stopped her.

"What?"

His hands slid to her face and he kissed her. "I promise you that nothing happened. Nothing. Babe, I love you more than anything in the world. You know that."

"And I know that she walked out of your locked office doing her shirt up. That's not the way it should be Emerson. You want to play the field then I move out. Easy as that," Lily replied.

She went to leave the room and he stopped her. "I don't want you moving anywhere."

"I need to take care of me Emerson. You want to..."

He kissed her. "I want you."

"Pass," Lily replied as she stepped away from him and went into the hallway.

"You ready," Addy asked.

"She's coming back to the house," Emerson said as he grabbed her hand. Lily shook her head and pulled away from him. She headed out and Emerson took her hand, walking her to the SUV and she shook her head.

"I said no."

"And I said get in. We can talk about it at the house."

Lily shook her head. "Emerson, I'm going with Addy."

"Get in the SUV."

"Emerson."

He picked her up and put her into the SUV. Addy went around the side.

"If you need me?"

Lily nodded. "Thank you for coming with me."

Addy nodded and headed off to her truck. "I need my stuff at Addy's."

"It's in the back," he replied. Lily shook her head and they went back to the house. Not the beach house, but the house that was far away enough from everyone that she would have to wait for anyone to come get her.

Lily barely said two words to him the entire drive home. She wouldn't come near him and when he tried to hold her hand, she pulled away. "Lily, please."

"Don't count on sleeping tonight in there."

"Lily."

"No."

They got to the house and Lily shook her head. "Come with me," Emerson asked.

"No."

"Lily, please." She shook her head.

"I don't want to be here," Lily said.

"Come inside. We can talk."

She took a deep breath, got out on her side, got her bag, and went and sat on the grass. She wanted to be away from him. Far away. He walked over to her. "Babe, please."

"I don't want to do this and you know I don't."

He grabbed her bag, handing it to his security and picked her up, carrying her inside and up to their bedroom.

"Emerson, what part of no didn't you understand?"

He closed the bedroom door and he slid her bag onto the counter in her closet. "The part where you think that you can walk out."

"Oh really? What are you gonna do Emerson? Tie me to the bed? I don't want to be near you right now. Maybe not..."

He kissed her.

Lily shook her head. "Go away Emerson. Go to the beach house. Go pick up some random bikinis and leave me alone."

He sat down beside her and Lily shook her head, getting up and sitting on the chair alone. "You can't seriously think that I would cheat on you in my office."

"I'm moving out Emerson. I'm leaving. Take the ring..."

He walked over to her and kissed her. "Don't leave."

"You were with..."

"No, I wasn't Lily. You want to know then I'll tell you."

Lily shook her head, got up and threw jeans, shorts, lingerie and shirts into her bag. "Lily."

"Leave me alone Emerson."

He picked her up and sat her on the edge of the bed. "She walked in and made a move. She locked the door and I told her that you were coming. She tried to pounce, and you tried opening the door. When you sent that text is when she ran out. I'm not letting you walk out because she's an idiot."

"Letting me? Since when do I have to ask permission Emerson?"

She went to grab her bag and he stopped her. "Don't do this."

She shook her head. "Just let go," Lily replied.

"I can't."

"Emerson, I can't be here."

"Then we go back to the beach house."

"No."

"Lily, I can't lose you."

"Should've thought of that…" He kissed her and slid her tight into his arms. "Don't do this." Lily shook her head and tried to break out of his arms. "Lily."

"Stop. I don't care what stupid lie that you're telling yourself about what happened. I don't. I don't want to hear about it anymore Emerson. Just leave me alone." He kissed her. One all-encompassing kiss that led him to pick her up and wrap her legs around him as he walked towards the bed and leaned her onto it.

"Emerson," Lily said as he came up for air.

"Babe, please. Please don't."

"I can't. I can't be with someone who thinks nothing of cheating on me when you spent all this time trying to talk me into a wedding and a baby and an engagement. I can't. Maybe you'll find someone that you're…"

"Don't. Don't walk away. Don't leave." Lily shook her head, pushed him off of her and got up. "Babe." She went to grab her bag. "Lily, don't leave."

"Then you're not staying in here."

"Lily, please."

She shook her head and made her way downstairs with her bag. She walked out the front door, put her bag in her truck and pulled out. She got to the gate and when he wouldn't open it, Lily snapped.

"I'm not letting you walk away. I'm not gonna watch you leave all over again. Don't do this," he said.

"You made your decision Emerson."

"Lily."

"Open the gate."

"No. Just come back up to the house. We can talk." Lily shook her head.

"Open it or I swear I'm ramming it."

"Come back up so we can talk."

"No Emerson."

"I'm not opening it."

He walked back up to the house and Lily shook her head. She parked her truck and burst into tears. She needed to be away from him. Far away. On another planet. Emerson went and sat on the front steps. He texted Lily:

> *I'll give you her contact info and you can get the proof. Please just come up here. I need you to stay.*

When he got no reply, he stared at the truck:

> *Please baby. Please just come up here.*

Somehow, all the noise from outside got quiet. Too quiet. He could hear her crying. Her truck wasn't running. He could feel the tears welling up in his eyes. He could feel her pain:

I need you like I need air. I always have. Please just come back up here so we can talk. Please.

Again, there was no reply, no read message. Nothing. He got up and walked down to her truck, then saw her in tears. He opened her door and she shook her head. "Come inside. Please baby."

"Go...away," Lily said between sniffles and tears.

"Babe, please."

"Just open the gate and let me go," Lily said.

"No. Baby, I get it. I promise you that nothing happened short of me telling her that I wanted her to leave. She tried to kiss me and I pushed her away. I didn't sleep with her. Nothing happened."

"I don't believe you."

"Move over then."

"Emerson."

"Move over." She shook her head and slid to the passenger seat. Emerson slid in and drove back up to the garage. He took the keys, slid them in his pocket, got her bag and took her hand. He walked her back inside and walked her upstairs to the bedroom, closing and locking the door behind him.

Chapter 5

"I need to leave," Lily said.

"This is your home as much as it's mine remember? Both our names are on the deed Lily."

She shook her head. "I don't want to be here with you."

"I didn't cheat Lily. I swear to you that I didn't." She shook her head and went to take the ring off when he stopped her. "Don't."

"Emerson, you talk me into a damn wedding and then you do that? Seriously?"

Lily took the ring off and handed it to him.

"Lily." She shook her head.

"Give me my keys."

"No." She shook her head and walked towards the door. "We're talking until we hash this out."

He slid the ring back on her hand, even with her fighting him on it. "If I have to put glue on it I will. Enough."

"I don't trust you Emerson. Not anymore." He took a deep breath, grabbed his phone, made one phone call, and put it on speaker.

"Emerson."

"My fiancée is now livid. I told you that she was coming and you tried to make a move. You did all of it to cause a damn rift. Tell her what you did," Emerson said as Lily tried to break away from him.

"I was attracted to him. I overdid it a little and pushed too far. I tried to kiss him and he pushed me away. I tried to show off the lace lingerie in hopes he'd agree, and he opened the office door and told me to leave."

Lily shook her head and locked herself in the bathroom alone. Part of her thought that somehow he wouldn't be able to hear her crying. She felt her pocket buzz and took a deep breath.

She looked and Addy had texted:

> *Are you okay? I know that he's not letting you leave his sight. I can come ram the gate if you need me to.*

Lily smirked:

> *I wish it were that easy. I already tried. Thank you for being there today. You're my best friend for a reason. Love you.*

When she got a phone call from Addy not two minutes later, she answered and went to the back corner of the bathroom.

"Are you alright?"

"No. He called whoever out on the crap and thinks that will fix everything. It doesn't," Lily said.

"Do you want me to drive up there?"

"It's not gonna fix it Addy. I wish it would, but it won't. I won't be able to leave."

"Lily, you're not being held hostage."

"He won't even let me go through the gate. I'm not gonna be able to go until all of it is handled Addy. Honestly, I'd leave at 2am if I had to."

"If you need me, I'm there. You need help getting your stuff, message me."

Lily hung up with her and heard Emerson at the door. "Babe, please come out here."

She took a deep breath. She splashed some cold water on her face and he knocked. "Lily."

"Leave me alone Emerson."

She sat down on the floor with her back against the tile wall. The cool tile was what she needed. At least that. "Lily, please."

She took a deep breath and got up. She didn't want to feel his lips on hers. She didn't want to feel him near her. She wanted to jump out of a window, but she couldn't.

"I need you to go," Lily said.

"Not until you come out here."

She shook her head and took another deep breath, opening the door. "Go."

He took her hand and pulled her to him. "I didn't do anything. Babe, I told you. She told you. Nothing happened."

"I'm not gonna be the fool Emerson. I'm not gonna be the idiot that lets you get away with cheating. I'm done." He kissed her.

"Babe."

She shook her head and pushed him away.

"Lily."

"Don't."

"I promise you that I didn't. She even said that we didn't. I don't know what you want me to do."

"Let me leave."

"I can't."

She shook her head. "This isn't gonna work Emerson. It's not. I need space. I need to be alone. Either you go or I do."

"I'm not losing you Lily. I can't lose you."

"You're still pushing too much."

"I love you. I can't walk away from that."

"I need space Emerson. Alone. Just go."

"Then stay here. I'll go to the beach house."

"I don't want to wake up with you here."

He walked over to her and kissed her. "I promise you that nothing happened. Nothing. Please just see that."

Lily shook her head, sitting down on the chair. "It's Wednesday. I'll come get you Sunday and we can go to church."

Lily couldn't even look at him. "Leave."

"Lily."

"Emerson, either you go or I am leaving."

"Baby." She shook her head and got up, walking out to the balcony, and sitting down. She couldn't even be in the same space as he was. "Lily," he said.

She shook her head and leaned back, curling up on the chair. When he came to the doorway of the balcony and saw her, he couldn't do it. He couldn't see her like that. It killed him seeing it. And he was the cause. When Lily heard the SUV starting, she exhaled and was in tears. Lily grabbed her phone and called her mom.

"Baby. What's wrong," her mom asked.

"You remember him right?"

"Of course I do."

"I need to know that I'm not going insane," Lily said.

"Baby, you're worrying me. What's wrong," her mom replied. Lily told her what had happened and when her mom was overtly quiet, she knew.

"Baby, it's up to you whether you trust him and believe him. Honestly, it's happened to a million guys in this world. If he's determined to make you believe him and trust him, then it's your choice. Honestly, after him reacting like that, I don't think he did. If he actually did sleep with her, I'd whoop him to the moon myself. Lily, he loves you. Your dad and I do too. If you need something, you tell me. If you need to leave, say it."

"Mom."

"Alright. I'm gonna come down. You and I can go have dinner somewhere just us. How does that sound?"

"I need you and dad."

"I'll make the reservation. Just send me over the address and I'll come get you," her mom said as Lily texted over the address. "I'll see you at 5 baby." Lily hung up with her parents and tried to relax as best she could.

When it got to dinner, Lily slid into her sundress and grabbed a sweater, slid her sandals on and went downstairs. "Miss Lily, can I get the SUV ready for you?"

"My folks are coming over. I'm going out," Lily said.

"I can set..."

"I have it handled. I don't need a babysitter out with my folks."

"Miss Lily."

"Don't," she said. When there was a buzz at the gate, his security let her folks in. Lily walked out the front door and got in the car with her folks, heading off.

"Alright, tell me what's going on," her dad asked. Lily told him and her dad almost snapped.

"And you didn't belt him," her dad asked.

"There's no point dad. It's not gonna change what happened, and it's not gonna make him realize what he's done. I can't just sit here and pretend that it didn't ruin everything. I can't be there when all of it is happening."

"What are you gonna do with all of it," her mom asked as they pulled into the restaurant.

"I don't know. He says that he denied her, and I think that he didn't. I can't just trust whatever he says. I don't feel like he's telling me the truth."

"Honestly, if you're that concerned, say it. I don't want you getting married to him when he's not gonna be faithful. My daughter deserves better than that. You know that," her dad said.

"I just wish that I could stop feeling like I just made the biggest mistake ever," Lily said.

By the time that she got back, Emerson was sitting on the front steps. She shook her head and her dad stepped out, walking inside with Emerson so they could talk alone.

"Come up here," her mom said.

Lily hopped in the front. "Lily, your dad has made a million mistakes, but that isn't one that either of us ever went through. He loves you. We both know that. Just do what your heart says. If you need me to come down here and steal you away, tell me. I love you," her mom said.

"I love you too," Lily said as she gave her mom a hug. She headed inside and heard her dad telling Emerson off. She walked upstairs and slid into joggers and a hoodie, grabbed her laptop and sat down to write alone outside on the balcony.

When she heard her mom and dad's car leave, Lily shook her head. She knew it was only a matter of time before Emerson walked upstairs. She moved over so she was out of his view. She needed the space and the peace and quiet. When she heard footsteps again, Lily shook her head.

Emerson came outside and saw her. "Are you talking to me yet?"

"No."

"Can you come in here for a minute?"

"No."

He walked out to the balcony and reached his hand out. "Please."

She shook her head. "Go back to the beach."

"Not when you went out without security. Come inside for a minute."

"No."

He walked over to Lily. "Please," he said.

"I said no."

"Lily, we aren't having this conversation outside. Come in here."

Lily shook her head. "I said no."

He reached his hand out and she shook her head. "What part of no didn't you understand?"

"Lily."

"Emerson." He shook his head, picked her up and carried her back inside, sat her on the bed and closed the door to the balcony.

Lily shook her head, got up and plugged in her laptop and shook her head. "We're talking," Emerson said.

"Go ahead Emerson. Do whatever you want like you always do."

"I didn't sleep with her. I promise you that I didn't. All I did was try and plan out the wedding stuff. She made a move and I said no. That's it Lily. I promise you that's all it was."

"Why are you here?"

"Because I was worried about you when I found out that you weren't with security."

"I was with my mom and dad Emerson. I don't need security."

"Yeah you do."

"Emerson, get out whatever..."

He kissed her, devouring her lips.

"What are you doing," Lily asked as she pushed him away.

"I don't want to fight anymore. I can't," he said.

"Emerson, you told me that you'd give me space."

He kissed her again and curled her into his arms. He wouldn't let go. When he leaned her onto the bed, she pushed him away.

"I can't do this," Lily said.

He kissed her again. "I love you. Please just stop pushing me away."

Lily shook her head, got up, grabbed her laptop and went to walk back outside. He slid the laptop from her hands, putting it on the chair and slid his arms around her.

"Stop."

He kissed her neck. "Babe."

"Either you..." He turned her to face him and kissed her, devouring her lips.

"I want my woman back," he said.

"Too bad," Lily said as he kissed her again and picked her up, wrapping her legs around his hips. "Emerson, just leave me alone."

He shook his head and leaned her against the wall. "Mine," he said.

"What are..." He kissed her again and slid her joggers off.

"Emerson." He kissed her again, pulling his shirt off, then going for her hoodie.

"What..."

He kissed her again, peeled his jeans off and his boxers. He slid her hoodie off and they had sex. Hot, he needed her sex that had him trying everything he could to get her back. They went from the wall to the bed to the floor. When they came up for air, Lily felt like she needed to shower. She needed to wipe the feeling off like he'd just slept with her to get what happened out of her mind. She got up and went to walk into the bathroom.

"Lily."

She closed and locked the door, had a long shower, crying on the bench of the shower. She felt sick. Sick that he'd probably screwed around on her, and now she had been with him again like it had never happened. She shook her head and finally flipped the water off.

She combed out her hair, freshened up and wrapped herself in the robe. "Babe, please."

She shook her head. She wanted more than anything to just leave, but she also knew that she wouldn't get that far. She took a deep breath and unlocked the door. "Come to bed," he said.

"Emerson, I told you that I didn't want you here. I told you..."

He kissed her again. "I love you. I get that you are so damn convinced even after I told you and she told you that nothing happened."

"I don't believe you."

"Lily, it's been a long day. Just come to bed and get some rest."

She shook her head, grabbed her pajamas and went into the guestroom, locking the door and putting a chair under it to make sure that Emerson left her alone.

She curled up on the bed, relaxed and got some rest. When she woke up the next morning, she was in the main bedroom and curled up in bed with Emerson's arm around her. She shook her head and got out of bed.

"Lily."

She shook her head. She went and slid on workout clothes, put her AirPods pro in, grabbed her phone and went downstairs to work out. When she was finished, Lily went to head upstairs and saw Emerson.

"What happened to you going and staying at the beach house?"

"I'm not playing anymore. I'm not letting you leave. Nothing happened with her, and if I have to sleep with you every damn night, I will. If I have to remind you that I'm yours for life, I will. I'm not walking away, and I'm not letting you leave me in the damn dust like you did in high school," Emerson said.

Lily shook her head and went to brush past him when he pulled her onto his lap.

"What," Lily asked.

"You don't get to walk out of here Lily."

"And? I'm not a hostage Emerson. I can leave…"

He kissed her, nibbling at her lips until he was pulling at her sports bra. She pushed him away and got up, walking up the steps to the kitchen. When she didn't see the housekeeper or the security guys there, she shook her head.

"Lily."

"No," she said as she walked up to the bedroom and locked the door behind her. She had a hot shower, got dressed and was about to do her hair when Emerson came up behind her. "What," Lily asked.

"Are you that damn determined to avoid me?"

She shook her head and he picked her up, carrying her to the bed. "Emerson."

He sat her on the side of the bed. "I'm not playing Lily. I meant what I said. I'm not letting you get rid of me. I'm not gonna sit here and watch you push me out of your life. All I want is you. What about that don't you believe?"

"The part where she was doing her shirt up," Lily said. She got up and walked off, going downstairs. She went and made herself breakfast then sat outside, as far from the door as possible. When Emerson walked outside, he shook his head. He vanished back into the house, emerging 10 minutes later with an omelet, coffee, and fresh fruit.

"Talk," he said.

"What part of go to the beach house didn't you understand? You agreed to it then end up back here? Seriously? I went out to dinner with my parents Emerson.

Leave me alone and just go back to the damn beach house and leave me alone."

He shook his head. "I'm not doing that."

"Then I'm leaving." She finished her breakfast, walked around the other way and went into the house. She put her dishes in the washer, walked upstairs and put her things into her bag, then packed the second one. She slid her electronics in the bag, found her truck keys and hid them in her pocket. She took her things downstairs, threw them in the truck and got down the driveway and through the gate before Emerson caught up with her.

She got out of town, attempting to be away from everything. She went to go to the one place that she knew she'd have space, but she couldn't. She found another spot that he wouldn't think that she'd go to, paying in cash for a week. She made sure that the location apps wouldn't give up where she was. She went into her quiet suite and relaxed, sitting down on the bed. Within a matter of 10 minutes, her phone was going off like crazy. First Emerson, then his security, then her parents, then Addy. "What's up," Lily asked.

"Mr. Ballistic is looking for you everywhere. Where in the world did you go?"

"Somewhere away from his stupid security and away from him."

"You do know that he's lost his mind right?"

"Addy, he said he would give me space. I went out with my folks for dinner and when I got back, he was sitting on the damn doorstep. I can't keep doing this. Until I am ready, I'm staying here. I'm not going back to that house."

"At least give me a hint."

"No."

"Lily."

"I have to go," she said as she hung up. Lily knew that he was gonna find her one way or another, but she prayed that maybe he'd actually listen for once.

She sat on her little patio, finished up the edits and by dinner, she was starting on the second run of her own edits. Her phone went off again at 6:30. One look and she pressed decline. She didn't want to talk to Emerson. She needed peace, and he was the furthest thing from it. She got room service from the resort and ate her dinner listening to the water. When her phone went off again at 7, she ignored the call. She made sure that any way of tracking her phone was fully off, knowing that he'd keep calling until she answered. She finished dinner, sat back with her ice water and relaxed. When the phone rang again at 8, she answered.

"Where in the hell are you," Emerson asked. He was passed irate. He was mad, worried, angry, and breathing fire into every word.

"Away from you. I told you that I needed space and you ignored me. You came back to the house when you promised that you wouldn't. Now I have space."

"Where are you Lily?"

"Somewhere that isn't near you."

"Lily, you're pregnant. I can't have you out there without..."

"Emerson, I'm not a child, and I'm not a toy you can play with. You screwed up. Large. I don't trust being alone with you. You were with..."

"I wasn't. I didn't do anything with her other than tell her to stop. You're my fiancée Lily. Get back to the damn house so we can end this stupid fight once and for all."

"No."

"Then tell me where you are."

"South Carolina," she replied.

"That's not funny."

"Wasn't meant to be. I'm away from all of it. You, Zack, everything. Just leave me alone Emerson. When I come back, I'll get my stuff and move into my place."

"No, you aren't."

"Yeah I am. I'm not marrying someone I don't trust. You caused the stress. You. I'm lowering my stress alone." Lily hung up. She burst into tears 2 minutes later, but she had space.

Lily slid her phone on her charger, locked the doors and flipped the fan on, curling up on the bed. Within a matter of 15 minutes, she was out cold.

The next morning, Lily woke up to 18 missed calls from Emerson, 5 from Addy and one from her Dad. She called her Dad first. "Hi," Lily said.

"Emerson called here 3 times looking for you. Everything okay?"

"No. I just decided that I needed time to breathe and be alone. He wasn't happy with it."

"I can tell. Where did you go?"

"I'm still in the state. I just got out of town. I needed to finish the edits uninterrupted."

"Did you at least manage that," her dad asked.

"Of course. I even got the dedication done. Now, the last read through and it's done," Lily replied.

"You need to call him."

"I will eventually."

"Lily, I talked to him last night. He knows how upset you are. I even see that what he did was really wrong. Even being in that position is, but you can't keep holding on to what happened. He told her to leave and she did. You have to let it go."

She talked to her dad a while longer and when Emerson called her again, and after an I love you to her dad, she answered. "What?"

"This is ridiculous. Where are you?"

"Like I said Emerson. Somewhere away from you."

"Lily, please just come home."

"That's not my home."

"Lily, we're having a baby. Please just come back so we can talk about this."

"No."

"Tell me where you are then."

"No."

"Please baby. I get it. I messed up. It happened and I can't change it. She even apologized for trying to. Please baby." Lily hung up, curled up on the bed and was in tears a few minutes later.

Lily managed to get her breakfast ordered and curled back up on her patio. Fine. She could hold a grudge, but she had a baby to think of. Her mind was overtaking her heart. It hurt too much to even think about what had happened. Just as she was calming down, Addy called her. "What's up," Lily asked.

"Other than Emerson ransacking my place looking for you? Nothing. I mean seriously Lily. You won't even tell me?"

"Because I know he'd drag it out of you."

"Lily."

"I'm away from the drama Addy. The doctor said lower stress so I am."

"She didn't say vanish on everyone and everything that you know and disappear into nowhere. I'm sure she meant stay near a hospital."

"I am."

"Lily."

"Addy, leave it."

"Then meet me for dinner."

"Not when his security will tail you."

"Lily, you do know that he's gonna keep trying to hunt you down until he finds you right?"

"Doesn't change anything Addy. I'm not going until I know what I want to do."

"You're seriously thinking about calling it off?"

"If he doesn't show me that he's not gonna cheat, yeah I am." Lily heard Addy walking across the floor that sounded way too much like she was in Emerson's house. "Where are you right now," Lily asked.

"He begged," Addy said. Lily shook her head and went to hang up when Emerson got her phone.

"Lily." She took a deep breath.

"So, now you're involving my friend in your scheme to get me back to the house? Really? A little high school of you Emerson," Lily said.

"If you're gonna up and vanish on me, this is what I have to do. I need you back here."

"And I need you to leave me alone and leave my friends out of your stupid scheme."

"Baby," he said as she heard a door close, knowing that he'd walked into his office and closed the door.

"Don't baby me. You're stupid plot to get some didn't work Emerson. Maybe it did with her. Who knows."

"Lily, stop. Please. I didn't. We didn't. Nothing happened other than her making a pass and me turning her down."

"I don't believe you."

"Where are you?"

"Bluffton."

"Lily."

"I'm not coming until I decide what I want. I can't be with you when I don't trust you."

"Lily, please come home. I get that you're mad. Come back so we can talk. Please baby."

"Goodbye," Lily said as she hung up.

Emerson smashed his hand on the desk. That woman had caused the last ounce of drama he was going to deal with. All he wanted was to plan a wedding that Lily would be stunned at. One that would not only sweep her off her feet but make her forget the stupid crap that his mom had done and said.

"Sam, find out where she is."

"Sir."

"Now." He handed Addy's phone to his security guy and looked at Addy.

"Don't you start. She's upset Emerson. I can't fix that for you. I can't do anything. I wasn't there to see whatever happened."

"I need her. I need her back here. Get her back here," Emerson said.

"I'm not doing that. All of that crap with her is why she ended up in the hospital. She's taking care of herself. Leave the woman alone."

"I can't do that," Emerson said.

"Emerson, we both know that she loves you. Just give her some space."

"No. I need her back here. I need to see her."

"She's off in the middle of nowhere Emerson. She doesn't want to be here. You should know that."

"I also know that she's my fiancée Addy. I'm going to find her."

There was nothing that Addy could say. He was as determined as he was the day that he'd proposed. The day that he'd asked her on that first date. He wasn't sleeping until he found her. He walked into his security office. "And," Emerson asked.

"Location is off on her phone. From what I would guess, she's at a private resort in Bluffton. She's definitely away from everything. If this is the place, they aren't gonna tell you if she's there."

"How far is it?"

"Two hours max. The montage. If I had to guess, a lagoon view."

"Then let's go," Emerson said as he handed Addy back her cell phone.

"What," Addy asked.

"I'm going to get my woman back."

"Emerson." He ignored Addy and headed off with his security.

Not 10 minutes later, Addy called Lily. "What? Are you gonna just tell him..."

"He thinks he figured it out. Be prepared. I think he's coming," Addy said as she got in her truck.

"I am so over this. If he shows up here, it's over."

"Lily, he's desperate. He doesn't look like he's slept since you left. He hasn't shaved, and probably hasn't had coffee either with that attitude. Just make sure you don't stress out alright?"

"Can you do me one favor?"

"What?"

"Get the truth from that woman."

"On it. I promise," Addy said.

"Where is this place," Emerson asked.

"Sir, honestly, I don't think demanding that she come home is a good plan. She doesn't need any undue stress. Whatever the reason for that hospital visit, I don't think getting in a fight with her is going to be a good idea."

"I need to know where she is. I need to see for myself."

"We know that Zack isn't there. Is it really necessary?"

"Fine. Stop and get something to eat and I'll try and call her," Emerson said.

When the SUV stopped, Emerson took a deep breath and called Lily. All he needed to hear was that she was safe. That's it. "What now," Lily asked.

"Come home."

"Emerson, we talked about this."

"No, we didn't. You left. You vanished to Addy's then who knows where."

"Emerson."

"I didn't sleep with her. She didn't touch me. I didn't touch her either. Please baby, just come back to the house."

"No."

"Lily, I love you. I have since we were kids. I wouldn't do that."

"I can't."

"Then let me come to you. I'll come out to wherever. We can do lunch. Please baby."

"Emerson."

"I can't do this without you. I can't do life without you. Please?"

"I can't. Not when I..."

"I promise you that nothing happened."

"Emerson, I can't trust that. I can't."

"Then at least come meet me. I'll get us lunch or dinner or breakfast. Whatever you want."

"Emerson."

"Please."

Lily knew it was only a matter of time until he found out where she actually was. Maybe it was the creek, maybe it was the rustling of the summer breeze in the trees. One way or another, he was gonna find out. "All I want is some time alone Emerson. That's it. I need time to think, to edit and finish the full edits of the book without interruptions. I can't do that when all I see is you cheating on me with someone else. Whether you did or you didn't, it feels like you did. I just want time," Lily said as she shook her head and curled back up on her screened in porch area.

"Baby, please. I get it. You're worried. You have to know that I would never do that. I can't live without you."

"I need to go Emerson."

"Then come home."

"Not right now."

"Lily."

"Emerson, I said no."

"Then I'm coming to get you."

His security handed him an iced latte and they made their way to the resort. Emerson shook his head, trying again to talk to her, but her phone went straight to voicemail. He finished his coffee then went through emails as they made their way to what he hoped was where Lily was.

Just as Lily was getting comfortable, Addy called. "What's up," Lily asked.

"He's determined by the way. I got confirmation. She didn't sleep with him or do anything. She tried to do a little tease, but he shot her down almost instantly. He basically said that you were on the way and if she didn't leave, she was gonna go out the window."

"Addy."

"I get it, but he didn't do anything. Lily, he has lost his marbles in more ways than one. Just talk to him."

"Thank you."

"Girl, I just want you happy. That's it. If being far from him is what you want, fine, but you still have to talk to him."

"Love you," Lily said.

"Back at ya. I mean it. He's a good egg even if he is a pain in my butt," Addy joked.

Lily took a deep breath, enjoying her little cottage for as long as she could before Emerson showed. She finished the second read-through, made the last of the edits and saved it in her laptop. She came inside, washed up and got changed when she got a call from the front desk of the resort. "Yes," Lily said.

"There's a Emerson Cartwright here to see you. Did you want us to let him know where..."

"No." Lily shook her head, slid her sandals on and walked up the back way to the front desk.

"Miss Lily, I couldn't..."

"It's fine," Lily said as she walked over to Emerson.

"What did you..." He kissed her, pulling her into his arms like she was the last oxygen there was. Like she was all that was left and he was holding on.

"Come with me," he said.

"Emerson."

"Outside."

She shook her head. "Fine. Pool."

"Emerson, stop." He kissed her again and walked her outside to the patio. Nobody else was there at that point, so they had all the space to themselves.

"I need you home."

"And I need space. I told you that."

"This is too much space Lily. Way too much." He kissed her again. "Please."

"Emerson, I get that you want what you want, but I can't do that."

"I need you home Lily. I need you. I didn't do anything with her. You know that. Please just let me take you home."

She shook her head. "I can't." Lily got up and he pulled her back to him so she was in his lap.

He kissed her, devouring her lips. He got up, picking her up and sat down on the chaise.

"What are you doing," Lily asked.

"Either we both stay wherever your stuff is, or I'm getting a suite. Your choice."

"Emerson."

He texted his security to get him a suite. When he got a reply 5 minutes later with the room number and digital key, he picked Lily up and carried her inside, up to the penthouse suite and through the door, straight into the bedroom.

"Emerson." He leaned her onto the bed and peeled his shirt off then went for her shorts. "We can't do this," Lily said.

He kissed her again and pulled her shirt off then kicked his jeans to the floor along with his boxers. "What are you doing," Lily asked.

He kissed her again and leaned into her arms. "Taking my wife back. I can't be without you anymore. I just can't," he said as he pulled her legs around his hips and made love to her. It was romance. It was passion, romance, and a million pounding hearts. When they came up for air, he pulled her to him and slid to his back. "Come home with me."

"Emerson."

"Please. I'll do whatever you want. I need you Lily."

She kissed him. "I'm staying. I'll be back next…"

"Lily."

"I'm staying and finishing the book."

"Baby."

She shook her head. "I need time to think. I need to know that what happened isn't gonna happen again. Right now, I don't think that you can…"

He kissed her again. "Lily." She shook her head.

She went to get up and he sat up, kissing her neck. "Please."

"In a few days."

"Lily."

"Emerson, leave it." His arms slid around her.

"I can't do this."

"I'm going. Just go home. Please."

She got re-dressed and he shook his head. "I can't Lily. I can't just sit and wait." She did her shorts up and slid her sandals back on. "Tell me where you're going then," Emerson asked.

She went to walk out and Emerson pulled his jeans on, grabbing her hand and pulling her back to him before she vanished again.

"What," she asked as his arms wrapped tight around her. His hands slid to her face, cradling it as he leaned in and kissed her.

"Please."

"Emerson."

"Please Lily. Please." He kissed her again. She shook her head and left, making her way to the elevator, and opting to go down the steps and out the back way to her cottage.

When she got there, she almost burst into tears. She closed and locked the door and sat down on her bed. Her phone went off and she saw Addy's name.

"Hey," Lily said as she sniffled.

"Are you okay? I've been trying to call for an hour and a half."

"He's here."

"In your suite?"

"In the hotel."

"Lily, I know as well as you do that he isn't gonna leave."

"What are you gonna do?"

"I can't do this Addy. I was single and happy. I was writing my book, I was fine being alone."

"And now," Addy asked.

"I can't. Every dang woman that passes him wants him. I'm just simple me Addy. Just a girl who writes romance novels. Lives in a house without an ocean view, wishes and dreams of beach houses. I'm not what he wants even if he says he does."

"Lily."

"I'm not what he wants Addy. He wants someone who's gonna be in that circle of wealth. I'm not that person and I never will be."

"Lily, he loves you. He loved you before you were the author. Before you were who you are now. He loved you in high school. He loved you when you were infatuated with the idiot football player. He loved you before we knew what love actually was. Why are you so dang convinced that he doesn't want you?"

"Because he wants something else. I know he does."

"That's it. I'm coming down there. Give me the address."

Lily messaged her the address and curled up on the bed. She cried until she thought she couldn't anymore. Just as she was about to nod off, there was a knock at her door. She shook her head and knew that it was either Emerson or his security. She didn't want to open it. Not in a million years. When she sat back down in front of it on the floor, she heard Emerson almost crumble.

"I know you're there Lily. Please baby. Talk to me."

Lily shook her head and the tears welled up in her eyes again.

An hour and a half later, Lily's phone buzzed. She got up and saw a call from the front desk.

"Miss Lily, there's an Addison..."

"She's fine. Just let her know." Lily hung up and threw cold water on her face. When she heard Addy fighting with Emerson outside, she shook her head.

"If you're going in there, so am I," Emerson said.

"If you want any damn chance of her coming back to Charleston, I'm going in. I need to talk to my best friend Emerson. Leave her alone."

Addy knocked and Lily let her inside, leaving Emerson outside intentionally.

Chapter 6

The minute the door was closed, Addy wrapped her arms around Lily and hugged her. "I don't want you ever talking like that again. That man is a dang mess. You know that and so do I."

"I'm not what he wants Addy."

"Then why is he sitting on the front steps of this cottage? He won't budge. Lily, he loves you. He doesn't care about anything else. He wants you."

"That's not enough Addy. You know it isn't. I'm not in..."

"Lily, his mom doesn't want to marry you. He does. Stop pushing him away."

"You don't understand Addy." She hugged Lily and shook her head.

"Lily, he doesn't love you because of your money or your house or your truck. He loves you because of who you are in there," Addy said pointing to Lily's heart.

"That's not what he wants Addy. You know that and so do I."

Addy hugged her. "Breathe. I'll help you pack."

"Addy."

She packed Lily's stuff back up and put it in her bag, sliding her laptop into the smaller bag.

"Addy."

"What?"

"I can't." Addy shook her head, opened the door, and handed Emerson the bags.

"What are you doing?"

"Lily, I get it. You're petrified that you're making the wrong choice. Right now, staying here? You are. You deserve to be with someone that loves you unconditionally. He does. I wish I could find that. Now go get in the SUV. Go home. Enough hiding out." Lily shook her head and Addy hugged her.

"Emerson, I swear, if you break her heart, I'll break every single bone in your body and throw you in a woodchipper," Addy said.

"I never will," he said as Lily saw his eyes red.

Addy got in her truck, and Lily saw that her truck was gone. "Where's my truck?"

"On it's way back to Charleston. Come with me," he asked as he walked with her to the SUV.

"Emerson." He got the door for her and helped her in. "Why could you not just leave me alone?"

"Because I can't be without you that long."

"Emerson." He kissed her and slid her into his lap. "What," she asked. He devoured her lips and held her tight to him. "Emerson."

He hugged her. "Don't leave me again. Not ever."

"All you had to do was give me space."

He shook his head and wouldn't let go of her hand. "I can't do that Lily. I love you."

She was quiet the rest of the way back, sliding into the other seat in the back. He still wouldn't let go of her hand. Not for anything. When they got back to the house, he walked her inside and up to the bedroom so they could talk alone.

"What," Lily asked as soon as he closed the door.

"What did you say to Addison?"

Lily shook her head. "Emerson."

"Tell me."

"That I'm not what you want. I don't have money or a fancy car or security or any of it. I'm not even in the same realm as you. I don't have a mansion or..."

He kissed her. "Yeah you do. Your name is on the deed of this house, and the beach house and everything else. It's ours."

"Yours."

He shook his head. "Tell me what you need me to do."

"Nothing. Emerson, even your mom says that I'm not in your league."

"I don't care what she says Lily. You're the only one I want. The only one I ever wanted."

Lily shook her head. "You don't want me Emerson."

"Yeah I do. Lily, why can't you understand that I never stopped loving you?"

"Because I know better."

He kissed her again, devouring her lips. "Baby, you're my fiancée. I wouldn't have asked just to make my mom feel like crap. I want you. Only you." She shook her head and he snuggled her to him. "I love you and I always will."

"Emerson, there are a million girls throwing themselves at you. Why me?"

"Because I knew you at your worst, your best and everything in between. I knew you when you were a mess after another breakup. The first time that you got drunk, you curled up with me because you couldn't get warm. I kissed you that night. That feeling never went away. I spent years trying to find that feeling. I couldn't. When we kissed at your house, there was a reason why it felt the way it did. Why you felt like a teenager again after we kissed. That feeling that night was what I'd been searching for since we had prom."

She shook her head. "I'm not..."

He kissed her again. "You're everything. You always will be. You always have been. Just stop thinking that I can do better. I can't. I never could."

Lily shook her head. He snuggled her to him and wrapped his arms tight around her. "You can change your mind Emerson."

He shook his head. "Never." He kissed her with a kiss that went from soft and sweet to passionate to making out, to curling up on the bed like two teenagers about to be caught home alone. "Lily."

"What?"

"Don't leave again alright?"

"I needed to be away to think Emerson."

He kissed her. "And?"

"And nothing. I couldn't finish the edits because of the distractions, then after what that woman..."

He kissed her. "You left in the middle of the night."

"Emerson."

"Don't do that again. I thought that he'd started something."

Lily shook her head. "I can handle him. I could when I broke it off with him. I still can. I get that you hate him, but I can deal with all of it."

He kissed her again. "No more leaving."

"Then what happened with that woman isn't happening again."

He kissed her. "Alright," he agreed.

"I can't deal with more drama. I just can't. If this peanut is gonna happen, then all of the drama has to stop."

He kissed her. "Just trust me alright? If I say nothing happened, nothing did."

Lily shook her head and went to get up. "Where are you goin," he asked.

"Food. Why?"

He kissed her again and got up. "Stay here. I'll get it," he said as he kissed her again. He went downstairs, grabbed the lobster rolls from the kitchen, bringing them upstairs for them both, along with a big ice water for each of them.

When he made it upstairs, Lily was curled up in bed in one of his t-shirts. When he saw the smirk, he knew she was still awake. "Come have dinner," he teased.

"Emerson."

He put the tray down and walked over to her, leaning over and kissing her. "Come eat," he said. Lily took a deep breath and came over and sat with him. "Babe."

"Don't Emerson. Just don't."

He handed Lily her plate and sat down with her. "Are we allowed to talk about it?"

"No."

She had her dinner and shook her head. She was torn. Now it was a problem between her and Emerson instead of everything else. She barely muttered a word. When she finished dinner, he kissed her. "I love you," he said.

"I know." Lily shook her head, put her leggings on and slid into her hoodie.

"Where are you going," he asked.

"Outside," Lily replied. She grabbed her laptop, walked downstairs, walked outside, and sat down on the chaise.

She wrote for a while, with no interruption, and when it started getting cool outside, she heard the swish of the sliding door. Lily shook her head and Emerson came and sat down on the chaise beside hers. "What," Lily asked.

"I get it. I do. I know that seeing that hurt you. Tell me what you need me to do so we're alright again."

"Emerson, all I wanted was time to myself. Alone. I needed it. You wanted me here. I'm here now. What else could you want," Lily asked as she closed her laptop.

"I want my fiancée back."

She shook her head. "Emerson, what you did whether it happened or not, was enough to put me in the hospital. Was enough to put the baby in danger. I can't keep pretending that everything is alright Emerson. You got what you wanted. I'm at your house. What else do you want?"

"Lily, I love you. I get it. You're pissed at me. I wanted you to be with me and be safe." She shook her head. He tried to hold her hand and she backed right off. "Lily."

"I needed time to breathe Emerson. If I'd lost it because of that stupid idiotic moment, you wouldn't have forgiven yourself and either would I."

"Babe, please. I told you before that I can't do this without you. I never could. I just want you in my life Lily. That's it. I want to marry you and forget all of the stupid crap that's happened. I wasn't with her. I never have been. You have to know that."

Lily grabbed her laptop and got up, walking inside. "Lily."

She walked up the steps to the bedroom, grabbed her phone and charger and went into the guestroom, locking the door behind her. She curled up on the bed and attempted to rest when her phone went off.

"Hey," Addy said.

"Hey."

"Lily, are you alright?"

"No."

"What's wrong," Addy asked.

"Just leave it."

"Lily."

"I can't Addy. I don't know if I can even trust him. The entire time I was gone, I kept thinking that he was with someone else. I could feel it. If that's what he wants, fine. I can just leave, but he won't let me. It's like he wants his cake and to eat it too," Lily replied. Little did Lily know that Emerson was right outside the door and heard the entire conversation.

"I'm coming over," Addy said.

"I wouldn't put you in the middle for anything. There's no point," Lily said.

"Be there in 20."

"Addy."

"I'm not letting you cry your dang self to sleep."

"Addy, please just leave it."

"No."

Lily shook her head and leaned back. She hung up with Addy and Emerson knocked at the guestroom door. "Emerson, just leave me alone."

He knocked again. "Open the door," he said.

"Addy's on the way here." He unlocked the door and walked in, grabbed her phone, laptop and her charger and walked into the bedroom.

"What are you doing?"

He came back in not two minutes later and kissed her. "I love you. You. Nobody else. There's nobody else Lily. I wouldn't cheat on you. You should know that."

"Emerson, after seeing that, I couldn't not think like that. That's all I saw. I couldn't concentrate. I couldn't be here."

He kissed her. "Lily, remember one thing alright? I love you. I put a ring on your finger even if you did try to hand it back to me. I don't know what else I have to do to prove to you that I'm not gonna cheat." Lily shook her head and tried to walk past him, but he wouldn't let her.

"She hit on me. I wanted you there with me. Not her. I wanted to look at wedding plans with my fiancée and the planner. Nothing else. If you'd been in that office instead of her, we would've been naked on the sofa in minutes."

Lily shook her head. "Move."

"No. For once, you're gonna hear me. I proposed to you because I love you. You said yes because you love me. It's not that hard baby. Please just be with me. Give me a chance to fix all of this."

"Move Emerson. She's on her way…"

He kissed her, devouring her lips. "You're the only one I want," he said as he kissed her again and picked her up, wrapping her legs around his hips and walking into the main bedroom.

He leaned her onto the bed and kissed her again. "I don't want my life without you in it. I don't want to lose you either. Please baby just give me a chance."

She went to shake her head and he kissed her again. "She's on her way here."

"I don't care." He kissed her, sliding her hoodie off and throwing it to the floor.

"Emerson," Lily said as she broke the kiss.

"What," he asked as he kissed down her neck.

"I can't." He kissed her again.

"All I want is you. Why can't you see that?"

"Because I can't stop seeing her leaving your office holding her shirt together with her hand. That's why," Lily said. She went to get up and he kissed her again.

"And all that I want is for you to stop leaving. Stop avoiding me."

Lily shook her head and slid out of his arms, getting up. "Lily." She grabbed her hoodie and walked out of the bedroom and went downstairs. She got herself a sweet tea from the fridge and sat down.

Emerson walked into the kitchen, got a double shot of Jack and an ice water, handing Lily the ice water and guzzling down the whiskey.

"What," she asked.

"No caffeine remember?"

He drank her sweet tea and got a refill of his drink. Just as Lily was about to flip a movie on, Addy showed up. "Great. Just what I need," Emerson said.

"Hey y'all," Addy said as she came in and hugged Lily. She gave Emerson a hug too, but she was not impressed.

"I'm going to attempt to get a few things organized. Are you two okay in here or do I need guards," Emerson asked.

"Not funny," Lily said.

"Wasn't meant to be," Emerson said. Lily walked Addy to the backyard, grabbing a blanket. They curled up on the chaises and talked. Little did Lily know that Emerson was sitting on the balcony.

"You gonna tell me what's actually going on," Addy asked.

"He eavesdropped. It's not that I don't love him. It isn't. It's that every time I try to look at what our future could be, I see that moment in his office."

"You do know that he didn't do anything though right," Addy asked.

"Not the point Addy. Any number of women could've come in there and actually succeeded."

Addy reached out a hand and held Lily's hand. "I know you don't want to hear this, but I don't think he could. I don't think he ever would for that matter. You didn't hear him desperate to find you. Lily, people dream of a love like that. Fine. Y'all fight. So does everyone else. I bet you that Jaxon Kent guy gets in fights with his woman," Addy replied.

"I just...I got scared. I was so scared that I almost lost it. How is that normal?"

"It's not. The difference is that he never left your side. That's the one you stick with even if he is a butthead."

Emerson could hear every word. Part of him was happy that Addy was at least on his side with it all, but the fact that Lily was so quiet was almost scaring him.

"Girl, breathe. I know that you love him. You wouldn't have come back if you didn't. You would've vanished into the sunset. I know you remember?"

"Addy, it's almost like it put the idea into my head and I can't shake it. I can't turn it off."

Addy got up and gave her a hug. "You are my best friend and always have been. If you decide that you don't want to be with him, fine. Just don't make a hasty decision. Don't do something that you're gonna regret."

Lily nodded and Addy looked at her. "What," Addy asked seeing the look on Lily's face.

"Zack told me that he would cheat. I knew then that it was a possibility."

"And you're seriously going to trust that idiot?" Lily looked at her. "He's wrong. Zack would've and did before he drove to Georgia. Emerson didn't. Try and remember that." Lily nodded.

Addy gave her another hug and saw Emerson at the door with his eyes welling with tears. "Turn around and tell me that's the man that would cheat and hurt you like that. Lily, every time someone broke your heart he wanted to hunt them down and hurt them like they hurt you. Nothing's changed. Just talk to him. Stop worrying that he's gonna do something he isn't capable of. Look at the man that loves you. He hasn't stopped since high school. Just breathe and go over there. Look at him and tell him how you feel." Lily shook her head and finished her water when she heard the swoosh of the sliding door. Addy gave her another hug and got up.

"Thank you," Emerson said quietly.

"Don't make me regret saying it. You hurt her and I'm throwing you in a piranha tank."

He hugged Addy and went out to the chaise by Lily. "Eavesdropping again?"

"Talk to me," he asked.

"I can't stop seeing it. I can't turn it off. If you could do that at your office, who's to say that you couldn't do it again? Even if nothing happened, it's putting yourself in a position to make me not trust you."

He got up and sat down beside her on her chaise. "How does this sound? Nobody else visits me at the office. If they do, door stays open. If it has to close, I have someone in the room with me. Would that work?"

"Even with meetings?"

"Baby."

"Alright. Just promise me that I never have to see that again."

He leaned in and kissed her. "The only woman I ever want to be left alone with is right here. Just you," he said. Lily nodded as she brushed a tear or two away.

He shook his head. "No more tears. No more worrying. No more storming off. Please."

"And what happens if something does happen?"
He kissed her. "It's never going to."

She shook her head and he kissed her again. "Am I allowed to carry my wife to bed?"

"Not your wife yet."

"Practicing."

He picked her up and carried her inside as his security opened the door for him, went outside and got the glass and locked up as Emerson carried Lily upstairs to their bed.

When he laid her down on the bed, Lily shook her head. "What," he asked.

"Promise me that it won't happen."

He kissed her. "I'm not gonna leave your side. Hell. I didn't even want to go into the office."

"You know that me coming back there isn't gonna happen right?"

He kissed her. "Next time you do, it's not gonna be like that."

"You can't..."

"Yeah I can baby. It's not."

"Did you find a backup?"

He nodded. "His name is Kyle Andrews. He loved the ideas and managed to find a way to show me how it would look. All you have to do is say that you'll still do it with me."

"Are you sure you even want to," Lily asked.

"More sure than anything in the world."

She looked at him. "What," Lily asked.

He kissed her, devouring her lips until he let her slide her shoes off. They dropped to the floor and he kissed down her neck. He slid her hoodie off and then kissed down her torso. Just as he did, his phone buzzed in his front pocket.

"Um," Lily said. When he ignored it and smirked, she shook her head. "Emerson." He took it out of his pocket, threw it in the drawer and slid her leggings and silky panties off, knocking them to the floor. "You know that you're gonna have to answer it sometime," Lily said.

"Right now, there's nobody and nothing else in the world that I want other than you," he said as he kicked his jeans off.

"Emerson, what..."

He kissed her again, snuggling her into his arms and pulling the blankets up.

"Determined," he teased. He devoured her lips and made love to her. This time, it was calm, full of love and passionate. One way or another, he wanted her back. He needed her and always had.

When they managed to come up for air, Emerson kissed down her neck and almost refused to move one single muscle. "What," she teased as he wrapped his arms around her. "You are my only, Lily. Forever. If I have to sleep with you every single day, every hour, I will. I'm not losing you to anything else in the world. Not a phone, not a business deal and not any other woman in the world. You're my forever love."

Lily nodded and he kissed her again. "I love you too. I never stopped," Lily said.

"I know. Part of me thought you hated me."

Lily shook her head. "I tried to. I tried harder than you think I did, but I couldn't." He kissed her again, devouring her lips.

They curled up together in bed and he didn't move. He didn't reach for his phone, and he didn't even care about work at that moment. He had all he could want or dream of in his arms. When his phone went off again, she grabbed it as he pulled her back so it was out of reach.

"Emerson."

"I don't care about work right now." She handed Emerson his phone and saw his secretary's name. He pressed answer and speakerphone.

"Miss Carter," Emerson said.

"You had a few missed calls that looked important. I'm sending paperwork over for you that came in as well. Did you want me to put the messages in with it?"

"Please. I'm gonna work from home for a week or two. Just let the staff know. If I have to come for a meeting, I can come in for an hour or what have you."

"Alright. Let Miss Lily know that we all said congratulations. I'm happy for you both," his assistant said.

"Thank you," Lily replied.

They hung up a few minutes later and he snuggled her to him.

"What," Lily asked.

"Like I said, everyone is on our side. They love us together. I love you, and I love being with you. I'll stay here every day if I have to. I want us to have a life together."

"Emerson."

He kissed her neck. "I want you to be okay. If that means staying because you're concerned, I'll stay. You tell me what you want."

He kissed her. "You can't avoid the office."

"Then you come with me. What about that idea?"

"Can we wait until Monday?" He nodded and kissed her.

"I know that you heard me and Addy," Lily said.

"Why didn't you tell me that?"

"Because I didn't even know until I got back here."

He shook his head and she turned to face him. "Look at me," he said.

She looked at him, staring him in the eyes. "What?"

He kissed her. "I'm never breaking your heart. What she said about the idiot guys in high school was true. One of them ended up with a black eye and a jaw bruise from me after breaking your heart."

She looked at him. "What?"

"I worked out with the football team. When he started telling all the guys about what you did, I tried by best to bite my tongue. When he came in early and saw me there,

I ripped him a new one. He boasted about you crying. I couldn't help myself."

"He said he'd been in a fight on the field." Emerson smirked. "He's the one that cheated with the cheerleaders?"

Emerson nodded. Lily shook her head. "I didn't want you to know that it was me. All I wanted was you to be happy again."

He kissed her. "I didn't even know."

He kissed her.

"There's a lot that you don't know. Every guy that broke your heart got me in their face from the moment we met. Even now. Zack is the only one I never threw a punch at, but he's intentionally taunting me."

Lily shook her head. "I don't want you punching anyone. A punching bag, fine. Nothing else."

He kissed her, devouring her lips. "As long as you don't leave again. I can't think without you. I can't even see straight. All I want to do is go after Zack. I wanted to whoop his backside to the moon then the damn sun."

Lily shook her head and he kissed her again. "What," he asked.

"Promise me."

He kissed her again, devouring her lips. "Anything you want."

"If it happens again, you won't keep hunting me down."

"That's like asking me to rip my heart out and hand it to you. I can't do that. I'm not losing you again."

She leaned him to his back and leaned her body against his, resting her head on his shoulder. His arm curled around her and he placed one finger to her chin, raising her gaze to meet his.

"There's never going to be another reason to. Never in my lifetime, yours or any other lifetimes."

She nodded and they both fell asleep curled up together. The only thing that he wanted. He nodded off and got the first decent sleep since she'd vanished.

The next morning, Lily woke up and Emerson was still wrapped around her. "About time you woke up," he teased.

"How long have you been watching me sleep?"

"An hour or so. Did you sleep better," he asked.

Lily nodded. "It's nice not being woken up by someone knocking on the door."

He kissed her. "Alright. Are you gonna come for breakfast," he teased.

Lily smirked. "I do kinda need a workout first," Lily said.

He shook his head. "I'll give you a workout alright."

"Emerson, if I'm gonna fit in that dress..."

He kissed her, devouring her lips. "If you're that determined, alright. You need a spotter though," he teased.

"Emerson, yoga doesn't need a spotter."

He kissed her again. "Party pooper."

She kissed him and went to get up when he pulled her back to him. "What?" He slid her leg over his leg. "Emerson."

"Mine," he teased.

Lily shook her head. "Think so do you?"

He kissed her and leaned her over, pinning her to the bed.

The sex was indescribable. They were back to being happy. At least he hoped so anyway. When they managed to come up for air, Lily shook her head and got up.

"What," she teased.

"I know what you're trying to do," he teased.

"I'm going to do my workout," Lily teased as she kissed him again.

"You sure you don't need company?" Lily nodded and kissed him again, got re-dressed, and headed down to the gym in the house. When she made it up to the kitchen after her workout, his housekeeper was making fresh waffles. "Miss Lily. Waffles or omelet," his housekeeper said.

"The waffles would be amazing."

"I have fresh peaches on top of them."

"Sounds amazing," Lily said. Just as she was getting herself some juice, Emerson picked her up and carried her to the table. "What are you up to," Lily asked as she took her vitamins.

"I was thinking. Did you want to go away for a while?"

"Meaning what? You have work."

He kissed her. "And I think we should go away somewhere. Alone."

Lily shook her head. "Maybe taking our time would work. We can save the travel for after the wedding you're so determined to have early."

He kissed her. "Are you sure you're up for it?"

"No, but I have time," Lily said.

"Babe."

"Time. We have a while. I just need to..."

He kissed her. "I have a solution," he said.

"What?"

"I need to go grab something from my office. Come meet me and we'll go have a day just us."

"Emerson."

"Try," he asked. She shook her head and he kissed her again.

"I don't know that you can handle that happening again," Lily said.

He kissed her. "It's not going to. I have to pick up a package that I left in my office. That's it."

"Fine," Lily said. His housekeeper brought the food over to them and they had a quiet breakfast together.

"I have to get the dress for Addy organized."

"I did kinda already handle that, but if you want to. After you can meet me over there. We'll do lunch. Addy can hang with her boyfriend."

"From what I heard, they may not be doing all that well. I know she bumped into Carter," Lily said.

Emerson smirked. "I don't even wanna know."

"What," Lily asked.

"Carter's had a thing for her since prom."

"What," Lily asked.

"I'm surprised you didn't notice. He was dancing with her at every chance that he could the entire night."

"Seriously?"

Emerson nodded. "Not that I'm pushing her in that direction or anything, but Carter's a good guy. He's working for me now in the music section of the company. He's president of that side."

"Since when?"

"5 years. We were joking before I saw you that getting your attention at the high school reunion would mean finding my forever. Luckily we didn't have to wait that long," he teased.

They had breakfast together then headed upstairs. Lily had a hot shower. Just as she was rinsing the conditioner out, she felt arms slide around her waist. "And what do you want?"

"My fiancée," he teased as he turned her to face him. She rinsed the rest of her conditioner out and he kissed her.

"I thought you had work to do," Lily asked. He kissed her again, devouring her lips. He picked her up and wrapped her legs around his hips. "What," she teased.

He kissed her and sat down on the bench in the shower. "I love you," he said.

"Why do I think that something else happened?"

"Nothing happened. I'm just reminding you. I'm all yours and always will be."

She got a feeling in the pit of her stomach. "Just say it."

"I have to go into a meeting."

"Then go."

"I still want you to come down. I'll be done by 1:30."

"Whatever you say," Lily said. He kissed her. "What," she asked seeing that he had something else on his mind.

He kissed her again and she shook her head. "Just say it," Lily said.

"I have a meeting after lunch too. What if you came down to the office and worked from there? We can do dinner after."

"You sure?"

He nodded and kissed her. "And?"

"Lily."

"And?"

"Zack's gonna be in the office."

Lily shook her head. "For what? Finalizing the contract?" He nodded. "Alright. You know I'm fine just staying here," Lily said.

He kissed her. "And I want you with me."

She shook her head. "Then get up handsome."

She went to get up and he pulled her legs tighter around him. "What?" He pulled her towards him and she shook her head. "Emerson." He kissed her again and stood up, leaning her against the wall of the shower. "I thought you had work?"

He shook his head and they had sex against the shower wall. When her legs started to crumble, he flipped her so she was facing the wall and they kept going until he crumbled to the bench. "Mine," he teased.

Lily kissed him and he shook his head. "You are so bad," Lily said. He kissed her again and she got up and cleaned off a little.

"Where are you going," he teased.

"Takes me longer to get dressed than it takes you," Lily said.

He pulled her to him and kissed her. "I love you."

"Love you back," Lily said as she shook her head and stepped out. She wrapped a warm towel around her and freshened up. When he stepped out of the shower, he wrapped the other towel around his hips and came up behind her.

"My sexy fiancée."

"Emerson, you have to go into the office," she teased.

"We'll be there." He kissed her shoulder.

"Emerson."

"Fine. I'm getting dressed," he teased. Lily smirked, kissed him, and went and got changed.

When she came out of the closet, she was in a pale pink satiny slip dress and her white heels.

"Damn," he said.

"Reminding you of what's gonna happen when you make another mistake," Lily teased.

He shook his head. "You sure you're gonna be comfy enough to work on edits?"

She nodded. "You sure you're gonna be able to concentrate?"

He shook his head. "Not really. You sure you want to wear that into my office?"

She kissed him. "I have a sweater," she teased as she slid her things into her other purse. She grabbed her laptop bag and he shook his head.

"Sexiest woman alive and she's my fiancée," Emerson said.

"For now," Lily teased. He kissed her, slid his dress pants, shirt, and shoes on and slid on a tie that got a smirk from her.

"What," he teased.

"I almost put on the silver dress," Lily teased.

"Sure you don't want to change?"

"Nope." He kissed her and Lily touched up her makeup, curled her hair and put on some of the perfume that was almost intoxicating to him.

"Ready beautiful," Emerson asked.

Lily nodded and he knew what she was up to. "You know what that perfume does."

"I know. Thought you might like the reminder," Lily teased.

"We're not even gonna make it in the door," he teased as he picked her up and carried her down the steps.

"What are you up to?" He smirked. "Making sure my fiancée doesn't trip," he teased.

They headed out, stopping and getting Starbucks on their way in. "You sure you can have it," Emerson asked.

"Decaf espresso. I'm fine. Promise."

He shook his head. "I sorta thought of something. Who do you want to have at the little ceremony?"

"You, me, Addy, your friend, our parents and that's it. I think my dad would be a little irritated if he wasn't included."

"Dinner at home after?" Lily nodded. "Church or home?"

"Church, so long as nobody else knows."

He kissed her. "Done."

He knew exactly what to do. He already had the bishop of her favorite church coming. All he had to do was make sure the flowers were where they needed them. His housekeeper was completely on board with setting the house up. Everything was perfect.

When they pulled up to his office, Lily was apprehensive. Part of her just assumed that when they would walk in, a half-naked woman would come running out of his office. They got through the front, passing the secretaries and receptionist. When they got to his office, roses were there waiting.

"And now you're sucking up with roses," she joked.

He kissed her and closed the door behind them. "You sure you're gonna be alright," Emerson asked.

"So long as some random women don't come in here announcing that you got them pregnant, yes," Lily teased.

He shook his head and kissed her. "Babe."

"I'm alright." He sat down at his desk and saw a pile of paperwork. "You work on the paper stuff. I'll edit," Lily teased.

"I know that you're worried baby. I promise that we will get out of here as soon as we can." Lily nodded. She sat down on the sofa, kicked her heels off, and went through her emails, seeing one from Emerson:

> *Looking sexy and beautiful as always. I can't wait to make you my wife. Am I allowed to ask if you're feeling okay?*

She shook her head and replied:

> *I love you but stop asking. I'm alright. Not nauseous yet. If it happens that this sticks, we go from there handsome. Just concentrate on your papers so we can get out of here.*

When Emerson's secretary came in, she smirked.

"How are you doing today Miss Lily," his secretary asked.

"Good thanks. I thought he might need a bodyguard today," she teased.

"Sir, the meeting starts in 20. Did you need anything," his secretary asked.

"I'm good. Just close the door please," Emerson said as he got up and followed his secretary, locking the office door.

"What," Lily asked.

He walked over to her, devouring her lips. "Emerson."

He smirked. "He's coming in. Just don't go near him."

Lily nodded. "I wasn't planning on it."

He smirked. "If you need something, message me."

Lily smirked. "Emerson, I promise nothing will happen. I just need to finish the last edits," she said.

"When it's done let me know." Lily nodded. He kissed her again. "You sure you're gonna be alright?"

"Emerson." He sat down with her. "I love you but stop. I'm fine."

He got up a little while later, grabbed his paperwork and went into his meeting, getting it done as fast as possible. When Lily heard Zack walking down the hallway, she shook her head. Zack walked into Emerson's office and Lily wanted more than anything to just hide in a corner.

"There is no way that I'm doing that. I told you. You want me and Lily to stop talking, you let her do what she wants. She'll come running to me in a damn heartbeat," Zack said as he walked into the office with Emerson right behind him.

"You think so do you," Lily replied.

"I know you miss me," Zack said.

"Not really to be honest with you. I think I'd rather dive into ice water."

"I know you want me. You know that you want me. Just say it so this idiot can get over himself already," Zack said.

Lily showed him the ring. "Enough said," Lily replied as she went and worked on the book some more.

"That's all he could do? I would've got you something you didn't need to squint at," Zack said.

"Making up for the lack of something? Oh right. Lack of a woman that's willing to date you."

Emerson had to hold back a laugh. "You wanted me when we were at that beach house."

"And then I found a real man who wasn't trying to show off. Who didn't need to go to the fancy restaurants. I'm good with what I have thanks," Lily replied.

"Whatever. Easily replaced. If I wanted you, I'd have you," Zack said.

"Keep telling yourself that," Lily replied. Zack shook his head.

"Now that you know that she doesn't want you around either, does that mean you're gonna do as I ask," Emerson asked.

"Fine, but if she decides she wants me back, she's mine."

Lily rolled her eyes. "Get over yourself Zack. I'd rather be single for life."

Zack signed the papers and shook his head at Lily, walking out the door.

Emerson shook his head with a grin ear to ear, sitting down at his desk. "Did you have fun," Lily asked.

"Honestly, yes. That was kinda fun," Emerson joked.

"You seriously put that in the contract?"

He nodded. "If that's what I have to do so that we're both safe from his stupid crap, I'll do it. I don't want him starting anything." Lily shook her head.

Chapter 7

By the time they headed off, Lily had just about enough of watching Emerson work. She had edits finished and he had decided to read it. Lily was determined to get her mind off it.

"You sure you want to read it," Lily asked.

"Babe, this is amazing," he said.

"Emerson."

He looked over at her. "What?"

"You don't have to."

He marked the page and walked over to her. "What's wrong," he asked.

"Nothing. I just don't think you want..."

He kissed her. "I'm reading it. Babe, this is the thing you've been working on for months. I want to."

"You don't have to," Lily replied.

He shook his head and kissed her. "What are you worried about," he asked.

"Because I don't think you're gonna want to read it."

He kissed her again and slid his hand in hers. "Come sit with me," he said as he took her hand and walked her outside, curling up on the chaise with her.

"What am I gonna read that you don't want me to," he asked.

Lily shook her head. "Some stuff that's not what you're gonna be happy with."

He kissed her and slid his arm around her. "Baby, we're good. It's a book. It's not me and you in there. From what I read, it's amazing. I didn't know you could write like this." She shook her head and he snuggled her tight to him. "Breathe," he said. Lily shook her head and he kissed her. "Tell me what you want me to say." Lily shook her head and got up, heading over to the pool. She slid her feet in and Emerson came over to her.

"Lily, what's really wrong," he asked.

"I can't believe that he actually said that about me."

He looked at her. "You stood your own. He deserved a butt whooping for what he said, but what's wrong?" Lily shook her head. "Baby."

"I've dated idiots before. I've dated guys who were just trying to get some. That is a whole new thing Emerson. He's gloating about being a psycho. I'm not stunned that he hasn't had a girlfriend in years."

"Baby, tell me what's going on."

"Just think it's rude. First he's saying that he wanted me to choose him, then he's saying all of that without knowing that I'm there? Did he seriously think that I wouldn't hear it?"

He kissed Lily.

"Which part are you mad at?"

"The disrespect."

He kissed her and slid her legs across his lap. "Babe, the man is an idiot. We both know he is. He never deserved to have you around." She nodded. "Lily." She shook her head. "Tell me what you need me to say," he said.

"How did I not even see it then," Lily asked.

He kissed her forehead and snuggled her to him. "You made a better choice. We've had fights, but I would never in my life ever disrespect you like that. You're too important to me."

"I know. You never have," Lily said.

"Not for a minute. I have my moments, but I'd never go there."

Lily took a deep breath. "Come with me," he said.

"Where?"

"Putting you in a much better mood."

"Emerson." He helped her to her feet, picked her up and carried her inside. "What are you doing?" He kissed her and walked up the steps. "What are you doing?"

He sat her on the bed and walked into the massive bathroom, flipping on the hot water in the tub. Lily shook her head, sliding out of the dress. When she walked into the bathroom a few minutes later in her satin robe, he smirked. "Give me 5 minutes. I'll come hop in with you." Lily nodded, kissed him and he vanished from the bedroom. Lily put the towels on the warmer, slid her robe off and slid into the water, bubbles and all.

He knew. She had no idea that he did, but he knew exactly what she needed. Would've been better with a few bottles of wine, but she was alright. When she heard music, she knew. He came in with two glasses of soda, in fancy glasses, handing one to her. He went and got undressed then slid into the water with her. "Better," he asked.

Lily nodded and leaned back a little. He slid in and rubbed her feet for her. "Babe, you don't have to keep holding it in. Just say it," he said knowing that deep down there was a reason behind the deafening silence.

"At least I made one really good decision," Lily said.

"Which was what," he asked.

"Giving you a chance."

"I'm really glad you finally did, even if we did have a few squabbles."

Lily shook her head. "Emerson."

He smirked. "We had a fight and a few big ones, but we came back together beautiful. I don't know what I would've done if I lost you."

"Other than ended up in a police cell for stalking or a psych ward," Lily teased.

"You're joking, but you're probably right. I don't think I can deal with losing you."

"Just remember that," Lily said with a smirk.

"And the smile is back," Emerson said as Lily sipped her drink.

"Well, now that we're both in a better mood, what do you have planned," Lily asked.

"I'm getting lobster for dinner. A nice quiet meal with just you and me. If we have dinner on the sofa, so be it," he teased.

"You know, we haven't really had a sit around and watch movies night," Lily said.

"Which movie were you thinking sexy wife to be?"

"Something relaxing. I just want to relax and be with you," Lily said.

"No phones?"

She shook her head. "Just us."

He kissed her. "That works," he replied.

She slid across the tub to him and he slid her legs around him. "Are you actually okay," he asked.

"I will be. It's just irritating. It's frustrating that he thinks it's okay to say any of it. He kept fighting to talk me into coming back to him and that's how he actually felt?"

Emerson kissed her. "I love you. I'm not letting anything like that said about you or anyone else. My mom is a royal pain, but at least she taught me not to treat women like that."

"Emerson."

"What?"

"Do you think that your mom is actually gonna calm down with all of that stupid drama stuff?"

"She's trying to protect me and my life, but I've told her a million and one times that being with you is the safest thing in the world for everything. Honestly, maybe it's because y'all don't know each other that well. She's just harsh with you for some reason."

"At some point, I'd kinda like to not have the hostility," Lily said.

"When we get baby, guaranteed she'd stop with all of it. She's gonna worry until we actually get married. She's gonna keep going until then."

"So, what's the plan with her then?"

"I came up with one idea, but I don't know what you'll think," Emerson said.

"Just say it Emerson."

He kissed her. "Let her take you out to look at flowers or something for the wedding."

"Really?"

He nodded. "Even if it's clothes for the honeymoon."

"Maybe," Lily said.

"Flowers are simple. The other option is she can go to a fitting with you."

Lily looked at him. "You sure about that," Lily asked.

"You aren't showing. It's fine baby."

Lily shook her head. She didn't need any negativity at the fitting. "What if I took her to lunch after my fitting?" "It's up to you. I just want her to stop seeing you as something that you aren't."

Lily nodded. "Emerson, promise me that if she still keeps going with her stuff that I can just leave it."

He shook his head and kissed her. "Babe, I love you, and I love that you're trying, but if she decides to cause more havoc, we are gonna have to do something big."

"I just don't want it to get worse."

He smirked. "Babe, it won't. If she does something that really ruffles those feathers of yours, I'll handle her."

Lily kissed him. "Alright," she teased.

They managed to get up from the tub and he wrapped her up in a warm towel, wrapping the other around his hips. "You know wife to be, I think that you are way too beautiful to be all cooped up here. You sure I can't talk you into going out of town somewhere alone?"

"Can't avoid her forever," Lily said.

He kissed her, sliding his hands to her face and cupping it as he deepened the kiss. "How's this? You do the fitting with Addy, then you can meet Mom and I at the hotel for lunch. I'll go back to work and you can have a little time. I'll be a buffer for a while."

Lily smirked. "You sure you want to?"

He nodded. "We'll do it Monday."

"The book is going to the publisher on Monday too."

"Then you two have a reason to celebrate."

Lily smirked. "When you finish reading it," Lily said. He snuggled her to him and gave her a hug.

"Lily, just so you know, every single word you wrote that I've read was like you were tapping into my soul. I know the woman who wrote those words. I know it all. I know where the pain came from, I know where the love in the characters comes from, and I know what makes you cry when you write it. That right there is the beautiful, breathtaking, amazing, talented, creative, passionate, and caring woman I know in words." She shook her head and he hugged her again.

She kissed him and they headed into the bedroom, pulling on something comfortable. Just as Lily was getting changed, she got a twinge. A sharp one. She took a deep breath. "If you're in there, stay in there," Lily said silently to the peanut in her belly. She took a deep breath, sliding the towel off and noticed one red spot. One. One that changed everything. One that said that no matter how happy she was, it was going over a speed bump.

Emerson came in and saw her on the chair. "What," Emerson asked.

"Nothing."

"Lily." When he saw the red spot on the towel, he looked at her.

"No."

Lily shrugged and slid her workout shorts on. Emerson picked her up and sat her on the bed, folding the towel and putting it under her. He grabbed his phone and called the doctor.

When Emerson came back to Lily, she was curled up on the bed. "Babe."

"What?"

"The doctor is coming here."

"Emerson."

"It's that or we go to the hospital. She suggested staying here."

"Go figure this happens." He kissed her and the housekeeper came upstairs with some ginger ale and a glass of Jack on ice for Emerson.

"Sip," Lily asked.

He shook his head. "Babe, you know this wasn't your fault right?"

Lily nodded. "Just wasn't the right time."

By the time the doctor headed out, she'd verified it. "Well, you're alright. It's fine. You'll have to try again but give yourself some time." Lily nodded.

"Thank you." The doctor nodded, headed out and Emerson laid down on the bed beside Lily.

"You alright," he asked. Lily shook her head.

"Like I said, there's no reason to get all excited until we knew it had stuck. That's why I didn't want to tell anyone. Addy knew, but that's it," Lily replied.

He kissed her shoulder and slid his arms around her. "Tell me what you need."

"To not feel defective." He shook his head.

It was the last thing that he wanted to hear, and the last thing he thought she would ever say. She had no idea. She was far from it in his eyes. She'd had heartbreak, pain, a loss of faith in men and had spent all of her teen years with the wrong ones. He'd always been the right one for her. He'd picked her up and held her until her tears stopped. He'd dried the tears. He'd turned her crying into her almost laughing. He'd been there through thick and thin already. What was a lifetime when he'd already had a lifetime of moments with her? He knew they'd never be apart again. That they'd be that team, those best friends that made a life full of love. At that moment, all she needed was someone who wasn't judging. He never had and he never would. All of the stress had built up, and all he could do was sit there in silence, holding the only woman he ever loved in his arms.

"You're being too quiet," Lily said.

"Just thinking."

"About?"

"All those times that you thought you wouldn't make it through."

Lily shook her head and turned to face him. "Meaning?"

"All those times that you thought those idiot guys in school had broken you permanently. They never did. You're still in one piece Lily. It's a blip."

"And if I said I wanted to wait a while?"

He kissed her. "Whatever you want. Gives us time after the wedding to just hang out and relax. We can just go do whatever we want to. We can fly somewhere for a weekend. We can go into the jungle if that's what we want."

"Emerson."

He kissed her forehead. "Tell me what you want baby."

"You and me alone."

"Like beach house alone, or cabin in the woods alone?"

"You and me here alone. No security, no nothing."

"Just want silence?"

Lily nodded. He kissed her. "What you want you get. I'll give them all the night off. We can just be on our own."

"I just need to be able to talk without them hearing it all."

"What are you worried about them hearing?" She looked at him. "Babe."

"Emerson, I want to be able to talk about it."

"Just between me and you, the housekeeper has an inkling, and security asked. They already kind of know." Lily shook her head and he kissed her. "Babe, they love you like family. They have since the first time you were here. They're my family. I love my folks and all, but this is my chosen family."

"And," Lily asked.

He kissed her. "You're the best part of it."

They relaxed and hung out alone the rest of the night. They had dinner on the sofa as planned, and they took it easy. They watched a couple movies, then just as the credits were rolling on the last movie, he looked down and saw Lily asleep in his arms. He saw her phone buzz, and looked, seeing Addy's name.

"Hey," Addy said.

"It's Emerson," he said.

"She alright?"

"Nope. She's asleep on the sofa with me."

"Emerson, tell me that she didn't lose..."

"Yeah."

"Crap.," Addy said.

"She's just resting. It's been a day."

"Alright. Tell her to call me tomorrow."

"I will."

They hung up and Lily's eyes opened. "Addy," Lily asked.

Emerson nodded. "Close your eyes. I'll carry you up to bed," he teased.

Lily smirked. "I can walk."

He shook his head, got up and picked her up, carrying her up the steps to the bedroom. He pressed the button to close the curtains and leaned her onto the bed.

"What are you doin," Lily asked.

"We're having alone time."

"And what did Addy want," Lily asked.

"She wanted to check on you and see if you were alright. That's all."

"Emerson."

"I told her. She told me to give you an extra hug. For you to call her tomorrow."

Lily shook her head and he curled up with her. "What are we really gonna do though," Lily asked.

"Wait until we're ready and try again. Take our time."

"You sure?"

"Babe, I told you before. When we got together, all I wanted was a chance. We're getting married now. We have all the time in the world. I want you. Baby, no baby, four-legged baby. I just want us. Everything else is just sprinkles on the sundae."

Lily shook her head. "What am I gonna do with you?"

"Snuggle with me and hear I love you every minute," he teased.

Lily shook her head. "I can do that," Lily said.

"Good." They snuggled up in bed, talked and made one large decision – they were going through with the wedding regardless.

When Lily got up the next morning, there was a latte on her side table with a note that he'd run into the office. She took a deep breath, got up and showered then got dressed and headed downstairs.

"My woman," Emerson said with a smirk.

"When did you get back?"

"Just. Did you sleep?"

Lily nodded. "I decided that we needed to go out and do something."

"Okay. What if we went to the beach?"

Lily looked at him. "Rain."

"What if we went for a drive? We can go up to Myrtle beach or something."

Lily looked at him. "What if we went to Cypress Gardens?"

He smirked. "Alright sexy fiancée. I kinda like that idea."

"Emerson, don't read anything else into it."

"Okay. You know I kinda thought about us having the wedding there."

Lily shook her head. "No. I love that you want to, but I don't want to worry about the weather."

"Okay. We have time."

Lily had breakfast with him then he ran upstairs to change into shorts and a tee. "How are you feeling," the housekeeper asked.

"Sore, but okay. I didn't want to say anything."

"I know. It's not getting out of this house. I'm sorry for the loss."

"I appreciate it. We have time to get that. I know he was happy when it happened. I just know that it's not the right timing." When Lily's phone buzzed in her pocket, she looked:

Come upstairs.

She shook her head and finished her food, then walked up the steps to the bedroom. "What did you want handsome?"

He kissed her. "I love you."

"I know you do. What's wrong?"

He kissed her again, devouring her lips. "What if we ran off to Vegas?"

"So, either you're determined to avoid your folks, or something happened."

"Last night was enough."

"Emerson."

"What?"

"We have two months."

He kissed her again. "Come to Vegas."

"Why?"

"Because I want to. Run away. They have a fancy spa, a really nice penthouse suite, sunshine..."

"Emerson, I love you. I do, but we can't outrun it. I think maybe staying around town is a good idea until all of this is cleared up."

"Do we have to?"

Lily smirked. "Yes." He kissed her again and pulled his swim shorts on. "What," she asked.

"Beach. I checked. It's not raining until later. We can hang out at the beach house."

Lily shook her head. "Alright handsome."

"And by the way, I finished reading it."

Lily looked at him. "And?"

He kissed her. "It's amazing."

She looked at him like he was just saying it to be nice. "Emerson, are you sure?"

He nodded. "Babe, it's amazing. My question is, when are you doing book 2?"

"I was gonna start on it, but I didn't feel like starting."

He kissed her. "It's what you love. We can go to the beach. You write, I'll get a few emails in, and we can go for a walk on the beach."

"If you really want to. Just don't be surprised if we bump into him when we're there. He's kind of determined remember?"

"I think after the tongue lashing that you gave him, he's not coming near you baby."

Lily couldn't help the smirk. She may have been beyond mad at Zack for the rude comments, but she also knew that her reaction and words hit him as hard as she'd hoped. Maybe he had got the point, but there was a little piece in her that said that it just made him even more determined to get her back.

"Do you think it's good enough to sell though," Lily asked.

"You mean since you already sent in the manuscript?"

Lily nodded. "Bestseller list right beside that Jaxon Kent guy. Babe, it's amazing, and I'm not just saying that because I love you."

"The first one was amazing too Emerson."

"You didn't have the right promo for it. This time, it's me. We already have the promotion stuff going. You're probably going to be doing the book tour too. I just hope that you're alright to do it."

"Depends on whether I have my handsome fiancée as my bodyguard."

He smirked. "If I can be there, I will. I may have to be here for a few of them, but beyond that, I'm all yours, beautiful wife to be."

It was the last thing she wanted to think about after the insane day that they'd had. They hung out for a while, then headed over to the beach house, laptops and phones in hand. "You sure that we don't need clothes," Lily asked.

"Bikini, shorts, pajamas and maybe a sundress. We have it all there."

Lily shook her head. "Alright then," she said as she went and slid into her bikini, pulling her shirt and tee overtop. "You sure," Lily asked.

He smirked. "Now that my woman is in a bikini, yes. By the way, did I tell you I love you today?"

Lily smirked. "Yes. I love you too handsome."

He handed Lily her laptop and the phones and carried her downstairs, sweeping her right off her feet. "Emerson." He kissed her as she slid to her feet in the foyer of the house.

"What," he teased. He kissed her, slid both laptops into his bag, threw in the chargers and the housekeeper came over. "I have steaks ready for you to barbecue. I have the salad that Miss Lily loves and the lunch all organized and ready to eat. I'll meet you over there before lunch."

"Thank you," Lily said.

"You're most welcome," his housekeeper said.

"I'll get the car," his security said.

By the time they got through the traffic jam and out to the beach house, they were both laughing and drinking their iced coffees. "So, I have to ask, are you still doing that whole iced Irish coffee thing at Christmas?"

"You mean the Irish cream coffee with the Baileys added in? Yes."

"For someone who barely even drinks..."

"I know. It's a holiday thing Emerson. You'll understand when it gets to December. The big tree, the Christmas music blaring while I decorate, the Irish cream coffee when I'm done. Then I watch all the old black and white Christmas movies."

"That part I remember. You seriously have to have watched those movies a billion times by now."

"When they come up with a movie as good as It's a wonderful life, then I'll add it to the rotation."

The fact that he'd remembered those traditions almost stunned her. When she was a teen, she'd snuck a little taste of Bailey's and when she was finally of age, it had become a tradition. He'd remembered sneaking the drink, but not what she'd made out of it on her 21st birthday. "What," he asked as she thought back.

"I remember the first birthday I had on my own. I made an Irish cream cake with Bailey's mousse and coffee flavored cake. It was one of my best," Lily teased.

"And now you can make it for my birthday this year."

Lily almost laughed. "You have a point." She kissed him as they pulled into the driveway.

"You know, we could just go to Ireland and get away for a few weeks Lily."

Lily shook her head. "If I have to do any press for the book, I can't just run away to the Emerald Isle."

He smirked. "Yeah we can. I know a guy that would give you the time off."

Lily shook her head. "That determined to get away?"

He nodded. "I thought it'd make the perfect honeymoon."

Lily smirked and kissed him. "It's up to you."

"Very good answer," he said as he snuggled her to him.

They headed inside as soon as they arrived, and he carried her up the steps. "Emerson."

"What?"

"Put me down." He kissed her and set her on her feet. "You are ridiculous."

"And that's just another reason why you love me."

She shook her head and looked outside. The waves were almost too big for her comfort level. "Are you sure that the storm isn't coming?"

Emerson nodded. "They said big waves, breeze, but no storm."

Lily shook her head. "Whatever you say." She sprayed on some sunscreen, slid her t-shirt off and walked outside. She knew. That storm was coming whether he thought it was or not.

When she walked inside, Emerson was putting the phones on the charger. "What are you up to?"

"Charging them. We forgot last night." She smirked. She grabbed them each a sweet tea, handing one to Emerson and grabbed her laptop, heading outside to the porch. She curled up on the porch swing, set her sweet tea down and flipped her internet on to see if the publisher had replied back:

> *Dear Miss Lily.*
>
> *I just wanted to say that we are thrilled with the new book. We already have a ton of promo ideas, and we have a few cover options. Please let us know which you like or if you'd like something altogether different. By the way, there has been talk of you doing a book tour to promote which would include a few TV show spots. Would you be comfortable with the travel, or would you rather do them from home? Just let us know. We can do half and half if you want to. By the way, the*

*dedication brought tears to my eyes.
Congratulations again. PS, we had 3500 pre-
orders for the book. Already on the bestseller list. –
E*

"Oh my goodness," Lily said as she covered her mouth.

"What," Emerson asked running outside.

"Um..."

"What baby?"

"3500 pre-orders."

"You're kidding me?" Lily shook her head and showed him the email. "Well dang. That's amazing."

"What do you think about the tour stuff?"

"Do as many as you can live. Easier to promote and take questions. If we sort of get that little peanut situation again, home might be good."

"Holy bananas," Lily said.

"Like I told you, the book is amazing. All it needed was promotion and you to have a little extra inspiration when you were stuck," he teased.

Lily kissed him. "Thank you for that by the way."

"Any time you want," he joked.

One more kiss and they curled up together on the chaise. "You know, we could just go down and dive into the water," he teased.

"Emerson, I have to try and at least come up with an idea for the next book. Something."

"Babe, you do realize that you can relax right? You've spent all this time writing. You can take a break between books and just enjoy the summer a little."

She smirked. "And what exactly are you hinting at that you wanted to do?"

"I'm glad you asked."

He slid her shorts off, slid her shoes off, peeled his shirt off and picked her up, running down the steps and out to the beach, then into the waves of perfect salt water. It wasn't just refreshing. It was like it was washing away all of the hurt about losing the baby. It washed away the anger, the pain, and the tears. When he got up to his neck in waves, he kissed Lily, wrapping her legs around his waist.

"What," Lily asked.

He kissed her. "Are you gonna let me marry you?"

"Depends. You sure you want to," Lily asked

He kissed her. "More than anything in the world."

"I guess. I mean, I have the dress already," Lily teased as he kissed her, devouring her lips as the waves crashed around them.

"Emerson."

"Soon to be wife."

"I think we need to head inside."

"Why?"

Lily pointed up. When he saw the clouds, and the sun almost vanishing, he shook his head and walked back up to the beach, putting her down and smirked. "You ready," he asked. Lily nodded. He put her feet into the water then picked her up and carried her to the deck. Lily grabbed the laptops and towels and they came inside, just as the storm was getting closer.

"Alright. I guess grilling is out," Emerson said.

"Good thing we can grill it in the oven," Lily teased. He smirked and kissed her.

"Fine. I'll make dinner tonight," he teased.

Lily nodded, grabbed her laptop, and headed upstairs, sliding into her shorts and a hoodie. When Emerson came upstairs, he smirked. "You that determined," he asked as he saw her writing on her laptop.

"I need an idea for something. I figured if I wrote, it'd come." He kissed her, devouring her lips, sliding the laptop to the side table. "What," Lily asked when he let her up for air. He took her hand, walked her to the bed, and they curled up on the bed together.

"Wife."

"I swear, you need to quit getting ahead of yourself," Lily teased.

"7 weeks."

"What?"

"7 weeks. You, me, Addy, Carter, my folks and my sister and yours and your brother."

"Did we send invites?" He nodded and pulled it up on his phone, showing her the invites. "And you did mention that we're keeping it very quiet right?" He nodded.

"I told them that we're having a quiet ceremony and a party later with all the friends and family. We just wanted to do this ourselves."

"And your mom is gonna be alright with it and not start an issue?"

He kissed her. "I'm gonna try baby. I talked to her and asked her to leave it be. We go from there," he said.

"Are you sure that doing all of this so fast is a good idea?"

He kissed her, devouring her lips. "I'm marrying you whether you like it or not sexy. Whether mom wants to be there or not. I told her that if she didn't want to be positive and cheer us on, to not bother coming."

"Still think I should go hang with her?"

"Since you have to do a dress fitting? Kinda might be a good idea."

"Alright," Lily said.

He kissed her again and snuggled her. "You okay?"

Lily nodded. "I wish it hadn't worked out this way. I would've loved having a baby with you."

He kissed her. "We still can. You know we can," he teased.

"But what happens if I can't?"

He kissed her again, snuggling her to him. "Stop. Babe, stop thinking that way. If you want a baby, we have one whether we need medical assistance or not."

"Emerson, please just let me say it."

He kissed her. "I love you. If we have kids, great. If we don't, we have each other. That's all I'm gonna say. I have you in my life, in my arms and in my life. That's all I could ever want. That's what I was dreaming of. I promise you that."

"And what happens when you change your mind," Lily asked.

"I give you permission to smack me into reality and knock my butt on the floor."

"Gee. That is a perk."

He kissed her. "Lily." She kissed him and they curled up together. "What would you think about maybe just hanging out a few days instead of rushing back?"

"So, now you're good with staying out here? You do know he's still one beach away right?"

"He's not interfering anymore. He does, I may have to drown his butt."

"Promise," Lily joked.

He kissed her. "Do you want to stay out here for a while?"

"You have work."

He looked at her. "I'm working from home."

"Oh really?"

He nodded. "I want alone time with my woman."

"I guess," Lily teased.

He snuggled her close and they talked through the things she hadn't wanted to talk about. From where they'd live full-time to Lily having time to herself. "All you have to do is say the word. Just tell me what you want Lily."

"And if I want to go stay with Addy for a night?"

He kissed her. "I'll miss you something crazy."

She kissed him. "I still want to be able to have some time just me and Addy."

"I know," he said.

"And if I want to stay at the house with her?"

"The house or our house?"

"The."

He shook his head. "If that's what you want, I can't stop you."

Lily smirked. "Good answer."

He kissed her and within what seemed like minutes, her phone was ringing. "You know it's Addy," Lily said.

He grabbed it, handing the phone to Lily. "Hey Addy."

"And how's my favorite person?"

"Funny. What's up?"

"You still keeping the house?"

Lily smirked. "Well, I am keeping it in my name, but I think that there are keys for you."

"Where?"

"I'll meet up with you tomorrow. That work?"

"I'll see you tomorrow. How are you feeling though?"

"I'm alright. We're just hanging at the beach house." Lily talked to her a little and Emerson got up and went to get his laptop.

"Seriously though. You're giving me the house?"

"Like I said, so long as Zack doesn't find out where it is, we're fine. I just don't want drama. That place is like a safe haven."

"Got it," Addy said as Lily heard the grin.

"This mean that you're gonna come hang with me?"

"Yes. I wanted to talk to him about it. I did."

"I still can't believe you two."

"What?"

"Girl, he had such a crush on you in high school. I remember him getting into the alcohol a little and telling me that he was gonna marry you one day, and now he is."

"Just remember one thing. You are still and will always be my best friend."

"I love you back my friend."

"I'll give you a shout tomorrow. I'll bring you the keys."

"Alright. I'll see you tomorrow," Addy said as they hung up.

When Emerson came back in, he looked at her.

"What?"

"I have to go into the office for a meeting."

"When?"

"Tomorrow." Lily smirked.

"I'm going to hang with Addy anyway. We can do dinner downtown or something. I'll make a reservation and meet you over there," Lily said.

"You sure you'll be alright?"

"I'm gonna take her to the house. Figure out the plan for the house I bought."

"You sure?"

Lily nodded. "I know that you aren't happy with me having that house, but for now this is what I have to do."

"Alright," Emerson said.

Lily looked at him. "I thought you were totally against it."

"It's gonna be Addy's right?"

"She's staying there. Still mine."

He kissed her. "Then it's still alright. I just don't want you vanishing on me."

"At least you'll know where I am."

"Not the point Lily."

He was more nervous that she'd actually take off to the house without saying a word. That she'd just disappear into the night. He wanted to beg her to give him the address, but he knew that after everything they'd already gone through, it was a fight not worth having. She'd had enough stress in her life.

"Emerson."

"Will you at least tell me where it is?"

She looked at him. "If you're that determined to know, yes."

"Good answer. When do you want to go?"

"In the morning?"

He nodded and kissed her. "What time do you have to be at the office?"

"10:30. We both get up too early anyway."

"It's not as big as your house. Not even here," Lily said.

"As long as it makes you happy, and it's safe. I know it's not gonna have the security that the big house does, but as long as it's safe I'm fine with it."

"Well, Addy isn't with Sam anymore, so at least it's Zack free." He smirked and kissed her.

Chapter 8

"You sure that you want to show me," Emerson asked the next morning as they were heading out.

"If you're that determined to see it, then yes. Honestly, it's like a third of the size of the beach house. It's something that was big enough just for me and Addy if it came to that."

"It's never going to. I'm glad that Addy has somewhere to stay, but I still don't think you even needed the house."

Lily shook her head. "Agree to disagree," Lily said.

He kissed her and they made their way over with security. When they pulled into the subdivision, Emerson smirked. "See, I kinda knew that you would like this kind of place. Neighbors that can wave over a fence and everything. Like your place when you were in high school."

"It's called being a normal kid. Not one with a paycheck that has a million zeroes."

He kissed her. "Babe, that never mattered. Nobody knew anything different at school. You didn't either. Now that you do know, it hasn't changed anything." When the car slowed, he looked and saw the home version of Lily.

The porch, the red door, the big windows, and the back porch looking out over the water. "Babe, this place is amazing," Emerson said as Lily opened the front door and walked him inside. Her furniture fit in perfectly. It was fully and completely her. "And now you know why I loved it. There are two freaking masters. One would be hers, the other would be mine for when and if I'm here. Easier for us," Lily said.

"And if she bought it from you outright?"

"That's up to her. Leave it be."

"Is there room for when baby comes?"

Lily smirked. "One small bedroom between them. Just the right size. Honestly, you and I both know that we're fine. If I come to visit, there's space."

When Lily heard a knock at the door, she smirked. "What," Emerson asked.

"I told her to come over," Lily replied.

She went and answered and Addy walked in. "What did you want to...."

"So, what do you think," Lily asked.

"It's beautiful. This is the house?"

Lily nodded and handed Addy the other key. "You sure?"

"We stick to our plan. Beyond that we're good," Lily said.

Addy gave her a hug and handed her an envelope. "What's this?"

"A thank you," Addy said. Lily gave her a hug and slid the envelope into her purse. Lily gave her the tour and Emerson went and talked to his security about upgrading the security system.

"I still can't believe that you're letting me stay in the house."

"Addy, we promised each other that we'd find a way. If I'm at his place and at the beach house on and off, there's no reason not to go through with the plan. I want you to be somewhere that is safe and makes you happy. If things backfire with Emerson, I have a landing pad."

"I gave you two months. The amount we agreed on."

"And you're good covering utilities and stuff?" Addy nodded as she gave Lily a big hug. Just as they were about to sit down and talk through everything, Emerson came in.

"So, if I upgraded the security for the house, would that be horrible," Emerson asked.

"I'm good with it if you're determined," Lily said. Addy nodded. Emerson kissed Lily and walked back downstairs.

"You sure you're alright," Addy asked.

Lily nodded. "I'm alright. It just feels kinda weird knowing what happened. I don't have to go into the hospital or anything. It's all passed. I have to wait a little while for anything exciting with us, but I just kinda think that maybe it's good. It was rushing into everything."

"Just remember one thing. He loves you whether y'all have kids or not."

"Well, I sorta have two. Two books," Lily teased.

"I'm glad you finished it. So, what's the plan with the next one since I know you can't possibly take a break."

"Trying to start. I wanted to show him the house. It gets him to cut back on the worrying. I got everything moved in here and put whatever way. I just wanted you to have the house the way you wanted. So it feels like home."

"This place is better than I could ever imagine. I love it," Addy said as she gave Lily a hug.

"Just remember what I said."

Addy nodded. "By the way, Carter is single right?"

Lily smirked. "Emerson said he wanted to talk to you about that," Lily said as she heard him coming up the steps.

"About what," Emerson asked.

"Carter." Emerson smirked.

"What," Addy asked.

"You don't remember Carter do you?"

"We were friends Emerson. Just like we were with you."

"But do you really remember?"

Addy looked at Lily. "Meaning what," Addy asked.

"You have no idea. You knew what a crush I had on Lily. Are you telling me that you didn't know he was crushing on you?"

Addy looked at him like he'd sprouted purple polka dots. "No, he wasn't. He had a crush on Sarah Carol."

"Who was Sarah," Lily asked.

"His codename for Addy. He had a crush the first time he saw you and all the way through high school."

"No he didn't," Addy said. Emerson nodded and slid his arm around Lily's waist.

"You're serious," Addy asked.

Emerson nodded. "I told him once that if y'all were meant to be, it'd happen. Now, he has his chance."

Addy shook her head and was about to retort with something when her phone rang. When she saw Carter's name, she smirked and walked downstairs and out to the porch to talk to him.

"You had to go and tell her."

"Babe, she needed to know. He should've told her himself a long time ago. I'm surprised that he didn't yet."

Lily shook her head and he pulled her to him. "What," Lily asked.

He kissed her. "I love you. Always have and always will."

"I know. I love you too even if you are..."

He kissed her again, devouring her lips then hugged her. "Even if I am a pain sometimes?" Lily nodded.

"Okay. Here's my idea. You and me and massages."

"You have work to get to handsome."

"Am I allowed to ask you to come to the office with me?"

"You mean since I'm not in the middle of the book writing stuff."

He nodded. "Come with me."

"And it's not just because you want company?"

He kissed her. "Partially. Come with me."

"Then we have to go back so I can change out of shorts and a tank."

He kissed her. "Luckily, your other stuff is maybe 10 minutes away," he teased.

Lily shook her head, they headed downstairs and Addy looked at Lily. "What?"

"Is it okay if he comes over?"

"Carter?" Addy nodded. "You may need some clothes here and a few other items, but sure. It's your place too." Addy smirked and went back to talking to Carter. "We're heading out. Go enjoy the house," Lily said.

Addy gave them both a hug and Emerson and Lily headed off to go back to the house. Emerson messaged security at the beach house to bring Lily's laptop over to the office. They got to the big house and headed inside, seeing three boxes in the foyer on the table. "What are those," Lily asked.

"I'll handle them. You go get more beautiful," he teased. Lily kissed him and headed upstairs. She slid into a soft sundress, grabbed her sweater and came downstairs to see Emerson coming out of his office.

"And what was in the boxes?"

"Presents for your birthday." Lily shook her head.

"Emerson, we're getting married. I don't need birthday presents on top of it."

"You're getting them anyway wife to be. My woman is having a birthday. We're doing all of it." Lily shook her head. "Just don't go overboard."

"Fireworks, flowers, fancy dinner, and hearts everywhere. That work?"

"Overdoing it as usual," Lily said as he looked up.

"Damn," he said.

"Are you ready to head in?"

Emerson nodded. They headed out, locking up behind them, and hopped into the SUV. "Coffee," his security asked. Lily nodded and Emerson snuggled up to her.

"What," he asked.

Lily kissed him. "Back to normal," Lily said.

"Still want us to try again."

Lily took a deep breath. "If it happens, we go from there. It can wait."

"You sure?"

"I can't do anything anyway right now. We have to take our time."

He nodded. "I know." Just as they got their coffees, Lily's phone went off with a call from her doctor.

"Hi," Lily said as she took a sip of her coffee.

"I wanted to check and see how you were doing?"

"No spotting. Nothing. Just yesterday. It's fine."

"I want you to come for an ultrasound then we can talk a little."

"What time?"

"Can you pop in at 10?"

"Sure. I'll be downtown anyway."

"Alright. I'll see you then," her doctor said as they hung up.

"What time," Emerson asked.

"10."

"That's the time of the meeting."

"Then I'll be back when you're done," Lily teased.

"Babe, I wanted to be there with you."

"She's just checking to see how I am," Lily replied.

Part of her was happy Emerson wouldn't be there. She could ask what she needed to without him interjecting and asking more questions. She needed to know that it wasn't because of her. That the miscarriage was just a bad moment instead of it being physically not possible.

"I still want to be there with you."

Lily kissed him. "I'm good. It's just a checkup."

"Promise me that you'll tell me what she says?"

Lily nodded. "Promise. What else do you need me to ask handsome?"

"You know what."

She shook her head. "I know what she's gonna say. Just give it time."

He kissed her and they pulled up to the office. Lily checked her watch. "Come up when you finish. Promise me." Lily nodded and kissed him. His security drove her over to the doctor's office and she headed upstairs.

"And," Lily asked.

"Well, it passed. Fully. You're still completely healthy. There is no reason to think that it was something with you that caused it. I know that it wasn't. We both know. Give yourself the full week before you attempt to try practicing again. I just want to make sure you're alright," the doctor said.

"I'm alright. I was a little disappointed, but I can't change what happened."

"Are you sure," the doctor asked. Those three words hit her like a brick. No, she wasn't alright. No, she wasn't happy with what had happened. She was more than miserable. The thing was that part of her was happy it was somewhat on hold. Part of her was happy that she wasn't pregnant. She wanted to spend time with Emerson without little feet following them. They needed that time together. Explaining it to his mom wasn't gonna happen either. Thankfully, she'd never need to tell her.

"What's wrong," the doctor asked seeing Lily's eyes welling up.

"Nothing. Just personal stuff. Is it bad that part of me is relieved?"

The doctor shook her head. "Lily, it takes time. It was a major surprise to both of you. I get that you were relieved. You'd be surprised how many people say that." Lily nodded. "Give yourself a little time. When you decide that you're ready, you can go ahead. Just make sure you're really ready."

Lily nodded. "Thank you."

"Keep on the vitamins just in case." Lily nodded. She went to head out, made another follow-up appointment and walked outside.

"Miss Lily," Emerson's security said.

"Am I allowed to just walk back?"

"It's a little too far. We can take the scenic route back if that's what you'd like." Lily nodded, hopped into the SUV and they headed off. Just as they were making their way past waterfront park, Emerson called her phone.

"Hey," Lily said.

"What did the doctor say?"

"Don't you have a meeting or something?"

She could hear his grin. "I do. How did it go?"

"She said we're fine. I can try when I'm ready. I just need time," Lily said.

"But everything else is okay?"

"Yes."

"Are you okay?"

"I don't want to talk about it."

"Okay," he said.

"We're heading to the office."

"I'll be here. The meeting will be short. You sure you're okay?"

"I will be."

"I love you."

"I love you too. See you in a few." They hung up a few minutes later, and his security intentionally went and got two iced lattes. "You didn't have to," Lily said.

"You needed one. It's fine. Just breathe. When you're ready to head over let me know." Lily nodded, took a deep breath and they went in.

When Lily got to his office, the door was locked and she felt like she was having déjà vu. When Emerson answered, he kissed her and walked her in. When she looked in his eyes, she could see they were red. "What's wrong," Lily asked as she gave him the extra iced latte. He took the glasses, put them on the table and kissed her. "Emerson."

He shook his head and hugged her. "I just wanted you to be alright. It's not easy. I get it. I'm just glad that you're okay."

Lily looked at him. "I'm okay for now. It's fine," Lily said.

"You sure," he asked. Lily nodded. He kissed her again and hugged her.

"If you want to put the wedding stuff on hold, just tell me."

"Emerson, it's fine. It just takes time. We have a lot of it."

He kissed her again. "Okay. I'm gonna go do the meeting. You sure you're alright?" Lily nodded, handing him the iced latte that they'd got him. One more kiss and he grabbed his papers and went to his meeting.

Lily sat down and saw her laptop on the sofa. She grabbed it and just let it flow. Whatever was going to spill out would. She kicked her heels off, slid her phone on the table and wrote. By the time he came back in, her latte was finished and she was 4 chapters in.

"And how much did my amazing talented woman get done," he asked.

"Chapter 4."

"And?"

"Came up with a good idea. How was the meeting?"

"The one that felt like it'd never end? Great. Now I have two more."

"I can go home," Lily said.

He shook his head. "Stay," he asked. Lily shook her head and he came over and sat with her.

"Honestly, lunch might be good, but I can stay if you want me to."

"Then I'll get us lunch and we can eat together."

"Emerson, you're working."

He kissed her. "My woman is just as important."

Lily shook her head. "I love you," he said.

"I love you too handsome."

He kissed her again and grabbed his phone, ordering lunch for them. "What did you get?"

"That seafood salad and lobster rolls," he joked. He kissed her and wrapped his arms around her. "Well wife to be," he said.

Lily kissed him. "Now you can stop," she joked.

"When did she say we can practice," he teased.

"When I'm ready. We're giving it time."

"So, would you be completely irritated if I said that I wanted to take you away on the weekend?"

"Emerson."

"We can drive."

"Where?"

"Two options. Blue Ridge or we go to the Outer Banks." Lily looked at him.

"You're being serious?"

He nodded. "Either way, we have a house to ourselves."

"I kinda like the North Carolina option."

"Good. That's the one that I was hoping you'd agree to."

"Emerson."

"We're getting away. No interruptions. Just you and me."

"Still."

He kissed her. "You deserve time. You deserve a break from life. I don't want you worrying about anything."

"So long as we have Wi-Fi in case we need it, I'm good."

"And if we don't?"

Lily looked at him. "I just want us to have some time really alone. I don't want phone calls, I don't want the drama. What's wrong with that?"

She kissed him. "You wouldn't last 24 hours without Wi-Fi."

"Still." Lily kissed him again. "I know what you're saying. We have the week to relax and for you get actual work done."

He smirked. "Lunch then we get back to work."

"What time is your next meeting?"

"1:30." He kissed her and just as he did, there was a knock at the door.

Emerson got up and answered as his secretary handed him lunch for the two of them. "Thank you," he said.

"Most welcome. I'll put your calls on hold for a little while so you two can enjoy."

Emerson nodded and locked the door behind her. He handed Lily her lunch and Lily kissed him. "Thank you handsome. I did kind of need this." One more kiss and they had their lunch. Lily smirked when they finished.

"What?"

"Nothin handsome. Kinda glad I didn't even have to tell you."

"Babe, I know you. This is your comfort food," he teased as he took a gulp from his water.

By the time they went to head out, Lily was exhausted. When they stopped off part way home, Emerson got a grin. "Where are we going?"

"You'll see when we get there." Lily shook her head and he slid her heels off and pulled her legs across his lap. When they pulled into a waterside restaurant, she got a grin.

"Emerson."

"I thought going for a walk by the water before we head home might be a good idea."

"Emerson, I know what you're up to."

He kissed her and they hopped out and went for a walk. His security nodded and left them on their own.

"A walk alone? Really," Lily asked.

Emerson kissed her. "What else did the doctor say?"

"So that's why."

He looked at her like he knew she wasn't telling him everything. "She said that I need to take time and let my heart heal from this."

"And?"

"Part of me was relieved. Part of me was upset. It's not easy either way," Lily replied as he hugged her.

"Just promise me that if you aren't happy with something you tell me."

Lily nodded and he kissed her as they walked down the boardwalk some more. "What would you think if we left Thursday instead to go away?"

"Are you intentionally trying to get me out of town for some reason?"

"Because it's your birthday next weekend. You know Addy is gonna want to be around for it, so it's a trip before your birthday," he said.

"I don't even really want to do anything for my birthday Emerson."

He kissed her. "You're getting something whether you want it or not beautiful. You deserve it."

Lily had never been a fan of her birthday. She'd never had a big party, she'd never really celebrated with anyone other than Addy. She knew that he was planning something. She also knew that within a matter of weeks, she would be marrying him. He'd never let her forget or brush off her birthday again.

"Well," he asked.

Lily kissed him. "I get what you're trying to do, but you know that I never really celebrate."

"You get a birthday 2-week celebration. That's just how it's gonna be. Babe, I want to celebrate you. To thank your parents for you. What's wrong with that," he asked. "You don't have to. Honestly, I'm fine just doing dinner with me, you and Addy."

"And Carter." Lily looked at him. "Carter's taking her out tonight," Emerson teased

"I swear, you are just the matchmaker aren't you?"

"With them? I don't have to be. I never did." Lily shook her head and they kept walking. When they got to the end of the boardwalk, Lily looked at him.

"What," he asked.

"Did you plan that out?"

"The part with her getting together with Carter? No."

"Emerson."

He smirked. "Part of me hoped it'd happen that way. It's up to them. We're kind of contagious like that," he teased as he kissed her. Lily shook her head and they looked out into the blue of the water. "So, you were relieved?"

"A little. It was too much all at once. That's all. We have time for the baby stuff. I also didn't want your mom interjecting that I was trapping you into a wedding."

He shook his head. "In other words, part of you is happy we never had to tell her."

Lily nodded. "I love you. You know that. I just want us to have time together before we throw a baby into the mix. I don't want a baby coming into this when your mom is so against us even getting married. My folks and my family are happy for us. Beyond your mom, I think that they're happy for us. Just that one problem with her. That's it."

Emerson kissed her. "We'll work on my mom. Everything else is fine baby. We can do whatever we want to. All I want is you."

He kissed her again and snuggled her into his arms. For once, instead of her anxiety running away with every worry, she was calm. Like he was her safe spot like he was when they were kids.

He kissed her and picked her up, wrapping her legs around his hips.

"What?"

"I missed that look. That one like you had back in high school when we were hanging out between idiot boyfriends," he teased.

"Emerson."

"I love you," he said.

"I love you too."

He kissed her again and he sat down on the porch swing by the end of the dock. "Are we still alright," he asked.

Lily looked at him. She knew him well enough to know what he was thinking. "We are." "I sorta think that we need to talk to my mom. Straighten all of this out. Are you good if we go over and see them?"

"Not today. We can go before we head away on the weekend."

He kissed her. "Because today's a good day and we're not ruining it?"

Lily smirked. "Something like that," Lily replied. He kissed her again, devouring her lips.

"Still gonna marry me?"

"I'll think about it," she teased as he snuggled her tighter to him.

"Lily."

She nodded. "Of course handsome."

"Okay."

He kissed her again. "Do you want to eat out here?"

He kissed her. "The big question. Beach house or the other house tonight?"

Lily smirked. "House. You don't have another suit at the beach."

"Yeah I do. If you want to go back to the house, just say it."

Lily smirked. "Part of me wants to, but I am in a beach mood."

He kissed her. "Good. We're having seafood on the grill. Just you and me and the beach."

"That works," Lily said. He got up, sliding Lily to her feet and they walked back down the pathway and went back to the SUV.

When they got in, the flowers that Emerson had got for her were sitting on the seat. "What's this," Lily asked.

"Just because," he said.

It had every flower that she loved. From the white Lilies to the lavender, the heather, the sterling roses, the lady Di roses. All of it was beautiful. "Those are all in that bouquet for the wedding."

"Emerson, this is too much."

"Nope. Like you said baby. You only get married once. I want it to be the wedding of your dreams."

"It's just us."

"I want both of them to be about us instead of everyone else. We're all that matters. If you want to, we can just have the ceremony just you and me and just have a party with everyone else. It's up to you."

"I still think that we don't need 2. I just don't want it to be insane. It was supposed to be about us instead of about the 300 people you invite."

"Then we have the wedding at the church like you wanted."

"Emerson."

"And we're having the reception at that restaurant that you love," he teased.

"Where?"

"Belmond Charleston."

Lily shook her head. "Just changed everything that fast?"

"Kinda had it booked."

Lily shook her head. "They go out tomorrow." Lily shook her head with a smirk. "Do you even have a list?"

"Your friends, mine, my folks and my sister and your folks and your brother. The bishop agreed to do the ceremony. Flowers done, food and cake done."

Lily looked at him. "So much for the bridezilla moment. It's the groomzilla," Lily teased.

He kissed her. "Planned. That's it. We still have to go get our marriage license."

Lily shook her head and leaned into his arms. "What," he asked.

"Nothin," Lily said as he kissed her.

"Babe."

"No more wedding talk," she joked.

He kissed her. "Done," he teased as they pulled into their driveway. They hopped out a few minutes later and his driver brought in the food. Lily came in and put the flowers in a vase and she saw his housekeeper setting a table for them outside under the awning.

"What's all of that," Lily asked.

Emerson smirked and kissed her, picking Lily up and carrying her upstairs. He closed the bedroom door, leaning her onto the bed. "Well, we're having some me and you time. That's just part of it."

"And?"

He kissed her. "I'm romancing my woman tonight."

She smirked and shook her head. "And what else were you planning?"

"No rain. Walking on the beach. Swim. Getting every ounce of relaxation in that we can."

"I know that you're up to something."

He kissed her. "I want you and me to be alone. Just us. No more phones, no computers. We get to hang out for a while without anyone else getting in the way."

"I'm waiting on the bomb to drop."

"My mom wanted to take you out tomorrow."

Lily shook her head. "To do what?"

"She said lunch. The café at the Belmond Charleston Hotel."

"So, in other words, you're sucking up to keep me in a good mood."

He kissed her, snuggling her into his arms. "Maybe. Honestly, lunch with her is never quiet and relaxing. It's always stressful."

Lily looked at him. "Fine, but if she starts a fight, I'm gonna get up and leave until she calms herself."

"I know. She also knows that if she starts a problem, I'm gonna come down there and get in the middle."

"Emerson."

He kissed her. "What?"

"I get what you're up to. A non-stress weekend after a really stressful lunch with your mom?"

He nodded. "I just wanted it to be about you."

Lily kissed him. "I love that you're trying," Lily teased.

He smirked. "And if she causes major problems, I'll bring you over to the office."

"I can handle it. I may need to punch something after, but I'll handle it."

He kissed her. "Security is gonna be there, at least nearby, anyway."

"Emerson."

He kissed her again, devouring her lips. "They're gonna be there anyway."

Lily shook her head. "Of course they will," Lily joked.

He shook his head and snuggled her. "What would you think about going back to the house tomorrow?"

"Stay out here tomorrow then go back before we go away."

"Okay. Perfect," he teased as he kissed her again. When she felt his phone buzz, she almost laughed. She knew that he was up to something.

"Are you answering it?" He shook his head and kissed her. When his phone went off again, he shook his head, grabbed it out of his pocket and saw that his mom was calling.

He kissed Lily and pressed speakerphone. "Hi Mom," Emerson said.

"So, are we still on for lunch tomorrow," his mom asked.

"You mean you and my wife to be."

"Are we still on for lunch or no?"

"Reservation was made. Lily's coming to the office with me tomorrow."

"When does all the book tour stuff start," his mom asked.

"Well, that's part of the celebration. It's coming out at the beginning of December if not earlier. She's doing a book tour starting in October or November."

"Then why are you really just jumping in and having this wedding now?"

"Mom, we talked about this," he said as he got up and took the phone off speaker, holding it to his ear.

"That wasn't an answer," his mom replied.

He kissed Lily and went down to his office. "I'm the one that wants it now. I waited 15 years to get her back in my life. I don't want to wait any longer mom. I'm not playing this stupid game. If you can't respect her then don't come to the wedding. You can't keep doing this."

"You want me to sit and have lunch with the woman who's after you for your money. That's ridiculous," his mom said.

"Then don't come. You don't accept her, you lose me. Which one do you want?"

"Emerson, stop being ridiculous. You're not gonna walk away from your family for her of all people."

"Either you stop disrespecting the woman I'm gonna marry or I swear, you're not gonna like my reaction."

"She's using you."

He took a deep breath. "Like you used Dad? You liked him, but you loved his wallet. Isn't that what you said to your friends when I was little?"

"Emerson."

"Treat her with respect. You don't, you lose your son."

"Then come with us."

"You say one thing that upsets her, and I swear I'll…"

"Emerson, I get it, but I know that she doesn't love you."

"Really? She told me she loved me. She knew she had. She'd always cared about me, but she had no dang idea how I felt. She didn't know when we met about the money. I promise you that. Leave her be."

"And if it turns out that I'm right," she asked as Emerson's jaw started clenching and his fist started twitching.

"You aren't. There's no if."

Lily walked downstairs and grabbed her laptop, walking outside. She curled up on the chaise and went through emails. When she got a chapter finished and he hadn't come outside, she shook her head. When she heard the whoosh of the sliding door, Lily took a deep breath.

"When did you come out here?"

"When you and your mom were reenacting world war two," she said as she continued to write. When she stopped, he closed her laptop and took it in the house.

"Babe."

"I'm good not doing lunch with her on my own. She doesn't want me there, I can stay here and write." He sat down on the chaise beside her and wrapped his arm around her, sliding her to him.

"Babe, I'm gonna come with you. If things get too intense, we leave. I'm not throwing you in the pit alone with her. Not after that," he said as he kissed her forehead.

"I can just chill here Emerson. Honestly, if y'all need time to talk all of it through, I'm good."

He shook his head. "Come have dinner."

"Emerson."

"Babe, come have dinner. We can talk about it when we go for a walk later." She shook her head, took a deep breath, and got up.

"She doesn't have to want me around all the time. All I wanted was for her to accept that we're getting married. That I'm gonna be part of your life. If she doesn't then you can find...."

He kissed her, leaning her against the wall by the door to head inside. "I'm not finding someone else. You're all I ever wanted. Period. I don't want something else or someone else."

"She's never gonna be happy with this."

"Then she's gonna have to get used to it." Lily shook her head and he kissed her again. "Get used to it wife. You're stuck with me forever. Longer than that. I'm never ever going away." She smirked and he kissed her again. He linked their fingers and walked her inside. He got her a glass of wine, poured one for himself and sat down in the table that his housekeeper had set up.

"Still not sure what she's gonna say. I don't want any insults getting thrown out," Lily said.

"Babe."

She shook her head, had her wine, and tried to just relax. "What," she asked.

"She's not starting anything with me there. That I can promise you." Lily took a deep breath, finished her wine and he poured her a second glass. "She's not coming after you and she's not going to disrespect you at all baby. That I do know. I promise you that. I'm not gonna let that happen to you."

Lily took a deep breath. "I love that you think that, but I know she's not gonna back down Emerson. That's why I've been avoiding it."

He looked at her. "Baby."

"I'm not talking about this."

"Lily, breathe. I love you. Even if she's gonna be a pain in my backside, she's not gonna come after you. She's not gonna say anything." Lily shook her head and took a sip of the wine, praying that it'd calm her now frazzled nerves.

"What threat did you make to her?"

He looked at her like she'd read his mind. Like she knew what they'd discussed on that phone call. "All I said was that if she didn't accept you, she'd end up losing me. That you're important to me and you always will be. I waited 15 years for us to be in the spot that we're in right now. I waited 15 years to tell you that I love you and I want to spend forever with you. Nobody is getting in the way of that Lily."

She shook her head. "Emerson."

"What?"

"You can't do that. That's your mom."

"You know that we've never been that close. She knows that I'm serious. That you aren't just in it for the money or the houses. You're in it because you love me. She knows that you do, but she needs to see it for herself. That's all," Emerson replied as he gulped down his wine.

Lily shook her head. They sat back down and had dinner, oddly, in complete silence. "I love you. You know that right," he asked.

"I do, but you can't threaten your mom into being nice to me. She's not gonna mean a single word."

He slid his hand in hers. "I promise you. One way or another, she's gonna see the real you. The one that got me tripping over my feet all the way through high school and got that big ole grin on my face when we saw each other again."

"I love that you're sucking up royally right now, but no. It takes more than one dinner to get her to stop seeing me like I'm destroying the relationship between you two. I love you Emerson, but trying to make her feel something she doesn't isn't fair. If she thinks I'm in it for the money, so be it. So long as she doesn't destroy the wedding, I'm fine," Lily replied.

He shook his head, refilled their glasses with the second bottle of wine and took the glasses to the steps on their deck as they sat down together. "Babe, are you really that concerned?"

Lily nodded. "If she knew me, she'd know that I'm not in it for anything but you. You can't force her to feel that way."

He slid his arm around her. "Baby, I just don't want her upsetting you. That's all."

Lily shook her head. "You can't control her Emerson. She's your mom for the rest of your life. She's why you're alive. She was the first woman in your life. Leave it. Don't threaten anything on my behalf alright?"

He nodded and took another sip of his wine. Lily kissed him and got up. "What are you doin?"

"Going for a walk." Lily walked down by the water. Emerson got up, grabbed a blanket, putting it on the bottom step and walked out to her, sliding his hand in hers.

"When do I start the book stuff?" "Probably before thanksgiving. Could be more after the holidays. I think you're done before the film premiere."

"Emerson."

"I'm gonna be out there with you as much as I can. If not, Addy can come out."

Lily shook her head. "And if it doesn't do well?"

He looked at her. "Even now you're worried? Babe, they've been promoting it for 2 months. The pre-orders are insane. We have the wedding, then a little time alone on a beach or something somewhere, then the holidays." Lily nodded as she got a little closer to the water. "Tell me what's wrong Lily."

He could see it. He knew her that well. Lily going silent and second-guessing herself and her book. She was second-guessing her life. "Emerson."

"Stop. Come here," he said as he pulled her into his arms and snuggled her to him. "You are an amazing writer. You always have been. You're an amazing woman. You have been the entire time I've known you. Tell me what you're worried about."

Lily shook her head. "I can't be what you deserve Emerson. All I can be is me."

He kissed her, picking her up and wrapping her legs around his hips. "All I want is you. All I ever wanted was you. I don't care about the money. I don't. I just want you baby." He kissed her again, devouring her lips.

"And if I can't?"

"Can't what?" Lily gave him a look as if to say that he knew.

"Lily."

She slid to her feet. "What if I can't?"

"Then we travel the world. We have cats. We do whatever we want. We can adopt. As long as you're happy I don't care."

"Are you sure?"

He watched her walk back down to the water and finish her wine. "Lily."

"What?"

"Come here." She took a deep breath, grabbing a shell as she tried to delay looking him in the eye. He sat down and she walked over and sat with him. "I know that you're worried babe. I do. I know that my mom makes you anxious. All I'm doing is lessening it."

"And I'm saying that maybe we should just wait."

He shook his head. "We waited 15 years. I love you. You love me. I'm marrying you. You're marrying me. It's not about money. It's not about security. It's about you and me. I already told you that I didn't care whether our folks were even there."

Lily shook her head and he pulled her into his lap. "I love you."

"I know. I love you." He kissed her.

"Tell me what you want Lily." She shook her head and he kissed her, pulling her to him and hugging her.

Chapter 9

"Tell me," Emerson asked.

"I know what you want even if you don't say it Emerson. I've known since the first time we were alone. I don't know if I can have kids. I don't know if I can change your mom's mind. There's…"

He kissed her, cradling her face in his hands. "Stop. I want you. I don't care what form that is, but I want to marry you. Whether we're here, on a beach somewhere, in a church, away from everyone and everything or with everyone we know. All I want is us. Everything else is just a bonus. No stressing baby. None."

"But, what…"

He kissed her again. "Stop. No more stress. No more worrying. That's all. You don't need it. The book is gonna be a bestseller. We all know it, and we all see it. You're worried. I get it. Breathe."

He snuggled her again. "You aren't gonna change your mind?"

He smirked. "Not in a billion lifetimes."

"Emerson."

He kissed her. "What?"

"Walk with me?"

He nodded, kissed her, and picked her up. "Wife."

Lily smirked. "Not until I say I do," Lily teased.

"Better?" She nodded. He handed her back her glass and they walked for a while more.

When they got back, the wine was in the decanter on the table with the flowers he'd bought for her. "Another glass?" Lily shook her head. She got the flowers, bringing them inside, Emerson put the wine onto the tray with the other decanters and they walked upstairs as Lily saw his security lock up the doors. When they got to the bedroom, there were candles, fancy sheets, roses and music. She smirked.

"What's all of this?"

"A no-stress night. Just you and me."

Lily kissed him. "You're sucking up."

"Nope."

"Making up for your mom being a pain?"

"Partially," he teased. Lily smirked. He picked her up, wrapping her legs around his hips, "Mine," he teased. He kissed her again before she could say another word.

"Emerson."

"What?"

"Bed." He smirked and leaned her onto it, leaning into her arms as he slid her to the pillows.

"You sure you're alright?" Lily nodded and kissed him.

"Phone," Lily asked.

"Why?"

"You're making a phone call."

"Not tonight I'm not. Phones don't exist right now."

He put it on the bedside table, put it on the charger and slid it into the drawer on silent.

"Tell me what you want," he asked.

"How do you know exactly what to say?"

"To you?" Lily nodded. "Because I know you. I know what's in your heart. You consider everyone and everything when you make decisions. That's why I loved you then. I've never seen you do something for selfish reasons. You've walked away when you worried, but I know that you never stopped caring. Babe, you bought a house and you're handing the keys to Addy."

Lily kissed him. "I don't think anyone ever noticed."

He shook his head. "Babe, we all see it. The people that you're close to and I'm close to are all that matter. Everyone else is just bonus. Even with me it's the same. I saw it in high school. I saw it with your book stuff. You going out to appease Addy when you wanted to be home instead. I'm surprised that you even left the house."

"What happens if I don't want to do the wedding?"

"Then we run off to Hawaii and do it alone just you and me on a beach."

"Emerson."

He kissed her. "Tell me where and when and we'll go."

She kissed him and he snuggled her. "You're ridiculous."

"You can't get rid of me beautiful. I'm yours until the end of time."

"You sure you want this?"

He looked at her and smirked. "The only thing in my entire life that I've been sure of since the minute we met."

He kissed her and snuggled her that much closer. "You didn't know way back then did you?"

He nodded and kissed her. "I knew the minute I saw you. You had that look like you do when you're determined to get your way. That same way that you were when I got you to my mom and dad's party."

She shook her head. "The one where your exes opted for a second try?"

"Where they all knew with one single look that you were and will always be my forever." She shook her head, running her fingers through his hair. "The one where you changed my life in ways you didn't even know," Emerson said.

"Meaning what," Lily asked.

He kissed her. "You did. You made me the man I am supposed to have been. I loved you then, and I love you even more now," he said.

"And if I changed my mind?"

"I'd drag you kicking and screaming all the way down the aisle."

"Emerson."

"Did you think that you maybe didn't want to get married?"

"I want you happy."

"Then marry me. Just be with me. If you want to run off and do it alone, we can. You want to do it with a thousand people, we do it. I want you just as happy. All that matters is me and you. I'm yours baby. I'm yours for the rest of time."

When she kissed him, something was different. He didn't know what it was, and he didn't care. She was his again. The woman he'd dreamt of for years. The smile was enough to tell him. This was the woman he proposed to. The one who loved him as much as he loved her.

"I see that look in your eyes Emerson. What are you thinking?"

He kissed her. "That I want you naked in 3.2 seconds."

"And the part of your brain that's on your shoulders?"

He smirked. "That I can't wait 6 weeks."

Lily smirked. "It's an insane busy 6 weeks coming, but I'll do it so long as it doesn't become stress."

"Then we're doing lunch."

Lily nodded. "So long as you and I are a team."

He nodded and kissed her. "Forever."

She kissed him. He leaned to his side and curled her into his arms. "Wife, are we getting sleep or are we watching a movie?"

Lily kissed him. "Movie or we talk through the rest of the wedding planning."

He kissed her. "Pajamas then curl up and do something."

Lily kissed him. "Whatever you say handsome."

He kissed her again, devouring her lips, and she managed to get up. She walked into her closet, slid into her satin chemise then came into the bedroom. She intentionally blew out the candles that were on the counters, leaving the ones on the bedside table and headboard lit. When he came in and saw Lily going through emails on her phone, he grabbed it, threw it in the side table with his, putting it on the charger and slid onto the bed and into her arms in nothing but his boxers.

"Now, where were we?"

"Emerson."

"What?"

He kissed up her chest, then her neck. "I know what you're up to." He kissed her and pulled her legs around his waist.

"And what would that be," he asked.

"Emerson."

"What? I'm not allowed to taunt my woman?"

"No," Lily replied.

"What if we just…"

He kissed her and pulled the blankets up, kicking his boxers off.

"Emerson."

He kissed her and snuggled her to him. "What?"

"You know we can't."

He nodded and kissed her. "I just want us back to normal."

Lily shook her head. "As in what?"

"Feeling your body against mine. Feeling your skin on my skin."

He kissed her again, devouring her lips until she sprouted goosebumps. "You're not behaving."

"Nope." He kissed her again and snuggled her to him, devouring her lips.

"You're not being fair."

"Miss me," he asked as he slid the strap of her chemise off her shoulder.

"Emerson."

He kissed her shoulder. "Wife." He could feel her heart fluttering like she was almost nervous. "What's wrong," he asked.

Lily shook her head. "You're taunting."

"You have no idea what's running around in my mind," he teased.

"Yeah I do. I've known that dirty mind for years," Lily teased.

He kissed her. "You have no idea," he teased as he snuggled her to him.

"We can't Emerson."

He kissed her again. "And?"

He pulled her legs tighter around his hips. "What," Lily asked.

He kissed her. "Do you want me?"

Lily smirked. "Not the point handsome."

He kissed her again and he kissed down her neck. "We can if you want to," he teased.

"Meaning?"

She felt his hand slide to her hip. "Meaning I want you."

"Emerson."

He kissed her, nibbling at her lip. "Say yes," he whispered as he kissed her again. Lily shook her head, or at least it felt like she did. He snuggled her in tight to him and they had sex. It was hot. It was toe-curling, body humming, heart pounding sex. He felt too good. Way too good. He wanted her, and his body wanted her too. He missed how she felt in his arms. His body gave in and she was wrapped tight around him. "I'm not letting you go."

"You better not," Lily teased as he kissed her again.

He leaned onto his back and pulled her to him. "You okay sexy?"

Lily nodded and he kissed her again. "Are you sure?"

"I promise. I'm fine," she replied as his hand slid to her backside.

"I love you," he said.

"Love you too handsome. You're still gonna need a big amazon box full of soap for that dirty mind of yours."

"Oh I know. Just happens to pop up every time I kiss you."

"Think so do you?"

He nodded. "No more taking a night for granted. No more taking each other for granted."

Lily kissed him. "I guess that means I'm stuck with you?"

He nodded. "For life."

Lily curled up with him and they fell asleep not long later. It was the first time in a while that she actually slept. When she woke up and he wasn't in bed, she was almost irritated. She opened her eyes and saw her coffee on the side table with a note:

> *I love you. Just went downstairs. Decided to go for a run on the beach. I'll meet you downstairs sexy.*

Lily smirked, got up and slid her satin robe on, freshened up and headed downstairs to see Emerson making breakfast. "What are you up to," Lily asked.

He kissed her. "Making my woman breakfast. I got some fresh fruit," he said as he kissed her again.

"Where is everyone?"

"Security's here, the housekeeper went to the house and we get to have breakfast alone." He finished cooking, plated the food and they curled up together and watched the waves while they ate at the counter.

"What time do you have to go to the office?"

"2. We're going for a walk or a swim or something this morning, then you have a fitting, then we go and do lunch."

"Who's coming with me to the fitting?"

"Addy. She said she wanted to ask you something according to her text. She messaged you this morning."

"Checking my phone?"

"Nope. I saw it when I took the phones off the charger in the drawer and turned the ringers back on."

Lily shook her head. "I may need a few shots before lunch."

"We both might," he joked as he kissed her.

"You sure we have to?"

He smirked. "I know you'd like to make a few excuses, but we can get it overwith then go away this weekend."

"You sure that's what you wanna do?"

He kissed her, devouring her lips. "Positive," he said. They finished breakfast, cleaned the dishes up together and headed upstairs to get ready. "Do I seriously have to do this lunch?"

He handed Lily her bikini.

"What?"

"We're going swimming. You, me and waves."

Lily smirked and slid the bikini on. When he came out of his closet in his board shorts, she shook her head.

"Emerson." He picked her up, carried her down the steps and straight out into the water. They fell into the salty bliss of the ocean water. When they surfaced, she smirked and he swam over towards her.

"What," Lily teased. He kissed her.

"Am I allowed to say that you are the sexiest woman I know," he teased.

Lily kissed him. "Sucking up," Lily teased.

He shook his head and Lily dunked him. She kept swimming and something surfaced behind her. When Lily looked, a dolphin was jumping out of the water. She heard Emerson laughing as she made her way back towards him.

"Had to swim with them," he teased.

"Not intentionally," Lily joked as he pulled her into his arms.

"You okay," he asked as he pulled her legs around him.

"I still don't want to."

He kissed her again and he smirked. "Still going."

"I know, but do I really have to be there?"

He kissed her and nodded. "I'm not going without you beautiful."

She shook her head. "Then we kinda need to go in and get ready."

"We will," he teased as he walked deeper into the water.

"What are you doing?" He smirked and kissed her as he was up to his shoulders.

"She's not gonna burst us into flames. I promise."

"Emerson."

He shook his head and devoured her lips. "We get ready, stop off at the office to grab my papers and then we go meet her."

"When?"

"11."

"What time is it," Lily asked.

He kissed her. "9:30."

"Then we're going in."

He nodded and kissed her again as he walked inside with her still wrapped around him. He set her down as they hit the warm wood of their deck. "Where did the towels…"

He kissed her. "I told them we were coming outside."

They headed inside, walked upstairs, and got undressed, hopping into a hot shower together. "You sure that I have to be there," Lily teased.

"I'm sure that you're going even if I have to carry you." She shook her head, rinsed out her hair and he kissed her. "Babe."

"Hopefully, there's no excess drama."

Emerson nodded. "I got you either way."

Lily kissed him and put her conditioner in. "Wife, you good," he asked as Lily washed up. Lily washed his hair for him.

"I'm good. I wish this was easier, but I'm good," Lily said. He slid his arms around her as she slid him under the water and rinsed the shampoo out.

"Just promise me something. You start feeling awkward, tell me." Lily nodded and kissed him. They finished their showers, hopped out and started getting ready.

Emerson shaved, freshened up and got dressed and when he was pulling on his shirt, he saw Lily come out of her closet in a blue dress. It hugged her curves but was so beyond beautiful. She looked like a princess.

"Wow," Emerson said.

"You think?" He nodded and kissed her. Lily went and finished doing her hair, put her lipstick on, and slid her heels on. When she came back into the bedroom, he shook his head with a grin ear to ear.

"Babe."

"What?"

"Just between you and me, you look like a princess." Lily kissed him.

"Good," she teased. They headed to go down the stairs and he picked her up and carried her. "What are you doin?"

"Making sure you don't nosedive down the steps." Lily shook her head and he kissed her. He set her on her feet and she grabbed her purse. "You look amazing."

"And you're pretty handsome there yourself husband to be." He looked at her.

"You just..."

Lily shook her head and he hugged her. "We ready," his security asked. Emerson nodded and they headed out the door, hopping into the SUV. Lily grabbed her phone and called Addy.

"What's up," Lily asked.

"What are y'all up to today?"

"Lunch with his mom. Why?"

"I need to ask you something. Are you okay if I kinda go out with Carter?"

"What happened to the boyfriend?"

"You mean the man that was cheating? Great. I moved into the house this morning."

"You sure you're alright?"

"Yeah. Are you alright with me hanging with Carter?"

"I don't see any problem," Lily said.

"Alright. Go do your lunch. Call me after," Addy said as they hung up quickly.

"And," Emerson asked as he went through his emails on his phone.

"She's going out with Carter." Emerson smirked and started laughing.

"Told ya," he teased.

"Emerson."

He shook his head as he slid his arm around Lily. "Like I said, we're contagious." Lily smirked. "And what happens if they end up getting hitched like us," he asked.

"Then we really are contagious," Lily teased. He kissed her forehead.

"Babe, he loves her. We both know that he does. When she sees it, and knows it like you did, there isn't gonna be any doubt."

Lily smirked and they went and tried to grab a coffee.

"I'm good," Lily said.

"Babe." She shook her head. He got her one regardless, handing the iced latte to her. She took a sip and was beyond glad he ignored her request.

They pulled up to Emerson's office and they ran inside. They got into his office and he had a mound of paperwork to do. He took what he needed off his desk and slid it into his briefcase.

"You sure you don't need to be back here after," Lily asked.

"I'm coming home with my woman," he teased.

"Emerson."

"I told them. That meeting I have is gonna be a call-in."

"And if today goes alright?"

"Then I'm still coming home with you."

"You can come back here."

He shook his head. "We're going to the beach house then we have alone time."

"Emerson."

He looked at her. "Babe, you're not gonna sit here all afternoon. We do the lunch then go home."

Just as he said it, his assistant knocked. "Quick question. Are you able to come back for a quick meeting after the lunch?"

"Half hour max." His assistant nodded. "Alright, but no longer than a half hour."

Lily almost laughed when his assistant left the room. "Fine. You're right," he teased.

"It's fine. I'll stay here with you until we head back."

"Did you want to go back to the beach or the house?"

"Up to you handsome. Honestly, either works."

"Beach so you have time to calm down?" Lily nodded and went through her emails. A half hour later, Emerson looked at her.

"What?"

"Nothin. Just keep seeing the sexy wife to be over there and you're distracting me," he teased.

Lily shook her head. "Concentrate on the paperwork handsome."

"Kinda can't. I just got the updated numbers on your pre-orders."

"Meaning what," Lily asked attempting to be nonchalant.

"Lily."

She looked at him. "What?"

"Do you want to know?"

Lily's heart started racing. "I almost don't want to."

"Comes out the first of November right?"

Lily nodded, gulping and trying to not get her hopes up.

"Babe." She looked at him.

"They told me 3500."

"Kinda went up.," Emerson said.

Lily nodded. He looked at her and shook his head. He took the piece of paper and walked over to Lily, sitting down beside her. "Tell me what's wrong," he asked.

"Just worried what it'll say."

"Baby, it went up. It went up more than you think. It's good."

Lily shook her head. "It doesn't matter. It's good reviews that matter."

"Well, we sent advance copies to a few papers and bloggers. Nobody can release their copy, but they can give reviews. Do you want to see it?"

Lily shook her head. "Okay, then I'm reading it to you."

"Emerson." He kissed her.

"One of the most romantic novels I've ever read. The main characters make you almost swoon. The love gets you crying, laughing, smiling and blushing within a few chapters. A beautiful second novel from my new favorite author. I can't wait to see this in film."

Lily looked at him. "Emerson."

He handed it to Lily.

"Like I said baby. Everyone loves the book like I do."

"This is insane."

"Okay. Here's another one," he said as Lily read it.

"Emerson, this...this is almost too much."

"Now look at the pre-order number."

He handed the paper to Lily. It was better than she could've imagined. "This is so much."

"And now we get to celebrate. I'm taking my woman to dinner by the house. What do you think?"

"She'll like it. I could go for a grilled cheese," Lily teased.

"Funny," he joked as he kissed her.

"This is big Emerson."

"Like I said. No more doubting that insanely sexy, smart, and inspiring brain of yours."

Lily kissed him. "Okay."

He shook his head, kissed her forehead and Lily's phone buzzed with a reminder of their lunch reservation.

They headed out and made their way over to the restaurant. "You okay," Emerson asked.

"Now that I got good news before this, yeah. Good timing," Lily teased.

He kissed her and Lily touched up her lipstick. When they pulled into the turnaround for the front doors, Emerson kissed her hand. "You ready for this," he asked.

Lily nodded. They hopped out and he took her hand. "We got this." Lily looked at him and took a deep breath.

They made their way through the mezzanine and came into the restaurant, sitting down in the quiet side of the restaurant. "You sure she didn't change her mind," Lily asked.

He shook his head. "We could only wish," he joked. When he heard his mom's voice, he kissed Lily's hand.

"She's here."

"I heard."

His mom walked over towards them and Lily was hoping more than anything that she'd changed her mind. Lily's phone buzzed that her fitting had been changed to 2pm. She sent the info to Addy and got up.

"Lily. How are you," his mom asked.

"I'm great. How are you," Lily said attempting to be nice.

His mom hugged her and they all sat down to eat. Lily knew that she'd have to mind her tongue, but the minute his mom sat down, Lily instantly felt like that awkward 15-

year-old. When Emerson's phone went off with a work call, she almost held on for dear life.

"Give me 5 minutes," Emerson said as he kissed Lily and got up.

"How has the planning been going," his mom asked.

"Doing a fitting this afternoon. Everything else is pretty much done. Emerson kinda took over the planning," Lily replied.

The food came to the table and Lily tried her best to stay positive. "I heard. I know that you didn't want to discuss this and either did he, but I need to know. You aren't with him for any bad reasons right," his mom asked.

"I just released my second novel and have thousands of pre-orders and reviews. I never was with him for the money. We've been friends since we were kids. I had no idea that he'd had a crush on me that long. Honestly, the money never mattered, and it never will. I have my own car. I have my own house. Like I said, his money is his. I just want to be with him because I love him."

"Lily, I get that, and it's all nice to say, but y'all are living at his house. How could you have a house of your own if you're living with him?"

"I bought a place a while ago. I'm renting it to one of my friends. The house is in my name. He knew that. He tried talking me out of it. He knows why I'm doing what I am. His stuff is his. All I want is his heart and his mind. That's all I ever wanted. I can't say that it's going to be easy for either of us. It's harder when you're so objectively against the relationship." Lily's hands were almost shaking as she took a sip of her water.

"I just don't want my son to end up penniless and homeless."

"If he is, I am too. Like we both said a long time ago. Even if we both end up in a cardboard box, we're good so long as we're together."

His mom started getting a little uncomfortable. "I just don't understand what happened after the two of you finished high school."

Lily knew it would happen. She knew the questions that his mom would say. "I made a lot of mistakes in my life. A lot of guy mistakes. They just don't make them like your son anymore. I had no idea that he knew where I was. Honestly, bumping into him on the beach was one heck of a moment. I didn't even recognize him."

"I know he missed you. All I worry about is that you two haven't been dating that long."

"I said the same thing. I do know that I don't want a life without him in it. He feels the same," Lily said.

"Exactly," Emerson said as he sat down beside Lily and kissed her.

"And, what happens if you two don't work," his mom asked.

"If we have struggles, we work at them. Walking away isn't an option," Lily said.

Emerson slid his arm around her shoulders. "What did you think was gonna happen," Emerson asked.

"I just worry that this is fast."

"Mom, I love that you're worried, but we've known each other since we were kids. I've loved her since we were kids. We struggled all the way through high school."

"You have both changed since high school," his mom said.

"And we still have a bond. It hasn't faded even a little," Lily said.

They finished their food and a fight hadn't happened. Lily was partially relieved. "What time are you doing your fitting," his mom asked.

Lily almost cringed. "Around 2. I'm meeting my maid of honor over there. She's getting a fitting for hers as well," Lily said.

"Would you like me to come," his mom asked.

Emerson squeezed her shoulder a little, hinting that she say yes. "You're welcome to join us if you'd like," Lily said as she wrote down the address for the bridal salon.

"I'll be there," his mom replied. When Emerson's mom looked at him, Lily knew. She wanted to talk to him alone.

"I'll be back in a moment," Lily said as she grabbed her purse and phone and went to the ladies room.

She called Addy back. "Hey. So, how was lunch with Cruella," Addy teased.

"It was alright, but I know they're having world war three now," Lily said.

"I'm coming down to the bridal shop for 1:30. Does that work?"

"Depends. You dropping Carter off?"

"We're going out tonight. He has a meeting with Emerson to be honest with you. I can come by the office if you want."

"What happened to work?"

"I took today off. Kinda had to meet this friend of mine," Addy joked.

"Come hang in Emerson's office with me then."

"Alright girl. See you then."

Lily touched up her lipstick, took a deep breath and came out of the ladies room to see Emerson waiting. "What happened," Lily asked.

"Nothing. Let's go."

"Did she leave?" Emerson nodded and took Lily's hand, walking her out to the SUV. "Emerson." They hopped in and headed back to his office. "What did she say?"

"It doesn't matter," Emerson said.

"She was nice to me for once. What happened Emerson?"

"She threw an insult or two out and I told her if that was how she felt, not to come to the wedding at all or the fitting."

Lily shook her head. "You know that you two are like fire and dynamite right?"

"Hopefully I'm the dynamite."

Lily shook her head. "Emerson, you two set each other off. You have since we met in high school. You always told me that y'all got into huge fights all the time."

"Because she stuck her nose in my business." Lily shook her head. They got back to his office and he headed upstairs with Lily hand in hand.

"At least this means that we have time before your fitting," he teased.

"And Addy is coming over with Carter."

"Here?"

Lily nodded. "While y'all are in the meeting, we're going to the fitting together."

"I could just do the meeting at home."

Lily shook her head. "If she shows at the fitting and starts a problem, I'll let you know and Addy can come to the beach with me."

"I can do…"

"Emerson, you have a career and they need you. All I'm gonna do is hang with Addy and write. I'm not going anywhere without you."

"Promise?"

Lily nodded and kissed him. "I promise."

He snuggled her to him and wrapped his arms tight around her. "I'm sorry about my mom."

Lily kissed him. "Here's the thing. If she decides she can respect us and show up, then she comes. If she doesn't, she doesn't come. You're fine, and I'm good. It doesn't matter. We tried."

He kissed her. "How'd you get to be the wise one instead of the panic mode one?"

"Just for today we changed spots."

He kissed her again, devouring her lips when there was a knock at the door. "Yep," Emerson said as his assistant came in.

"Sir, there's an Addison here to see you and Carter Sams is here for the meeting."

"Bring them in."

She nodded and Lily smirked. "I love you," he said.

"I love you back fiancée. Go do your meeting and I'll see you after. If anything happens, I'll come over here and let you know." Emerson nodded, kissed her again and hugged Lily like he was walking into the death chamber.

"Do I get a hint about the dress?"

"It's white." He shook his head, kissed her and Carter and Addy came in.

"What are we interrupting," Addy teased.

"Nothin. Long time no see Carter," Lily teased.

Emerson guy hugged Carter and gave Addy a hug.

"What are y'all doin showing up together," Emerson asked.

"Well, we were kinda talking. We went out for breakfast and I figured that we could do lunch then come over," Carter replied.

Lily smirked and grabbed her purse and phone. "Leaving me already," Emerson said. One more kiss and Lily headed out with Addy, and Emerson and Carter got prepped for the meeting.

"So, what actually happened," Addy asked. Lily told her everything as they made their way to the bridal shop for the fitting.

"I don't even know if she'll show, but he is still mad. She was fine with me for once."

"Miss Lily, I'll wait outside for you both if that's alright. Saves me a little travel time," Emerson's security said.

"Alright. Thank you," Lily said.

They pulled up to the shop and Lily and Addy headed inside. "Miss Lily. How are you," the saleswoman said as they came in.

"I'm good. I'm hoping the dress looks amazing," Lily said.

"6 more weeks. We're gonna get Addy into hers first, then we're moving to yours." Lily nodded and Addy went in to change into the dress. When Addy came out, she had a smirk.

"Well," Addy asked.

"It's perfect."

"It's a little loose in a spot or two, but it's alright. I'm kinda glad that we got the flowy like you said. I'm comfy in it." They pinned the last changes, Addy got dressed, then Lily went and slid into her wedding dress. Just as she was getting changed, Emerson's mom showed up.

When Lily came out and saw her, she was almost stunned. She could see that Emerson's mom had been crying. "You came," Lily said.

"Oh my goodness," she said as Lily stood on the pedestal in the dress.

"What do you think," Lily asked.

"He's gonna be a mess when he sees you. It's beautiful," his mom said as the seamstress pinned where Lily needed it a little tighter.

"Thank you," Lily said.

"I'm still a little surprised that you were willing to let me come." Addy was about to roll her eyes when Carter messaged her. "What did you get for your veil," Emerson's mom asked.

"I'll get it," the seamstress said.

She put the headpiece and the veil on and his mom got a grin. "Are you sure you don't want to add some sparkle," his mom asked.

"I have a dress with the sparkle. I'm alright. Emerson got me a necklace a while ago that he thinks I forgot about that I'm gonna wear."

"You sure you don't want a tiara or something?"

Lily smirked. "I'm alright. I appreciate it though."

"Then what about shoes?"

Lily smirked. "I had my eye on a pair," Lily said.

The seamstress got the shoes and Lily slid them on. "What do you think?"

"Perfect. I'm buying you the shoes," his mom said.

"You don't have to." His mom got up and hugged Lily for including her.

"I'm gonna call Carter. I'll be back in a few," Addy said.

Lily slid out of the dress and got re-dressed then came and sat with his mom. "Thank you for this," his mom said.

"You're welcome. Thank you. I know that it didn't exactly go the way you were hoping."

"We've had spats before. I'm just worried about him." Lily knew what she wanted to say, and she hoped it'd come out the way she wanted.

"When you met Emerson's dad, was everyone in support of it?"

"His mom was irritated. She demanded I sign a prenup. I actually signed it, and thankfully we never needed it. It calmed her down, but she always gave me the evil eye."

"And," Lily said.

"I expected the worst. All it was there for was to protect the family and for you two. If something ever happened, one of the two of you would be lost."

Lily smirked. "We'd be lost without each other, not the money."

His mom nodded. "Thank you."

Lily nodded. "I don't want him regretting having you there or not having you there. He would regret it if you weren't. All I ask is for happy and positive."

His mom gave her a hug. "I can't wait to see you at the wedding. I can't wait to see his face."

"You and me both. He's already started asking for hints," Lily joked.

"Is there a specific color that you'd prefer for me to wear?"

"Burgundy or silver. If that works."

His mom nodded. "Perfect. Let me know the rest of the details?" Lily nodded and they headed out together and Lily hopped in the SUV with Addy.

"Okay. Where did the attitude go," Addy asked.

"We talked."

"Twice in one day," Addy joked.

"I sorta made her see it from our point of view."

"So long as she doesn't object to the wedding, she's safe," Addy said sarcastically.

"That's why I talked to her."

"Dude, you're the new and improved cranky mom whisperer!"

"I know what you really wanted to say. Honestly, I didn't even want to go to lunch, but for now it's fine."

"Still stunned y'all weren't fighting," Addy replied.

They made their way back to the office when Emerson called. "Hey handsome," Lily said.

"Are you heading back?"

"To the office. Why," Lily teased.

"Just checking. How was the fitting?"

"Yes she came, no there wasn't a fight. She actually bought me shoes for the dress. We were good. I talked to her about the lunch stuff and it's good," Lily said.

"So that's why she called me."

"See you in a few minutes."

"Alright beautiful."

"Even Emerson is in shock," Addy joked.

"Girl, I'm stunned, but at least I got it all out. I told her I wasn't intentionally trying to upset her. We talked like two adults instead of a mom and kids. If it fixed the riff between Emerson and his mom even temporarily, I'm okay with it."

"The mom-in-law whisperer. That's your new nickname."

Lily shook her head. "So, what's up with you and Carter?"

"We were talking. Honestly, we were talking all night. We both fell asleep on the sofa." Lily smirked. "What?"

"You remember him from high school right?"

Addy shook her head and laughed. "I remember him. He was a lost puppy dog," Addy said.

"Who had a giant crush on you."

Addy shook her head. "Barely."

"Worse than Emerson." Addy looked at her like she'd sprouted purple, green, and orange polka dots.

"No, he wasn't," Addy said. Lily nodded. Just as they pulled up to the building, Addy looked at Lily.

"Seriously?" Lily nodded and they hopped out and headed up to Emerson's office. "You're joking aren't you?"

Lily shook her head. "Emerson has decided us together is contagious," Lily replied. They went up the elevator and when they stepped off, Emerson was waiting in the lobby. "Hey..." He kissed Lily, taking her hand and walking her into his office. Carter grabbed Addy's hand and walked her to the empty office.

Chapter 10

"What," Lily asked. "First off, thank you for talking to her. I seriously thought she wouldn't come."

"Emerson, I knew she'd been crying."

"You got her to stop being insane. Whatever you said, she actually heard it. She stopped thinking that you were gonna take my money and run."

"I guess whatever I said clicked."

"And what did you say?"

"That if everything was gone, we'd still be okay because we'd still have each other."

He kissed her and hugged her. "We're good. Babe, you made her put the snarky mood aside. You are the miracle lady."

"And what's the second thing?"

"Well, that idea we had about going to the outer banks is working. The house is called Pinch me. Right on the beach, pool, and lots of room. We can do whatever we want and walk over to the beach."

"And?"

"Us. We're bringing security and the housekeeper, but we're good."

"What's the third?"

He kissed her. "No more stress."

"And?"

"He's asking Addy to be his girl."

"What are you doing," Addy asked.

"I still can't believe that we're standing here right now."

"About that. Lily was telling me that you actually had a crush on me in high school."

"I was too nervous to even ask you out. Now, not so much."

"What are you saying Carter?"

"I'm done being nervous around you. What would you say if I wanted us to date just you and me and nobody else?"

"Like I want to just be with you and never leave?"

"Something like that."

Addy smirked. "You sure," Addy asked as he kissed her hand.

"Never been more sure."

Addy kissed him. "Okay," Addy said as Carter picked her up and spun her around.

"Good. By the way, we're going to dinner tonight."

"Why," Addy asked.

"Because I'm celebrating with my woman."

Addy smirked and kissed him. "Okay." Part of her wanted to run in and tell Lily, but she knew that Lily and Emerson needed to talk too.

Addy and Carter headed off, opting to celebrate just the two of them, leaving Lily and Emerson to hang out alone. "So, now what," Lily asked.

"Now, I grab my papers and we get out of here before I get dragged into a meeting."

He kissed her and they headed out. "And," he asked as they stepped onto the elevator with his security.

"And where are we headed?"

"Beach then home tomorrow and packing for the weekend. Honestly, you moved mountains today baby." Lily smirked and heard the elevator ding. They headed out of the office, hopped into the SUV, and went to the beach house.

"What," Lily asked as they pulled into the driveway a little while later.

"Nothin," he said with a huge grin ear to ear.

"Emerson, just say it."

"Who knew that you'd be the one to get my mom to stop being a pain."

"I'm not even gonna tell you what I said," Lily said as he kissed her.

"Babe."

"No. It's between your mom and I."

"Hint?"

"No. She loves the dress though." He shook his head and snuggled her to him.

"Alright. Swim then we come in and relax."

"What are we doing for dinner?"

"I was gonna suggest going out, but I offered up the reservation to Carter and Addy," Emerson said.

"And what did you know about what they were talking about," Lily asked as she got them each a sweet tea and handed one to Emerson.

"They're officially boyfriend and girlfriend. If they weren't, we would've heard and he probably would've banged on my office door before they left."

Lily shook her head. "And of course, the matchmaker strikes again."

He kissed her. "You love my matchmaking and you know it."

Lily smirked. "You need to let them have their own relationship Emerson. Leave them be. If they're gonna work, they will. Leave it at that."

"You know, they could..."

Lily covered his mouth. "Emerson. Leave them be." He kissed her hand and sat her up on the high-top chair. "What," she asked.

He kissed her. "Wife."

She shook her head. "Not yet."

"Soon enough baby."

"And?"

He kissed her again. "You, my love, are my inspiration. Still stunned you pulled that lunch off."

Lily smirked. "Well, we're home. What do you want to do," Lily asked.

"Bikini." She smirked and hopped off the chair, heading upstairs.

****

The weeks that followed were filled with Lily writing, and Emerson doing his best to spend every minute he could with Lily. The holiday away was peaceful and quiet, and felt even better noticing that they had the place completely to themselves. Two weeks before the wedding, Lily went in for the last fitting with Addy.

"And how was the vacation?"

"You mean since I've barely seen you since then? Good. How's Carter," Lily said as they walked in.

"He's really good."

Lily smirked. She knew that Addy was happy. She could see it all over her face. "I bet he is. How are you doing otherwise," Lily asked as the saleswoman went to get the dresses.

"I'm good. I got a raise at work, which always works, plus I can now work from home 4 of the 5 days. Perfect," Addy said.

"That's good. Less outside time."

"Something like that. Go get that dress on," Addy said.

Lily gave her a hug and went and slid into the dress, sliding into the shoes that Emerson's mom had bought her with it. When she slid in, it fit like a glove. She slid the heels on and came out to see Addy in her dress.

"Well," Addy joked.

"As long as you're up there with me," Lily teased. The seamstress got a picture of them with Addy's phone and Lily smirked.

"We ready for this," Addy asked. Lily nodded.

Despite Emerson's planning, the last two weeks before their wedding were taken up with smaller details, writing of vows, way too many questions from friends and family that were coming and a few nights of taste testing what they'd have for the meal for the wedding.

"I tried for your favorites," Emerson said as they had the entrée.

"It's almost sinful it's so good," Lily said.

"Exactly what I planned," the chef said.

"I'm loving this," Lily said.

"And the wine choices. Are we good with those as well," the chef asked as they went through the rest of the dinner options.

"We're good. They'll match up. Thank you for all of this by the way," Emerson said.

"Most welcome. Y'all enjoy and we'll see you at the rehearsal dinner."

"Well," Emerson teased.

"I had no idea that you were planning this. The food is better than half the restaurants that I've gone to with you."

He smirked. "That was the plan babe. We are only doing this once. There's maybe 50 of us total. We can splurge a little," he teased.

"And?"

"Part of me is still worried that Zack is gonna cause another problem." Lily smirked. She remembered telling him off in Emerson's office, and she remembered how good it felt to tell him off.

"He's not gonna say a single word," Lily replied.

"Good," Emerson said.

He kissed her and once they finished eating, he got her on her feet and kissed her, pressing something on his phone.

"What," Lily asked.

"Dance with me." Lily smirked and kissed him as he pulled her into his arms and danced with her.

"I know this song," Lily said.

"Written by Jaxon's fiancée," Emerson said.

Lily shook her head. "Did you ask her to?"

Emerson shook his head. "I heard her singing it when I was talking to him."

Lily shook her head. "Emerson."

"What? I just like the song. That's all baby."

"I know you're up to something." He smirked and kissed her, holding her close to him.

"There's a lot that you have no idea about."

"Such as," Lily asked as she teased him.

"I have surprises. You'll find out at the wedding."

"Emerson, you do realize that whatever you're planning is sort of for both of us right?"

He kissed her. "I know. I'm still planning something that you'll see at the wedding. It's for us. Nobody else will know what is going on."

"You're so full of it," Lily said. He kissed her again and danced with her to another song. "Emerson."

"What beautiful?"

"Are you ready for all of this?"

"I'm ready for another vacation just you and me." "Did you decide where we're going?"

"Yep."

"And?"

"You'll find out after the wedding."

Lily shook her head. "Just full of secrets."

They finished their dance and grabbed their things and headed off to the house instead of the beach.

"We're going home," Lily asked.

He nodded. "I wanted to get my girl home. You'll be closer to Addy," Emerson joked.

"Something tells me she's a little more distracted than normal with Carter. She only called once when we were away."

"From what I heard; I'm surprised if she manages to get up. The two of them are stuck together like crazy glue."

Lily smirked. "All I ever wanted was to see her happy. If she's happy, I'm good."

He kissed her and slid his arm around her, snuggling her to him in the backseat. "If they're as happy as us, we seriously may be having a double wedding."

Lily shook her head. "They're not you Emerson. They're not gonna jump into a wedding," Lily teased.

"Babe."

"They aren't going to. She thinks we're nuts for jumping into a wedding this fast. She's not gonna do it," Lily replied. He smirked and Lily knew. She knew a mile off that he was keeping something quiet. Something that concerned Addy and Carter.

"What," he asked feeling her staring at him.

"What aren't you telling me?"

"Nothing. Last I heard they were good. That's all. He's been staying with her."

Lily looked at him. "What?" He nodded and they pulled through the gates and headed up to the house.

"Did you just say what I think you did?"

He smirked, hopped out and helped her out of the SUV. "Emerson."

"Just don't get mad when they move into that house together," he said.

Lily shook her head. "You're so bad," Lily said. He picked her up and carried her inside, walking up the steps. "What are you up to?"

"Finishing the night on a good note," he teased.

Emerson walked upstairs and leaned Lily onto the bed. "Now, wife, what are we doing tonight," he asked.

"Sleeping."

He shook his head and kissed her as he slid her heels off. He slid his suit jacket off, then his tie, putting it on the bed beside them. "Strip tease," Lily joked.

"All yours," he said with that sexy smirk. He'd had the same smirk the first night he'd shown up at her condo. When he'd kissed her the first time, that kiss gave her goosebumps from head to toe. It wasn't one kiss. It wasn't one moment. It was how she'd felt in his arms. How she'd wanted him and hadn't known that they'd met long before that moment on the beach.

"Where are you staying the night before the wedding," Lily asked.

"Up here. Why," he asked. Lily smirked. "You can get ready at the beach if you want to. Just make sure you let security know where you're going." Lily nodded as he threw his shirt into the laundry. Lily looked up at him. "What," he asked.

"Just remembering when you showed at the condo that first time."

He smirked. He remembered the moment well. He thought he'd hallucinated her when he saw her on the beach. The closer he got, the more hot and bothered he was. He wanted to kiss her the moment he'd seen her. He wanted to pick her up and hide her away from the world. He'd almost wanted to propose at that exact moment. When he'd written his phone number on her hand, he thought that there was no way she wouldn't have put two and two together. When he'd called her, he had no idea that she hadn't figured it out. When he showed up and kissed her, making out on the sofa like he'd dreamed of when they were in high school, he thought she'd know. When she didn't, he just made the gestures bigger. The day that he'd proposed, he was sure that she'd say no. That she'd walk off and never come back. Every move he made; he was unsure. Now, he had the woman he'd dreamt of. He had the life he'd always wanted. He had the woman that he never thought he'd have, and a life he never thought would ever be possible. It was that moment. That big moment that he imagined his entire life.

"I know that look Emerson."

He kissed her, devouring her lips and leaned into her arms. "What look," he asked as he propped himself up on his hand.

"That same look that you gave me on the beach. What are you up to Emerson?"

He kissed her. "Getting my fiancée naked." He slid his arms around her and unzipped her skirt.

"Emerson."

He slid it off then went for the silky tank top that should've been illegal. He slid the tank off, revealing the lacy lingerie that he didn't even know she had.

"Lily."

"Emerson."

He shook his head. "Mine." He kissed her again, throwing her clothes to the laundry basket and pulled her legs around his hips.

"What," Lily teased.

"Had to taunt me with all this lace."

Lily nodded with a smirk ear to ear. "Part of my plan to taunt you into making sure you show up."

He kissed her. "Babe."

"What," Lily replied.

"I'm coming. I'd run down the aisle if you didn't kick my butt."

Lily kissed him. "Good. I expect you to be there with Kleenex and all."

He shook his head, kissed her, and peeled the last of her clothes off. "Emerson." He kissed down her torso and Lily's toes almost curled into pretzel-like knots. Just as he was going for her bra, his phone rang. "Emerson."

He kicked his dress pants off, throwing them onto the pile with his suit jacket. "I'm not answering it."

Not two minutes later, Lily's phone went off. "If we don't, they're gonna keep calling," Lily said.

Emerson grabbed his phone, seeing the missed call and shook his head. He called Carter back with a smirk and put it on speaker phone.

"Hey," Carter said.

"So, you and Addy are intentionally interrupting date night why," Emerson asked.

"Well, we sorta decided to move in together," Carter said.

Emerson almost laughed. "Meaning what," Lily asked.

"We're both gonna live at the house together if you're okay with it," Addy said.

"Are you sure," Lily asked.

"I don't think she can really get rid of me," Carter teased.

"And why is that," Emerson asked as he smirked and kissed up Lily's neck.

"Because I can't. We were sorta talking and we're gonna try living together," Addy said.

"Then what," Emerson teased as he kissed Lily.

"We were talking about other things I need your assistance with buddy," Carter said.

"I'll meet you tomorrow morning. Workout then we go run the errand."

"Done," Carter replied.

Lily shook her head and they managed to get off the phone.

"I know what you were talking about. Don't you…"

He kissed her before she could object to one more thing. "Date night. No talking about them."

Lily shook her head and he peeled the lacy bra off. He devoured her lips again and he made love to her. Romantic, passionate, goosebump causing, toe-curling sex that made two into one. He knew at that moment that they were going be together forever. She wasn't going to walk out, she wasn't going to leave, and she was going to be his wife until they were old and grey. Babies or not, they had each other. Now, she was going to officially be his wife. Not just in heart or in mind, but in soul. He had her, and she had him.

They had a life and they would always be those same two people that had met in high school. The same guy who had comforted her during every heartbreak, the same woman who had finally given him a chance. They were meant to be, and now they got to tell everyone in the world – Lily was going to be his wife. He would be her husband. Together forever.

By the time that the rehearsal day came, Lily had butterflies. It wasn't nerves, it wasn't panic. She took her bag to the beach house and saw the flowers and the champagne. The chocolate covered strawberries, and the rose petals in a heart on the bed. It was everything she could want, plus a lot more.

"You didn't have to do all this," Lily said as the housekeeper came in behind her.

"You two are only getting married once Miss Lily. You deserve everything and a lot more."

"Thank you," Lily replied as she gave her a hug.

She headed off with Emerson, making their way back to the house, and slid his present into his drawer in the bedroom. When she looked, she saw something she didn't expect. "Emerson," Lily said.

"What, beautiful love of my life?"

"What's this," Lily asked handing him what looked like a little black book of women's phone numbers.

"A little tradition that one of my friends joked about. Burn the book with all the old girlfriend's numbers. I have the one I was meant to be with. I don't need the book," Emerson teased.

"And should I be concerned with this little tradition?"

He kissed her and opened it, showing her the name on the page. Every one of them said 'I love Lily'.

"So bad," Lily teased.

"And what were you sneaking into the drawer," he asked.

"You can't open it until tomorrow."

"Babe, we agreed to no presents," Emerson said.

"And I got you something anyway."

"You'll see yours in the morning."

Lily laughed. "Neither of us can follow rules. Go figure," Lily teased.

He kissed her. "I love you," he said.

"Love you back handsome. Do you need anything for tonight?"

He smirked. "Always, and I don't know that I can sleep without it."

"One night, then you get me all to yourself for the rest of time."

"Promise?"

Lily nodded and kissed him. Not two minutes later, there was a knock at the bedroom door.

"Yes," Emerson said.

"Sir, Carter is here to speak to you. He's in your office."

"Thank you," Emerson said.

"What are you doin?"

"Two minutes. I promise," Emerson said.

"Fine. I'll meet you outside."

Emerson walked into his office and closed the door. "I wasn't sure which one. I can't make a damn decision. I winged it, but I need your advice on how to do this," Carter said.

"Which one do you know is totally and completely her?"

"Both," Carter teased.

Emerson looked at the two platinum rings staring him and almost blinding him with the diamonds. "I say this one," Emerson said as he pointed to the diamond that was cushion cut with a brilliant diamond.

"I thought so too. I think the other one is more Lily," Carter teased.

"Are you doing it tonight or when we leave?"

"I'm hoping that Addy catches the bouquet, then I can do it right then and there," Carter said.

When Lily heard the swoosh of the sliding door, she looked over. "Hey handsome," Lily said.

"Hey yourself beautiful wife to be."

He sat down behind her and snuggled her into his arms as she leaned against his chest.

"And what did Carter need? Last minute tux problem?"

"Something like that. He wanted to make sure I was okay with the bachelor party plan."

Lily turned to face him. "What plan?"

"The one where we hang and play poker and have a little guy time."

"Including a few naked women?"

"Nope."

"You better not," Lily teased.

He kissed her and slid her closer. "Back at ya wife."

"I wouldn't even look. I can't."

"Meaning what," Emerson asked.

"The only guy I'd stare at was you. I mean, unless one of the male characters from my book come to life, you're safe," Lily teased as he kissed her.

"Had to throw that in," he teased.

Lily nodded. "You inspired the good guy anyway."

He shook his head. "What am I gonna do with you?"

"Walk down the aisle and wait for me."

He nodded. "Anything you want."

She kissed him and his phone buzzed. "Yes," Emerson said.

He put it on speaker. "I wanted to make sure that the dress was alright. I also have a little something for each of you for tomorrow. Are you both alright with me stopping by," his mom asked.

"I'll be at the beach house with Addy and my mom and Cara. You're welcome to come by," Lily said.

"And if you really want to come to the house, let me know. I'll make sure we're decent," Emerson teased.

"Alright. I'll see y'all in a bit. Lily, please let me know if the dress is okay. I have another option as well," his mom replied.

"I will and thank you again," Lily said as they hung up. He showed Lily the dress his mom had.

"Just reply back that it's beautiful," Lily said.

He smirked. "Who knew that you and mom would actually get along," Emerson teased.

They got up a while later and headed downtown to the church for the rehearsal. When Lily walked in, the church was covered in red roses. The aisles had her lilies, red roses and flowers that made the entire room smell like a meadow in the summer.

"Wow," Lily said.

"And they just got started," the bishop said.

"Thank you for all of this," Lily said.

"You two are most welcome. There's one other thing that I have for you Lily. Your grandfather and grandmother came to this church, as you know. They asked me then to give something to you if you ever decided to marry here. It was brought to my attention by your grandfather's attorney in town."

He handed Lily the envelope and her hands almost trembled. "You two, have a seat. I'll be up at the front if you need me."

> *Dear Lily.*
>
> *Right now, I imagine that you're writing and doing what you always loved. I remember you being so loving and so creative. There was always a chance that what we thought might happen would, so I hope we were right. Your grandmother and I had a once in a lifetime love. I knew from the minute I met her. You have been there since the day you were born, always being with us and taking time*

out to spend with us when high school got busy. I want you to have these. They're the wedding bands from when we got married. Whether you married well or not, these have 75 years of love in them. I hope they have another 50 or more for you too. We love you. I love you. I always have. To the best hugger in the world, I wish you a lifetime of love. – Grandpa.

Lily shook her head, holding the rings. "Wow," Emerson said.

"Something old, something new," Lily said. When her grandfather's ring fit Emerson perfectly, she almost cried.

"Do you think he was talking about me?" Lily nodded.

He took a deep breath, holding Lily in his arms as she hugged him. "What are you two crying for," Addy asked as she came in.

Lily showed her the rings and Addy almost burst into tears.

"They aren't," Addy asked as Emerson nodded. "Oh my goodness," Addy said as she started crying and hugged them both.

"Alright. What's with the crying," Carter asked.

"Her grandfather left her their rings," Emerson said.

"Now that was a good idea," Carter teased. When Lily saw the bishop head towards them, she smirked.

"Are you ready to get this started," the bishop asked. When Lily nodded, he smirked and they started the rehearsal.

Emerson watched her make her way down the aisle. Every step, she got closer to him and he got closer to his dream coming true. They got to the end of the aisle together and the bishop walked them through the easy part of the ceremony, then they walked back down the aisle. After 3 more practices, they had it down perfectly.

"Follow me," the bishop asked as he walked them to the side of the church.

"Is something wrong," Emerson asked.

"You have your license yes?"

Lily nodded and handed it to the bishop. "Do you want to sign it with everyone here?"

Emerson shook his head. "I wish we could just do it now," Emerson said.

The bishop smirked. "We'll do it quickly before you leave the church tomorrow. Lily, do you have your things here or are you getting ready somewhere else," the bishop asked.

"I'll be at the beach house. When I get here, there will probably be pictures and stuff, but that's it." The bishop nodded.

"We have everything together then. Do you have any questions," the bishop asked. Both of them shook their heads. "We will see you tomorrow." Lily nodded and they headed off.

"Tell me that I don't have to actually attempt to sleep without you," Emerson said as they drove over to the hotel.

"Tradition handsome."

"I don't want tradition."

"You'll be busy with the guys anyway," Lily said.

"Not fair. You know that right?"

Lily nodded and kissed him as they pulled up to the light. "You'll be so distracted, you will barely miss me," Lily teased.

"I doubt it," he teased.

He linked their fingers and kissed her hand as he pulled in the driveway of the hotel. "I know that you're determined to have all the traditions going, but can we just bypass one of them?"

"Which one husband to be?"

He kissed her, the SUV stopped and they hopped out. "Follow me," he teased as he grabbed something from the front desk and walked her to the elevators.

"Emerson."

"Just come with me." The elevator stopped and they headed down the hall to the presidential suite.

"What are you doing," Lily asked.

"This is where the backup plan for the first night was," he teased as he walked in and she shook her head.

"Emerson."

"I wanted to do something for us."

"What are you doing?"

He kissed her, picking her up and walked to the bed, leaning her onto it. "Emerson."

"Ours."

Lily shook her head. "We're going to our rehearsal dinner."

He kissed her and snuggled into her arms. "What are you up to really?"

He motioned to the closet and saw the red dress. "What is that?"

He kissed her. "For tonight," he said as he kissed down her neck.

"Emerson, what are you up to?"

"Nothing. I wanted you to have something you like to wear tonight."

Lily shook her head and he undid her skirt. "We aren't doing this here."

"We have an hour before everyone's gonna be here."

Lily shook her head and he kissed her, pulling her shirt off then undoing his and putting it on the bed beside them. "I know what you're doing."

He kissed her and peeled the last of her clothes off. "I know. I'm taunting you so you show up tomorrow," he teased. Lily shook her head.

"And you think that's gonna do it?"

Emerson nodded as he kissed his way down her neck then down her torso as she saw his dress pants pile on top of his shirt. "Now, where were we," he teased as he slid into her arms and pulled her legs around him.

"So dang determined," Lily said.

"Mm hmm." He kissed her again, devouring her lips until they were making love. Every ounce of blood was rushing through her body. Her hands were almost trembling along with her stomach. He was so overheated, he almost felt like they would both burst into flames. When they came up for air, he pulled her with him and leaned onto his back.

"Emerson."

"I love you."

"I love you too. You know we still have to get up right?"

"Power nap," he teased.

Lily smirked. "Then I'm getting up to get dressed," Lily said. He kissed her.

"You sure you're okay?"

"I'm good. I think the dress was a little much though."

He kissed her, cradling her face in his hands. "I wanted you to feel beautiful. You are. You always have been."

"I love you for that. I'll be alright," Lily said.

"I'm gonna miss you."

"Emerson."

He kissed her again. "You sure you can't just stay with me?"

"I'm sure. We'll be alright for one night."

She kissed him and got up, cleaning up and touching up her makeup, then slid into the dress.

When he got up and walked into the bathroom, he shook his head. "Even sexier than I thought you'd be." Lily smirked.

"This mean you like," she teased.

"This means I'm not sure that I want to share you with everyone."

"Sorta late to make that decision," Lily said.

He kissed her and sat her on the bathroom counter. "Am I allowed to sneak over later?"

Lily shook her head. "Emerson, you'll be a half hour away. You're not sneaking over."

He kissed her. "Party pooper."

"My mom, Addy and your sister will all be at the beach house. I can't exactly sneak out. You can't sneak in either."

He kissed her again. "You sure?"

Lily nodded. "I love you, and I love that you can't live without me, but that book tour means being apart when you can't come."

"I'm coming with you."

"Meetings and you have a career Emerson. They need you."

"I need you more," he replied.

Lily shook her head and he kissed her. He got dressed and she slid off the counter, putting her clothes into the suit bag. "You ready," Lily asked as she put some of her perfume on and fluffed up her hair.

"I guess." She redid her lipstick and they headed downstairs, hand in hand.

"Still pretty handsome there husband to be."

"Too tempting," he teased as he slid his arm around her instead.

"You started it with this dress."

He smirked and kissed her forehead as his hand slid to hers and they hopped off the elevator. He handed the suit bag off to his driver and they made their way into dinner. When they walked in, everyone was just starting to make their way in.

"Told you," he whispered. Lily shook her head and she saw her parents getting a soda.

"I love the dress," her mom said.

"Thank you. It was a little surprise," Lily teased as she gave her mom and dad a huge hug.

"You two alright," her dad asked with a sense of pride on his face.

"Yes. He just surprised me with the dress before we left. How are you two doing," Lily asked.

"Good. Excited to see what tomorrow brings," her mom said.

"Emerson has a bunch of surprises that he put together. He barely let me hear any of them."

"So, you're getting even more surprises," her dad teased.

"He's kinda the big grand gesture type. I hope you two get to enjoy the day too. No stress allowed," Lily said.

"And what's the plan for you tonight," her dad asked.

"We're having a little pampering night. Relaxing and massages. Nothing too wild. I have no idea what the guys are gonna be up to, but I have a feeling it'll be semi g-rated," Lily said.

"I heard poker, swimming and hanging by the fire," her dad said.

"Sounds good. Y'all will need some actual rest for tomorrow." Emerson came over a few minutes later with his folks and re-introduced them.

When the planner came over to let them know all their guests had arrived, everyone grabbed a seat and sat down. Emerson smirked.

"Quit," Lily said.

"Never," he teased as he slid her chair a little closer. The meals came out, the wine was poured and the speeches started. By the time they were done, Lily and Emerson had their turns.

"You go first," Lily said.

"I can do it for both of us." Lily nodded and he snuggled her to him and kissed her, holding her hand.

"Alright. The last speech of the night. When Lily and I were talking about the wedding we wanted, we agreed on the only important thing. Everyone in this room is family. Whether you're blood family, or friend family, each one of you is important to us. Addy, I don't know that Lily would've ever given me a chance if it wasn't for you. You're her best friend, her confidant and her ride or die since high school. You knew how much I loved Lily even in high school. I never had the guts or the right timing until you talked me into being with her. Thank you for being my friend too. Carter, we were best friends since we were little. Now, the best part of hanging in the office. You still are my best friend. Now, you realized just how strong that feeling was in high school when you found Addy again. Thank you to both of you for being the voice of reason with Lily and I. Thank you for being our family. To all of you, thank you for being part of our love story. Thank you for cheering us on and being supportive of my crazy schemes. Thank you for our past, our present and our future."

Emerson looked at Lily and she took a deep breath, nodding. He had said exactly what was on her heart. "Good," he asked. Lily nodded. They all finished dinner and Lily and Emerson brought over the gifts for the parents and for Addy and Carter. They all got packed up and headed out to get some sleep and Emerson slid his hand in Lily's pulling her away from everyone. "What's wrong," Lily asked.

He kissed her. "You can't just come stay at the house?"

"If I stay at the house, you're at the beach house."

"Babe."

"It's one night. One. We have the rest of our lives," Lily said.

He kissed her again, devouring her lips. "Come with me."

"Where?"

"Lily." She shook her head.

"I love you. You know I do. We're good Emerson. You can call me and we talk until you fall asleep."

"Promise?"

She nodded. He hugged her again, kissing up her neck. "Emerson."

"Promise that you'll be there?"

Lily nodded. "If I go for a walk, I take security. I'll be fine." He kissed her again.

"Dude, are you coming or what," Carter asked as he found where they'd hidden away. "Yes. Just saying goodnight to the woman," Emerson said with a smirk as he kissed her one more time and slid his hand in hers. "If you need anything, call me alright," he asked quietly. "I'll call you in the morning." He nodded and kissed her again. "I hate this," he said. "I know. I'll see you in the morning," Lily said as she headed off with Addy.

Chapter 11

"I still can't believe you two are really getting hitched. 15 years in the making girl. 15."

"Back at ya Addy. You two finally started really dating instead of just being in the friend zone. How are you two doing," Lily asked as they sat down on the porch with a glass of wine each and waited on Addy's mom and Lily's.

"He's good. Honestly, it feels like I've known him forever," Addy said.

"Because you have."

Addy smirked and they sat and talked until they were both two glasses down and going for another bottle. "Miss Lily, Miss Addison's mom and your mom are here," security said.

"Thank you. Come on in. We're just hanging outside and watching the water," Lily said. Everyone came outside and they relaxed by their fire pit and talked. When the masseuses came, Lily let everyone else go ahead, giving herself a little bit of quiet time. She sat down with her notebook and wrote out the vows. She had already delayed it too long.

She wrote it out, rewrote and edited and re-read it. Within 3 drafts, she had it. Addy came outside in the fluffy robe that Lily had got her and sat down.

"You alright," Addy asked.

Lily nodded as she brushed a tear or two away.

"Girl. What have you been crying about now?"

"Just finished writing the vows. It's fine," Lily said.

Addy gave her a hug. "Do you want me to read through it?"

Lily shook her head. "You'll hear it tomorrow."

Addy smirked and gave Lily a hug. "You sure you're okay?"

Lily nodded. "I promise. Just thinking about how different things would be if I hadn't seen him."

"Girl, y'all were meant to be forever. Even when you were just friends in high school, I always saw you two as the forever couple. After every idiot guy that we both broke it off with, he was holding your hand. He was right there."

Lily smirked. "Remember the look on your face when he showed at the condo?"

Addy nodded and laughed. "I'm still stunned that you didn't recognize him."

"I just can't imagine how insane life would be if I hadn't seen him. I probably would've got that book finished faster," Lily teased.

"Girl, you needed his inspiration. He isn't the type to stop you when it's something you love."

"I know. I just don't know how different life would be."

"You'd be in my shoes. With a man that you love, living with him and knowing that he's keeping secrets," Addy said.

"It hasn't been that long girl. Y'all are good together and you know it."

"I just think that he's hiding something," Addy said.

"You told me if I start worrying that I should just remember that sometimes it's a good secret. One that was going to surprise you and make you extatically happy. Like the day that Emerson proposed."

"You called me laughing. You thought it was a dang joke."

Lily looked at her. "It wasn't," Lily replied.

Addy gave her a hug and poured them each another glass as their moms came outside in their fluffy robes. "Miss Lily, I'm ready for you," the masseuse said.

When Lily finished her massage, she slid into the fuzzy robe and watched the masseuses pack up and head out. The manicure and pedicure people came in and got set up and they all came in and got their nails done together. Lily was almost too quiet for Addy's liking. Lily finished getting her nails painted and dried and took her wine, walking outside. When Addy saw her sit down on the steps, she smirked.

"Is she alright," Lily's mom asked.

"She's just all in her head. She's re-thinking what she wrote for vows and clearing her mind. That's all. I've seen her quieter than this. Trust me," Addy said.

"I know, but are you sure," Addy's mom asked.

"She's alright. I'm almost done. I'll go check on her," Addy said. Addy finished up, made sure her toes were dry and slid her flip flops on and walked out the back to where Lily was.

"You know that we're all worried right," Addy said.

"I'm fine. I'm just thinking too much again."

"What's wrong?"

"Am I doing the right thing?"

Addy looked at her. What's going on Lily? You were fine. You were happy before we left. You were excited for it. What happened?"

"I love him, but what happens if we don't work?"

"Take a chance for once. The guy has been in love with you for 15 years. He's told you hourly even at nauseum. He made us all nauseous with all the mushy stuff. How could you really be second-guessing that?"

"Because I don't know if I can even have kids. He wants a family. I might not be able to give him that."

"Girl, he loves you. He doesn't care if y'all have kids or not. He just wants you."

Lily nodded and looked out into the water, watching the waves roll in and out. Watching the moon reflect on the water.

When Lily heard the swoosh of the sliding door, her mom and Addy's came outside and handed Lily a box. Addy's mom handed her the other. "What's this," Lily asked.

"One is from your dad and I," her mom said.

"And the other is from Paul and I. You've always been like my other daughter," Addy's mom said.

"You guys," Lily said. She got up, put the boxes on the table and hugged them both.

She opened the box from her mom and saw a quilt that her aunt had made. Then, she saw the cookies.

"Mom."

"The molasses ones that you loved. Your recipe." Lily hugged her. When she got to the bottom, there was a note from her mom and dad. "Open that part later," her mom said.

Lily nodded and gave her a hug. Lily smirked and opened the one from Addy's parents. The blanket that came out had photos of her since she'd met Addy.

"This is really cool mom," Addy said.

"All the photos from when y'all were growing up are all on there. In the middle, it's you with Emerson and your first book cover," Addy's mom said.

"I love it," Lily said as she gave Addy's mom a hug.

"If all of y'all are gonna do this, then I'm giving you mine," Addy said.

"We can wait until tomorrow," Lily said.

"Nope," Addy said as she slid it out of her pocket and handed it to Lily.

"What's this?"

"Just open it," Addy said. Lily opened it and saw the charm bracelet.

"Addy."

"The feather is for your book, the seashell is kinda obvious. The key is the first condo. The house is for the house you bought. Sorta something to remind you of where we started," Addy said.

Lily hugged her. "Seriously?" Addy nodded.

"I was gonna give it to you for your birthday, but this kinda came first," Addy teased.

"Y'all are too much," Lily said.

"So, what has you all quiet and worried," Addy's mom asked.

"Just overthinking. Honestly, I think I may need a walk on the beach later. Maybe I'm just tired," Lily said.

Addy's mom gave her a hug. "From what I see with you two, you found a good one. I still can't believe he's the same Emerson that you two hung out with in high school."

"He's not the same guy, but he's the same on the inside," Lily replied.

"Has he changed that much," Lily's mom asked.

"He grew up. That's about it. He's smarter, has an amazing company and he's marrying a bestselling author. He kinda lucked out in life university," Lily teased.

"Everyone grows up. Even you," Addy said.

By the time her mom and Addy's headed out, Addy was giggling on the phone with Carter. Lily curled up and got a little writing in, then realized that she was stuck. The story wasn't flowing like it had with the last book. She needed something. Addy turned in and Lily went upstairs to their bedroom, sliding into her silky pajamas. She tried to sleep, but she was tossing and turning within an hour. She shook her head and went into the closet. She needed the salt air and the waves. She needed the sand between her toes. Without even thinking, she slid his dress shirt on over her satin shorts and tank and walked downstairs to see security in the living room. "Miss Lily," security said.

"Just going to sit on the deck for a few." He nodded and Lily grabbed a glass of sweet tea and walked outside, closing the door behind her. She took a gulp of her sweet tea, put the glass on the table and walked down to the sand.

The pristine sand had cooled from the daytime. It still felt way too good. Even the water against her ankles felt good. "You do know that it's not exactly safe being out here at night alone right," she heard like Emerson was standing behind her.

"The sand cooled off. What's to complain about," she said like he was there.

"I mean, you even picked the nice shirt."

Lily thought she was hearing things. When she felt arms slide around her torso, and a kiss on her neck. "Aren't you supposed to be at home with the guys?"

"You mean since Carter is talking Addy's ear off? Nope. This is where I wanted to be," he said as he kissed her neck again. Lily smirked and turned to face him.

"Emerson."

He kissed her, devouring her lips. "What," he asked as they came up for air.

"What are you doing here?"

"I need my woman. I couldn't sleep anyway. I tried. What are you doin up sexy wife?"

"I was just thinking all night. Addy's mom gave me a blanket with a bunch of pictures of me and Addy. Mom gave me a quilt with a bunch of pictures of us through the years. I completely forgot to open the note," Lily said as she walked onto the deck and grabbed it. Emerson grabbed the beach blanket and laid it on the sand, walking her over to it as they curled up on the blanket while she read it to him:

> *To my daughter:*
>
> *You have become one amazing woman. Your dad and I are so proud of the woman you've become. Things haven't always been easy, but I know that things will only get better. You found your forever person, and he found his forever love. The advice I'd give is to never forget to be best friends. Squabble, scream and yell, but never ever go to bed mad. Never attack. Your dad and I met in high school just like you two did, and I've never ever walked away from your dad. You're gonna become even more than you are. Next it'll be a mom, then a grandma, then a great grandma. Don't let go of his hand. Say I love you every day. You can do whatever you set your mind to. I know that you'll be an amazing mom and wife. If all you do is teach*

*your kids to be the way you and Emerson are,
you're ten steps ahead of everyone. Even if it's just
the two of you, cheer each other on. Don't forget
your past, and always look forward to your future
together. I love you, and Dad loves you. Neither of
us could imagine a world without you in it. Just
don't forget that the door is always open to you if
you need us. — Mom and Dad*

Emerson snuggled Lily closer. "And," he asked.

"They're psychic," Lily teased.

"What are you worried about?"

"I love you. I do. I'm just worried that we're gonna regret
all of this being so fast."

He smirked. "When you see that reception and the church,
you won't think like that. Babe, people plan things for
years and still don't get what we're gonna have. It'll be
fine. I promise you that. We're still gonna be there. Like we
both said, all that really matters was that you and I were
there. We didn't care who else was," Emerson said as he
laid down beside Lily.

"It's still true. I just worry."

He kissed her, devouring her lips. "You're stuck with me
baby. I'm not leaving your side. You need to know that."

"Just jitters," Lily said.

He leaned into her arms. "Then stop worrying. I can't sleep
without you. I'm not about to do life without you." Lily

kissed him and he snuggled her. "You feel any better?" Lily nodded.

"Maybe I need you more than I think," Lily teased.

"Did you write the vows," he asked.

Lily nodded. "Did you try to write them?"

"I've had them written for years. I rewrote them and tweaked a little. They're done."

Lily smirked. "Just remember, I'm the one in the fancy suit," he teased.

"I'm the one in white," Lily joked.

"One dress or two?" "One for the ceremony. You'll see tomorrow."

He kissed her. "The housekeeper packed a few last things. We're leaving after the wedding."

"Do I get to know where we're going?"

"Somewhere away from everyone and everything. Still phone access if needed though," Emerson replied as he kissed her. Not two minutes later, Lily heard someone on the deck.

"I totally knew you'd show up. Aren't you supposed to be at the house," Addy asked.

"Needed Lily for a minute," Emerson joked. Lily kissed him and they got up. He shook off the beach blanket and put it on the deck.

"I'm coming," Lily said as Emerson smirked.

"Good," Addy said as she went inside. Lily kissed Emerson. He picked her up and wrapped her legs around his hips walking her out of eye sight. He devoured her lips and was about to pull the shorts off of her. "We can't do that out here," Lily said. He kissed her again. "I need my woman," he said. She shook her head and she felt his hand slide down her back. "Emerson."

He taunted her and she couldn't stop him. "Stop."

"Nope," he teased. He undid his jeans and they had a quickie on the beach, away from everyone. When he managed to stand back up, Lily shook her head.

"Bad," she teased. He kissed her again and he got semi redressed. "You never behave."

"And I hate traditions. You sure you're gonna be okay for tomorrow?"

Lily nodded. I was a little worried, but I'll be okay."

"No worrying. It's gonna be beautiful," Emerson said.

Lily kissed him and he shook his head. "Before she comes back out here, I'm goin. I love you wife."

"Love you too handsome." He set her on her feet and headed off, and Lily grabbed her sweet tea and came inside.

The next morning, Lily woke up and was still in his shirt. She grabbed her phone and saw a text from Emerson:

Good morning wife. I love you. Just thought I'd remind you. If we hadn't been disturbed last night I could've shown you. Lol. I promise you a forever that you can only dream of starting today. Forever. I'm yours. — Your husband that loves you more than life

Lily smirked and got up, freshening up, and slid her robe on as she came downstairs. When she walked into the kitchen, there were fresh croissants, mimosas, a heart-shaped omelet and bacon and fresh strawberries and peaches waiting for her. "This is beautiful," Lily said.

"Glad you like it. I thought I was better off over here. Miss Addy is still asleep," the housekeeper said.

"Thank you."

"Most welcome. Are you excited for the day?"

"Getting there. Partially I kinda want a workout."

"Well, you could go swimming," the housekeeper joked as she saw the water. Everything was calm, but she knew the sand was steaming hot already.

Lily had her breakfast and cleaned up a little. "I can take care of it," the housekeeper said.

"Thank you. This was amazing and exactly what I needed."

"I was told to tell you to check your texts. I also emailed you a list of what I packed up for you. If there's anything missing, let me know."

"Thank you for that. Honestly, I'll probably be fine. I'm gonna go have a shower and freshen up."

"Hair and makeup are coming at 8. Mrs. Cartwright is coming around 11. She wanted to come and check in on how you were doing and drop off something she got for you."

"Thank you," Lily said as she headed upstairs and got changed, opting to do a hair treatment and pamper herself a little. She hopped in the shower a half hour later, washed up, intentionally putting Emerson's favorite perfume on, and came out of the master bath, putting her lotion on. Not two minutes later, there was a knock at the bedroom door.

"Morning Addy," Lily said as Addy came in.

"Why are you up so early?"

"Couldn't sleep. Breakfast and mimosas are downstairs."

"You doing okay?"

Lily nodded. "Better now," Lily replied.

Addy came and gave her a hug. "Carter told me that Emerson had gone out for a drive last night. I figured he'd end up here. You sure you're alright?"

Lily nodded with a smirk. "Just ready to get all of this done and overwith so we can go start married life," Lily said.

"Y'all already did, just without the paperwork," Addy teased as she gave Lily another hug.

"Hair and makeup are coming around 8. Meaning, go eat and get showered," Lily teased.

"I will."

"Oh, and this is for you," Lily said as she grabbed a small box from her drawer.

"What's this," Addy asked.

"Open it," Lily said as she got her jewelry out.

Addy opened the small box and saw the bracelet with a single diamond on it. "Lily."

"I wanted to get you something," Lily said.

"You didn't need to," Addy replied.

Lily helped her put it on and hugged her. "You are like my sister Addy. You always will be."

"I can't believe you went and did this. Thank you," Addy said.

"You're welcome. Now get goin," Lily teased.

Addy headed out of the room and security came up the steps. "Miss Lily, there's a package here for you."

He handed it to Lily and she sat down and texted Emerson:

> *Good morning handsome soon to be husband. I knew you'd beat me to the text this morning. Thank you for that last night. I think I kinda needed the surprise to be honest. My barefoot billionaire sneaking up behind me. I can't wait for us to start forever. Do we really have to go to the reception? PS You realize that I still don't know where we're going right? I love you more than you even know. I miss you already. I love you and I'll see you soon – your wife to be.*

She pressed send and opened the box that was delivered. When she pulled the lid off, she saw a jewelry box. One that he shouldn't have gone to. She opened the smaller box and saw a bracelet. It said 'Forever' on the front and the date on the back. She opened the second box and saw diamond stud earrings. When she opened the last, there was a triple diamond pendant on a beautiful necklace. She shook her head and saw a card:

> *I promised you long ago that I'd never walk away, and I promise that I never will. I promise that you'll know how much I love you. That you'll know that I'll always be your person, and your cheerleader. I promise to kiss you every night, to wake you up with a kiss, and to never let you go a moment without knowing that I love you. You're the most amazing woman I've ever known. You're the only woman I want, the only one I need, and the only one I'll ever need. I can't wait to see you. I'll be the one in tears at the end of the altar. The one that's holding your hand through life.*

Lily grabbed tissues and dried her tears and called Emerson. "Hey wife," he said as she heard his huffing and puffing.

"Doing a workout?"

"I have to do something. Holding myself back from sneaking over there again," he teased. When she sniffled, he got concerned.

"Baby, what's wrong?"

"You and your mushy card. You went overboard."

"Babe, you deserve to hear those words. I wanted to surprise you with the gifts, but I wrote that one night when you were sleeping. It was when we were away to be honest with you."

"Are you upstairs or in the gym?"

"Heading upstairs. Why?"

"Go look in the bedside table drawer on your side," Lily said.

"What did you do?"

"Go see. I'm going to get ready. I'll see you in a few hours."

"Alright beautiful. I love you."

"I love you too," Lily replied.

Emerson went and saw the box in the drawer with a card. When he opened it, he saw a photo of the two of them. He got a grin ear to ear. He couldn't help it. He sat down on the bed and opened the card:

> *To the man who will be my husband:*
>
> *The day we met, I thought that I'd met my forever. Little did I know I already had. Thank you for loving me the way you do. For never letting go. For reminding me that you and I have already had a lifetime together. Here's to the next half of it. To the man who deserves all the love. I promise to wake up and kiss you, fall asleep in your arms, remind you every day that I love you and intentionally steal your hoodies. You are the love of my life, and you always have been. That will*

never ever change. I promise when we're old and gray, sitting on the porch, I'll still hold your hand and snuggle you. I promise a day will never pass without an I love you. I'll see you at the altar handsome. Look for the lady in the veil. – The woman who loves you – your soon to be wife.

When he opened the box, he saw a watch. One that he never even thought to buy himself. There was a note that there was an inscription. He flipped it over and saw the engraving:

Forever starts now.

It had the date on it then the words – about time.

He smirked and shook his head then saw another box. He opened it and saw cufflinks with a single diamond. He got a grin ear to ear. He was missing her already. He was missing her something bad. He shook his head, got up and showered and got a call.

"Yep."

"Sir, your barber is on the way."

"Thank you," Emerson said as he saw her body wash and took one deep inhale of it. He shook his head. He was beyond missing her. He was craving her. He shook his head, finished his shower, and dried off, freshening up and throwing his toiletries into his bag.

He walked into the bedroom and pulled his jeans on with a t-shirt. He came downstairs and ate, seeing the fresh fruit and a note from Lily on his coffee cup:

I love you handsome.

He smirked and Carter came downstairs. "Barber's on his way over. You need a cut," Emerson asked.

"Probably," Carter said.

"Go get showered. I'll grab your coffee," Emerson said as Carter ran upstairs to shower and get changed. Emerson finished his breakfast and the barber showed.

"How are you doing groom," the barber said.

"Good. Just need a cleanup for the wedding."

By the time he was done, Emerson looked great. Carter got his done while Emerson went and got the confirmations done for the hotel and the honeymoon.

"Dude, are you using the company plane to head out," Carter asked as he got his haircut.

"Yep. I need alone time with my girl," Emerson replied as he printed everything out and slid it into his laptop bag.

When Emerson and Lily's dads showed, and Carter's folks showed, Emerson smirked. "Perfect timing," Emerson joked.

The dad's had brought their suits and Carter's mom gave Emerson a hug. "My other son," Carter's mom said.

"And how are we doing," Emerson asked.

"Good. Excited for the wedding. How are you doing? Any jitters," Carter's mom asked.

"Not a one. She's always been the one for me," Emerson said. They had a coffee and hung out and then the guys started getting ready. The pictures of the guys were intentionally at the big house. The view was to kill for anyway, and it was perfect for the day.

By the time it got to 1:30, the bridesmaids were ready, the moms were ready and Lily's dad was on his way. Lily slid into her dress and got her hair touched up, got her makeup touched up and they slid the veil on. The photographer snapped a few photos and went and got Lily's mom. When her mom was almost instantly in tears, Lily smirked.

"Does it look okay," Lily asked. Her mom nodded and hugged her. "We're not even at the church yet," Lily said.

"Baby, you are beautiful," her mom said.

"Thank you." When Lily came into the hallway, the bridesmaids all started to get welled up.

"Y'all, quit starting. We're not even there yet," Lily said. When her dad showed, his jaw hit the floor. "What do you think," Lily asked.

"You look like a princess," her dad said.

"I take that as a good sign," Lily said as she came down the steps. Her mom got everyone the bouquets and pinned the boutonniere onto her dad's lapel, the photographer snapped some more photos and they made their way outside and to the two cars that Emerson had set up to take them to the church.

"I still can't believe the dress," her dad said.

"I wanted to surprise everyone. Mom saw it when I picked it out with Addy."

"You surprised me. You literally look like a princess."

She dried his tears. "I love you Dad. You know that right?" He nodded. "Always have and always will. You were my first best friend. You always will be."

Emerson pulled into the church early and saw his mom pulling up with his dad. "Looking amazing as always. Good timing," Emerson said.

"Is she here yet," his dad asked.

Emerson shook his head. "She's going in a separate door to get touched up a little. Whatever that means. I'll find out what the plan is."

He walked them inside and the wedding planner came over to him. "Is she here," Emerson asked.

"She's pulling up in a half hour. She's on her way," the planner said.

"My mom was looking for her."

"She's fine. I'll show you to the groom's room," the planner said as she walked him and Carter to the room.

When Lily got there, the photographer snapped a few more photos as they came inside then went straight to the bride's room. "Emerson was looking for you," the planner said as she came in.

"I know. I guessed he would be," Lily said.

"Alright. So, there's a few things we need before the wedding. Something old, new, borrowed, blue and a sixpence," her mom said.

"Dress is new," Lily said.

"Something old and borrowed," Lily's mom said as she slid her bracelet on Lily's wrist.

"I have something blue," Addy said as she handed Lily a blue garter. Lily almost laughed. When there was a knock at the door, Addy answered and saw Emerson's mom.

"Oh my goodness," she said.

"Do you like," Lily asked.

"Just absolutely amazing," his mom said.

"We're just giving her the traditional stuff," Lily's mom said.

"I have the sixpence," Emerson's mom said.

"Are you sure," Lily asked.

"The same one I had when Emerson's dad and I got married," his mom said.

"Thank you." She gave Lily a hug and went back in to see everyone coming in.

Lily's mom got a grin ear to ear. "Well, that's more like it," her mom teased.

When Lily's cell buzzed that it was 3pm, she started getting even more jitters. She slid her phone on silent, sliding it into the secret pocket of her dress.

"You ready for all of this," her mom asked. Lily took a deep breath and nodded. She touched up her lipstick and after a quick hug, Lily's mom headed out with Lily's brother. "

You ready," Addy asked.

"This is insane. We both know it. I think I'm okay," Lily said.

"Breathe. This is all the stuff you wanted. The church is absolutely beautiful. What do you need," Addy asked.

"Ring."

"I have it."

"Vows."

"In your other pocket and I'm holding your phone in my pocket," Addy said sliding it from Lily's pocket.

"Mint," Lily said.

Addy popped two Altoids into her mouth and into Lily's. "Ready," Addy asked.

"Flowers."

Addy handed Lily her bouquet. The planner knocked and Addy came out, followed closely by the vision in white. The veil almost shimmered in the sunlight. The lace with the shimmer of sparkle glistened like she was covered in diamonds. The dress was that perfect A-line dress that we all dream of. It made her look like a princess. Addy knew that Emerson would be in tears.

"Bring him the little pack of tissues," Lily said. Addy nodded and Lily saw Emerson come down to meet her and the doors closed as Lily's dad came out to meet her.

"You alright," her dad asked.

Lily nodded. "Ready for forever," Lily replied.

Emerson was watching the door as Addy made her way down the aisle with Carter. When Addy took her place, Carter slid tissues into Emerson's pocket.

"From your wife," Carter teased as everyone stood up and watched the door. Emerson started to fidget. He couldn't imagine what would happen when those doors opened. He took a deep breath and closed his eyes, willing his heart to calm. When he opened his eyes, the door opened and he could barely see. The photographer snapped a few photos and Emerson saw Lily walking with her dad. When he saw her, his heart almost skipped a beat.

The light from the stained glass was shining on Lily like she was an angel. The dress looked like it sparkled with a personal spotlight. When his eyes started welling up, he brushed tears away. It was as if time slowed down to a snail's pace. He watched the dress and the veil almost glisten and Carter handed him another tissue. Emerson got a grin ear to ear and watched her take every step. When he shook her dad's hand, it's like the bishop's words were drowned out by the racing heartbeat pounding in his ears. Everyone sat down and Lily handed her flowers to Addy. She brushed Emerson's tears away and he shook his head, mouthing the words 'I love you'.

Lily smirked. Emerson slid the veil over her head, determined to see her face without any obstructions. She smirked again. The bishop did the first half of the ceremony, including Addy's mom reading an excerpt that they'd chosen. When it came time for the vows, Lily started to get nervous.

"Lily and Emerson have vows they've written for each other. Lily, go ahead," the bishop said as Lily took a deep breath.

"Emerson. When we met, way back in high school, you were my best friend. I had no idea that we would end up here someday. I knew that with every heartbreak that I endured; we got that much closer. After seeing each other again, it's like time hadn't moved. We both looked a little older, and grew up a lot, but you were the same Emerson. That first kiss gave me goosebumps from head to toe and it still does now. I promise you that I will tell you I love you every day. I promise to dry your tears when you're crying happy tears or sad. That I'll kiss you goodnight every night. I promise to hold your hand through life whether we have good, bad, sickness or health. I promise to be your best friend, your love, and your wife with all my heart until the end of time."

When Lily looked up, Emerson was wiping away tears. She brushed his tears away. He shook his head.

"Emerson, your vows."

"Lily, when I first saw you as a teenager, you took my breath away. Every heartbreak you had, just made us closer. You were my angel then and you still are now. That first night that we saw each other again, I truly thought you were a mirage. Like a man seeing water while walking in the desert. You were my water. You saved me from a life of loneliness. Everything I've done always had a spot for you in it, and it always will. I promise you that you will always feel loved, honored, cherished and safe in my arms. I promise that you'll never go a day without an I love you. You'll never cry tears unless they're happy tears. I promise to tell you every day that you are amazing and inspiring. I promise to be your cheerleader, your best friend, your forever love and your family until the end of time. I promise good and bad, sickness and in health to never ever walk away. Life wouldn't be life without you in it. I love you Lily. I always will."

Even the bishop was getting a little choked up. They exchanged rings, did the last of the ceremony and Emerson wanted to kiss her so badly he could feel it. When he heard the words, 'You may kiss your bride', he kissed Lily, giving her a hug.

"I love you," Lily said.

He kissed her again and Lily got her flowers then walked down the aisle as husband and wife. They went into the alcove, not noticing the photographer or anything in their way. Emerson kissed her again as the bishop's assistant walked them into the bridal room to sign the papers that they hadn't signed the night prior.

"It had to be signed the day of the wedding. Thank you for staying here. I wanted the two of you two know that I said a special prayer for you both and your marriage. I know that you'll be together forever. If you need anything at all, come see me."

"Thank you," Lily said as she headed outside with Emerson to everyone throwing lavender.

"Emerson," Lily said as she saw the car at the side of the road. He kissed her as the photographer snapped away. When they finished the photos at the church, they all headed off and made their way to the waterfront park for the wedding photos.

When they got into the SUV, Emerson kissed her, devouring her lips. "I really thought that you were an angel," he said.

"So, you liked your surprise."

"I did. What did you think of the lavender idea?"

"I can't believe that you actually got lavender and lilacs and the red roses. I'm still stunned."

He kissed her hand. "We're married," he said.

"I know. This means I'm actually stuck with you for life," Lily teased as his driver almost laughed and Emerson shook his head and kissed Lily.

They talked and snuggled their way over to the park. When they got there, Emerson picked Lily up and carried her down to where they were doing the photos. "Emerson."

"Didn't want to get the dress dirty," he teased.

"Oh really," Lily asked.

He kissed her. "Partly."

One more kiss and she touched up her lipstick while they shot a few photos. By the time they were done, Emerson wanted more than anything to just vanish into the sunset with Lily. He knew that the reception would blow her mind, but he also wanted them to be alone.

They pulled up to the hotel and Emerson walked Lily inside, then straight up to the same room they'd been in the day prior. "What are you up to?"

He unlocked the door and they walked in to see champagne, roses and a beautiful view. "I'm getting my wife to myself for a while before I have to share you again," he said as he kissed her again.

"Happy I gave him the Kleenex?"

Emerson nodded. "Babe, you were glowing like you had a heavenly spotlight following you down the aisle. I couldn't help those tears. It's like your grandparents were giving us their blessing. Like mine were cheering us on."

Lily kissed him. "Dad said that we were something special when he was walking me down the aisle."

"I love your Dad."

"I know."

Emerson kissed her again. "Is it bad that I really don't want to go downstairs?"

Lily smirked. "Still have to. I wanna see what you did with the reception."

Emerson kissed her and flipped music on, having their first real dance as husband and wife just the two of them, alone in the hotel suite. When she heard At Last by Ella Fitzgerald, she smirked. "Had to?" He nodded. They danced, kissed, danced and kissed. When All of Me by John Legend came on, she shook her head.

"All yours," Emerson said.

"I'm all yours," Lily replied as he kissed her again and danced as close as they could get.

"I don't want to share you tonight," Emerson said.

"Then we should probably let the people downstairs know."

He smirked. "Party pooper."

"Plus, Addy has my phone."

He shook his head. "I can get you a new one."

Lily shook her head. "I want to see it," Lily said.

He kissed her, devouring her lips. "You sure?"

Lily nodded. "Your dress for when we leave is up here. You okay with it," he teased.

"In other…"

He kissed her. "I'll help you out of the dress," he teased.

"I knew that's what you were planning," Lily teased.

He kissed her again, devouring her lips until he almost picked her up and carried her to bed. "Emerson."

"You're such a party pooper," he teased.

Lily motioned for him to come closer. "I have a garter for you," Lily teased.

"Damn."

"Yep." She'd intentionally bought the lace lingerie. The one that he said had to be illegal. If nothing else, he'd be surprised.

"You sure I have to share you?" Lily nodded and kissed him. "Fine. Let's get this insanity overwith." She kissed him, touched up her lipstick and he kissed her neck. "You put on that perfume again."

"Your favorite," Lily teased. She slid the veil out of her hair, laid it on the bed and walked down to the elevator hand in hand with Emerson.

"Did you see the inscription," he asked. Lily slid it down her finger enough to read it:

>*Forever my love – forever my best friend.*

"Did you read yours," Lily asked. He looked at it:

>*My forever love*

He smirked. "We share a brain," he teased.

"Something like that. Do I get to know where we're going on the honeymoon now?"

He smirked. "Nope." Lily shook her head and he kissed down her neck. "You'll need your passport," he teased.

"Emerson."

"We're going somewhere with water." She shook her head and the elevator opened. They stepped off and walked into the lobby, then down the hall to the reception room. "They set up a cocktail hour area then this for the reception," he said as he walked her in and showed her.

"Emerson."

Chapter 12

They walked into the reception room and it was like they were in a magical forest of white lilac, red roses, and white lilies. The fairy lights made it feel like it was almost magical. Even the branches looked like they'd grown there. "Emerson, this is…"

"Like being in a park?"

Lily smirked. When she saw the magnolias on the main table, she looked at him. "Emerson, this is beautiful. I couldn't have even thought this up," Lily said. He slid his arms around her and hugged her.

"Now, come look at this," he said as she saw the cake. Red roses, magnolias, lilies, and lilacs were on the cake. It was beyond beautiful. "Midsummer nights dream but in Charleston," he teased. Lily kissed him. She brushed her lipstick off his lips and he snuggled her to him.

"I love you," Lily said.

"I love you more," Emerson teased as they snuck into the hallway. Addy and Carter saw them and came over.

"And where did y'all vanish to," Addy asked.

"We needed a little alone time," Emerson joked.

Addy gave Lily back her cell phone. "Thank you," Lily said.

"Most welcome Mrs. Emerson Cartwright," Addy teased.

Lily gave her a hug and Carter gave Emerson a look. Emerson smirked and shook his head, kissing Lily's hand.

"Whatever you two are up to, cut it out," Lily teased.

"Alright. Everyone ready," the planner asked.

Lily nodded and hugged Emerson. Addy and Carter went in, then Lily and Emerson came in. They opted for their first public dance before the meal. When Lily saw a stage, she looked at him. "Emerson."

He smirked. When Adele came onto the stage, Lily almost lost it. "You get two songs Emerson. Congratulations you two," Adele said.

She sang 'Make you feel my love' then sang 'When we were young" where Lily was almost in tears.

"That's where this life started baby. You and me against the world since we were 15," he said.

Neither of them even noticed anyone else. They didn't notice the photographer, the camera flashes, or even Addy and the moms crying. When the song was over, he dipped her and kissed Lily.

"I love you," she said.

"Love you more," Emerson said. They thanked Adele for that surprise gift, invited her to stay with her boyfriend for dinner and went and took their seats. The main table even had sand from their beach. It was in a clear tray that looked like a seashell, with the branch of the magnolia over it. "Wow," Lily said.

"I love you," Emerson said.

"I love you too husband." He smirked and poured them a glass of champagne, pouring one for Carter and Addy as well.

Emerson looked at Lily. "What?"

"Speech."

Lily smirked. Carter got up, taking over that situation.

"Now, before we get going with a meal that we all know is gonna be amazing, I have a little speech. I've known these two since I was a kid. I almost idolized how much Emerson loved her even when he was a fledgling teen. He never gave up hope. He never ever thought that they'd just be friends forever. He knew somehow, he'd find a way into her life that would mean a day just like this. When he told me that he'd found Lily again, just a short few months ago, I knew. I knew that my crazy, impulsive friend would put a ring on it to quote Beyonce. They've already gone through the good and bad, the sickness and the health for that matter. I know that they'll be together forever. Lily, the man was lost without you even when it was for one night. I know that you two are going to be an amazing example for me when I get married. Just be prepared," Carter said as Emerson and Lily gave him a hug and Carter handed the mic to Addy.

"If y'all don't know who I am, I'm surprised. I've been Lily's best friend since we were in grade school. I'm Addison. What can I tell you that you don't already know? Lily may not seem it, but she's just as impulsive as Emerson. She broke hearts in high school, and Emerson became the caretaker afterwards. That's why they're so close. Everyone figured that they'd at least dated, but it took a crappy date, and a moonlit walk on a beach for them to find each other.

I can remember Emerson surprising Lily at the house and I almost laughed. She hadn't recognized Emerson, and Lily was giggling like she did in high school. When she did realize that it was him, she was pretty much stunned....and giggling. You managed to win her heart, but you never did read the rules. You break her heart, I break your bones. If Lily gets upset, coffee Haagen-Dazs. If she's really upset, don't get between her and Jack. She walks on the beach at midnight, but the Barefoot Billionaire already knows that," Addy joked. "And lastly, don't ever think that you can just walk away. She'll chase you down just like you chase her down. Just remember to always dust the sand from your toes, always find the love in everything, and never ever forget the I love you's. To Lily and Emerson, may you have a lifetime of love, a forever of happy tears and every dream come true."

Everyone clinked glasses and Emerson and Lily hugged Addy and Carter. "Had to," Lily asked.

Addy nodded. They all sat back down and the bishop said grace. They had their dinners and Lily smirked.

"What," Emerson asked.

"I still can't believe that you did all of this."

He got a smile ear to ear. "Babe, if it means a smile ear to ear on your face, I'll do anything."

"I love you," Lily said.

"I love you too beautiful."

"Y'all are making me nauseous," Addy teased. Emerson smirked and kissed Lily.

"You sure you don't want to just tell me where we're going," Lily asked.

"Nope," Emerson replied. They finished their appetizer and main course when the last two speeches started. First was Lily's dad, then Emerson's. Both had everyone reaching for the tissues that each table had. When they opted to get up, they made their way over to the cake.

"It's too pretty to cut," Lily said. Emerson kissed her.

The photographer came over, and everyone crowded around them. They cut the piece and he fed her a piece, then she fed him a piece. He kissed her while everyone snapped photos and walked her out to the dance floor. They had another dance, then Lily took her dad's hand and brought him onto the dance floor for the father and daughter dance. When she heard 'What a wonderful world', she smirked.

"Are you happy," her dad asked.

"Way beyond. He did all of this for me."

"For both of you," her dad said.

"This is all like a fairy tale."

"I'm proud of you. You stood your ground with him and you always have. Just don't forget that. You can do whatever you need to," he said.

Lily nodded. "I'm still your favorite daughter," she teased.

"Always."

When she saw her dad getting a little teary-eyed, she brushed his tears away. "You didn't lose me, dad. You gained Emerson," Lily said as he held on a little closer.

"As long as you still go to the opening day game with me."

"You mean you didn't notice that everything was Falcons colored," Lily joked. Her dad smirked. "I love you Dad," Lily said.

"I love you too baby girl," her dad said as they finished their dance.

When Emerson walked onto the dance floor with his mom, Lily hoped that he wouldn't end up in a fight with her. He'd picked Landslide by Fleetwood Mac intentionally, and Lily knew what the undertone really was. If they hadn't ended up having world war three during the planning, it would've been so much easier. His backup had been You Raise me up by Josh Groban, and he was pretty sure that he was sticking with Landslide.

When the song finished, he gave his mom a hug, grabbed Lily's hand and pulled her into his arms. Everyone joined in and danced. "I love you," Emerson said as he held her as close as they could while they danced.

"You two okay?"

He nodded. "Honestly, I'm just glad that we're done with the wedding stuff."

Lily kissed him. "You could just tell me what else you're planning," Lily said.

"I'll give you a hint. Bikini, shorts, sunshine and me all to yourself," Emerson whispered in her ear.

"That works."

"And we're only taking two security people. We have a housekeeper slash chef," Emerson said.

"You rented a house?"

"Cottage."

"With 3 bedrooms?"

"6," he replied.

"Good. I can kick you into one if you snore too loud," Lily joked.

He held on a little tighter. "You couldn't get rid of me if you tried," he teased.

Lily kissed him. "So, I'm stuck with you." He nodded and kissed her.

By the time that Emerson was almost itching to leave, there was one last thing to do before Lily could run off hand in hand with Emerson. They did the garter removal game, and Lily smirked. Emerson threw it out and it was as if he was intentionally throwing it to Carter.

"What are you up to," Lily asked.

He kissed her. "Nothin," Emerson said. When Carter walked over to Addy, Lily shook her head.

"Tell me that you didn't," Addy said. Carter slid something into Addy's hand and Emerson smirked.

"What's this," Addy asked.

"Just open it," Carter said.

When she saw a ring, she looked at him. "Carter."

"Promise ring. When we're ready, this is what I want."

Carter brought Addy to the dance floor, slid the ring on her finger and danced with her. "Carter, are you being serious," Addy asked.

"If I proposed now, you'd kick me right out the window. It's too soon for it. I want us to have this when we're ready," Carter replied. When Addy kissed him, Lily knew they were safe to sneak out. They headed up to the hotel suite and Emerson practically carried her down the hall to get her alone faster.

"What are you up to," Lily asked.

Emerson closed the door to the suite and kissed her, devouring her lips. "I love you. I couldn't wait anymore," he teased.

He kissed her again and Lily smirked.

"Can you unzip," Lily asked.

He kissed her with a grin ear to ear. He unzipped the dress, seeing the lace lingerie under it. "Damn," he said.

"What?"

"Had to do it?" Lily nodded and he kissed her again as she stepped out of the dress and put it on the hanger. Before she turned around, his arms wrapped around her and he kissed her neck, down to her shoulder and went to slide the lingerie off.

"Emerson."

"Wife, you and this lingerie is..."

She kissed him and smirked. "Still getting dressed."

"Lily, nobody knows..."

She kissed him and her phone buzzed. When she saw the text from Addy asking where she'd vanished to, Lily almost laughed. "We're going back down."

He slid his casual pants on and he shook his head. "Such a dang party pooper," he teased.

Lily kissed him and went to slide into the going away dress. When he saw it, he shook his head. "And you actually expect me to not flip you over my shoulder," he teased as he almost drooled over his wife in the way too deep of a V top and lacy shorts.

"When we leave you can." He shook his head and kissed her, picking her up.

"Shoes," Lily said as she put the shoes in the bag and hung it on the hanger with the dress. She slid the heels on and he sat down on the bed.

"You sure I have to share you?"

"Saying goodnight, throwing the bouquet to Addy and we're out of here," Lily said. He kissed her again and Lily got up.

"What?"

"Touching up lipstick then we go," Lily said as she touched it up. He handed Lily the flowers, got Lily's phone, handing it to her, and they headed downstairs for goodbye's.

When they came in, Lily said goodbye to her folks and her brother, Emerson said his goodbyes to his folks and his sister and they went and talked to Addy and Carter.

"Y'all are vanishing before midnight," Carter asked.

"Yep," Emerson joked. He took Lily's hand and they walked towards the door.

"Single ladies, who's ready for the bouquet," the dj asked. When Lily tossed it directly to Addy, she smirked. Emerson picked Lily up and they headed outside, getting directly into the SUV. They waved goodbye and took off.

"Will you finally tell me where we're going?"

He shook his head. "Nope."

"Emerson."

"Wife, you'll know when we land. It'll be a while." She looked at him.

"Meaning what," Lily asked. He kissed her. They pulled into the airport a little while later, going in the private entrance to the runway. "Emerson."

He smirked and the SUV stopped beside a plane. "What did you do?" He kissed her again and hopped out, helping her out. "What's this," Lily asked.

"Sir, we're loaded and ready. The bags have been loaded."

"Thank you," Emerson said as one of his security hopped on.

"What are we doing?"

"Flying." She looked at him and he picked her up, carrying her onto the plane.

"Phone?"

"Got it organized wife."

He sat her on the sofa and the rest of security hopped on and the door closed as everyone buckled in. The airline attendant gave Emerson and Lily a glass of champagne and Lily curled up with Emerson. "Did you like the dress," Lily asked.

"It was beautiful. Babe, you looked like an angel. Honestly, I'm surprised I could speak." He kissed her.

"And now you're stuck with me." He smirked and they clinked glasses. They had their champagne and the plane headed down the runway. "What time will we be getting in," Emerson asked as the attendant looked over.

"Around 2pm." Emerson nodded.

"Emerson." He kissed Lily and when they made it to the right elevation, he got up, taking Lily's hand. "What," she asked as he walked her over towards the back of the plane where there was a much bigger sofa so they could curl up together.

"Why are we landing at 2pm?"

"Because there's a 6-hour time difference." Lily looked at him.

"You do realize that you have to tell me right?" He kissed her, snuggling her to him. She looked at him. "Say it Emerson."

"No. When we wake up, we'll be there. I even got us Eggs Benedict for breakfast, and your favorite grilled cheese for lunch," he teased.

"Emerson."

He kissed her, devouring her lips and leaned into her arms. "Where," Lily asked when they came up for air.

"Fine. The city of lights."

"As in Cali or Paris?" He smirked. "Emerson."

"Wife."

She shook her head. "Paris?"

He nodded. "Then south of France to the beach. We're staying in a fancy house. Lots of room, a pool and hot tub and we can walk to the beach."

Lily shook her head. "I had no idea this is what you were planning."

He kissed her. "I wanted to take you somewhere we could really be alone." Lily shook her head.

"Just full of surprises." He kissed her, devouring her lips. She went to get up and he shook his head. "What?" He grabbed the blanket and they curled up together.

"Emerson."

He kissed her again. "What?"

"We aren't," she said quietly. He kissed her again and took her hand, walking her into the bathroom. He closed the door behind them. "What," Lily said.

He kissed her and she felt the hem of her dress slide up. "Emerson."

He kissed her. "What?"

She shook her head and he kissed her. "We…" He shook his head and picked her up, sitting her on the countertop. "We aren't."

He kissed her. "Says who," Emerson teased.

Lily shook her head. "Stay there for a minute," he said. He stepped out, and when he came back in a minute or two later, he handed Lily her shorts and a hoodie.

"Emerson, what are you up to?"

He kissed her and peeled the lace panties off and she felt his hands slide up her inner thighs. "I'm reminding you of something."

Lily shook her head and they had sex in that way too small room. The fact that her toes almost curled into triple knots wasn't lost on him.

He slid her dress off, sliding the last of her lingerie off and slid the hoodie over her head. "Taunting on the plane," Lily asked.

"You have no idea what I have in store for you wife." She shook her head and he slid her legs around him.

"I missed you this morning."

Lily smirked. "I bet," she teased.

He kissed her again and he handed Lily the shorts. "And you brought these why?"

"In case we have a hang out inside night. My hoodie that you love."

Lily kissed him. "And what are you changing into?"

He devoured her lips. "Jeans and my hoodie," he replied. Lily kissed him. "Then I'll grab your jeans." He shook his head and kissed her again. "Emerson." He smirked. "Fine," he teased. Lily kissed him, grabbed his jeans and hoodie and handed them to him as he closed the door behind her.

"You know they're out there sleeping right?"

"Noise cancelling earpieces and sleeping masks. Gives us a little privacy."

Lily shook her head. "I'll meet you on the sofa," Lily said.

He kissed her, changed out of his dress pants and into the jeans, peeled his shirt off and slid the hoodie on and kissed her. He folded everything and grabbed her dress and the lingerie he'd refused to let her put on and put it into his bag, curling up on the sofa with her so they could get a little rest after the insanity of the day. He curled her into his arms and he smirked.

"What?"

"Nothin. Just thinking."

Lily shook her head. "Close your eyes and get some sleep."

He kissed her again. "Never waking up alone again."

"Until the book tour."

By the time they got back from the whirlwind honeymoon, they were back to their normal giggly and happy selves. They came into the house to see a room full of gifts.

When Emerson intentionally carried her over the threshold, she almost laughed. "What is all of that," Lily asked.

"They were from the wedding. I thought you both would like to open them," the housekeeper said.

"Thank you for all of this. How was your short vacation," Emerson asked.

"You're most welcome. It was quite nice. I got to visit family and some friends I hadn't seen. I have some mail for you both whenever you're ready," the housekeeper said.

"Thank you," Lily said as Emerson kissed her and walked her upstairs.

"What are you doing?"

"Have a surprise for you," he teased.

"We just got home from a million and one surprises. What did you do," Lily teased as he kissed her and walked her into her closet. He picked her up, wrapping her legs around his hips and flipped the light on, sitting her on the new sofa.

"Hold on. Where did this come from," Lily asked.

"The sofa or the new clothes?"

"Emerson."

"You're going on a book tour. I found some stuff for you to wear."

Lily got up and looked. "You did all of this without me?"

"It was stuff you already tried on when we were away. Just different colors."

"Emerson."

"What?"

"Are you intentionally trying to drive me bananas?"

"Nope. Just making sure that you have the clothes that make you feel good when you're doing the events. I want you comfortable."

Lily kissed him. "No more buying clothes. I already have too much."

He kissed her, picking her up and carrying her to their bed. He leaned her onto it as she slid her shoes off and he kicked his sneakers off.

"When am I supposed to leave," Lily asked.

He kissed her, disregarding anything she was about to say. "I don't want you going without me."

"Then come with me," Lily said as he snuggled her legs around him.

"Babe."

"You can't?"

"You're getting a bodyguard and me."

Lily smirked. "What's the problem?"

"What happens if we get pregnant?"

"Then we handle it. I'll be home before Christmas. We can figure it out then," Lily said.

"Babe."

She smirked. "I love you, but there's no guarantee that it's gonna happen the way you want. I have to go out there and do my job," Lily said.

"And when you get back, I give you a little inspiration for the next book."

She smirked. "So, that's what you're up to," Lily teased. He kissed her and they relaxed when her phone went off.

"I know who it is," Emerson teased.

Lily grabbed her phone. "Hey Addy," Lily said.

"And you're finally back. Took you two long enough. I need to hear all about the world tour. What are y'all up to tonight," Addy asked.

"Being alone with my wife," Emerson teased.

"Carter and I were gonna come by and check in on y'all. We sorta wanted to tell you something."

Emerson smirked and shook his head, determined to have his wife all to himself. "Fine, but dinner is at 7. No earlier," Emerson said as Lily shook her head.

"Alright. Don't forget to open the wedding presents y'all. Sorta looked like there was a ton of them. I did see one that I don't think you wanted to open, so I got security to put it in their office," Addy said.

"Thank you," Lily said.

"Welcome. See y'all at dinner," Addy said as they all hung up and Emerson kissed Lily.

"Now, where were we?"

"I know what you're up to husband."

"I know you do wife," he said as he peeled her shirt off and threw it to the floor. He went to peel her shorts off and his phone went off.

"I'm not answering it. Don't even try," Emerson joked. He was kissing up her torso when it went off a second time.

"Emerson."

He nibbled. "Not happening," he said as he peeled the way too sexy lingerie right off and peeled off his t-shirt. He leaned into Lily's arms and devoured her lips as his phone went off a third time.

"Fine. Don't move one single muscle." He grabbed the phone from his back pocket, looked and answered.

"Yes."

"Mr. Cartwright, I'm sorry to interrupt. We're having a small issue at the office. Zack Fairchild is in your office, demanding to speak with you. What do you want me to do?"

"Tell security to remove him."

"Sir, we tried that and one of the security staff is on the way to the hospital."

"Fine. I'll be there in 45 minutes. Not one second later. Tell him to cool his jets," Emerson said as he hung up with his secretary.

"I guess..."

Emerson kissed her, kicked his jeans off along with his boxers and they had sex. Hot, he was pissed off, sex that had her body throbbing in his arms. Every movement made her toes curl even tighter. When he finally collapsed into her arms, she couldn't let go, and she didn't want to. Not for a second.

"What," Emerson asked as he kissed her again.

"Don't go." He got a look like he'd finally heard the words he wanted to hear.

"You're all mine. I'm all yours until the end of time baby. I'm not doing anything."

"Emerson."

"Then come with me." She kissed him and he curled her to him.

"Baby."

"Don't. He's just gonna..."

He kissed her and devoured her lips until he was getting turned on all over again. She slid into his arms, almost stopping him from leaving. "Babe."

"He's just going to cause another problem. Leave it at that," Lily said.

He took a deep breath. "Don't feel like sharing," he teased.

"Not with him."

He smirked and kissed her. "Then we get dressed and get it overwith. You and I as a team."

"I don't even want to be near him, and I don't want you near him either."

He smirked. "I don't exactly feel like having to see him right now either," he teased.

They managed to get up and Lily got cleaned up and changed. She intentionally put on something that looked nice, but that was more to stand her ground. She went to slide her heels on and Emerson grabbed them. "What are you doin?"

He zipped his jeans up, slid his dress shirt on and picked her up. "You aren't walking down the steps in those heels."

Lily kissed him as he slid her phone and his into his pocket and walked down the steps.

"Sir," his security said.

"I have to go into the office. Lily is coming. Are we good for Addy and Carter coming for dinner," Emerson asked as his housekeeper smirked.

"I had a feeling. I got extra steaks. It's fine. I'll get the table set and ready," the housekeeper said.

"Do you want me to get a wine out," Emerson asked. Lily smirked. He kissed her, grabbed the wine that she loved and put it on the counter. His security got the SUV, Lily grabbed her purse and his wallet, and they headed off hand in hand. They took the fast route as best they could, but Emerson was almost happy that they had intentionally come back to the main house instead of the beach. Things were quiet for a while, then he started wondering what Zack was actually up to.

"You sure that you want me in there," Lily asked.

"Nobody is causing a problem the day we get home from our honeymoon. If he doesn't want you there, he can leave. We're a team and we're staying that way," Emerson said as he slid his arms around her.

"I swear, you're seriously eating this up."

"Yep," he teased as he kissed her forehead.

"Now, really, what do you think is going on with Addy and Carter?"

"I have a feeling," Emerson teased as Lily shook her head.

"I swear, if you say that you think they're getting hitched, I may have to kick you."

"Could be. Could be that they're pregnant. Could just be that they're buying a place together. Could be anything," Emerson teased. Lily shook her head and looked out the window as they made their way over the Ravenel Bridge.

"Did you miss home," Emerson asked.

Lily nodded. "I will even more when the book tour starts."

"At least you get the best piece of home with you," Emerson joked.

Lily smirked. "Very true. That built-in bed warmer will come in really handy." He shook his head and snuggled her into his arms.

They pulled up to the office and he hopped out, helping her out of the SUV. They headed up to his floor and when they walked off the elevator, his assistant almost jumped out of her seat. "Welcome back," his assistant said as Lily slowed Emerson down.

"Thank you. Is he still being a pain," Emerson asked.

"We got him to go into the meeting room."

Emerson nodded. "Did you need a drink at all," his assistant asked.

"Just an ice water if you can," Lily said as he held her hand a little tighter. He got his paperwork he'd intentionally left on his desk, sliding it into his bag that he'd left in the office. He walked down to the meeting room with Lily.

"Breathe," she said.

"He's being this much..."

Lily kissed him. "Breathe husband." He took a deep breath and walked into the meeting room with her.

"Zack," Emerson said as Zack looked at Lily then at the ring.

"I can't believe that you married this idiot when you could've had so much better," Zack said.

"I married better. I'm not playing a game with you Zack. You don't deserve a woman. You deserve to be alone," Lily said as she sat down as far from him as possible.

"I heard about the book," Zack said.

"You can talk to me Zack. You wanted me to talk to you, speak. Get it out of your system and get out," Emerson said.

"I want the publishing side back."

"Nope. You already signed the contract. There's no renegotiating. I know the reason, and that isn't happening either. Stay away from my wife," Emerson said.

"I want to buy it back," Zack said.

"Answer is still no. Next time you decide that you want to be an idiot, make an actual appointment. Second, might want to get a lawyer. Assaulting security in my office?"

"I need to talk to you alone," Zack said.

"No," Emerson replied.

"Whatever you're gonna say, just say it Zack. You're still an idiot," Lily said as she shook her head and went through way too many emails.

"You stole Lily out of my dang life," Zack said.

"So, this is about me," Lily asked.

"Partially," Zack said.

Lily shook her head, got up and went to leave the room when Emerson stopped her. "I stole her? Seriously? I've known her..."

Lily stopped him. "This isn't the who's dick is bigger moment. Zack, grow up and grow a pair. Either you walk and get the hell over it or find meds that will get you there. You want to be served a restraining order, you're headed down the right pathway. Leave. Get out of the office, go home, move. Vanish into the ocean somewhere. Leave me alone and quit trying to buy a woman. Nobody wants to date you because you're a self-absorbed idiot. You're a narcissist. Just go away. Nobody wants that here, and nobody wants that anywhere. Go," Lily said, reprimanding Zack like he was a child. In her eyes, he was. An overgrown, spoiled rotten, narcissistic idiot. When Zack got up, Lily glared at him. When he walked towards her, she put her hand up.

"Go."

Zack shook his head with a scowl and walked out.

Emerson closed the door behind him and walked over to Lily. "What," she asked.

Emerson kissed her, devouring her lips. "I think I may need to make you president or something," he teased.

"Top negotiator?"

He smirked and wrapped his arms around her. "Baby."

"What?"

"Can we go home?"

Lily smirked. "I was waiting to hear you say it," Lily teased. He kissed her again, took her hand, grabbed his bag from his office and went to say goodbye to his assistants.

"We're heading out. If you need anything, we're at the house."

"We did get the dates for the book tour for Lily. I made a few copies so you have dates. Hotel suites are booked, and the transportation is booked. It's in two week blocks as per your email," his assistant said.

"Thank you. I'll be in later next week before Lily heads out."

"Yes sir, and congratulations again," his other assistant said.

They got down to the SUV and hopped in. "I still can't believe that he was doing all of that to get your attention," Emerson said.

"I was seriously going to call the damn lawyer," Lily said.

"I know. Thank you for staying," Emerson replied. He kissed her.

"I had a feeling that's what he was up to. Somehow, a wedding photo ended up in the paper," Lily said.

"Sorta like dumping salt on a wound for him."

Lily nodded. "At some point, he has to stop. We both know that."

Emerson kissed her. "I'm just glad that we can relax," Emerson said.

"And be butthead free," Lily teased. He smirked and snuggled her to him as they drove through the live oak pathway towards the house.

When they pulled in, Emerson smirked. "What," Lily asked.

"Now we can actually have some alone time," Emerson said as they made their way to the front door. They stopped, hopped out of the SUV and went inside, opting to try and go through at least some of the presents. They got most of the way through, laughing through some and writing it all down. When they got to the one that was from Emerson's mom and dad, he opened it and saw a platinum frame with a picture of Lily and Emerson in high school.

"Oh my goodness," Emerson said as he showed Lily.

"That was...that was summer formal when we were going into senior year," Lily said.

"Like I said beautiful wife of mine. I loved you even then."

Lily smirked and kissed him. "I kinda like it," Lily said.

"Good because it's going on the bookshelf." He got up and put the picture on the shelf beside their wedding photo.

When they got to the one from her mom and dad, it was a little book of all the advice for their marriage with his and hers robes. "See, this can come in handy," Emerson joked. Lily shook her head and saw one that was from Addy and Carter. They opened it and saw a bottle of Dom Perignon and two champagne flutes. Emerson smirked.

"What?"

"I have a feeling that this will need to be opened tonight," Emerson teased as he went and put it in the cooler to chill before they showed. They only had a few left when Addy and Carter showed up.

"About time you two got here," Emerson said as he got up and gave them each a hug then they both hugged Lily.

"What do you have left there, bud," Carter asked.

"Three," Lily replied.

They all sat down. "Drink," Emerson asked.

"Sweet tea," Addy said as Lily smirked, kissed Emerson and got up, grabbing sweet tea for her and Addy.

"Carter," Lily asked.

"Jack," Carter joked. Lily got him a drink and handed a glass of red to Emerson, handing a sweet tea to Addy.

"So, what were you two gonna tell us," Emerson asked.

"Well, we were talking. We're sorta thinking that we might want to have you two as godparents," Carter said.

"What," Lily asked looking at Addy.

"It's early, but we sorta decided that we were gonna be together anyway. We wanted kids, and we're planning a future and stuff," Addy said.

"Meaning," Emerson asked.

"Meaning we're engaged and pregnant," Carter said.

Lily got up and hugged Addy and Carter, and Emerson hugged them both. "So, we are contagious," Emerson joked as he slid his arm around Lily and they sat back down together.

Lily shook her head. "Are you gonna stay at the house," Lily asked.

"It has 3 bedrooms, but we're kind of thinking we may stay until we need to go," Carter said.

Emerson smirked. "This mean that you're buying that house you sent me a picture of," Emerson asked.

"Thinking about it. I don't know if that's gonna happen. That house is kinda perfect where it is. For now, we're happy there. I just sorta think that maybe we should just buy it from you," Carter said.

"What?"

"If you're okay with it," Addy said. Emerson got a grin ear to ear. He kissed Lily's forehead. "That's kinda up to you," Emerson said.

"If you want," Lily replied.

"I was kinda hoping you'd say that. I just think it's fair," Carter said. "Meaning," Emerson asked. He handed Emerson an envelope and he handed it to Lily. When she opened it, there was a check for $200,000 over the price she'd paid. "Carter." "That's what it's worth now according to the real estate agent friend of mine," Carter said. Lily slid it in her purse and nodded. "If you want it, it's yours," Lily said. "Good. And what about the godparents thing," Addy asked. "When y'all get there, I'd be honored," Lily said. "Me too," Emerson said.

Lily got up and grabbed herself an ice water instead of the sweet tea and Addy got up and came into the kitchen with her. "You okay," Addy asked.

"Are you sure you want to do this," Lily asked.

Addy nodded. "I wanted to buy it when I moved in, but you weren't sure."

"As long as you're alright."

"Girl, I know something else happened. What's going on?" Lily shook her head.

"Outside," Addy said as they walked outside and sat down on the porch.

"Say it."

"Zack tried to buy the publishing part back."

Addy shook her head. "And you were there?"

"He assaulted security at the office."

"I'm so glad that he's gone from your life. The man was an idiot and so was Sam. He got someone else pregnant," Addy said.

"What happened to the chef?"

"You mean the one who was sleeping with the sous chef?"

Lily almost laughed. "You sure that you two are alright?"
"Better than alright. I still can't believe that he had a crush on me in high school. In grade school too!"

"And you're happy?" Addy gave her a hug.

"Way beyond. I love him," Addy said.

"As long as you're sure. All I wanted was you happy."

"Are you alright? How was the honeymoon?" Just as she said it, the guys came outside.

"You alright," Emerson asked as he put the steaks on. Lily nodded and Carter came and sat with Addy. They talked and when Emerson sat down with Lily, he snuggled his arms around her. He knew what had her in a funk, and it wasn't Zack. When he kissed her shoulder, he knew. "Refill," Emerson asked.

"Please," Carter asked as Addy smirked.

"Do you want some more sweet tea," Lily asked.

"I'm good, but thanks," Addy said as Emerson walked Lily back inside.

"What's wrong," he asked as he closed the sliding door.

"Nothing. I just can't believe that they're actually pregnant and engaged," Lily said.

Emerson kissed her. "We were. Babe, it takes time. We have a ton of time."

Lily kissed him. "I know. It's just crazy. Part of me wanted to hold onto the house in case something..."

He kissed her. "Babe, nothing is gonna happen. Breathe."

"Emerson." He shook his head and hugged her.

"No more worrying. It's good news not crappy. Just enjoy the night," he said as he grabbed the corn to put on the grill and Lily made the salad.

Chapter 13

They took everything outside to the screened-in porch and Emerson flipped the steaks as Addy came over to Lily and Emerson handed the refill to Carter. "Everything good," Carter asked quietly.

"Crappy afternoon. We were planning to just relax and be alone for a while and ended up having to go in and deal with the idiot at the office. He threw a punch at security and sent him to the dang hospital," Emerson said.

"And?"

"He wanted the publishing half back. Partially because of Lily. Mostly to be honest."

Carter shook his head. "Am I dealing with him?"

"Nope. My amazing wife put the idiot in his place. Honestly, it was almost a dang turn-on," Emerson joked.

"I can imagine. Everything else okay," Carter asked.

"We lost one before the wedding. Just a reminder," Emerson said quietly.

Lily went inside and got a refill of her ice water and topped up Emerson's glass of wine. When he slid his arms around her waist, he snuggled her to him. "What," Lily asked.

"I love you," he replied.

"I love you too," Lily said.

"Come," he replied as he walked her over to the grill.

"Emerson."

He kissed her. "You okay?"

Lily nodded. "I will be."

He slid his arm around her shoulders and snuggled her to him as he plated the steaks. Lily took two over to Addy and Carter and Emerson put theirs on the table.

They talked through dinner, talking about the things that Addy wanted for her wedding. Talking about work and business stuff took up most of Emerson and Carter's conversation. When the housekeeper came out with chocolate silk pie for dessert, Lily smirked.

"You didn't," Lily said.

"With strawberries in it," the housekeeper said with a smirk.

"Thank you," Lily said.

"Most welcome," she said as she took the dishes inside and left everyone to hang out and talk.

"So, when does the book stuff start," Carter asked.

"Next weekend I think. At least I have a little time that I can be back here," Lily said.

"Then you can come to my doc appointment maybe," Addy said.

"You really should figure out when you wanted to do the wedding. We kinda lucked out with that hotel situation," Emerson said.

"Why," Addy asked.

"Someone had cancelled their event the day I booked it all. I kinda had it booked pretty quickly anyway. Where were you thinking of doing it," Emerson asked.

"We were thinking Cypress Gardens to be honest. It's quiet and there won't be a ton of people anyway. If we can get the whole thing in one spot, it kinda works," Addy said.

"It'd be really beautiful. Hopefully no alligators would request a plus one," Lily joked. Emerson snuggled Lily to him knowing that she was finally okay with all of it.

By the time Addy and Carter headed out, Emerson was ready to turn the phones off and go get some rest. Lily cleaned up the dishes and Emerson came up behind her. "What," Lily asked.

He picked her up, walked into the house and sat her on the high-top chairs at the counter. "Emerson."

"Stay there," he teased as he kissed her. He brought the dishes in, got Lily a glass of wine, refilled his and handed the glasses to her.

"What are you up to," Lily asked. He picked her up and carried her upstairs. He sat her on the bed, putting the wine glasses on the bedside table and leaned into her arms. "What," Lily asked.

"No more stress, no more phone, no more interruptions."

"Oh really?" He nodded and kissed her. He peeled his shirt off and Lily shook her head. When he went for her shorts, she stopped him.

"What are you up to?" He kissed her and walked into the master bath, drawing them a bath in the massive, oversized tub. When he came into the bedroom, Lily was hanging her shorts up.

"Well dang," he teased as he smirked and leaned against the door frame.

"Emerson, cut it out." He shook his head and walked towards her as she went into her closet and hung the shorts up. She slid off her shirt and went to pull her robe on when he stopped her and sat her on the sofa, pulling her into his lap.

"Yes handsome."

He kissed her. "I love you. You know that right?"

Lily nodded and kissed him. "I know. Just kinda felt a little jealous for a minute there," Lily replied.

"Then we go curl up in the tub and relax, have our wine, and curl up in bed together. Babe, we deserve to have a baby when it's time. Whenever that time is, it'll happen. We both know it will. It's alright baby."

"Emerson."

"What?"

"Are you gonna be okay if it doesn't?"

He kissed her. "Bathtub conversation."

He kissed her again and they got up. Lily peeled the last of her stuff off, throwing it into the laundry bin and walked into the bathroom, sliding into the hot water. He kicked his jeans off and grabbed the glasses of wine, sliding into the tub with her. He handed one to Lily and pulled her into his arms.

"You want to try, then we try. Babe, you thought you'd never finish the book. Then you thought that it wouldn't sell. Then you thought you'd never get married. All of it happened. We'll be fine."

"And what happens if it doesn't?"

He kissed her. "Like I said, we go adopt or get a bunch of dogs or cats. Whatever you want as long as I get to wake up and see that smile every morning," he teased.

Lily kissed him. "Determined."

He nodded. "I have what I want. All I ever wanted. Your turn," he said as he set his glass down and pulled her into his lap so they were face to face.

"I still think that the book tour is a little much," Lily replied.

"Well, it's that many stops because they're all selling out. The book sales are insane. They released it early. I got us the first 15 copies for friends and family and stuff. We can do anything."

"You sure?"

He nodded. "They also know that I'm gonna be with you for most of it. Luckily, a lot of the signings are at night which means I can get work in during the day if I need to. It's all you. I get to show off my sexy, talented, creative, amazing, gorgeous wife to the world. I'm happy with that," he said.

Lily kissed him and he snuggled her in even tighter. "Mine," he said.

"And?"

"Tell me what you want. Name it," he said.

"I'm worried that things aren't gonna go the way you want. The way we want."

He shook his head. "Babe, tell me what you're actually worried about."

"Is the book worth it?"

He kissed her forehead. "Lily, I'm not the only one saying it's amazing. I read you the reviews. It's amazing. I don't know why you don't agree."

"Because it's part of the job. It'll never be all rainbows and butterflies Emerson."

He kissed her. "The book is really good. I promise you. They wouldn't have published if it needed work. You're fine. What else are you worried about," he asked.

"Us."

He looked at her. "Babe."

"Emerson, I want kids. If I can't, I'm gonna feel like crap. I'm..."

He kissed her. "Don't say it."

"You know what I'm saying."

"You are an amazing woman, you're gonna be an amazing mom whether we adopt or not. We'll be alright baby. I promise you we will. I'm not gonna be all upset if we don't. It means I get to take you on vacations more," he teased.

"Emerson."

He kissed her, put her wine glass with his and slid his arms around her. "We got married because I'm not leaving your side. Because I love you with all that I am. Having kids or not doesn't change anything. I still have you. That's what I wanted. You wanted us right?"

Lily nodded. "I just don't want you to regret us not..."

He kissed her. "It'll happen. I promise you. We have time."

Lily kissed him. "Just don't rethink that feeling."

"Never. Don't be stunned when it does happen. Babe, if it takes a while, it means more us time. It will happen. I know it will."

He kissed her and his hands slid down her back. Lily smirked and he devoured her lips. "All yours," he teased. Lily smirked and he snuggled her.

When he wrapped her legs around his hips, Lily smirked. "Wine," she joked.

He kissed her neck and she finished her wine, putting the glass on the counter behind him. "Up," he said.

"What?"

"Up," he repeated.

Lily got up and he stood, grabbed a towel, wrapped it around his hips and picked Lily up, wrapping the other around her. He drained the tub and sat her on the bathroom counter.

"Emerson."

"What?"

"I know what you're doing."

He kissed her. "Practicing," he teased with a wink. He kissed her with a kiss that had goosebumps appearing on her body and got that much closer. "Tell me what you want," he asked.

"I already have it," she teased.

He kissed her again. "Good answer wife." He pulled her legs around him, knocking his towel to the floor and they had sex. Her body was almost shaking in his arms, and her toes were knotting themselves tenfold. They kept going until he collapsed in her arms and she held on that much tighter. He didn't dare move. Not at that moment. Not for anything in the world. He just felt her almost clench around him and he kissed down her neck.

"Damn you're addictive," he teased.

"Good," Lily replied as he kissed her again.

When he was able to move, he managed to pick her up. He carried her to bed, leaning into her arms as they rolled into the blankets. "Lily."

"Husband."

"I love you."

"Love you more," she replied as she ran her fingers through his hair. He kissed and nibbled down her neck, down her torso and she tightened her legs around him. He leaned back into her arms and propped himself up on one hand.

"You, my wife, are perfect to me. I'm not leaving your side and I'm not going anywhere except maybe into the gym downstairs. I promised you that. I'm not gonna stop just because we aren't pregnant yet."

"Yet?"

"We have lots of time to practice sexy." He kissed her again, devouring her lips and slid the blankets over them in bed.

"Think so do you?"

"And in fancy hotels," he teased.

Lily shook her head. "I love you, but you're ridiculous."

"And sometimes you need a little bit of a laugh," he said.

Lily kissed him. "You sure you want to come with me on the signing stuff?"

He nodded. "I wanted to be your cheerleader, and I'm gonna be. I may have to maybe miss one or two if I have to be at a meeting or something, but I'm gonna be there as much as I can."

"If you can't, it's fine."

He kissed her. "Can't get rid of me that easily beautiful. I'm right beside you like it or not."

"I guess I can put up with you," Lily teased as he shook his head and smirked.

"Put up with me?"

Lily laughed and he shook his head. He kissed her and cradled her face in his hands. "My forever love," he said.

"Promise," Lily said. He kissed her again and they curled up together, falling asleep on the bed. They were still entangled, still inseparable and still head over heels.

The next morning, Emerson woke up and she wasn't in bed. He saw a note that she opted to do a workout and smirked. He got up, sliding his joggers on with his sneakers and walked downstairs, seeing Lily finishing a workout. He leaned over and kissed her. "Morning sexy," he said.

"So, you got my note?"

He nodded and smirked. "I still can't believe that you're up this early," Emerson said as he started doing a warmup.

"I couldn't sleep. Someone was snoring," she teased as he shook his head.

"You tired me out. All your fault wife." Lily shook her head then did her yoga stretches.

"And now you taunt me while I'm working out. So fair," Emerson teased as she intentionally changed position so he was staring at her backside.

He shook his head, stepped off the treadmill and came up behind her, wrapping his arms around her waist. "Wife."

"Husband."

"What's up," Lily teased.

"You started it." Lily smirked.

"I'm doing yoga."

"I'll give you yoga alright," he teased. Lily went to turn around to face him and he kissed her neck, stopping her.

"Emerson."

"Yep."

"What are you doin?"

"Nothing," he teased.

"Husband."

"You and your yoga."

He pulled her tight against him. "What are you up to?"

"It's a really good thing I closed the door." He walked her towards the wall of the gym and she shook her head.

"Not gonna behave at all are you?"

He shook his head and slid her leggings down. "Husband."

He kissed the back of her neck and she could feel the heat radiating off of him. When she felt him against her back, she shook her head. "What?"

"Mine."

"Ditto," Lily teased as they had sex against that wall. It wasn't rough, it was just hot as all get out. Really hot. Her legs were almost shaking and her belly was trembling when he ended up pinning her against the wall.

When he turned her to face him, he picked her up and wrapped her legs around his hips as they kept going. When he finally gave way, he kissed her with a kiss that overheated every cell in her body. They slid to the floor and he barely managed to let her up for air. She grabbed her leggings and he shook his head.

"You started it," he teased.

"How?"

"Yoga."

Lily kissed him. "I thought you were doing a workout," Lily teased.

"Something like that. Got distracted by this sexy woman I married. I can't help it," he teased.

Lily shook her head. "Water," Lily asked.

He nodded and she grabbed her water, handing it to him. When he tasted peach, he smirked. "Peach water?"

Lily nodded. "While we still have them," Lily replied.

He kissed her again and when Lily tried to get up, he pulled her back to him.

"What?"

"I love you."

"I love you too handsome. Always."

He devoured her lips. "Do your workout. I'm going to get food."

He kissed her again. "Nope."

"Emerson."

"Not allowed," he teased as Lily got up and slid her leggings on as he pulled his joggers up.

"You're not seriously gonna eat without me are you," Emerson asked. "

Getting something then I'll come sit with you," Lily said. He kissed her and she went up and got a protein shake and came and sat, watching Emerson do a workout. He was almost too sexy. The muscles, the ring on his finger, the eyes that could make her melt. She loved him more than he even knew.

"Drooling yet," Emerson teased.

"A little. That ring just makes you even sexier," Lily teased. He smirked, walked over, kissed her, and finished his workout and his stretches.

"You ready to eat," Lily asked.

He picked her up and carried her up the steps to the kitchen. "I can walk."

"I know," he teased as he kissed her.

"Omelets and bacon are ready. I chopped up some peaches as well," his housekeeper said as Lily smirked.

They had breakfast and Emerson couldn't get the smile off his face for a second. "So, what's the plan for today," Emerson asked.

"Hanging out with my husband, writing, figuring out what to pack and relaxing," Lily said.

"What if we went out to the beach?"

"Up to you. We could go walk downtown," Lily replied.

"Hmm. No. We can go for a swim," he teased.

Lily smirked. "You and that bikini."

"Dang right sexy wife of mine."

They finished breakfast and the housekeeper brushed them out of the kitchen and sent them upstairs.

"Seriously though. Bikini?" He nodded. They went and got showered, and just as she was about to step out, he pulled her back to him. "And what do you want," Lily teased.

"Better today," he asked.

Lily nodded and kissed him as he picked her up and wrapped her legs around him. "Good. No more worrying.

Babe, we're fine. We always will be. So long as you keep that bikini around, you got me."

"And if I get something else?"

"Nope. Still wearing it."

"The same one I had to stop you from undoing in the ocean and when we were away?"

He nodded and kissed her. "I guess I can keep it." He smirked.

"Wife, I love you. I love us. That's all I've ever needed."

Lily kissed him and he slid her to her feet. She grabbed the shower sponge, put his body wash on it and washed his back for him. When her arms slid around his waist, he linked their fingers.

"You know if you start something you're gonna be finishing it right," he teased.

"Yep," Lily teased as she smirked and kissed his back. He slid the sponge from her hand and turned to face her, rinsing out the shampoo.

"What," Lily teased.

He kissed her. "If we don't stop, we're never making it to the beach," he teased.

"You started it," Lily said. She kissed him and stepped out. She saw him shake his head with a grin that said she was gonna end up being late to head out to the beach. She slid her hair up in a towel, went into the bedroom and into her closet, sliding on her bikini with her tank top overtop. She slid her jean shorts on that Emerson loved and put her sunscreen on. When she took her hair out of the towel, she felt arms slide around her and pull the t-shirt off.

"Emerson."

"Wife."

"What are you up to?"

"Retying this for you," he teased as he undid the tie on the back.

"You are so bad." He kissed her and slid his arms around her.

"Yeah. This bikini is definitely illegal. 100%," he teased.

Lily shook her head and he pulled her tight to him. "Mine. All mine," Emerson joked.

"And you need to get dressed."

"We have time. About this though," he teased as he pulled her bikini top right off.

"You are so bad."

He kissed her and walked her to the bed, leaning her onto it. "Emerson."

He kissed her and was going for the zipper of her shorts when his phone went off. "Seriously. Can we not just throw them away?"

Lily laughed and he shook his head. Lily handed the phone to him and he put it on speaker, putting it onto the bed.

"Yep," Emerson said.

"How was the honeymoon," his mom asked as Lily grabbed her bikini top out of his hand and went to get up when he pinned her to the bed.

"Still kinda on it still at home. What's up," Emerson asked.

"Well, I was going to see if the two of you wanted to come by. We're having a charity dinner on Friday," his mom said.

"Which one," Emerson asked.

"One that goes to the homeless," his mom said.

"Black tie?"

"Yes. Would you two like to come?"

"I'll talk to Lily. Should be fine," Emerson said as he slid Lily's jean shorts off.

"And where did you two go for your honeymoon," his mom asked.

"South of France. Went on day trips. We went to Paris and went to London for a day or two on the way back," Emerson said as he went to untie her bikini bottoms.

Lily tried to stop him and he smirked. "Tell Lily I said hi. I'll see you Friday," his mom said.

"Will do. Love you guys," he said as Lily shook her head and he hung up. He undid the bikini bottoms and threw them on the floor.

"You are so bad," Lily said.

"And? You married me. The man who wants you 24-7. For life," he teased as he kissed from her ankle all the way up her body.

He taunted, teased, and taunted some more. "Emerson."

"Wife," he said as he got to her breast.

"You are so not playing fair."

"Didn't realize that I had to," he joked as he leaned into her arms. He devoured her lips and they had sex on that bed. He didn't care about leaving that room. He could've gone without the phone. The only thing he knew he couldn't go without was Lily. She felt so good, he wanted to have sex with her practically every second of the day. They taunted each other, but all of the worry she'd had just melted away. When they came up for air, Lily's toes were curled into double knots and her body was still throbbing, wrapped around him.

"I can't move," he said as he kissed up her neck.

"I think my legs locked into place," Lily teased.

"Think so," he teased as he smirked.

"You're bad," Lily said.

"And you love it."

He kissed her again and she let him up. He curled her into his arms and kissed her. "You okay?"

Lily nodded. "We're going to the beach still right?"

"Yep. It's only 10. We're good babe."

Lily shook her head. "Where did you throw my bikini?"

He smirked, kissed her and grabbed it, handing it to her. "You wearing it," he asked.

"Considering wearing the red one instead," Lily teased.

"Party pooper."

"Safer option," Lily joked as she slid the bikini on, then her shirt and shorts. She slid her red one in her bag. When he came out with his red shorts on, Lily smirked.

"Had to," Lily asked.

He nodded and smirked, sliding his shirt on and walked over and kissed her. "Laptop," he asked. Lily nodded and they got their things and headed downstairs.

"Can we just drive the truck out on our own," Lily asked.

Emerson smirked. "You sure," he asked. Lily nodded. He kissed her.

"I'll follow you out. Are you planning on staying," his security asked.

"Never know. Might just for tonight," Emerson replied.

"We'll meet you there then," his security said as Lily handed him the truck keys.

They left and made their way out to the beach hand in hand. "Nice idea," Emerson said.

"This way, we actually have a little time really alone."

"Something you wanted to talk about that you didn't want anyone hearing?"

"I just wanted actual alone time. That's it. Just you and me being us." He kissed her hand as they stopped for a light.

"What do you want to do for dinner," he asked.

"Shem creek," Lily said.

"Islander is a better option. Not really in the mood for drunk people," he said.

"Okay. Islander it is then handsome," Lily said. He smirked.

"Must be feeling better," Emerson joked.

"Just was a little stunned. Did you seriously go look at rings with him?"

"He had questions that I could help answer. That's all. You love your ring, and Addy always commented on it. Easy to find a happy medium."

"You two picked a beautiful one."

"I was gonna ask. What did you want to do for your birthday on Wednesday," he asked.

"Emerson."

"We promised to go to mom's thing on Friday next week, but we still have your actual birthday to celebrate."

"Emerson, I don't want a party. Honestly. We just had the wedding. I just want to have a laid-back birthday just us."

"Well, I could technically do that. Sorta changes a few things I planned." Lily shook her head.

"I leave the Sunday after your mom's party. I don't want anything big. You and me on the beach with seafood is good enough for me. I got what I wanted when we got married."

He smirked and kissed her hand. "I get it, but you're still getting a party."

"Emerson." He smirked. "Who," Lily asked.

"Does it matter?" Lily shook her head.

"Family that includes Addy and Carter."

"As in my folks and brother and your folks and your sister?"

"She went back to Australia, so my sister isn't coming. Your brother can't fly out. Our folks, Addy and Carter." Lily looked at him. "We can give them the books."

"Emerson, can we not just be alone?"

He shook his head. "Nope. Not this year. Next year, we do something just us."

Lily shook her head and he kissed her at the light. "You deserve a party. You always have and you just didn't have one. Addy even said you hadn't."

"Husband, I get it, but it's because I don't want to celebrate it. I would just rather have something small. That's all I want."

"Then we do something at the beach. We still have the fire pit and, we still have the sunset."

Lily smirked. "Fine, but nothing massive." He nodded and they headed over the bridge and made their way to the beach house. When they got there, Lily saw a truck on the street that looked way too familiar.

"What," Emerson asked.

"Just put the truck in the garage."

"Babe, talk." She shook her head and he parked the truck, turned it off and closed the garage door. He hopped out, went around to her side, and opened the door, grabbing the bag.

"What did you see," he asked.

"It's gonna sound really weird, but that looks like Zack's truck."

Emerson called his security. "Sir," his security said.

"How far out are you?"

"We'll be there in 5. What's the problem?"

"Truck parked across the street from the beach house. Possibly Zack."

"It'll be handled. Just stay inside until we're there please."

Emerson walked her inside and they went into the bedroom. He took a deep breath, making sure that the doors were secured. Lily shook her head and curled up on the bed, grabbing her laptop and turned it on, checking emails for any stupid emails from Zack. When she saw one, she showed Emerson:

> *I think that you made a mistake. You should've married a real man. I know it was all a game at his office. Just come over and see me. I'll be over at my friend's place. He's a few doors down from the idiot you married. – Z*

Emerson shook his head, forwarding the email to his security. He blocked the email from her email account and deleted it.

"Emerson." He slid her laptop to the side.

"He's not messing with us. Not today."

He grabbed his phone, messaged someone and put the phone down. "Who were you messaging?"

"That idea that you had. It's gonna happen," Emerson said.

"Which one?"

He kissed her. "The one where he isn't within 1000 feet. No contact."

Lily shook her head. "Just what I always wanted," Lily said sarcastically.

Not 2 minutes later, security came in. "It's being handled," security said.

"I'm going outside," Lily said.

"Miss Lily." She peeled her shirt off, kicked off her shorts and walked outside. Emerson shook his head, grabbed the towels, and by the time he got outside she was already in the water.

Emerson put the towels down and dove into the water, trying to catch up to her. When he got closer, he pulled her into his arms. "Babe."

"Emerson, just leave it."

He pulled her to him. "I get it. I do. Breathe."

"No."

"Lily, please."

"He just shows up and throws a wrench into everything all over again. I thought that his stupid crap was done. I thought maybe he might grow a pair and go away. Instead, he keeps going with all of this stupid crap."

Emerson kissed her. "He's been handled."

"Emerson."

"Babe, he's not coming near us again. It's fine. We're safe."

Lily shook her head and he hugged her. "What did I do that was so earth-shattering that makes him not screw off," Lily asked.

"All it took for me was one kiss. One kiss in your tv room of your condo that night. To be honest with you, all it took was one look in your eyes when you were in tears in high school. I wanted you then, I want you now even more. I get that he thinks he cares about you. The fact is, he knows that it's pointless to even say it. You and I are married. He can't destroy that. That's why he's so dang frustrated. I get it. I'd be the same way if you'd married him instead of me. I would've fought to the ends of the earth to get you back. You're the only woman I love. The only woman I ever loved. You get that right?"

Lily kissed him and he hugged her.

When Emerson saw security nod on the porch, he kissed her. "He's gone. Handled. Are you okay," he asked.

"Promise me something."

He looked at her. "What?"

"If you change…"

He kissed her. "Stop."

"If you change your mind, tell me."

"I haven't changed my mind since we were 15. I never stopped loving you and I never will. I've been in love with you for over 15 years. I'm not turning that off. It'll never stop."

"Emerson."

He kissed her again, devouring her lips until he felt her legs slide around his as he moved in enough that his feet touched the bottom of the water. They were up to their necks in salt water and he didn't care. As long as they were together, he didn't care. "We okay," he asked.

Lily nodded and hugged him. "Swim or coming in to write the next million copy book," he teased.

"Swim," she teased.

He shook his head. "You sure?"

She nodded and he felt her feet against his back. "What," he asked as he saw the smirk.

"Nothin," Lily said. When he went to grab her foot, he knew what she was up to.

"Really. Out here?"

Lily kissed him.

"Nope. We're going inside." She shook her head and he walked in, walked across the beach and up the steps to the house, slid a towel around her and walked upstairs, leaning her onto the bed and kicking the door closed.

"Now, what were you saying," he asked.

"Nothin," Lily teased.

He shook his head. "Lily." She smirked and went to slide her shorts on. "So, now you're just gonna tease and taunt me all day?"

Lily nodded. He kissed her and leaned her back onto the bed, pulling the jean shorts off. "Woman, you intentionally taunt me and think that I'm not gonna react?"

"Nope," Lily said as he kissed her and leaned into her arms, pulling her legs back around him.

"Tell me what you want."

"Inspiration for writing," she said almost laughing.

"Well then," he teased as he kissed down her neck and undid the bikini.

"Emerson." He kept going, nibbling as he knew her toes would curl into pretzels.

When he kissed her hip, Lily shook her head and he handed her the bikini bottoms. "Emerson," Lily said as her toes were almost curling into double knots. He kissed her inner thigh and Lily grabbed for him.

"You think you're the only one that can taunt anyone," he teased as one warm breath against her had her legs shaking.

"Funny. Come here."

"Nope." He kept going until Lily went to sit up. He stopped her and it got that much more intense.

"Emerson, please." He smirked and looked at her, kissing his way back up her torso. He kissed her and they had sex on the bed. Hot, intense, goosebumps and passion, sex that had her legs shaking around him. When he collapsed into her arms, he almost laughed.

"You are so grounded," Lily said.

He kissed her and slid to his back, pulling her into his arms. "Wife."

"Husband, we need to actually..."

He kissed her. "You putting it back on?"

"Red one," Lily said as Emerson smirked.

"Party pooper," he teased. Lily kissed him and he snuggled her to him.

"Feel any better?"

"I'm literally surprised if I can walk." He kissed her and his hand slid to her backside. "Emerson." He kissed her again.

"What," he teased.

"I know what you're doing."

"Distract you long enough," he teased. Lily nodded and he kissed her again. "No worrying. No stress. That's what we agreed when we went away. It's the same now. If you look like you're getting stressed, tell me that you're worried. We have to talk to each other," he said as she snuggled into his arms again.

"Okay," Lily said.

He kissed her again. "I love you."

"And I love you handsome." He kissed her and Lily managed to get up.

"Can't change your mind on that bikini," he asked.

Lily shook her head and went and slid it on, noticing her sliding shorts on top. "Babe."

"What," Lily asked as she watched him get out of bed and pull his swim shorts on.

"You sure," he teased. Lily nodded.

They headed downstairs and walked out to the patio and curled up on the chaises side by side. "You writing," he asked.

Lily smirked and he kissed her shoulder. "Trying to. This handsome guy keeps distracting me," Lily joked.

He smirked and went through emails. When he got to one from the lawyer, he smirked. Seeing the words 'it will be done today' was the icing on the cupcake of the day. When an email popped up from Lily, he smirked:

> *I know that smile. Lawyer reply with some good news?*

He replied:

> *The words 'it will be done today' just made me happy. Almost as happy as this morning with you doing yoga.*

Lily smirked and replied:

> *And now you know why I work out before you wake up handsome.*

He kissed her shoulder and read the email. "Think so do you," he teased.

"Yep," Lily replied as she went back to working on the book. He kissed her shoulder and Lily kept going. When he got another email from his mom with the information for the event, he shook his head. "Of course she doesn't bother to tell me that part," he said sarcastically.

"What," Lily asked.

"I'm now being forced into a speech at that event. I'm so not in the mood for it," he said.

Lily smirked. "We could just tell her we're busy that night," Lily teased.

"And never hear the end of it?" Lily smirked. "I could duck out early and fake laryngitis."

Lily shook her head. "Emerson."

He kissed her. "I could say that you're not feeling well and bail altogether," he joked.

"Just blame that one on me," Lily teased. She got a little more writing in when Emerson got up.

"Where are you going?"

"Food," he teased as Lily slid out of the chaise and opted to sit in the shade a while.

When Emerson came out with chicken Caesar salad for each of them, Lily smirked. He handed her a glass of peach sangria and slid a beer out of his pocket.

"Beer?"

He smirked and nodded. They had their lunch then opted to go for a walk. "We going down to the other side," Lily teased.

"No." She smirked.

"Emerson, it's not like we're gonna get killed walking down the other beach."

"We aren't. I'm not pushing our luck being over there."

"Fine," Lily said as he smirked and kissed her, pulling her into his arms. They walked, then wandered through the water a little, then turned and made their way back towards the beach house.

By the time they made it to dinner, Lily was 3 chapters into the new book and Emerson was grilling. "What are we doing tomorrow," Lily asked.

"I may have to go in for a quick meeting, but after that, whatever you want. Why," he asked.

"Kinda need a dress for the party at your mom and dad's."

"You have a few already."

"What?"

"At the house. There's a bunch. I have to go to charity stuff all the time."

"Emerson."

"What? Did you think you'd seriously have to go out and get a dress?"

"Kinda," Lily replied.

"We can look through what's already there and see if you need to. If you do, go for it," Emerson said as she smirked.

"I get that you think that I'm being ridiculous."

"You have dresses and stuff for all the signings. You have something for the press stuff. There are dresses in there, but if you want something new then go with Addy," Emerson said.

"You sure," Lily asked.

"Want me to come," he asked.

"Addy needs to look at wedding dresses. I don't want to add that to it," Lily said.

"Then you and I go. Either that or I can get dresses sent over for you to choose from sexy. Up to you."

"Do you want to come or do you want me to take Addy?"

"She's kinda going to the same party. Carter emailed me to let me know."

Lily shook her head. "I guess I can go with her."

"And I get a fashion show when you're back. I know y'all are gonna end up coming back with more than one dress."

"I only need one Emerson. You know me. I don't need much."

He smirked. "Just me?" Lily nodded.

Chapter 14

They finished dinner and Lily curled up on the chaise again and kept writing. "What," he asked as he noticed her staring into the waves as they lapped at the pristine white sand. He shook his head, poured them each a glass of wine and put them on the table beside her, sliding onto the chaise behind her. "You alright," he asked. Lily nodded.

"Trying to write while it's in my brain," she said as he handed her a glass of wine. "Thank you."

He kissed her neck and then down her shoulder.

"Babe."

"Yes handsome husband." He smirked and slid his arms around her.

"Are you okay?"

Lily nodded. "I had an idea for the book and I wanted to put it down before I forgot," she said.

"You okay," he asked. Lily nodded. He kissed her and snuggled her into her arms. When he saw what she was writing, he almost questioned it, but he knew better.

"Come inside with me?"

Lily smirked, nodded and he took the glasses inside with him as she followed, putting her laptop on the charger. He handed Lily her glass and they curled up on the sofa, just as they both heard thunder. "Good timing," Lily said as he snuggled her to him.

He kissed her. "How much did you get done?"

"Couple chapters. I got a little distraction today that kind of set me back a bit," Lily teased.

"A good distraction though?"

Lily nodded and kissed him. "Emerson."

"Wife."

"What do you want to do now since we can't go for a walk on the beach, and we can't really go anywhere?" He smirked. He got up, flipped on the gas fireplace, grabbed blankets and pillows and flipped on Casablanca.

"You coming to sit," he asked as he went and got them each another glass of wine and some popcorn. He slid under the blankets with her and slid his arm around her. "Well," he asked.

"And he thinks on his feet." He kissed her and snuggled her as they both took a sip of wine.

By the time the movie was over, they were alone. Complete peace and quiet, no interruptions and nobody to see what they were up to. She smirked and looked at him. "I know that look Emerson. What are you up to?"

He kissed her, leaning into her arms and devouring her lips until he felt her leg slide around his. He pulled the blanket up and curled her other leg around his hip. "Wife of mine," he said as he kissed down her neck.

"Husband."

He kissed her. "We could still go outside if you want to," he said with a smirk. She shook her head and he almost laughed.

"Emerson."

"What?"

"Flip the fireplace off." He smirked and kissed her, flipped it off then picked her up and carried her upstairs to the main bedroom.

He leaned her onto the bed as he heard the rain hitting the upstairs balcony. "I can shut it," he said.

Lily shook her head and pulled him to her. "Leave it. It's kinda relaxing," Lily said.

He smirked and kissed her. "You warm enough?"

Lily kissed him. When he leaned into her arms, she curled around him like she was quicksand and he was melting and sinking into her arms. He kicked his shoes off, peeled hers off and pulled the faux fur throw blanket on top of them. They were making out until he peeled his jeans off, kicking them to the floor. He pulled her shirt off, slid her shorts off and peeled his shirt off, throwing that and her bikini onto the floor.

"Wife." Lily kissed him.

"Husband." He kissed her again, devouring her lips until he could feel her toes curling into knots.

Just as he was about to make his move, her phone went off. Lily didn't let go of Emerson and didn't break the kiss. He kept going and when his phone went off again, he wanted to stop, but Lily wouldn't let him. When his phone went off a second time, Lily kissed him until they were making love again. It was pure passion. There was no intensity. It was just making love. Neither of them cared about phones or the outside world. What mattered was the two of them. When she curled into his arms, and they cuddled up under the blankets, he looked over at his phone and saw 5 missed calls from Carter and two from Addy.

He called and Carter sounded way too scared. Like something had happened that was terrifying. "What's wrong," Emerson asked.

"Dude, we've been trying to call you for an hour," Carter said.

"Phones were spotty during the storm. What's wrong," Emerson asked yet again.

"Is Lily with you," he heard Addy ask.

"She's right here. What's wrong?" He heard Carter walk over to Addy as her voice started getting louder.

"I need Lily," Addy said.

He put the phone on speaker. "What's wrong," Lily asked.

"I'm at the hospital."

Lily shook her head. "We were in a freaking car accident. I lost it," Addy said.

Lily shook her head and covered her mouth in shock.

"Which hospital," Emerson asked.

"St. Francis," Carter replied.

"We'll be there in a few," Emerson said.

"Let me know when you get here. I'll come get y'all from the waiting room."

Emerson got up and Lily shook her head. "What," he asked. Lily shook her head. She got up, slid her jeans and a shirt on with a hoodie on top to cover her head.

When she looked at Emerson, she almost wanted to laugh.

He was in his beat-up blue jeans, tee and a red hoodie with his sneakers. He handed Lily the cell phones and her purse and they went to head out.

"Sir," his security said.

"St. Francis. Carter and Addy."

"I'll get the SUV."

They came outside, hopped in, and got to the hospital as fast as they could. When they pulled into the ER, Emerson and Lily headed inside and security parked the SUV, waiting on them. Within minutes, they were at Addy and Carter's sides. "What in the hell," Emerson said as he saw Carter with stitches and bandages.

"Tell me what happened," Lily asked as she took Addy's hand.

"We got a green light, went through the intersection and this truck comes out of nowhere and hit us," Addy said.

"Did he take off?"

Addy nodded. Lily shook her head.

"Are you alright," Lily asked.

"We were alright. We were happy."

"I know. What matters is that you two are alright. Everything else we can fix."

"But…"

"Addy, you can still try. We always wanted to have them together anyway," Lily said. Seeing Addy with a bandage on her forehead, a bandage on her arm and bruises was so very unlike her. Lily sat with Addy and tried to calm her down, reminding her of how many miscarriages that she'd had. When she knew Addy was calmed down, she checked on Carter and Emerson.

"You seriously think it is," Emerson asked.

"What," Lily asked as Emerson slid his arm around her and snuggled her to him.

"Carter thinks it might've been Zack."

"I swear, I saw him and said silently for him not to run the light. Honestly, the guy looked pissed as all get out," Carter said as Lily made him sit down.

"Probably because the cops gave him a warning and served the cease and desist. At least y'all are alright. The car can be replaced. Y'all can't," Emerson said.

Lily shook her head. "If it was him, I will rip…"

Emerson covered her mouth. "He'll be handled," Emerson said.

"When are y'all allowed to go home," Lily asked.

"Probably tomorrow. As long as we're good and someone doesn't flip out."

"I'll send security over with the SUV to get you both home. If you want, you can stay at the house so you have someone there just in case," Emerson said.

"We'll be fine I think. May take you up on the ride home when we can go," Carter said. Emerson nodded and Lily gave Carter a gentle hug then kissed a sleeping Addy's forehead. She headed out with Emerson and when they hopped into the SUV, Emerson spilled what he wanted to say.

"You can't say you're gonna whoop Zack's butt. Let the police handle it."

"Emerson, if it was him, I'm telling the dang cops."

He kissed her. "Breathe."

"Emerson, if he…"

He kissed her again. "They're alright. Nothing time won't heal. They'll both be alright."

Lily shook her head and he slid her closer to him as they made their way back to the beach house. "Can we drive past his beach house to check," Lily asked.

Emerson shook his head. "Yes Miss Lily," his security said. When they saw Zack's truck with a banged-up bumper, she looked at Emerson.

"And you're thinking that it wasn't him why," Lily asked.

"Babe, let the cops handle it."

They got back to the beach house and Lily shook her head. She hopped out and walked into the house with Emerson right behind her. "Lily." She ignored him. "Lily, stop," he said as he pulled her to him.

"If it was, then what?"

He kissed her. "Babe, the cops will handle it. Like you said to them, they're still alright. They're okay. Shook up, but alright. Breathe," he said.

"Why? Why would he do that to them," Lily asked.

He pulled her to him, wrapping his arms around her. "Because he's an idiot. Maybe he thought it was us. We never know babe. We can call the cops, but they've already talked to Carter and Addy. They talked to them when they got to the ER."

Lily shook her head and he walked her upstairs. He got changed for bed and saw her staring out the balcony door, watching the rain. He walked over, shirtless and slid her shirt and hoodie off.

"Come to bed," he said.

Lily shook him off. He hung up the hoodie, threw the shirt into the laundry and walked over to her. "Babe, we can't fix this. Come to bed."

"Emerson, stop." He shook his head, picked her up, carried her to bed and handed her a t-shirt, pulling her jeans off.

"Neither one of us can change this. We can't fix it. The cops can. It'll be alright."

Lily shook her head. "Why her," Lily asked.

He took a deep breath, slid his jeans off and slid into the bed, sliding her into his arms. "Babe, she is now going through what you went through. It happened. We can't fix this, and we can't change anything. It's alright."

"It's not."

He kissed her. "He'll be handled. I promise you that. You and I have our own stuff to handle," Emerson said.

"Such as?"

He kissed her. "Such as your birthday, planning for mom's event, the book stuff. All of it."

"I feel bad even thinking about going to your mom's."

He kissed her. "We'll figure it out. I'll get dresses sent over to the house. If Addy does stay, you two can look at them. If not, you can always bring her over and have a day just the two of you."

"Or," Lily asked.

"Or I could just go with you to look," he replied.

Lily looked at him. "Up to you. You have a meeting or something don't you?"

"I messaged my assistant to move it a few days to give them time to recover. I don't want him rushing into the office."

"Are you gonna come with me then," Lily asked as she snuggled in a little closer.

"Depends. Do I get to pick the dress?"

Lily smirked. "Depends. Are you gonna choose something sexy or classy?"

"Something that makes you look beautiful. Something where you have all the confidence in the world."

Lily smirked and he kissed her, cradling her face in his hands. One kiss led to them curled up in bed. "I love you. You know that right," he asked.

Lily nodded. "I love you too," Lily said.

"No stress. We can look, and if we don't find anything, we look somewhere else. Babe, I promise you that everything will be alright. We can get the dress anywhere. We can get them brought in if we don't find anything. No stressing."

Lily nodded. He knew how much she hated dress shopping. He also knew that without Addy, she was never gonna find anything.

"How dressy is the party?"

He smirked. "Your birthday or the charity event?"

Lily shook her head with a smirk. "Emerson."

"Tux."

She took a deep breath. "Do we have anything red at the house?"

"There's silver, one or two red ones then a few black. The red ones are more signing level though."

"Then we're going," Lily said.

He nodded and kissed her. "Do you want to look yourself or get some sent over?"

She smirked. "I'll get them sent." Lily almost laughed. He knew that she didn't want to spend all day looking, and either did he.

"You sure you can take time off?"

He kissed her. "I'm taking time off with my wife. Anything major fine, but beyond that, everything can wait."

Lily shook her head. "Determined?" He kissed her. She knew how he felt. How he'd always felt. Everything else could wait, so long as it wasn't an emergency.

The next morning, Emerson woke up and Lily wasn't in bed. He shook his head, pulled his joggers on and walked downstairs to see her coming in from the water with his security keeping an eye out. "What time did she head out," Emerson asked as he came outside.

"An hour or two. She was sitting out here for a bit doing writing, then went into the water to swim. She's okay though. She just wanted to relax a little."

"No power walk on the beach?"

His security shook his head. Emerson grabbed a towel and walked out to her, wrapping her up. "What are you doin up," Lily asked.

"Bigger question. What are you doing out here," Emerson asked.

"Opted to go for a swim. Addy messaged. They are staying today. Carter passed out and bonked his head last night. They're in the same room, but they're keeping him to make sure he's alright," Lily said.

"Come inside," he said. Lily shook her head and Emerson's phone buzzed in his pocket. He answered and looked at Lily, grabbing her hand and walking her inside.

"What does this mean," Emerson said as Lily dried off and sat down beside him on the chairs by the counter.

"Okay...well, we sort of noticed last night when we were on the way back from the hospital. She was suspicious of him, but we weren't sure," Emerson said as Lily looked at him.

"Will do officer."

Emerson hung up and Lily looked at him. "And," Lily asked.

"They saw the damage and saw the paint on Carter's truck. They got the information from us yesterday and they want to talk to us about it," Emerson said.

"I guess we aren't shopping," Lily teased.

"They're bringing dresses to the house. I don't want us here when we finish with the police." Lily nodded.

She went to walk upstairs and Emerson grabbed her hand. "Babe." She walked up the stairs, breaking away from him and went and had a hot shower. Just as she was about to step out, he took her hand and tried to get her to step back in. She broke away from him and walked into the bedroom. When he stepped out, she was dressed and pulling her hair into a ponytail. "Babe."

She looked up at him. "Yep."

He kissed her. "You okay?"

"I told you," Lily said.

He shook his head and tried to hug her but she wouldn't. "Lily."

"He did it because he thought that it was my truck. Emerson, don't doubt me."

He kissed her. "I didn't. That's why I texted my lawyer. He passed the information to the police. It's done." Lily shook her head.

"If he did this to get back at us..."

Emerson pulled her into his arms and hugged her with nothing between them but his towel. "Let the police handle it."

"I will seriously..."

Emerson kissed her again. "No you won't."

Lily shook her head and walked downstairs. Emerson shaved, got dressed and packed up what they'd brought with them. When he went downstairs, Lily was on the deck.

"Where's her truck," Emerson asked.

"Took it back to the house. I'll get the SUV ready. I take it we're going to the main house?"

Emerson nodded, made omelets, grabbed some bacon and warmed it up then poured two coffees and took it outside, sitting it on the table.

"Come eat and we'll head over," Emerson said.

Lily took a deep breath and got up, grabbing her plate. "Lily, please just sit down," he said as he sat her plate back on the table. She shook her head and sat down. She ate in silence. "You do realize that you kicking his butt would put you in a cell beside him right?"

"Emerson, he did it because he was getting back at us. What do you want me to do? Pretend that it didn't happen?"

Emerson shook his head. "Breathe."

"How?"

"He'll get what's coming to him in spades babe. I promise you that."

Lily shook her head, finished breakfast and her coffee, and went to get up. "What are you doing," he asked.

"Dishes." She got her dishes and went inside, putting the dishes into the washer. When he came in and put his dishes in, Lily almost wanted to step out of the kitchen.

"The bag is already in the SUV. We can leave now if that's what you want."

Lily nodded and he pulled her into his arms. "Promise me that you don't threaten to kick his butt."

Lily shook her head. He almost laughed, sliding his arm around her. "I love you."

"I love you too. Just...let's just get this overwith." Emerson nodded and kissed her.

They locked up and left to head over to the police station. They walked in, went straight into the officer's room, and went through what had happened since the beginning. The more they talked, the more it felt like Lily had let all the anger go. When they finished and headed out, they got back into the SUV and headed back to the main house. Lily curled up in Emerson's arms in the back seat. "You okay," he asked.

Lily nodded. "I didn't know anyone that could be that callous. That he could be that vengeful."

Emerson snuggled her, not saying anything. He knew better. He could've let a rant go faster than she could imagine. Instead, he just said a quiet prayer, thanking his lucky stars that he had been there that night on the beach when she'd taken off from Zack's house. That he'd been the one to find her. If he hadn't, he was petrified thinking of what could've happened to her.

He knew at that moment that Zack was gone from their lives. He didn't have to watch over his shoulder, and either did Lily. When they pulled through the gates and made it to the front door, Emerson hopped out, got her door for her and they headed inside. When she saw the housekeeper coming down the steps, Lily looked at Emerson.

"The dresses are upstairs. Whenever you're ready, head on up," the housekeeper said. Lily smirked. Emerson kissed her, went and got them each a sweet tea and went upstairs. When he came into the bedroom, Lily was looking through the dresses then stopped and saw one of the price tags.

"What," Emerson asked as he put the sweet tea down on the bedside table.

"Do you realize what that tag says?"

"Yep. It is kind of nice. It'd look amazing on you," Emerson said.

"It's an $8000 dress."

"Nice," Emerson said as he smirked and handed her one.

"Try it," he said as Lily shook her head.

"I don't need one that badly," Lily said.

"Woman, put the thing on. Let me see," he said. Lily shook her head, got changed and slid the dress on while he did the back of it up. She turned to face him and he got a grin ear to ear.

"Sexy, classy and hot. Perfect. Okay, try the silver one," he said.

"Emerson."

"You'll need a few. Just try it." He took a sip of his sweet tea, checking through emails when she walked over and sat down on his lap so he'd zip the back up.

"You're taunting Lily."

"And," she asked as she stood up and faced him.

"Damn. You may not make it out of the bedroom in that one."

"And," Lily asked as she looked at him.

"Closet. Next." He unzipped and she tried on 5 others. Every dress was sexier than the last. When they got to the last one that she liked, she slid it on and when she walked into the bedroom, he saw the slit. He saw the way too skinny straps, her leg, the back completely bare of material and the thin line of sparkle down her spine.

"If you wear that, you may be pregnant before the signing stuff starts."

"Perfect for the event then," Lily said.

"You wear that, I'm warning you now, you're gonna end up in my room at my mom and dad's in nothing but the g-string I know you'd wear to taunt me with."

"Still like it. It's in black and red," Lily said.

He shook his head and came into the closet with her. "I wasn't joking."

"I know," Lily teased as she slid it off. He kissed her, hanging up the dress and sliding it onto the rack.

"And what did you..."

He kissed her, devouring her lips and picked her up, sitting her on the counter. "Emerson."

"You started it," he teased as he peeled off the barely there lace panties so she was naked in his arms. He unzipped his jeans and kissed her. She slid off the counter and went to grab her robe when his arms slid around her waist. "What are you doin?"

"Answering your phone."

He shook his head and Lily grabbed his cell phone and handed it to him. He pulled her to him and answered. "Yes," Emerson said.

"That paperwork from the lawyer is here. Do you want me to send it over for Lily to sign," his secretary asked.

"Please," Emerson said.

"Yes sir," his secretary said as he hung up and kissed Lily, throwing his phone onto the chair.

"What," Lily asked.

He kissed her and leaned into her arms, leaning her onto the bed. "Now you're taunting intentionally."

"I mean, you were the one that said to try them on," Lily teased. He shook his head and devoured her lips. He slid her across the bed and kicked his jeans off. "Emerson."

He kissed her again and pulled her legs around his hips. "Wife."

"You sure you don't want me to try another one on?" He kissed her and shook his head.

"I swear you do it intentionally," he said as he kissed down her neck and was already past the point of being turned on. They had sex. It wasn't romance, it wasn't joking around and it wasn't passion. It was carnal. Neither of them could even think to let go or stop. He kissed her again, devouring her lips as he kept going until his body couldn't hold back. Lily's legs were almost shaking, and his heart was racing. It was as if the heat had overheated the bedroom. Like they were surrounded by a wall of fire. When he leaned onto his back, he pulled her with him and Lily smirked.

"What are you smirking at sexy wife?"

"Maybe that dress is good for the party."

"I'm not joking. You wear that, you're never making it downstairs. You won't even make it out of the house."

"Perfect," Lily teased.

He shook his head. "Lily."

"I can wear it on my birthday."

He shook his head and snuggled her closer. "Babe, if you start that, you're gonna seriously end up pregnant before we even leave for your book tour."

"Promises, promises," Lily joked as she kissed him.

"Wife."

"Husband," she said.

"Those dresses are for you and me nights."

Lily smirked. "And what about the ones I haven't tried on yet?"

He kissed her. "I may need a power nap before you try them on." Lily smirked and he snuggled her to him.

She pulled a blanket up a little and he flipped the bedroom fan on. "Overheated," Lily asked.

He nodded. "And it's all your fault."

Lily kissed him. She went and slid out of bed, cleaned up a little, and went and tried on the last 3 dresses. One was technically perfect for an event with Emerson's mom and when she came out to show Emerson, he was out cold. Lily smirked, looking a little more, came out and slid a blanket over him and went in to try on the last 2. Every single dress was perfect. She loved all of them, but she didn't think that she should even think about all of them. She slid out of the dress and sat down, pulling on a pair of jeans and a tee. When she came into the bedroom, he was staring at her.

"By the way, yes I know the prices and yes you're keeping them."

"Emerson, there's enough dresses there for a dang down payment on a house."

"And you're keeping them."

She shook her head. "I don't need all of them."
"Considering that I have 12 events between now and Christmas, then that movie premiere before Valentine's Day, yeah you do. Just don't wear that one to my mom and dad's. I beg you."

"Maybe." He shook his head and reached out a hand, pulling her to him.

"Where are you going?"

"Figured I'd get dressed in case Carter and…"

He kissed her. "Nope. They're at the hospital tonight."

"I can get writing in."

"Nope."

"Emerson, I get that you're all hot and bothered, but we can't stay in bed all day." He kissed her again and leaned into her arms.

"We can do whatever we want to," he teased.

Lily kissed him and he kissed down her neck.

"Emerson."

"Wife."

"I want to get writing done."

"Nope."

"Emerson."

He kissed her again. "Stay."

Lily kissed him. "Come downstairs with me. I thought you had paperwork coming or something."

He shook his head, kissed her, and got up. He cleaned up and pulled his jeans on with a t-shirt and walked downstairs with Lily. "Sir, some documents from your office showed. They said to ask you both to sign them and send them in," his security said. Lily smirked and Emerson took her hand, walking her into the office and closing and locking the door behind them.

"What," Lily asked.

He slid the papers out of the envelope and put them on the desk, sitting down and pulling Lily into his lap. "Sign them."

"Why?"

"Read and sign," he said again. She looked at them and saw that it was changing the deed to every piece of property that he owned.

"Emerson, why," Lily asked.

"Like I said, it's all ours. Not just mine."

Lily shook her head. "And that document from Carter is in there. The lawyer got it for you to sign."

"Why do you need me to sign them all?"

"Because if something ever happens to me, they're yours. If something happens to us, they're ours. Period."

"It's too much Emerson. I can't do this."

He handed Lily the pen. "I want you, not the stupid property."

He kissed her. "And that's why your name is gonna be on the deed with mine."

He kissed her and she shook her head, signing the papers then signed the one for her place for Carter.

"We have to go over to the bank too," he said.

"What for?"

"To get your bank card, credit cards and to deposit that check sitting in your purse."

"You do realize that all of this is nuts right?"

He kissed her. "Like I said before. All I ever wanted was you. Just you. Nothing else. I don't care what happens. If you're not with me, I don't want any of it."

Lily kissed him and sat back down on his lap. "Why do you have all this property anyway?"

"Because I wanted us to be able to go wherever we want to. If we don't have to be in a hotel, we have peace and quiet and safety. That's all I want."

"We're gonna be at some of them on the book tour. Wherever we don't have a place, we stay in a hotel with major security."

"Why?"

He kissed her. "Because I said so," he teased as he snuggled her back into his lap.

"Can we just go and get it overwith? I don't need 2 months away."

He kissed her. "Birthday, charity thing then we head out."

"Emerson."

He kissed her. "We still have to figure out the holidays."
She shook her head and he kissed her.

By the time her birthday came, she was more than willing
to just ignore it, but Emerson was determined to do
something special. She woke up and did a workout and
when she came upstairs, there were not only flowers and
candles, but the bed had a breakfast tray and a gift on it.
Lily shook her head and Emerson came up behind her,
sliding his arms around her.

"About time," he teased.

He kissed her shoulder and she turned to face him.
"Emerson."

"Wife. Happy birthday," he said as he kissed her.

"Remember when I said not to go overboard?" He nodded
and sat her on the bed. He took the cover off her breakfast
and saw eggs benedict and bacon with fresh peaches for
two.

"Your favorite breakfast," he teased. Lily shook her head
and they curled up together and had breakfast in bed.

"And," he asked.

"I like. Honestly, I'm fine if this is all we do."

He kissed her. "You don't get off that easy this year wife."
He handed Lily the box and put the tray on the table by
the chair she loved to write in.

"Emerson."

"Mm."

"I love you."

"Love you more beautiful." She opened the card:

> *To the woman who has always been my forever. A day to celebrate you. You're worth every second. Open the gift. I get that you hate celebrating but just humor me.*

Lily looked at him and he slid the card onto the bedside table. "Open." She shook her head and opened the box, seeing a note:

> *Look in the one place that most women dream of having. PS it's not in the truck.*

Lily shook her head. "Emerson."

"Go."

"You made a treasure hunt?" He nodded with a smirk as he took a gulp of his coffee. Lily shook her head and got up, walking into the closet and saw a suit bag. She opened it and saw a white satin version of the dress that he'd drooled over the day prior.

"Now, this is a gift for you. Not me," Lily teased.

"True. Look on the hanger." She saw another note:

> *We have a morning ritual. The gym, breakfast than this.*

Lily shook her head with a smirk and walked into the bathroom. Right beside her bathrobe was a little blue box with a white ribbon. He walked in, leaning against the door frame and watched her open it. When she saw the diamond earrings, she looked at him. "Emerson."

"What? You're not allowed to sparkle when you're doing signings?"

"It's a little much."

"Nope." She saw the note attached to them:

> *We never get in there, except for rare*
> *opportunities. Normally keys are involved.*

Lily shook her head. "Emerson."

He smirked and kissed her. "What?"

"Tell me you didn't." He smirked and followed her outside to the garage. When she saw her truck and an SUV that had keys hanging on the side mirror, she shook her head.

"What's this?"

"It's electric. Easy for going back and forth to the beach or appointments. We have a charger for it too."

"Emerson."

He smirked. "Yours. Nobody else other than maybe me will be driving it."

"Emerson, this is way too much."

He kissed her. "Just say thank you and read the note."

"All of this is too much," Lily said as she read it:

I've loved you since the first time I saw you. Where did we sit that first time that I got you to the house?

She shook her head and he took the keys and the note from the SUV and walked inside with her. When she walked into the TV room, he smirked and she saw boxes laid out in a heart shape with a single note in the middle:

I went overboard, but you deserve every one. Open them, then you get your last present in bed.

Lily smirked and shook her head. He kissed her, sliding down onto the sofa beside her. "This is still too much," Lily said.

"Want me to take the last one back?"

"Funny." He kissed her. She saw the fancy pen for autographing books on the tour, a new iPhone, a necklace, AirPods Pro earbuds, a bracelet with a single quill charm on it, an apple watch and the last one was a note:

You are my world. You always have been, and you always will be. Come upstairs.

She smirked and he picked her up and carried her upstairs to their bedroom. He sat her on the bed and leaned into her arms. "Do you like your birthday surprises part one?" Lily smirked.

"Part one?"

"Yep. This afternoon is part two, tonight is part three."

Lily kissed him. "I think you might've gone overboard." He kissed her, devouring her lips and peeled her workout shorts, lacy panties and the rest of her clothes off. "Emerson."

He kissed her and kicked his jeans off. "What," he asked as he almost cradled her in his arms and slid her legs tightly around his hips.

"What are you up to," Lily asked.

He kissed her again and they had sex. It was passion, love and toe-curling sex that had her body almost throbbing. He picked her up and carried her into the bathroom, flipping the hot water on and continuing in the shower. The mirrors were fogged up and neither of them even cared. When he almost slid to the floor with her still wrapped around him, she finally said something.

"Bench," Lily said.

He sat down on the bench in the shower. When she tried to get up, he wouldn't let her. "Mine. All mine forever," he teased.

Lily kissed him. "We have..."

He devoured her lips. "Don't move."

"Emerson." He kissed her again.

"Don't," he said. She kissed him and he wrapped his arms tight around her.

"Happy Birthday beautiful," he whispered as she almost got goosebumps.

"Thank you handsome." He kissed her again and she got up. She washed her hair and washed his for him. He teased as she rinsed out the shampoo. "Emerson."

He kissed her breast and pulled her back to him. "What," he asked. Lily kissed him.

"We're gonna run out of hot water."

"Don't care," he said as he kissed her again. He smirked and Lily went and flipped the water off, handing Emerson a warmed towel, and sliding the other around her. He smirked and wrapped his arms around her from behind as she freshened up and combed her hair. He kissed her shoulder. "Wife."

"Husband."

"Ready for part 2?"

"Depends." He smirked and kissed her neck.

"Just put on something comfy."

"Where are we going?"

"Spa." Lily looked at him.

"Are you coming with me?" He nodded. Lily kissed him and she finished getting ready, intentionally wearing a sundress.

"Wife."

"What," she asked as he watched her in her closet and leaned on the door frame.

"You're seriously wearing that?" Lily nodded. He shook his head. He kissed her again, slid his jeans on with his t-shirt and dried his hair. Just as he was about to shave, she shook her head.

"What," he teased.

"Nope."

"Lily, I love you, but I'm shaving."

"I like it spiky."

"I bet you do. Still shaving," he joked. Lily grabbed his razor and walked away.

"Lily."

"For one day."

"Fine. Just give me the razor." He kissed her, slid it from her hand and put it in the drawer, putting her favorite cologne on. When he came into the bedroom, she was checking emails. He walked over, picked her up and walked down the steps.

"Emerson, put me down."

"Nope." He headed out the front door, sat her in the backseat of the SUV and slid in beside her as his security took them to the spa. "You are such..."

He kissed her. "The most amazing husband in the world."

"That too." He smirked and kissed her.

Chapter 15

They got to the spa and went to change. When Lily came out with a robe on, and saw him in the same, she smirked. "What are we doing?"

"Massages, then manicure and pedicure. If you're signing all those books, you're gonna want your nails done."

"You don't have to do all of this. You know that right," Lily asked. He nodded.

"Happy birthday beautiful." She kissed him and they were walked into the massage room.

By the time they were massaged into bliss, they got up and went down for manicures and pedicures. "I may just need a power nap," Lily teased.

He smirked. "A day with no stress and just relaxation. That's all I wanted for you. You deserve a little time to take care of you," he said as they got started on both of them. When they brought Emerson and Lily each a peach mimosa, she shook her head. He kissed her.

"Happy birthday wife." Lily smirked.

"I'm definitely liking the pampering."

"Good. You needed it as much as I did."

They finished at the spa then went and had a quiet lunch alone. They walked around a little, stopping to intentionally get Lily new lingerie then they headed back to the house. "Are we allowed to just relax for a while," Lily asked.

"Power nap for a while?" Lily nodded. "Sure," Emerson said as he slid his arm around her shoulder and snuggled her to him as they headed back to the house. When they got there, Emerson walked her inside and she saw roses and lilies and birthday presents.

"Did you?"

Emerson shook his head. "There were a few deliveries. Here are the cards," the housekeeper said as Lily went through them. Some were from family, some from friends and one from Emerson. She felt like Miss America. Way too many flowers, but they were beautiful. "Alright beautiful. Power nap before the big dinner," Emerson teased.

They headed upstairs and she saw her dress hung up on the door frame of her closet. "At least it's not the white dress," Lily teased.

"Nope. I don't know that you can wear any of them outside the house," he joked. Lily kissed him and she slid her shoes off and sat down on the bed. She went through her emails, seeing a bunch of birthday messages, then one from the publisher:

> *Your book hit #1 on the New York Times Bestseller list. And on your birthday. Congrats!*

Lily showed Emerson the email. "Babe."

"How is that even possible," Lily asked.

"That's huge."

"Emerson."

He kissed her. "And you thought nobody would like it. Holy crap," Emerson said. He picked her up and practically spun her around. "Baby, this is amazing."

She kissed him. "How on earth did I manage to pull that off," she said still stunned.

He kissed her. "Because you had inspiration." He shook his head.

"I need..."

"We can tell everyone tonight." Lily nodded and he kissed her as they curled up on the bed.

By the time everyone showed that evening for dinner, Lily had a perma-grin. Emerson shared the news with everyone then they sat down to relax and have dinner. She never wanted a party, so having dinner was the option that was left. They had seafood, steaks and a little of everything that Lily loved. The meal was topped off with a chocolate silk pie. It was her favorite and was quickly becoming Emerson's too. She opened gifts from her folks, Emerson's folks and from Addy and Carter who were finally feeling up to going out. All of it was more than she could hope for. From the new suitcase, to the new laptop that Emerson had snuck into the pile, all of it was way too much. She gave everyone a copy of the new book and signed them for everyone then little by little, everyone started heading out.

When they were finally alone, Emerson walked her upstairs. "What," Lily asked as he slid his arms around her.

"I love you," he said as he snuggled her to him.

"I love you too handsome. Thank you for all of this today."
He kissed her and hugged her.

"You deserved all of it. You don't even know how much
you are loved do you," he teased.

"A little," Lily said. He kissed her, holding her face in his
hands.

"I love you more than you even know. I always will," he
said as he kissed her.

"I love you too," Lily said as he hugged her.

"Bed?"

"I'm exhausted," Lily said. He peeled her out of her
sundress and she slid his shirt on and curled up in bed.

"And she steals the shirt," he teased.

"Yep."

"Lily."

"Husband. Get into bed and stop complaining," Lily teased
as he shook his head and kicked his jeans off, snuggling
into bed with her.

"How was your birthday sexy," he asked.

"Relaxing, fun, and exactly what I knew you were planning.
It was nice to have everyone here without the stress."

"That's what you wanted," he said as he snuggled in tight
to her.

The next morning, Lily woke up just as Emerson was pulling his joggers on. "Workout without me," Lily asked.

"I was just about to wake you up," he teased. Lily smirked and he kissed her. "Coming?" Lily nodded and got up, slid into her joggers and a tank top, freshened up and put her hair in a ponytail and walked downstairs with him. He handed Lily a water from the fridge and they made their way downstairs. "You do know you could've slept in right?"

Lily nodded. "If we are gonna be on a book tour then I need to do a workout."

He shook his head and she stretched out and tried to get a workout in without taunting Emerson. He watched her stretch out and shook his head, trying not to trip over his feet on the treadmill. "You okay," Lily asked.

"Taunting me intentionally," he joked.

"Trying not to." He shook his head and Lily got going on her actual workout, opting to do her yoga stretches facing the other way.

"Still taunting," he joked as Lily finished her stretches.

"And your mind needs to be washed out with soap."

"True." He laughed and Lily shook her head, finishing her yoga and sitting down to watch Emerson.

"What are you doing today," Lily asked.

"I have to go in and drop off that paperwork and grab a few things so we have them when we head out. We're getting the itinerary too," he said.

"Good. I'm thinking that I might just hang out and pack," Lily said.

"Kinda being done already. Anything extra, just let Sara know."

"Sara as in your housekeeper?"

He smirked. "Yes beautiful."

Lily shook her head. "We do have free days right," Lily asked.

"A couple, but not many. They were trying to get things done so you were back in time for thanksgiving."

Lily smirked. "Are they daytime or evenings?"

"A little of each from what I originally saw. The passes for them are sold out for the evening ones and almost sold out for the day signings." Lily shook her head and leaned back on the steps. He finished his workout and walked over to her, leaning into her arms, and kissed her, grabbing her water and guzzling it down in what seemed like one gulp.

He kissed her again and she shook her head. "Upstairs?" Lily shook her head. She went into the kitchen and saw breakfast being plated.

"Thank you," Lily said.

"Most welcome. I have your clothes for the tour packed, steamed and clean for you. If there's anything else you need me to add in, just let me know," Sara said.

"Thank you. I appreciate it," Lily said.

"Saves you a little time," Sara replied. They had breakfast, cleaned up and Emerson chased Lily upstairs.

"What are you doin?" He caught her in his arms and picked her up, leaning her onto the now perfectly made bed. "Emerson."

He kissed her, devouring her lips. "What," he teased.

"You need to quit."

"Nope." He smirked and slid her shirt off. "Come with me," he said.

"What?" He pulled her to her feet and walked her into their bathroom.

"What are you doin," Lily asked. He sat her on the counter. "Don't you have work?" Emerson pulled her into his arms and wrapped her legs around him.

"I'm the boss. Nobody there to tell me I'm late," he teased as he kissed her, devouring her lips. He pulled her sports bra off and went for her shorts.

All it took was one kiss and she was having sex with him on that counter, then the shower. Neither one of them even cared that he was running late for work. All he wanted was Lily, and all she wanted was him. Lily's legs barely stopped shaking enough for her to finish her shower. She went to hop out and he kissed her shoulder, sliding his arms around her waist. "Yes," Lily asked.

"Do you want to come with me," Emerson asked.

"I thought you were just going to grab some paperwork."

"I am. Come with me." Lily shook her head.
"Emerson, you're not gonna be there that long. It's…"

He kissed her. "Come with me." Lily shook her head and he kissed her.

"You can go in. I'm just gonna stay here and relax. I promise."
"Come with me," he replied.

"Emerson, I can chill and work on the book. It's fine."

"Lily, I want you there with me. Please?"

"What are you worried about," Lily asked.

"Come with me." She shook her head and he kissed her again.

"Why?"

"Because I don't want him showing up here when I'm not here."

Lily kissed him. "If you're that worried, say so," Lily said as he sat her up on the counter.

"Secondly, I get out of the office faster when you're with me," he teased.

"Emerson."

"I don't want to get dragged into a meeting. I want us to have some time alone before you have to do the book tour stuff."

"Fine, but I'm bringing my laptop."

He smirked and kissed her. "Done," he teased.

"Coffee?"

"Okay," he replied.

"Then fine. I'll come with you," Lily said.

He kissed her. "Nice negotiations sexy." He kissed her again, devouring her lips and wrapped her legs around his hips. "Emerson."

He smirked. "What," he teased.

Lily kissed him and shook her head. "Don't start. I need to be able to walk," she joked. He kissed her again and they both started to get ready. When he kissed her shoulder, she shook her head. "I know what you're doing husband." He kissed her neck.

"Which is?"

"Making sure you're actually late," Lily replied. Emerson smirked and turned her to face him.

"Think so do you?" Lily nodded. He kissed her and walked her backwards into the bedroom, leaning her onto the bed. "Then I guess I'll be late."

They curled up on the bed and he was just about to make his move when his phone went off. "Not answering," Emerson said as his arms wrapped around her. He kissed her, devouring her lips and his phone went off a second time.

"Determined," Lily joked.

He kissed her and grabbed his phone. "Yep," Emerson said.

"Sir, we have a quick meeting at 11am. Are you able to come in for it," his assistant asked. Emerson shook his head.

"We'll be there. My wife is coming with me."

"I'll get the Starbucks," his assistant said.

"Is Carter coming in?"

"He said he was. He was bringing his fiancée."

"Alright. I'll see you around 10:30." Emerson hung up with her and kissed Lily.

"We can just go," Lily said as she went to get up.

"Where are you goin?"

"Getting dressed." He shook his head and kissed her.

"It's only 8. We have time sexy wife of mine." Lily smirked and he slid his arms around her, pulling her legs back around him. Before she could say a single word, they were having sex again on their bed. She was an addiction to him. Now more than ever.

They finally made their way into the office, curled up together in the back seat. "You're staying while I'm in the meeting right?"

Lily nodded. "I'm writing. I wasn't to get a head start on it before we leave."

He kissed her. "Addy's coming."

Lily smirked. "So, while I'm thinking of it, is there any days that you know you have to be in the office?"

"One or two. They're both close to one of my places so you and Addy have somewhere safe. Most of it I'll be out there."

"Okay," Lily said as she kissed him.

"Did you tell Addy the dates?" He smirked and nodded. He kissed her again and they hung out.

When they managed to make it into the office, they were only alone a few minutes when his secretary came in with paperwork and coffees. "Good morning Miss Lily," his secretary said.

"Good morning."

Lily shook her head. "Sucking up," he teased. Lily nodded. He kissed her and sat down with her while he went through his papers.

"What," Lily asked.

"Well, one of my ideas actually happened. That is handy," he teased.

"Which one?"

"Covering costs for a battered women's shelter. Being a sponsor for them for a year. That, then we have another one to help with food issues for the homeless. All of the ideas went through," he joked.

"And," Lily asked.

"I got the woman and I got the funding for the projects. Now we just have to finish all of the signings and we get our life back," he teased.

"Then we have Christmas and Thanksgiving, then new year's eve and valentine's day."

"Sorta have plans for that last one."

"Which will be?"

"That movie premiere." Lily smirked.

He kissed Lily just as he heard Carter and Addy. Carter went into the office next to Emerson's and came over to his office. "Long time no see," Lily joked.

"I didn't know you were comin," Carter said as he gave Lily a hug.

"Someone wanted company," Lily joked. Emerson smirked and Addy came into the office. Lily gave her a hug.

"About time y'all got here," Emerson teased.

"We ready for this meeting," Carter asked.

"I guess," Emerson teased as he showed Carter the updates. Emerson kissed Lily, gave Addy a hug and they headed out to the meeting.

"How are you feeling," Lily asked.

"Tired. I still can't really believe it."

"We did hear that they think it was Zack. They arrested him or something," Lily said.

"I know. I heard. Still surprising that he would do it," Addy said.

"How are you feeling about that party tomorrow?"

"I'm gonna rest. See how I feel. I did find a dress though. Emerson sent it over."

"What color is it?"

"Dark charcoal grey. It's beautiful." Lily smirked. Emerson was past just being a good guy. He was an amazing guy. One she was lucky that she fell in love with.

"If you're not up to it tomorrow, it's fine."

Addy shook her head. "I'm coming. Still a little stunned that Emerson is letting me come out on the book stops with you. It's like once every other week, but I'm stunned he isn't gonna come."

"Realistically, he can get Carter out there with us and you. They can talk business while we do the book stuff."

By the time the meeting was over, Lily had a chapter finished and Addy was completely relaxed on Emerson's sofa. She was going through emails and looking up wedding ideas. Emerson came into the office with Carter and the two of them were laughing and cracking jokes.

"I gather the meeting went alright," Lily teased.

"Better than I could've imagined. How are you two doing," Emerson said as he leaned over and kissed Lily.

"Chapter in and Addy's doing wedding plans," Lily teased. Emerson smirked and shook his head.

"What else is on the schedule," Lily asked.

"No idea. I'll check," Emerson said as he logged into his computer.

"Crap."

"What," Carter asked.

"Two more meetings. One is the publishing end, one is the movie end," Emerson said.

"Addy and I can go do lunch," Lily said.

Emerson shook his head. "I'll get it brought in. Seafood or chicken," Emerson asked.

"Salad," Addy replied.

"Chicken Caesar for Addy. Babe?" She looked at Emerson. "Lobster salad for my woman. Carter?"

"Wrap," Carter replied as Emerson sent the lunch order to his secretary.

By the time they made it out of the office, it was close to 2pm. Lily gave Addy a hug and they all headed off. Emerson intentionally opted to go to the house. "Wife."

"Husband."

"Cannonball," he said.

"Might want to take the suit off though," Lily teased as he started sliding his suit jacket and tie off. Lily almost laughed and he kissed her.

"You're comin in with me wife."

"At least let me change out of the dress." Emerson nodded.

"Maybe," he teased.

When they got back to the house, Lily ran upstairs and slid her dress off, sliding into his favorite bikini and came downstairs. She grabbed the towels and walked outside to see Emerson already in the water. His dress pants, boxers and shirt were on the chair.

"Couldn't wait two minutes," Lily teased. He motioned for her to come closer. Lily smirked and sat down on the side of the pool in front of him. "And what did you want," Lily asked.

He pulled her into the pool and right into his arms. "Overdressed," he teased.

"I swear, I'm stitching this bikini up so you can't keep undoing it," Lily joked. He kissed her, silencing her. He pinned her against the side of the pool and undid the bikini bottoms. "Emerson." He kissed her, devouring her lips and he taunted her. He was beyond happy at that moment. He just wanted time to themselves like she did.

They had a quiet, relaxing night and they got everything together for what they needed for the book tour. "What else did we pack?"

"Sharpies, your pen, a bunch of dresses and jeans and the leather pants and tops. We're good."

"And what are you wearing?"

"Suits, dress pants, jeans, wine, jack, champagne and my razor."

Lily smirked. "So not fair," Lily said.

He kissed her. "You, my sexy, beautiful wife, are the center of attention. I'm there as your bodyguard and assistant. I'm your cheerleader."

"And," Lily asked.

"And as your husband who loves you."

Lily kissed him. "I love you. You know that right?" He nodded and kissed her.

The next day, Lily woke up and went and did a workout, and tried to figure out what she was going to wear for the party. She grabbed the shoes, putting them on her counter and the lingerie to go under it, then went through the dresses again. Part of her wanted to taunt Emerson, but since they were leaving the next morning, she opted for the classy dress with the slit that he drooled over. She put it out and came into the bedroom to see Emerson waking up. "What time did you wake up," he asked as he looked over at her, rubbing his eyes.

"6. I guess you were tired," Lily teased.

"Did you eat," he asked.

"Shake. Waited for you to get your butt out of bed," Lily teased. He motioned for her to come closer.

"What," Lily asked as she kissed him. He pulled her into bed and devoured her lips.

"Wake me up when you're going to workout."

"You were sleeping so peacefully. You needed sleep." He kissed her and leaned her onto her back, leaning on top of her.

"Wake...me...up," he said as he devoured her lips.

"Emerson."

"Wife."

"Relax. I was just figuring out what to wear tonight."

He kissed her. "The G-rated dress preferably."

"The red one."

"Lily."

She smirked. "The black heels."

He shook his head. "You're seriously asking for it," he teased.

Lily kissed him. "Come have breakfast."

"Babe."

"We're eating. We have to go to the..." He kissed her again as he peeled her t-shirt and sports bra off. She kissed him and he was about to go for her shorts when his phone went off.

"Don't move," he said.

Emerson grabbed his cell and saw 2 messages from his assistant and his phone went off again. Lily kissed him and got up while he made his call. She walked into the bathroom and showered. When she stepped out, she wrapped herself in a warm towel and freshened up when he came in behind her.

"And? Have to go back in?"

"Two meetings and a bunch of paperwork. Do you want to come with me?"

"Okay. First, is Carter in the meeting?"

"Yeah, why?"

"Tell him to drop Addy off here. We can get ready for your mom's thing," Lily said.

"Babe, please."

She shook her head. "It gives us girl time. We'll stay here."

"Come with me wife."

She shook her head. "Emerson."

He kissed her and pinned her against the counter. "Emerson."

"I want you there."

"Emerson, we're doing hair and makeup. We have to be at your mom's for 7."

"Hair and makeup are coming at 2."

"And you have meetings. It's fine. I'll stay here." He shook his head. "I love you, but I'm not going. It gives me a chance to make sure I have everything before we leave."

"Already packed and loaded. Come." She shook her head and he kissed her. "Please?"

Lily shook her head. "Fine, but I want to be back by 1." He kissed her again and showered.

Lily slid into her jeans and silky top and when she walked out of the closet, Emerson was in his suit. "Well would you look at that. All dressed and sexy," Lily teased.

"Skirt," he joked. Lily shook her head and he smirked.

"Fine, but you're behaving." She went and slid the jeans off, sliding on her skirt and grabbed her purse and laptop. She headed downstairs, went into the kitchen, and made them breakfast, intentionally letting the housekeeper relax. When Emerson came downstairs, she was plating them. She handed him a plate and coffee and sat down with him.

"You do know that I can be here on my own right," Lily said.

"After everything he's done, I just don't want you here on your own."

Lily shook her head and kissed him. "Your security is right here. We're not gonna just vanish." He kissed her.

He didn't want another fight before they left for the book tour. Either did she. They finished breakfast, headed out and grabbed coffees then made their way over to his office. "And why did I have to change," Lily asked with a smirk.

"Because," he teased. Lily shook her head and he snuggled her closer. "

What," she asked. "Because I want you. Woke up without me. Not fair," he teased as he whispered in her ear and almost gave her goosebumps. She shook her head and sipped her drink as they made their way to his office.

"You know I get absolutely no writing in when we're at your office right?"

He kissed her neck. "And," he teased.

"And I don't get anything done. I need to write handsome." He smirked and snuggled her. When they pulled up to the office building, they hopped out and went inside, heading up the elevator. They were the only ones in there, since it wasn't even 8am yet. He turned to face Lily and kissed her, devouring her lips. When the door opened, they stepped off and walked into his office. He closed and locked the door, closed the blinds, and leaned Lily against the wall, devouring her lips all over again.

"What are you up to," Lily asked as he slid the strap of her top off her shoulder.

"Making up for you not including me in the morning workout," he teased as he pulled at her panties and slid them off, sliding them into his pocket.

"Emerson." He kissed her again, wrapped her legs around him, undid his dress pants and they had sex against that wall. Hot, urgent, wanting and needing kind of sex. Her legs were almost shaking. When they stopped, she slid to her feet and kicked her heels off. "Damn," Lily said.

"You're an addiction wife."

"Back at ya husband," Lily teased as he walked into his bathroom and cleaned up.

"You forgot something," Lily said.

"Nope." She walked in there and went to grab her panties.

"Not happening," he teased. Lily shook her head and he kissed her again.

"Emerson, this is not Fifty Shades. Give me them."

"Nope."

She shook her head. "I could just go home." He kissed her and walked over to his desk, sitting down. Lily followed him and sat down on his desk.

"Lily."

"Husband." He shook his head.

"Those are kind of the papers I need for my meeting."

"Then give them back."

He kissed her, sliding them out from under her. "No. Mine."

"Next time I'm wearing jeans." He kissed her again and his hand rested on her leg. "Fine. I'm wearing the dress tonight then," Lily said as she walked and sat down on the sofa, stretching out. She flipped the lock on the door and his assistant knocked.

"Come on in," Emerson said.

Lily shook her head. "Miss Lily, good morning."

"Morning," Lily said.

"Your meeting is in 10. Did you want coffee," his assistant asked.

"I'm good. If you can grab Lily one of the lattes," Emerson asked. His assistant nodded, handed him the paperwork he needed and headed out.

"I'll meet you at home," Lily said.

He walked over to her and kissed her, devouring her lips. "Just stay. I'm not gonna be that long."

She looked at him. "Then hand them over." He shook his head and kissed her again, wiping the lipstick from his lips and went into his meeting.

Lily shook her head and her phone buzzed. "Hey Addy," Lily said.

"You went into the office with him again didn't you," Addy asked.

"Didn't have a choice. What are you up to?"

"Trying to determine how dressy I should go tonight."

"I'm doing a red dress. Little sparkle, silky and intentionally taunting my husband."

"So, the charcoal grey is alright?"

"You'll look amazing. What are you worried about?"

"Hair and makeup."

"Meet me at the house at 2. I have hair and makeup coming. We'll be fine," Lily said.

"And," Addy said.

"I tried to tell him I wanted to stay at the house and he was determined."

"He loves you. Carter is having issues. He almost left the house without even a goodbye kiss."

"Girl, breathe. We're all determined to get as much done as we can before we head out. That's all it is," Lily said trying to comfort Addy.

"Are you sure I'm not gonna be interrupting anything if I come get ready with you," Addy asked.

"I'm just getting writing in before we go. Hair and makeup is just a distraction."

When Emerson came back into the office, she could see a mile off that he was beyond stressed. "What's wrong?"

He shook his head. "I'm gonna end up being here all damn day at this rate," he said.

"Emerson, what happened?"

"Zack tried to buy the damn company."

Lily looked at him. "He what?"

"He tried to sue me for buying his damn company." Lily shook her head.

"What's the plan," Lily asked.

"Lawyers. I have to meet the lawyer here and go over the counter claim. It's gonna end up including you in it, which I don't want to do. He can kiss my butt," Emerson replied.

"Emerson."

He shook his head. "I will be a while. The lawyer isn't even coming until 12."

"Do you want me to tell your mom we can't go?"

He shook his head. "I'll find a way. I mean, you can stay if you want, but I can't guarantee that I'm gonna be home before 2."

"If you need me, call me. I'll go get Addy and we can relax and get ready. I'll get your tux out," Lily said. He closed the door and walked over, sitting down with her.

"I think he did it so I couldn't go on the book tour with you. I'm going. We know that. That's how it's gonna go. I'm gonna be in meetings all day." Lily kissed him.

"And when you get back, you get your sexy wife waiting on you."

"You sure," he asked.

Lily nodded and kissed him. "We'll be alright."

"Promise me something."

"What?"

"Wear the dress." Lily smirked.

"And how did you know I hadn't already planned to?" He shook his head and kissed her, devouring her lips, away from the prying eyes of anyone else in the office.

"I love you," he said.

"I love you too handsome. Just remember to breathe. He's an idiot and always will be. You got me all to yourself for life. Forever." He kissed her and locked his office door, drawing the blinds.

"What?" He picked her up and leaned her onto the sofa, curling up with her. "What," Lily asked again.

"I love you. I get that he's being an idiot, but he's tipped over logic. He's acting like an insane person. I don't want you getting hurt in the middle of all of this. I don't want it messing with the book tour. Nothing."

Lily nodded. "Just remember one thing handsome. You have a ring. He doesn't. He is striking back to be an idiot. That's it. He wants what you have. He's not getting it," she said.

He kissed her again and snuggled her. "If the lawyer needs you, I'll get him to call. Tonight, we are totally getting our minds off it." Lily nodded. She kissed him again and his phone buzzed. He shook his head, seeing a message from Carter that he'd handle things. He shook his head replying:

My problem. My issue. I'd rather bury him in red tape.

Lily kissed Emerson, reminding him what he should've been concentrating on. "I can go if you need to concentrate."

He kissed her. "Promise me that you aren't gonna be mad if I have to come back and deal with this when you're doing the book stuff."

Lily kissed him. "I can get Addy to come if you have to go back. It's fine."

He hugged her. "Okay beautiful," he said as they got up.

"By the way, I'm taking the lace panties back." He shook his head. Lily looked at him.

"Emerson."

"Wife." Lily shook her head and he walked her out to the lobby. "Babe." Lily kissed him and she headed down to the SUV. His security took her to the house and when she walked in, his housekeeper had lunch waiting.

"Miss Lily," she said.

"Hi. I need your help with something. Can you assist," Lily asked.

"What do you need?"

Lily walked her upstairs. "Do we need to get his tux cleaned?"

"I can freshen it up and get it pressed. Is everything alright," his housekeeper asked.

"He got dragged into something really stressful at the office. He may not be able to make it back in time."

"I can get his tux brought over to the office for him." Lily nodded.

"If we haven't heard from him by 3:30," Lily asked. The housekeeper nodded. She went and freshened up his tux, and Lily put a note in his pocket along with his tie and dressy socks. She grabbed his shoes and Lily put them with the dress shirt, laying them on the bed.

Lily headed downstairs, got a bit of writing in, had lunch and around 1:30, Addy showed with her dress. "About time," Lily teased.

"Hey," Addy said as she gave Lily a hug and almost started crying.

"What's wrong," Lily asked.

"Something's not right. I haven't even heard from him." Lily took a deep breath and walked Lily upstairs, steaming her dress.

"They're kind of in the middle of talking to the lawyers. Emerson hasn't called me since I headed home."

"Why are they talking to lawyers?"

"Zack. He tried to force Emerson into selling his company to him. He doesn't know what he's doing. I don't know why Zack is being an idiot, but he's causing stress for both of them. It's alright. Let them deal with that. We can have some girl time."

"I don't even know if I want to go."

"Addy, here's an idea. Take it or leave it. We go all out. Glamorous, fancy, over the top and have him drooling when he sees you."

"You sure," Addy asked. Lily nodded. They had a sweet tea and relaxed a bit. When hair and makeup showed, Lily told them what Addy wanted.

By the time they were both glammed and ready, Lily got a text:

> *What's my sexy wife up to?*

She got a smirk and replied:

> *Hanging with Addy. She now looks like a supermodel. How did the meeting go? Miss you.*

She knew his reaction. She also knew that he was probably on his way home:

> *This stupid meeting with that idiot has been going for 2 hours already. I'm ready to get out of here. Which dress are you wearing?*

Lily smirked and replied:

> *My husband requested the red, backless, way too sexy for a party with his mom dress.*

Emerson called 2 minutes later.

"Hey handsome," Lily said.

"Hey sexy wife. Are you really gonna wear it?"

"You made a request. You're gonna be at my book stuff. It's the least that I could do," Lily said as the hairstylist put the last touches on Lily's hair.

"Wife."

"Husband."

"I need a favor."

"Which is?"

"Um. Can you grab my tux for me?"

"Do you want me to send it over to the office?"

"Nope. Just faster when I get home."

"You on the way?"

"Leaving in 20. I guess Carter's coming?"

"Addy's all ready. I'm just finishing the last touches." She knew how badly he wanted to be at home.

"Emerson, hurry home okay?"

"I will beautiful. I love you."

"Love you too handsome."

When Lily headed back upstairs, she saw Addy sliding into the dress. She helped her zip it up and was loving the dress on her. "It looks amazing," Lily said.

"Are you sure," she asked. Lily nodded.

"You look like you walked out of Fifty shades Darker. Perfect," Lily teased. Addy went downstairs and got herself a sweet tea, waiting on Lily.

Lily walked into the bedroom, slid her jewelry on, slid her lingerie on and slid into the dress. When she went to leave the bedroom, Emerson was coming up the steps. He looked up and gulped.

"Um....I think...."

"What," Lily asked.

"I don't think we're gonna make it."

"And why is that," Lily asked as he walked towards her, and she walked backwards into the bedroom. He kissed her, pulling her into his arms.

"I don't know that we're gonna make it out of bed in time," he teased. Lily smirked and kissed him.

"We kinda have to go. Addy's downstairs." He kissed her again and he saw his tux laid on the bed.

He took her hand and smirked. "What," Lily asked.

"Shower."

"Emerson, I just got my hair done." He walked her into the bathroom and sat her on the counter. "Emer..." He kissed her again.

"And no lipstick. Good," he teased. Lily shook her head and he slid the dress up her legs.

"Emerson, we have to be there in an hour."

"90 minutes."

"And it takes 30 to..." He devoured her lips and slid the dress up her legs as he kicked his dress pants off, putting them on the other side of the counter. When she felt her lacy panties slide off, she knew. They had sex on the counter, being careful not to mess the dress. When he finished, Lily's legs were shaking.

"I might have missed you today." Lily kissed him.

"I missed you too."

"By the way, that dress you have on is officially illegal." Lily smirked.

"Your fave." He shook his head, kissed her again and hopped into the shower, while she cleaned up a little and slid into lacy panties that would taunt him to no end.

When he stepped out of the shower, Lily handed him a warm towel. "You look too sexy," Emerson said.

"You picked the dress. It was your request husband." He smirked and shook his head.

"I still think that you are way too sexy to go to my moms, of all places." She kissed him.

"I'm going to check on Addy. I put something in your pocket by the way."

"Which was what," he asked.

"You look. I'll meet you downstairs." He shook his head, freshened up and slid his hand in hers, walking her into the bedroom.

He hung up his towel on the door and slid into his tux, feeling the note in the pocket. Lily touched up her lipstick and put his favorite perfume on and he slid his arms around her waist. "Emerson."

He kissed her neck. "Yeah, I'm thinking we should definitely stay home."

"We're not staying when Addy and Carter are here." He kissed the back of her neck.

"You are leaving me a note like that and you really think that we're gonna end up at the party?"

Lily kissed him. "We're still going."

He shook his head. "Nope."

"Emerson, you promised your mom. Come on handsome." He shook his head, kissed her and went and slid his dress shirt on, slid the tie on and pulled his shoes on. He grabbed his jacket and slid his arm around Lily.

"I swear, you're gonna end up..."

Lily kissed him. They came downstairs and Addy and Carter were making out on the sofa. Lily smirked. "Are you two gonna make out all night or are you coming with us," Emerson teased.

Chapter 16

They got to the party a little while later and Emerson had barely been able to keep his hands off of Lily. He tried, but when they all pulled into the house, Emerson helped Lily out and instead of walking in and saying hi to his mom, he walked upstairs hand in hand with Lily. He walked into his bedroom and locked the door behind him. "What," Lily asked.

"Yeah, you may have to wear my jacket."

"Emerson." He pulled her to him, devouring her lips again.

"Since when do you ever listen to me when I pick out something for you?"

"Decided to placate you tonight. Special night," Lily said as he kissed her again.

"Lily."

"Husband."

He devoured her lips. "I don't think we're gonna make it downstairs." Lily smirked.

"You can hold off for a little while right?"

He shook his head. "Not with you in that," he teased as his hand slid to her back, then downwards.

"Emerson." He kissed her shoulder, brushing her hair off her shoulder.

"You're wearing lace? The naked lace."

"Emerson."

"What?"

"We're going downstairs." He turned her to face him and devoured her lips.

"Fine, but no phones tonight. All mine," he replied.

"Always."

He shook his head. "If we're doing what I think we are for dinner, we're coming upstairs after. A dance or two and we're leaving."

"Emerson, it's for charity."

"Don't care right now. I want to just be with you. Nobody else in our way."

"Was your day that bad," Lily asked.

"The beginning, no. After that stupid meeting, yes." She gave him a hug. "That dress is seriously illegal," he whispered.

"Good thing you get to take it off when we get home."

"Or sooner," he teased. Lily shook her head, touched up her lipstick, making sure none was on his lips, and they went downstairs.

"No stress. Just relax and pretend to enjoy yourself handsome." He kissed her hand as they made it down the steps.

They walked into the event, seeing it decked out in black, white and gold. When Lily and Emerson walked through the crowd, everyone was staring. They gave his mom and dad a hug and took a seat at the table with Carter and Addy. Even Emerson's mom was staring at Lily's dress.

"You look beautiful tonight Lily," his mom said.

"Well thank you. You do too. It's a beautiful dress on you. Almost like you're floating on air," Lily said as Emerson's hand slid up Lily's leg via the slit of the dress. His dad went up on stage and did his speech, then asked Emerson to come up. He kissed Lily and hit the stage, did his quick speech and came back down to the table.

"I think we need to leave," Emerson whispered as the steaks came to the table.

"Eat dinner first," Lily teased as she whispered in his ear. He shook his head and they all had dinner, then Emerson's dad asked Lily to dance. Emerson almost clamped down on her leg. "Sure," Lily said. She kissed Emerson and walked onto the dance floor with his dad.

"He was very, very lost without you. I don't think I've ever seen him this happy," his dad said.

"That's a good thing right," Lily teased.

"You blossomed into a beautiful lady. I'm so happy you two found each other again. We actually found photos the other day of the two of you in high school. He still has eyes only for you," his dad said as they finished their dance. When Lily went to head back to the table, Emerson took her hand and walked her onto the dance floor, as Addy and Carter followed suit with a ton of other people.

"And," Emerson whispered.

"They found pictures of us in high school," Lily teased.

"Oh geez. Of course he went looking," Emerson joked as he spun her around the floor. When they came back to the table, Emerson whispered that he wanted to head back. Lily smirked.

"It's not even 9," Lily said.

He kissed her shoulder. "You're way too tempting."

"That was the plan handsome." She sent him a text and within a minute or two, he got it:

> *Visit for 30 minutes then we can make an excuse to leave. Wait until you see the lace*

He shook his head and replied:

> *You mean the lace that will be on the floor of the SUV?*

Lily smirked and he kissed her hand. "I meant it," he whispered as he finished his glass of wine and Lily finished hers. "How is work going," his mom asked.

"It's okay. Happy to be off for a bit. We're heading out tomorrow for Lily's book tour," Emerson said as his hand slid up Lily's thigh.

"Wow. How long are you going to be gone," his mom asked. "Probably a few weeks. I have days off in between so I can come home for a while and see you and a few of our friends," Lily replied as she tried to stop his hand from inching up her thigh.

"Great. We'll have to do dinner when you get back." Lily nodded.

"I was actually going to ask what your plans were for the holidays," Lily asked.

"We always have a big thanksgiving at the house and we go away for Christmas and have presents at the cabin in Aspen," his mom said as Emerson's hand reached the lace.

"Sounds like a beautiful holiday."

"We were going to change it up this year since it's your first official Christmas with the family. Whatever the two of you want to do," his mom said as Emerson's finger reached the edge of her panties.

"I will come up with an idea. Maybe Christmas at the house. Nice and quiet," Lily said as she stopped Emerson's hand.

"Sounds fantastic. Let me know if you need me to help," his dad said. When her phone buzzed, Lily smirked.

"Excuse me for one minute:

We're leaving so I can slide that dress off.

"We're actually gonna head out in a minute. We're up and leaving early tomorrow," Emerson said.

"Alright. Have fun and be safe," his mom said as Lily and Emerson gave them a hug. Lily grabbed her purse and they gave Addy and Carter a hug.

"My driver can come get you whenever you're ready," Emerson said.

"Thank you," Addy mouthed as Lily smirked.

Emerson slid his hand in Lily's and walked her outside to the SUV. They hopped in and as soon as his driver and his security hopped in, Emerson slid her closer to him. "What," Lily teased.

"You and that dress." Lily shook her head and his hand slid to her leg.

"We're not doing this in here," Lily whispered. He nodded and kept going, skirting his hand up her inner thigh. Before she had a chance to say no, he kissed her and pulled her legs over his lap.

"Thank you for putting up with this tonight," he said as he kissed down her neck.

"Gave us a chance to dress up," Lily said as he kissed her.

"No more sharing my wife with the riff raff," he teased. Lily shook her head and he kissed her neck, then down to her shoulder as his hand slid to the lacy panties. She attempted to stop him and it was no use. He kept going. He taunted that much more.

When they got to the house, Emerson shook his head, helped her out and carried her inside and straight up to the bedroom. He closed and locked the door and pinned her onto the bed, pulling his suit jacket and shirt and tie off. "Emerson."

He kissed her and she went to get up. "Where are you goin?"

"Taking the dress off."

He shook his head, got up and followed her into her closet, unzipping the dress.

"Lily."

"What," she asked.

"You did that intentionally," he said.

"Yep," Lily replied as he slid the dress off and Emerson shook his head. He picked her up, walked her back to the bed and leaned her onto it, kicking his dress pants off.

"Emerson." He kissed up her leg and just as he was about to peel her lace panties off, his phone buzzed. He pulled them off, ignoring the phone and peeled his boxers off. He shook his head with a smirk. "What are you smiling at," Lily asked as he pulled the lacy panties off.

"How on earth did I get the hottest woman in the world as my wife?"

"Very, very lucky," Lily said as he leaned into her arms and devoured her lips. He slid her legs around him and shook his head. "Emerson."

He kissed her again and wrapped his arms around her. "Mine," he said. Lily smirked and he shook his head, pulling her to him as he sat up a little.

"What," Lily asked.

"No more taunting me," he teased as Lily shook her head and leaned him backwards on the bed.

"Who was taunting? I remember someone determined to..."

"And I would've in a heartbeat," he teased as he undid the rest of her lingerie and threw it on the floor.

"Emerson," Lily said. He pulled her to him and leaned her onto her back and they had sex. It wasn't just hot, it was intense and mind-blowing. It was like he'd been holding it back for months. He kept going until he felt her body give in then let go, holding her as tight to him as he could. "Emerson, I don't think I can even move."

"Good. Me either," he teased as he almost laughed and kissed her again.

He wouldn't move a single muscle. "Had to taunt me the entire time we were there."

"You did kind of ask for that dress."

"I'm still thinking that we shouldn't have got the other ones. I may have to hide those away."

Lily kissed him. "I'm glad you liked your surprise," Lily teased.

He shook his head and kissed her neck. "I swear, that dress is gonna be how you get pregnant," he teased.

Lily smirked and kissed him. "Your little dream," Lily teased. He nodded. They curled up in bed and he had her curled up tight to him, kissing her neck before he nodded off.

The next morning, Lily woke up and went to head downstairs for a workout when she heard steps behind her. She walked downstairs and Emerson's arms slid around her waist.

"Did you seriously try to sneak off and workout without me?"

"Yep," Lily teased as she did a warm-up. He walked up to the door to the workout room and closed and locked it, flipping on the stereo. "Emerson."

"Wife," he teased.

"What are you up to?"

"Taking full advantage of the little time we have before we leave." Lily shook her head and started her workout while he did a run on the treadmill. When she finished her weights and started her yoga, Emerson shook his head and did his weights.

"Emerson, stop." She almost laughed, seeing the look on his face.

"Can I help it that I have a sexy wife?"

"Control the hormones," Lily replied.

She finished her yoga and he sat up from his crunches. "Come here for a minute," he teased as he pulled her onto his lap so she straddled him.

"Yes handsome husband."

He kissed her. "Nervous?"

Lily shook her head. "I have the best husband in the world with me."

"Not even a little?"

"So long as it's not a room of 1500 people, I'm fine." Emerson smirked. "Don't go there."

"I mean, it's possible."

Lily shook her head and his hands slid to her backside. "And what do you want," Lily asked.

"You." He kissed her and picked her up, sitting her on the bench.

"What?" He devoured her lips and went to peel her shorts off when his phone went off.

"I'm not answering it, so don't ask."

He pulled them off and kissed her inner thigh. Lily shook her head. "Emerson."

He taunted and teased until she was pulling his shirt towards her. "Yes sexy wife," he said as he kissed up her torso and peeled off her shirt and sports bra. She went to shake her head and he kissed her, peeling his shorts off. He wanted her. Every single inch of her body wrapped around his. They had sex in that workout room again. Hot, intense, spur of the moment sex that drained both of them of any energy they had left. When they curled up together on the floor, she smirked.

"And why are you smiling," Emerson asked as her chin rested on his chest.

"I'm almost thinking I get a better workout in when you're in here."

"Understatement, he teased. He kissed her again and they sat up.

"You sure you want to come with me," Lily asked.

He nodded and devoured her lips. "I'm not letting go for a dang minute," he replied.

"Good," Lily joked as he handed Lily his t-shirt, pulled his shorts on and got up, carrying her up the stairs to their bedroom.

"Emerson."

"Mm."

"What time are we flying out?"

"When we get there." Lily shook her head and slid her robe on.

"Where are you going," he asked.

"Food." He shook his head, grabbed her hand, pulling her to him, and kissed her.

"I'll get it." He kissed her again and walked downstairs seeing his housekeeper putting two plates and two mugs onto the tray. "Thank you," Emerson said.

"Most welcome. The pilot called and said that he's ready with a flight plan when you arrive. What time should I tell him that you're coming?"

"Hour and a half depending on traffic."

"I'll let him know," his housekeeper said. "

I meant what I said the other day about taking some time off if you wanted to," Emerson said.

"I'll keep that in mind," the housekeeper said as Emerson headed upstairs and brought breakfast. When he walked in and saw Lily with his phone in her hand, he shook his head and put the tray on the table.

"What's wrong," he asked.

Lily handed it to him and walked into the bathroom. Before she could close and lock the door, he came in and grabbed her hand. "Lily."

"Who is she?"

He shook his head. "Babe, I don't know who it is. I've never seen them before."

"Then why is there a photo on your phone of you with this person?"

"Lily." She shook her head and went and got in the shower. She washed her hair, washed up and was about to step out when he stepped in behind her and slid his arms around her. "Emerson, stop."

He turned her to face him. "That picture was from 5 years ago. I didn't take it. I told you. Idiot exes." Lily shook her head and stepped out of the shower, slid her robe on and walked into the bedroom.

By the time he came into the bedroom, she was dressed, her laptop was gone and so was the charger. He shook his head, pulled his jeans on, and grabbed a tee, his phone and his shoes and walked downstairs. When he saw her about to walk outside, he grabbed her hand and walked her into his office.

"What," Lily asked.

"Breathe. Old photo. She's doing it to be an idiot. We talked about this before."

"Maybe you should stay home. I'll go do the first ones alone," Lily said as he shook his head.

"I'm going with you whether you like it or not."

He finished getting dressed. "What," Lily asked.

"Stop."

"Stop what? Seeing that my..."

He kissed her. "Watch," he said as he deleted and blocked the message.

"Done. Now, come eat breakfast," he said. Lily shook her head. He picked her up, flipping her over his shoulder and walked upstairs. He sat her on the bed, handed Lily her omelet and sat down on the chair. "I'm not hungry," Lily said.

"Woman, you don't eat, you won't be able to walk. Eat."

"Emerson."

"Woman, don't start. We were fine until she texted. The problem has been handled." Lily shook her head, had her omelet, and walked back downstairs, cleaning off her dishes.

Emerson walked downstairs with the tray and before Lily could walk out, he grabbed her hand. "Laptop, chargers, notebook," he said.

"In my bag. I'm leaving," Lily said.

"Lily, stop." She shook her head and he grabbed her hand again and pulled his shoes on. His housekeeper handed Emerson his chargers, laptop and briefcase and they got in the SUV.

"I can go by myself," Lily said.

"Why are you being so irritated? It's not like I asked for the reminder," Emerson said as he went through emails.

"Because when I grab your phone to throw it on the charger, I don't expect to see that. I don't want to see it." He slid his hand in hers, with her trying to pull away.

They got to the airport, pulled up to the plane and Lily grabbed her bag, hopping onto the plane. She didn't have a chance to sit away from him. The minute he came on board, and put his bag into the chair, security hopped on and they headed for the runway. Emerson was sitting right beside her.

"Let go of my hand," Lily said.

"No."

They got up in the air and Lily wanted more than anything to just hop off. She walked to the back of the plane, changing seats and Emerson grabbed her hand and walked her into the back. "What," Lily asked.

He walked her into the bathroom and closed the door, knowing it was the only area that was soundproof. "Enough," Emerson said.

"I don't want to wake up to that Emerson. You should know that."

"So, me seeing a text from Zack on your phone how many times means nothing? Lily, I can't stop random people from acting a damn fool. Just breathe. She's blocked. She can't message me. Just come and sit with me and stop. You're flipping out because you're nervous and taking it out on me."

Lily shook her head. "No, I'm not. I don't want to see..."

He kissed her. "I can't stop the world babe. I know that the only woman I want is in my arms right now. Period."

Lily went to step out of the bathroom and he stopped her.

"Talk."

"No." He shook his head.

"Lily."

"I'm not playing a game with you Emerson. I don't want to see those..." He kissed her again.

The kiss deepened and he picked her up and sat her on the counter. He pulled her jeans off, peeled the way too sexy panties off and they had sex on the counter. It was past hot. It was like he was making a point. A big one. It wasn't tender. It was almost mad sex that had her body throbbing in minutes. When his body gave in, Lily's toes were already in knots. He devoured her lips and pulled her to him, wrapping her legs around his hips. "I'm not fighting about it anymore with you. This is all yours. Just yours. Always yours. Stop worrying."

"Emerson."

He kissed her again. "What," he asked.

"I don't want to see it again."

"Okay," he replied. He kissed her, nibbling at her lips.

"You alright?"

"My legs are shaking. No," Lily said as they both almost laughed. He pulled his jeans up and handed Lily her jeans.

"I'm not playing with you today," Lily said.

"Mine."

She shook her head, slid her jeans back on and he kissed her. "No more fighting either," he teased.

Lily smirked, shaking her head again and they went back into the main cabin, sitting down. "When are we landing," Lily asked.

"3 hours," his security said. Lily shook her head, got comfortable and he handed Lily her laptop. He kissed her neck then down her shoulder.

"Cut it out," Lily said as he raised the arm rest and slid his arm around her as he went through emails.

When they landed at the first stop, Lily started getting nervous. "Babe, your fine. There's a ton of people in there and they all love the book. Breathe."

"What if I screw it up?"

"Take a deep breath. I love you, they love your writing. That's all that matters. If you want me in the front row, I'll be there." Lily hugged him.

"I think I'm okay," Lily said. He walked out of the back with her, walking her onto the stage and putting the sharpies out for her to sign the books. He put a bottle of water beside her. She did her reading, got a ton of applause, and started signing books. By the time she left, her arm was sore and she was exhausted. They did the same thing again and again, 26 times, until she had finished every stop. Emerson barely left her side.

When they got back to South Carolina, Lily was ready for some down time. She got her Christmas gifts ordered, giving the list to security so they knew what the deliveries were. Lily tried getting her thanksgiving ideas put in place, and Emerson's mom came and helped, realizing how many people would be there. By the time they made it through Thanksgiving, the tree was up, the presents were wrapped and Emerson was ready for an early gift for Lily.

"Emerson, Christmas isn't for another few weeks. What are you doing?"

"Open the envelope."

"Emerson."

"Open it." She shook her head and opened it, seeing legal documents.

"What's this?"

"Read it," he said. Lily read through it and saw the words for the plaintiff.

"Meaning what," Lily asked.

"Restraining order and he's banned from the building. He's not allowed near either of us or any kids we have in the future. He's not allowed to come to the office either," Emerson said.

"He's gone?"

Emerson nodded. "Thought it couldn't wait for Christmas," he teased.

Lily shook her head. "I can't believe they…"

He kissed her. "Zack free for life."

Lily shook her head. "Kinda makes going to the beach a little easier," Lily teased. He hugged her and kissed her again.

"You never did tell me what you wanted for Christmas," Lily asked.

"Already have what I want. That's all I need."

"And what can I put under the tree?"

He smirked. "You in a big red bow."

"With your parents and your sister in the house."

"I have something."

"What?"

"Boxers."

Lily smirked. "And what else that's G-rated Emerson?"

"New laptop."

Lily shook her head and he got up. "What?"

"Follow me," he teased as he walked upstairs.

"I kinda wanted to get writing in."

He kissed her as he walked her into the bedroom. "You'll get writing in. There's time," he teased as he showed her one of her early gifts.

"Emerson."

"Hand carved wood, soft cushion, sturdy so it can't be knocked over, and this slides around so you can use it as a desk," he said showing her the shaker style chair that was perfect.

"And, I found something else. It's getting too cold to try it out, but I got this," Emerson said walking her out to the balcony and showing her the porch swing.

"Emerson."

"I wanted to surprise you. It makes you feel like home having one like at your place when we were kids. It's a duplicate of it." Lily kissed him. He picked her up, wrapping her legs around his hips.

"You like your surprise I gather."

Lily nodded and kissed him again. "I can't believe you did all of this," Lily said.

"My thank you for having to go to the company party this weekend. Your second freaking week back and we have to go to the party."

"This mean you're going into work today?"

"I have to go get the paperwork to work on. Beyond that, I can relax. I'm trying to close the office until after the holidays."

"No more morning calls," Lily teased.

"Funny. My assistants will still be logging in and checking things on and off. I may still get calls. Never know, but I'm determined to have Christmas be phone-free."

"You do realize that's not exactly gonna work right," Lily asked.

He kissed her. "Trying. Carter and Addy are permitted, but if they get…"

Lily kissed him. "Before you say it, they will be calling at a bad time."

He shook his head. "Not allowed. Not even a little."

Lily smirked. "Emerson, we're gonna be with everyone. You invited your folks to stay. You invited my folks and my brother to be here."

"They're staying in Charleston. I got them a suite at the waterfront." Lily smirked.

"And?"

"And my mom and dad are staying at their place, we're staying here alone. You, me, security and that's it. Solution solved."

Lily smirked. "Emerson, I love that you're trying so hard to be alone, but we're having the holidays here. Your folks are gonna be over here."

He kissed her. "About that. What if we go to church on Christmas Eve? The family can come if they want to," he said.

"I kinda like that idea."

"We never get to go, and we haven't been in person since we were away for a while."

"I love the idea," Lily said.

"Good. Also means you in a dress. I'm always good with that," he teased.

Lily shook her head. "Behave for once."

"Nope." He kissed her and gave her a hug. "Were you surprised?"

Lily nodded. "The best surprise ever. Honestly, I never expected any of it."

He kissed her again and snuggled her to him. "Good. I have a million and one more surprises," he teased.

"You always do handsome."

They curled up on the bed and just relaxed. "What were you thinking about going out tonight," he asked.

"And do what," Lily asked.

"Beach," he asked.

"It's cold."

"And? We can be alone for a while. Really alone."

Lily shook her head. "If you want to. Honestly, I'm okay staying here."

"We haven't gone out anywhere since you were doing the book tour, and even then it was restaurants or Christmas shopping."

"If you want to. I may need sweaters." He smirked and shook his head. "Emerson."

He put two into a bag with two pairs of her jeans and went and packed his bag. "Why two?"

"Because we're having a weekend away. No drama, no stress and no phones." Lily laughed.

"Fine. Less phones." She slid her dress pants in her bag with something for church and he shook his head, putting his clothes into a suit bag. "Why do you have a cat that ate the canary look," Lily asked.

"Because I have a few more surprises."

"Emerson."

"I found out I have to go to Cali after new years."

"Okay. And?"

"Big meeting."

"Emerson, I write. I can literally be anywhere."

"It's a 4-day meeting. I won't be there at all" It starts at 6am and goes until 7 at night."

"Emerson."

"You don't want to sit in the condo for 4 days without me."

"So, you're vanishing to California without me?"

"Babe."

"Really?"

"When you see what I got you…"

"Emerson, I'm fine writing there."

He kissed her. "As soon as it's done I'm coming straight home."

Lily shook her head. "Fine. I guess I'll just have to hang with Addy."

He kissed her. "Come on sexy wife. We're going to the beach."

They hopped in Lily's truck and made their way to the beach with security following behind them. "Seriously taking off to beaches and sunshine without me. So not fair," Lily said.

His hand slid to her leg. "Babe, it's work. I'm gonna go in, work, come home and sleep. I'm gonna be too exhausted to do anything else."

"And you don't want me to go. I get it," Lily said sarcastically.

"Lily."

"No. It's fine."

"Wife, stop." She turned the radio up and heard news about a film premiere.

"That's the reason I'm having that meeting."

"Meaning what?"

"Jaxon is doing the premiere in LA and a bunch of interviews. On top of that he's doing promo. I have to be there for that, then the end of year stuff," he said.

"And I can't go to the premiere."

"He's doing another one here for Valentine's Day. We're going to that one." Lily shook her head.

"Lily." She stared out the window. He shook his head and they finished making their way to the house. Every time he tried to hold her hand, she pulled away. When he pulled in the driveway, she was still mad. "Lily, it's work."

"Maybe you'll just find someone else to take to the red carpet." She hopped out of the truck when it stopped, grabbed her bag and her laptop, and went inside.

"Lily."

"You sure you're okay with me sleeping in the same bed? Might be too much," Lily said. He shook his head, following her inside, locked the truck and handed the keys to security. He grabbed her hand and walked her upstairs, suit bag in one hand and her hand in the other. "Emerson, let go."

He walked into the bedroom, closed the door, and put his bag on the chair. He put her bag with his and she walked off, walking outside. "Wife."

"It's fine Emerson. Have fun." He slid his arms around her and she shook her head. "Don't."

"Lily, it's work. That's all. You don't want to sit out there."

"I've been to the condo Emerson. There's a ton of stuff to do."

"No."

"Fine." Lily went to walk out of the bedroom and he stopped her.

"Let go," Lily said.

"Woman, come and sit for 5 dang minutes." Lily shook her head and went and sat on the bed.

"What? So, I'm fine to be with when it's my stuff, but not when you're working."

He kissed her. "You're acting ridiculous." Lily shook her head. She got up and walked out of the bedroom. She walked downstairs, grabbed a sweater and went outside.

It's not like it was summer warm, but she needed the air. When she heard steps behind her, Lily shook her head and walked down to the beach.

"Lily." She ignored him and sat down in the sand. "Babe, it's not even warm out. Come inside."

"No." He shook his head and handed her a glass of wine. "I don't want alcohol," Lily said.

"Babe."

"Emerson, go away." He sat down beside her and she went to get up when he grabbed her hand and pulled her back down.

"Sit and drink the damn wine."

"No." He shook his head.

"When you see what I had planned, you won't be mad."

"Says who," Lily asked.

"Babe, you don't wanna sit there all day."

Lily shook her head, got her wine, and got up. "Lily." She walked inside, went upstairs and walked into the bathroom, locking the door behind her and drawing herself a bath. She slid out of her jeans, sweater, and tee, kicked her lingerie off and curled up in the hot water, adding her vanilla bubble bath to the water. When she heard the door, she shook her head. "Lily, you do know that I have the key for the bathroom door right?" She ignored him. She had her wine, ignoring him.

Emerson sat down on the bench by the bed. He wanted more than anything to unlock the door and walk in there, sitting down in the tub with her. If she knew what he had planned, it wouldn't have been an issue, but it really was the first time they would've been apart since they got married. Spending one night without her was torture. He never even managed to make it through the night before their wedding without seeing her. In the back of his mind, he asked himself what he was thinking. He shook his head and heard the tub draining. He got up, grabbed her robe, and knocked, handing the robe to her. When she still wouldn't talk to him, he grabbed her hand. "Emerson, leave it."

"I was rethinking it."

"Too late. You want to go without me then go," Lily said. He turned her to look at him. "What?"

"I changed my mind." Lily shook her head and grabbed joggers and a hoodie from the closet. "Lily."

He blockaded her in the closet. "You want to go then go Emerson. I'll stay here by myself. I'll hang with Addy. We can always go to a bar downtown," Lily said to push his buttons.

"You're coming."

"It's fine. I'll go out and hang with Addy. Never know how…"

He kissed her and pinned her against the door. "Why would you go to a bar downtown?"

"Because I had so much fun last time," Lily said sarcastically. He kissed her again and picked her up, wrapping her legs around him. "Emerson."

He walked out of the closet, leaned her onto the bed and pulled his hoodie off, then went for hers and the joggers. "What," he asked.

"What do you want?"

"I barely made it through the night before our wedding without seeing you."

"You wanted to go solo then go."

He handed her a box. "Emerson, Christmas is…"

He kissed her, devouring her lips. "Open it." She shook her head, sitting up while he pulled the joggers off and threw them in a pile with his jeans.

"I'm not…"

"Woman, open it." She opened the box and saw something that she almost laughed at.

"Emerson, when would I even need that?"

"When I'm not home. You can call me and we can talk," he teased.

"You're ridiculous. You know that right?"

"Molded to be the exact same."

Lily shook her head. "Emerson"

He smirked. "What?"

"You do realize that I don't need a replica right?"

"If I have to go to overnight meetings, you might." Lily shook her head.

"Making a regular thing out of vanishing on me?"

He kissed her. "My wife. I wouldn't if I didn't have to do it for work."

Lily shook her head. "Still not using it."

He pulled her to him.

"Emerson."

He smirked. "You sure," he teased.

He started taunting her even more, showing her how it felt. "We're not…"

He kissed her, put it on the bed and they had sex. Hot, even more intense than usual and kept going until her body was trembling and her toes were curled. "Maybe you're right. You're better off with the real thing," he teased as Lily pulled him to her.

He devoured her lips all over again. "I love you," he said.

"I love you too. Stop teasing. If you want to go then go."

"Babe." She shook her head and pulled away when he tried pulling her tighter to him.

"Emerson, don't."

She got up and walked into the bathroom, cleaning up on shaky legs. When he came in behind her, Lily shook her head and left the room, sliding back into the joggers and hoodie, and walked downstairs, sitting back outside with a throw blanket and her laptop. She got a few pages in when she heard the swoosh of the sliding door. "What?"

"Your phone was going off. I think it's Addy," Emerson said as he slid her forward and slid onto the porch swing behind her. She looked and it was an unknown number. Lily handed it back to him.

"Hello," Emerson said. When he heard the phone hang up, he shook his head. His arms slid around her and he kissed her shoulder.

"Emerson, if you're gonna go there without me then go. Not my fault if you can't sleep," Lily said. He kissed her shoulder.

"You sure?"

"I can't demand that you stay. It's work. Just don't have any fun without me."

He kissed up her neck. "It's not like there's any option here. It's work. It's his movie premiere. The actors will be there, and Jaxon and Mia. I can't do anything about it. I'm not going to the UK one or the New York one. Just LA and Chicago and Charleston."

"Why would he even do one here?" He kissed her.

"Because this is where the story began for them."

Lily shook her head. "Who's going to the one in the UK?"

"Carter and Addy. It's a surprise for her."

"Is he going to LA with you?"

"Yes. Addy's gonna be here with you. There's no reason to be all mad."

"And if you change your mind and bring me?"

"Then she's coming."

Lily shook her head. "Just go Emerson. You want to be there, then be there."

She went to get up and he pulled her back. "It's work."

"And so was the book tour stuff Emerson. You wouldn't even come home so Addy could come out."

He kissed her shoulder. "Because I realized that I can't live without you. I don't want us to be apart that long." Lily got up, closed her laptop and walked inside, putting her phone on the charger. "Babe," he said as he followed her.

"Emerson, stop."

He grabbed her hand. "Then stop walking off."

"When are you leaving?"

"First week of January."

"Date."

"January second."

Lily took a deep breath. "Fine."

"Lily." She shook her head. She broke away from him, got a big glass of ice water and went and sat on the chair alone. She looked at her phone and started going through emails when she saw one from an unknown email address:

> *I know and you know that marrying him was a mistake. I'll meet you on the beach tonight. By the way, nice joggers.*

Lily got creeped out, went and showed security and they grabbed her phone, pulling up all the information and forwarding it to the police.

"I'm upgrading your email filters. I'll bring it out to you," the security team said. Lily nodded and walked back to the sofa, curling up with her blanket.

"What," Emerson asked as she saw him with a glass of Jack.

"Nothing," Lily replied as she took a sip of her water. He shook his head and walked into the security office.

"What was it," Emerson asked.

"An email from Zack that he managed to send via a burner email. It's been handled." Emerson shook his head and walked over to Lily.

"What?"

"Come." Lily shook her head. He picked her up and walked upstairs, sitting her on the bed.

"What," Lily asked.

"You realize you could've just told me." Lily shook her head and he kissed her.

"Emerson, just stop." He slid his arms around her and Lily pushed him away. She got her bag and walked downstairs, walking out the front door. She put it in the truck, grabbed her keys, her laptop and purse and left.

Chapter 17

By the time it got to Christmas, Lily was still irritated. When she'd taken off that night, he was at least thankful that she'd gone back to the house. Seeing that email from Zack had started a major issue with the police and had explained why she'd left. She wasn't comfortable anymore. Lily was baking with the housekeeper and determined to keep her mind off of Emerson leaving.

"Lily," Emerson said as he came up behind her.

"What?"

"Come here for a minute."

"Emerson, we're..." He took her hand and walked her into his office. She'd barely even slept beside him since that fight at the beach. "What?"

"He was arrested."

"And? What does that have to do with anything?"

Emerson shook his head and sat her on the sofa. "Violation of restraining order and harassment."

"What's your point?"

"Lily, we're not fighting about him anymore. Done. You want to come to LA, then come. You don't want to, don't. I'm not playing this game anymore. I don't want to fight with you. I thought that maybe you'd want time alone to hang out. You don't, it's fine."

Lily went to leave the office and he grabbed her hand, pulling her to him. "Emerson."

"Talk to me."

"Why? It's not gonna change anything. You went as far…"

He kissed her. "Babe."

"Emerson, just don't." She pulled away and walked out of the office and went and sat outside with her blanket, trying to work on some writing while she had time. Everything was perfect and ready for Christmas. The last of the cookies were done, the champagne was chilling, the food was ready. Everything was done, short of them managing to actually get along.

"Do you need me to get anything before tomorrow," Emerson asked trying to come up with a reason to go out. The housekeeper shook her head. "I have everything together for Christmas Eve, Christmas Day and the Hoppin' John to make for new year's eve. There's steaks, chicken, seafood, and everything else you could possibly need. Two appetizer trays to take out for Christmas day," the housekeeper said.

"Give me something," Emerson said. She smirked.

"We even got enough coffee, Bailey's and vodka for you to do the espresso Irish cream martinis you'd mentioned. You can for a walk, but that's all I have." Emerson shook his head and walked upstairs, seeing her reorganizing drawers.

He walked over to Lily and looked at her. "Can we at least talk without you leaving the room?"

"No."

"Lily, come on. We're married. This isn't high school where you can vanish." Lily shook her head. She wasn't avoiding him. She was trying to make sure that if she had the flu, he wouldn't get it. She'd felt sick since she came back from the beach house. "Lily."

"Emerson, why can't you just leave me alone?"

He picked her up and sat her on the bed. "Talk."

"Just stop."

"Why do you look all nauseous?"

"Because I am," Lily replied as she went to get up.

"Flu?"

"Got the shot when we were on the book tour."

"Migraine?"

"If you don't go away, yes." He sat down in the chair and pulled it closer.

"I love you. All I was doing was keeping..."

"Emerson."

"I didn't think you'd want to be out there alone."

"Then go. Why send Addy and Carter. You can fly out to the UK and spend new year's alone."

He shook his head. "Lily, I'm not avoiding you. I'm not leaving because I need space. It's work. If you really want to be there, fine. Come with me. After the beach and that present you got, I kinda guessed that you were right. I couldn't sleep without you."

"And?"

"Come with me to LA."

"Wouldn't want…"

He kissed her. "Woman, quit prolonging the fight when you know you won."

"And if I say for you to go so I can torture you?"

"I'd drag you kicking and screaming." He kissed her again and pulled her onto his lap. "I don't want us going through Christmas in the middle of world war three. I want us to open presents together, alone in the morning."

"Why? Come up with some other sex toys?"

"Funny," he teased.

He kissed her again. "Have to undo the big red bow that's gonna be wrapped around you."

"And you think that you're getting that do you?" He nodded and undid her shirt. "Emerson." His hands slid to her backside and he slid them under her jeans. "What are you doing?"

"Making up," he teased as he kissed her. She shook her head.

"You realize the door is open." He nodded and unzipped her jeans. She managed to get up, closed the door and went to walk back over to him when he grabbed the belt loop of her jeans and pulled her into his lap.

"What," Lily asked. He devoured her lips and his hand slid her jeans down just enough to taunt her and get her as turned on as he was. When she went to break the kiss, he bit her lip and deepened the kiss. She squirmed and he intensified the teasing. She went to slide the jeans off and he kept going. "Emerson," she said as the kiss broke and her body started throbbing.

"Wife," he replied as he undid his jeans. "Take them off." Lily kicked the jeans off and he shook his head and watched the lace from her panties slide to the floor. He pulled her to him as he slid his jeans down. She slid into his lap and his hands slid to her backside so she was straddling him. "Mine," he teased. She shook her head and he devoured her lips again and teased.

"Emerson," she managed to almost cry out when they started having sex. It wasn't exactly slow and passionate either. It was harder, but more intense than ever. They kept going until her body was almost shaking in his arms. He taunted over and over until she was completely spent. He'd lost every ounce of energy he'd stored from the nights of sleeping alone. "I can't move," Lily said.

"Good," he teased as he pulled her to him.

"You totally enjoy taunting me," Lily said as she tried catching her breath and he pulled the throw blanket on top of them.

"I could taunt you all night until your body was almost convulsing," he teased.

"Maybe you should go to LA alone," Lily joked. He kissed her again.

"Mine."

"Don't start."

"You want to pick a fight, I get to taunt you until you can barely move. New rule," he teased.

Lily shook her head. "Not a fair rule."

"And if I do, you get to taunt me." She shook her head and he kissed her. "You know, there are things we haven't even tried right?"

Lily shook her head. "And you can..."

He kissed her. "Try them on Christmas Eve when you're in a bow and naked." Lily shook her head and he pulled her legs around him.

"Emerson."

"Mm." When she felt his hand starting to taunt her all over again, she tried pulling away and he held on tighter.

"We aren't..."

"Yeah we are."

"Emerson." He kissed her again, teasing her all over again until he was too turned on to stop.

When they managed to get up, Lily could barely walk and he was exhausted. "Dinner," he asked.

"I can go grab it." He shook his head. "Rest. I'll get it," Lily said as she got up and grabbed her fluffy robe from her closet. She came downstairs and saw the steak sandwiches.

"Really," Lily asked.

"I was about to bring it upstairs for you. Wine or sweet tea," the housekeeper asked.

"Water would be perfect," Lily said. She took the tray upstairs, thanking the housekeeper, and walked into the bedroom. When she was through the door, he took it from her hands and slid his arms around her, kicking the door closed. "Emerson."

"Wife," he teased. He put the tray on the counter and undid the robe.

"We could eat first." He kissed her shoulder then down her back. "What are you..." His hand slid between her legs and he bent her over the bed. "Emerson, food."

He smirked. "Hungry?"

Lily nodded. "She made..." She barely managed to mutter the words before they were having sex again. Her body throbbed around him and then he went one step further. It wasn't a feeling she'd ever felt. When her knees started shaking, he kept going, taunting her even more. He collapsed on top of her when his body couldn't hold back anymore.

"I don't think I can move," Lily said as he kissed her shoulder then up her neck.

"Good. Either can I."

"Food," Lily said. He leaned onto his back and Lily got up with even shakier legs and brought the tray over to the bed as he pulled the blankets back and pulled her into the bed and under the blankets. They finished eating and he smirked. "Emerson, stop with the smirk. I'm saying enough," she teased as she had her water.

"And since when do you not have wine with…"

"What," Lily asked when he looked at her.

"Are you?"

"Emerson, you know that the doctor said it'd be difficult." He kissed her.

"Never know," he teased. She shook her head and finished her food, giving the last bite to Emerson.

"Thank you sexy wife."

"Welcome sexy husband."

He kissed her shoulder. "We're staying up here tonight," he teased.

"Why?"

"Because we have a lot more making up to do," he teased. Lily shook her head.

"I don't know if I can take any more making up."

He kissed her. "We'll see," he joked.

Emerson got up the next morning, running off to do the last of his paperwork and pick up a surprise for Lily. When he came home, he saw her sitting on the sofa and texted her:

> *Come upstairs. I have a surprise for you.*

Lily shook her head:

> *I had all the surprises last night. I don't think I can walk if there are any more.*

When he replied, she almost laughed:

> *I was just getting started. We're going to church tonight remember?*

Lily shook her head. She got up, plugging her laptop in, and walked upstairs to the bedroom. "And what are you surprising me with now," Lily teased as he closed the door behind her, locking it.

"Emerson."

He handed her 3 dozen red roses. They were in a fancy crystal vase with a red bow that made Miss America's flowers look like a bunch of weeds. "What is all of this?"

"I wanted you to have something special." Lily kissed him as he put the flowers onto the counter.

"You didn't have to," Lily said.

"For being an idiot. I kinda did."

She shook her head and he kissed her again. "What time are we leaving for church?"

"11." Lily shook her head. "And you're wearing a dress." Lily shook her head.

"You never behave do you?"

"Around you? Never." He kissed her and walked her backwards to the bed.

"You know, you left before I woke up," Lily said.

"Had to go get them before they closed," Emerson said as he leaned into her arms and they curled up on the bed.

"And what did you have planned for the rest of the day?" Just as she said it, she felt something vibrating against her leg. He grabbed his phone and kissed her. When he saw the work phone number on his call display, he shook his head.

"What's up," Emerson asked.

"I just wanted to say thank you for the Christmas bonus. Everyone received theirs and we wanted to make sure you received your gift," his assistant said.

"I did. Thank you. Go home and enjoy your holiday. Close up for the holidays. Make sure the alarms are all on and the doors are secure. Enjoy your Christmas and New Year's break."

"Thank you again and happy holidays to you and your wife too."

"Thank you," Emerson said as he undid his jeans and Lily smirked.

He hung up and Lily shook her head. "We're not starting that again," Lily said.

He kissed her and undid her jeans, pulling them off. "I'm just helping," he teased.

"I know what you're up to. Behave."

"Nope." He thew them into the laundry and went for the lace panties. "I swear, you wear them to taunt me."

"Partially," Lily replied as she slid his jeans down.

"What are you up to," he asked.

"You started this." He shook his head and he grabbed Lily's hand before she did what he knew she would. He leaned into her arms, kicking the jeans off and pulled his shirt off.

"Wife."

"What?" He kissed her, devouring her lips and started taunting her all over again. "Emerson, we can't do this."

"Why?"

"Because I need to walk into church," Lily said as he pulled her shirt and bra off and nibbled at her breasts.

"Over-rated," he teased as they had sex in bed. She felt way too good. Way too addictive. She was all his. Every warm, throbbing muscle, every inch of her silky skin. All his.

When he came up for air, her phone went off. "Like I said. I hate phones."

He saw the call display and saw Addy's phone number pressing speakerphone. "Addy," Lily said as Emerson kissed down her torso.

"Hey. What time are we supposed to be there tomorrow," Addy asked.

"Whenever. We're sorta having Christmas just us in the morning. Maybe 11," Lily suggested.

Emerson nibbled and watched her get that much more turned on. "Is 10 alright?"

"Sure," Lily said as he licked and her toes curled.

"Emerson said he had a special surprise or something for me. I have no idea what he's up to. How are you and Mr. Happy sunshine," Addy asked.

"Good. Can I talk to you tomorrow? We're just getting stuff together."

"Sure. Hi Emerson," Addy said.

"Hi," he replied as he nibbled her inner thigh.

"I just bet that you two are gonna end up pregnant before the end of December. Have fun." Emerson smirked and they hung up just as they started having sex all over again.

The rest of the day, they were curled up together in bed while he told her about work and other plans he had. "You know, at some point I'm gonna want to actually see these other houses right," Lily asked.

"Just let me know when and we'll go Christen them," he teased.

"Do you ever get your mind out of the gutter?"

"Around my sexy wife? No."

"And what else is happening with work?"

"Well, I was kinda gonna tell you tomorrow, but an email came in you might want to read."

"About what?" He kissed her. He grabbed his phone and showed it to her:

> *We're interested in turning her new novel into a full-length film. If the books are going to be a series, we would be willing to do a three-book deal to be adapted to a film. Please let us know how she would feel about working on it with us.*

Lily looked at Emerson. "My book?"

"Books."

"Are you serious?" He nodded. "Emerson."

He kissed her again, devouring her lips. "I told you that everyone loves the book. It took a book tour and an email to convince you. Do you believe me now?"

Lily nodded and snuggled up to him as he pulled her legs around him. "Baby, you can do anything you set your mind to. Start trusting your husband." Lily nodded and they had sex again.

When they managed to come up for air, both of their stomachs were grumbling. "What time is it," Lily asked.

"5:30," he replied.

"Food."

"And we need to get ready for church." Lily almost laughed.

"You have a lot to confess husband."

"Ditto wife." She shook her head and they managed to get up. Lily went and slid into the shower and within minutes, he was in there with her, washing Lily's hair for her.

"I swear, if you start again, I'm not gonna be able to walk," Lily said.

"That's always an option."

"Not funny."

He kissed her, rinsing the shampoo from her hair. She washed his hair for him, then slid the conditioner in her hair. "Wife."

"Yes sexy husband."

"Promise me something."

"What?"

"That if you are, you tell me."

Lily kissed him. "I'm not."

He shook his head. "Just tell me." Lily nodded and snuggled him as he picked her up.

"Emerson." He smirked and slid her under the stream of water, rinsing her hair then his then walked over and sat down on the bench.

"What," Lily asked.

"Merry Christmas." She kissed him.

"Merry Christmas handsome."

By the time that they got back from church, they were both exhausted. They got changed for bed and curled up together on the bed and Emerson smirked.

"Would you cut it out," Lily teased.

"Was just gonna say that it's officially Christmas. You can open…"

She kissed him and he shook his head. Lily looked at the tree in the bedroom and he snuggled her to him. "I forgot something," Lily said.

"Which is what," he asked as Lily got up.

"You'll see in a minute," she joked as she grabbed the bow from the bag in her closet and told him to close his eyes.

"Babe."

"Do it," Lily said. He did and she came into the bedroom, sitting by the tree in nothing but the red bows.

"Okay. Come open your gift." He shook his head and saw her in three red bows. One around her chest, one around her hips and the last around her head.

"Well dang. I kinda love that present," he teased.

"Oh really," Lily said as he nodded and came over to her. He kneeled down and slid the bow from her hips down to her feet.

"I knew I should've waited until tomorrow night," Lily said. The one around her head slid off and he undid the one around her chest little by little. "Emerson." He kissed her and smirked. "What," Lily asked as he slid the one out from her feet and pulled her legs around him. "Emerson."

"I'm cherishing this moment. My wife as my present. Kind of love that idea."

"Behave."

"Never," he teased as he devoured her lips and made love to the best Christmas gifts that he'd ever got.

The next morning, Lily woke up to Emerson kissing her shoulder. "Husband."

"About time," he teased as his hand slid over her hip.

"I know what you're doing."

"Is it working," he said almost purring in her ear.

"Emerson." He kissed her neck and kept going, making her toes curl all over again. "Had to didn't you," Lily said as they came up for air.

"Most definitely had to. Every time I got close to you last night I was all hot and bothered," he teased.

"You know that we have to get out of bed right," Lily teased.

He kissed her shoulder. "I don't want to," he teased.

"Your folks, Addy and Carter and their folks plus my family. We kinda have to," Lily said.

He slid his arm around her and she linked their fingers, seeing the sparkling item on her finger. "Emerson."

"What?"

"Where did this platinum thing come from?"

"The skinny band one?"

She turned and looked at him. "Merry Christmas."

She kissed him. "Thank you handsome."

"I was gonna get a tracker put in it, but I thought it might get me put in the doghouse."

"It would've." He smirked.

"Alright party pooper, you ready for all of the insanity of my insane family Christmas?" Lily nodded.

They had a hot shower, got dressed and Emerson watched her slide into a red satin shirt and leather pants. "Damn," he said.

"What?"

"Yeah, I don't think that I can share you. We're gonna have to stay up here." Lily kissed him and put her red lipstick on.

"Wife, you're way too tempting," he said as Lily put her hair up. He kissed the back of her neck and she smirked.

"And," Lily asked.

"I do not want to share you today."

"Surprised you didn't request a skirt without anything under it."

He handed her the skirt. "Wear it," he asked. Lily shook her head.

"Not happening. You're behaving."

"We have 3 hours before anyone gets here. Put it on." She shook her head and he kissed her neck. She stood up and left the bedroom before they ended up back in bed. When they made it downstairs, a bunch of extra presents were under the tree.

"Where did those come from," Lily asked.

"Santa," Emerson teased. He walked into the kitchen, grabbing a few bags from the chair. He handed the housekeeper one, taking the rest into the security room, handing them out to everyone. When he came back in, his housekeeper was in tears.

"Sir," she said.

"Enjoy it. You deserve it," Emerson said as she plated the eggs benedict.

"This is too much," she said.

"You're family. You always have been," Emerson said.

He brought over the breakfast and his housekeeper brought over peach mimosas, putting them on the table and headed off.

"The roast will be done at 3. I put a timer on for it. Everything else is ready to go. Just has to be heated up. I put directions on the dishes."

"Thank you for all of this," Lily said.

"Most welcome and Merry Christmas," his housekeeper said.

"You too. Have a great holiday," Lily said as she gave the housekeeper a hug.

"Like the daughter I never had," the housekeeper said as she let go and headed out.

They had breakfast in peace and quiet and Emerson turned the music on. Lily cleaned up and he picked her up, walking her to the sofa. He sat her down and curled up with her as they had their mimosas. "You sure you're ready," he teased.

"For what?"

"All of it. A bunch of those have your name on them."

"And the other half have yours," Lily teased.

He kissed her. "I love you," he said.

"I love you too handsome."

He got up and grabbed a few for Lily and she grabbed a bunch that were for him. "Seriously," he asked.

"You didn't give me a single hint," Lily teased.

"And you did all of this?"

Lily nodded. She opened the first one and saw a bracelet.

"Emerson."

He smirked. "The one you kept staring at." She leaned over and kissed him and made him open his. When he opened it and saw a fancy pen that he'd always wanted, he looked at her. "Look at what it says." He saw the engraving:

For you to write love letters.

"Lily."

"Since you're gonna have meetings away from me." He kissed her. They opened a bunch of them, opening everything from a new iPhone for him, to new AirPods for her and a bunch of other things that were almost too much. The last one was intentionally hidden in the back.

"And where did you find that," he asked.

"Something for you from me."

He looked at her and shook his head. "I swear, if this is what I think it is…"

Lily kissed him and he opened it. When he saw what was in it, he looked at her.

"Lily."

"Husband."

"When did you do that," he asked seeing 3 pictures and a new wallet.

"When you were at work. Addy took them. She did photography in college." They were overly hot photos. Ones for his eyes only. He sat up and kissed her. "What," Lily asked.

"What time is it," he asked as she looked at her new Apple watch.

"8:45." He smirked, got up and picked her up, carrying her upstairs.

"Emerson."

"What?"

"We're having..." He kissed her and walked upstairs, kicking the door closed and leaning her onto the bed. He undid the leather pants, slid them off and peeled off the lacy panties that were underneath. "What," Lily asked.

He kissed her, devouring her lips. "All mine." He leaned into her arms and undid his jeans, kicking them off.

"Emerson, we..." He devoured her lips. One moment later, her toes were curling all over again. "They're coming Emerson." He kissed her again, devouring her lips until he was about to collapse. Her body throbbed around him and he held on a little tighter.

"Wear the skirt."

She shook her head. "I know what you're up to husband."

He kissed her again and smirked. "Good," he teased.

"So, you liked your presents," Lily said.

He nodded. "And you," he asked.

Lily nodded. "You went overboard as usual," she teased. He kissed her.

Addy and Carter showed at 10:30 and they hung out and visited for a while. "I have a few things for you," Lily said as she gave them each a few things from her and Emerson. When Addy opened the book and saw the dedication and what Lily had written, she almost burst into tears.

"I can't believe you did that," Addy said as Lily gave her a hug.

When Carter opened the gift from Emerson, he shook his head. "You didn't," Carter said.

"Being delivered on the 27th," Emerson said.

"I can't believe you," Carter said as he looked at the keys to the top-of-the-line Audi SUV that he had planned to get when he settled down.

"And I have something for you two," Addy said as she handed it to Emerson.

"What's this," Lily asked.

"Open it," Addy said as Emerson opened it. When he saw a baby sized falcons jersey, he looked at them.

"A baby jersey," Emerson asked.

Addy nodded. "There's something else," Addy said. He opened it and saw a sonogram photo that said 'Will you be my godparents'.

"Addy, are you saying what I think you are?"

Addy nodded. "We found out when I was sick. That's why I couldn't fly out to meet you," Addy said. Lily shook her head.

"Congrats mama," Emerson said as he went and gave Addy and Carter a hug.

"When's the due date," Lily asked.

"July 12th," Addy said.

Emerson smirked. "The anniversary of the day we got engaged," Emerson said.

Lily shook her head. "Alright, Carter, there's one there from me," Lily said as he opened it and Emerson curled up beside Lily. When he saw the tickets, he smirked.

"Thank you," Emerson said as he showed the tickets to Addy. It was a reservation for a spa near where they'd be staying for a massage for two.

"A little treat since you two are doing that end of the premiere," Emerson said.

"Thank you," Addy said.

"Most welcome. And there's one last one for you two," Carter said as he handed the box to Emerson.

"What did you do?"

"Just open the dang thing." Emerson opened it and saw a fancy bottle of whiskey that was a vintage and two glasses.

"You found one," Emerson asked.

Carter nodded. "Had to order it from the company, but yeah," Carter said.

"Thanks buddy," Emerson said.

"Most welcome."

"And thanks for inviting my folks," Addy said.

An hour or two later, the rest of the family showed. They went through a bunch of gifts, opened up almost everything under the tree and Emerson and Lily took care of the dinner together. When she went to check on the roast, Emerson snuck into the kitchen behind her. "I know what you're doing," Lily said as his arms wrapped around her and turned her to face him.

"Thank you," he said.

"For what? Making Christmas special?"

He nodded. "And for that other secret surprise that you gave me before they got here."

"You started it," she teased.

"And tonight neither of us are gonna get any sleep. You may not even be able to feel how tight those knots are in your toes," he whispered as he leaned her against the edge of the counter.

"Now you're just taunting." He nodded and devoured her lips.

He smirked. "I thought you had to leave," Lily said.

"They're going to the UK. You and I are doing the Cali part." Lily shook her head.

"You're going all alone."

He shook his head. "Nope."

"Yep. I'm staying with Addy."

He kissed her and whispered. "You're coming in more ways than one wife."

He smirked and they got the dinner together. They intentionally ate around 4:30. He wanted them gone and to be upstairs in bed with his wife.

They relaxed, had a nice dinner and even dessert. "Staying home is almost better than being so far away isn't it," Emerson said as he slid his hand under the table and slid it up Lily's leg.

"It was very relaxing. Thank you for having everyone," his mom said.

"You're most welcome. It's kind of nice to have it at home," Emerson said.

"Very," Lily replied. Everyone finally started heading out, leaving them in an empty house. Lily put all the dishes into the washer and he came up behind her. "What," Lily asked. She turned to face him and he sat her on the countertop, wrapping her legs around him. "What would you like husband?"

He kissed her. "Thank you for all of this."

"You have two more to open," Lily said.

"Where? All the ones under the tree were unwrapped." Lily shook her head.

"Lily."

"Go look if you don't believe me."

Emerson walked upstairs and saw two boxes under the tree. "Lily."

"Go open them."

"What else was there to even get me?"

"Go look," Lily said as he shook his head and kissed her. She kissed him and went and took the makeup off, changing into a lace chemise that had red bows all over it. He wasn't even watching when she came out of her closet.

"Lily."

"Husband."

"Come sit with me while I open..."

"What," Lily asked.

"Damn."

"Open it," Lily said.

"Which one," he asked.

"The box in your lap."

He opened it and saw a faux fur blanket that was red. "I like," he teased.

"I know."

"And what's the other one," he asked as Lily handed it to him and sat down beside him. "Do I want to know what you hid in here," he asked.

"Open it," Lily said as she curled up beside him.

"No, you didn't," he said as he saw the label. "Isn't that..." he slid her legs across his lap. "

You said that you wanted one." He shook his head, seeing the iPhone.

"Turn it on," Lily said.

He kissed her. "What did you do?"

"That's why your phone didn't ring all day," Lily teased. He turned it on and the screen in it was one of the hotter pictures that she hadn't given him. He looked at her then looked at the photo.

"You seriously did that?" Lily nodded and slid into his lap.

"Like your present?"

"More red bows?"

He devoured her lips and slid the lacy nothing right off.

"What," Lily asked.

He shook his head and pulled his shirt off then went for his pants. He kicked them and his boxers off, kicking them to the floor and pulled her on top of him. "You, wife, are the most amazing woman in the entire world. Nobody even got in a fight."

Lily smirked. "And what did you want to do now? Sleep," Lily teased knowing that he'd had his fair share of alcohol. He shook his head and pulled her tight to him. He was more than just hot and bothered. They had sex. He kept going until they were on the floor in front of the fireplace and still going. When they managed to come up for air, there were only embers left.

"Damn," he said.

"Emerson."

"Wife."

"You okay?" He kissed down the back of her neck and then down her back.

"Better than okay. I get this sexy woman all to myself."

He leaned on top of her. "Em..."

He kissed her again, devouring her lips and pulled out one of the gifts he'd got her.

"What are you doing?"

"Showing you your toy," he teased as she heard a buzzing. When she felt it against her leg, she shook her head.

"Emerson."

"Wife," he said as it taunted her until her legs were shaking again. He picked her up and carried her to bed, continuing the taunting until her legs were shaking and her toes had turned into pretzels. He kissed her and they curled up on the bed and fell asleep.

The next morning, he woke up and she wasn't in bed. He shook his head, pulled his joggers on and heard her sick. "Lily."

"Yep."

"You alright?"

"Just nauseous."

"Babe."

"Don't. We overdid it yesterday. That's why I wasn't drinking," Lily said.

"You sure that there wasn't another reason?"

"Of course that's what you think."

"You sure you aren't?" Lily shook her head and kissed him. "You coming to workout?"

Lily nodded and they walked downstairs and went and did a quick workout together. When they came upstairs, he made them breakfast and Lily made him a latte with his new espresso maker. "Where's yours?"

Lily looked at him. "I'm having juice."

He shook his head. "You sure you're not thinking what I am?"

"Have your coffee and your food," Lily said. He kissed her, handed her the omelet with spinach, and kissed her.

They had breakfast alone together. There were no interruptions, no phone calls interfering, and nothing to stand in the way of them just relaxing. They curled up and he made a fire in the fireplace. "You sure you don't want to take a test?"

Lily shook her head. "Not right now I don't. It's just running around all day and all the stress from yesterday. Beyond that I'm fine," Lily said.

"There's a lot of reason for you to be pregnant. I mean, you and I..."

"I know what you're about to say. I'll check after New Year's."

He kissed her and snuggled her to him, curling up on the sofa with her as he flipped on a movie on his new TV.

"I still find it amazing that you hid the TV in behind the other one."

"That was sort of planned by security. They thought it was a good idea," Lily joked.

"Did you like your surprises," he teased.

Lily nodded. "You did good handsome."

"By the way, that thing last night...it stays with you."

"Meaning?"

"If I go without you…" Lily shook her head.

By the time he left to head to LA, he had figured out another surprise. The toy he'd bought had a way for him to control it from a distance. He loved it. Lily just played along. The morning he left, Lily went and did the test. She didn't want him in the middle of it. When she got the result, her jaw hit the floor. Telling him when he wasn't home wasn't going to be an option either.

******

Emerson came home and Lily had a grin ear to ear and intentionally met him at the airport. He ran into her arms like he'd been gone for months. "I missed you," he said.

"I know. You and your toys," Lily teased. He kissed her and they hopped into the SUV and headed home. "What," Lily asked.

"He moved up the premiere in Charleston."

"To when? It's like the 19th of January this weekend."

"It's Saturday night."

"Seriously? You just got home."

"I know. He was going to do it later, but Mia hasn't been feeling well." Lily shook her head.

A few days later, the premiere day had come. She was beyond nauseous but managed to hide it from Emerson. Instead, they ended up bickering. She slid into the dress and didn't like how it looked. She almost hoped she could find a way out of it, or at least get him alone for a while. "What are we doing then?"

"Going to the premiere."

"I was kinda thinking we could just go away somewhere."

"I can't do that. You know that."

"Fine."

"I need my wife with me at this."

"Then we go after. I just want to be somewhere away from everyone like we talked about last year."

"I can't. It's way past busy now. You're gonna end up busy too."

"Maybe I'll just go away on my own then," Lily said teasing.

"Lily. You know how busy I get at work. I can't leave."

"All I'm saying is that I wanted to go away somewhere alone. I don't want phones there. I just want us to go away."

"And I have a film premiere to go to. I'm not going anywhere. It can wait," Emerson said as he put his suit on.

Lily slid into a dress that he almost drooled over. She slid into her heels, did her hair and makeup and they headed off. They made their way to the carpet and Lily saw all of the security and fans that were there. It was too much for her. Way too much. Emerson talked with the press a little and was in his element. Lily went and got a soda and got

Emerson a double shot of Jack. When he came over to her, she handed him the drink. "I was wondering where you vanished to," he said as he took her hand and walked her into the theater.

They sat down to watch the film and Emerson raised the arm rest between them. "You okay," he asked. Lily nodded, trying to say what she wanted to really say.

"What's wrong?" Lily kissed him and rested her head on his shoulder. At that point, telling him wasn't happening. Until she knew she was in the clear, she wasn't telling him anything.

The more she watched, the more she was in tears and snuggling with Emerson. When the film finished, they headed off quickly, ducking out ahead of the rest of the crowd and made their way back to the house. "I know something's going on baby. Tell me what's going on."

She shook her head. "It's fine."

"Lily." She shook her head.

He slid her to him. "Tell me." Lily shook her head and stared out the windows at the live oaks that they passed by. He took her hand when they got to the house and walked in. "What," Lily asked.

He picked her up and carried her upstairs. "Tell me what's wrong," Emerson said.

She shook her head. "I need to get away."

"Where?"

"Somewhere just you and me. Alone."

"Like where?"

"Even if it's the beach."

He kissed her. "Lily, I'll take you to the beach. Tell me what you want. Tell me what's going on."

"We're going tomorrow." She had a plan.

The next morning, they woke up and after a quick breakfast, they went out to the beach. It wasn't warm, but he didn't care. Either did she. "Come," Lily said.

"Where are we going," he asked.

"Walk with me," Lily said as they headed outside. They walked down the beach to where they'd seen each other that night. Where he'd written his phone number on her hand. Where he'd wanted to kiss her and steal her away from Zack.

"Babe, why are we all the way down here?"

"Emerson, just come with me." They got to the spot and Lily sat down. He sat down beside her and kissed her.

"What's wrong baby? Just tell me."

"The day that we bumped into each other here, I had no idea who you were. I could barely even see you. There was just something about you at that moment."

"And then this beautiful woman that I saw in a men's dress shirt. I thought you were a mirage. I'm still stunned that I found you."

"And then that night, you showed at the house and had me giggling like a teenager," Lily said.

"That's how I knew that I had the woman of my dreams. I wanted to carry you to bed and remind you that I loved you."

"And I said then that I thought I was in love. Addy laughed because she recognized you before I figured it out."

"So, why the walk literally down memory lane?"

Lily took a deep breath. "That day, I had no idea what was going to happen. I just knew I wanted it to be with you. When we got married, you turned it into a dang fairytale. Now, I get to surprise you."

"Babe, I love you, but you're making me nervous." She handed Emerson a box. "What's this?"

"From before we got together." He opened it and saw a sample of the cologne he wore in high school. He shook his head.

"Lily."

"Keep going." He saw a photo of the first movie they'd seen, the first concert they went to together, the first dance ticket, then saw the note that he'd given her at prom.

"Lily."

"Keep going." He saw the first note he had given her when they were at the house and he'd gone to do a workout. He looked at her.

"Emerson."

He saw a printout of the first text he'd sent, the card from the first flowers, then came the wrapper from the first condom they'd used. "How in the world?"

"Keep going."

"Lily."

"I've been sentimental since high school. You know that." He kissed her. When he got to the bottom, there was a note in an envelope. He looked at it and opened it:

> *We've squabbled like an old married couple since we were kids. I've loved you since that first moment in this spot. How fitting that the next part of our lives starts here too. – Lily*

"Meaning what," he asked.

"Keep opening." He kissed her and saw another envelope. Inside was a picture of a baby sock. He kissed her again.

"Baby, this is too much," he said.

"There's something else in there," Lily said.

He kissed her and pulled her into his lap. "What's going on," he asked.

"Keep opening." The last thing in the box was another envelope.

"Lily."

"Open." He took the envelope out and looked at her.

"You know you don't need to do all of this right?"

"Open it." He smirked and opened it.

It was multiple pages intentionally. The pages said:

First came friends

Then came love

Then came prom.

After prom came Charleston

Then came the first kiss

Then came moving in

And putting a ring on it.

The Barefoot Billionaire became my husband.

The only way

To make it even better

Is to know

That this little

Surprise is

All you've ever wanted.

The final page of the list had a sonogram photo on it. He looked at her. "Lily."

"What?"

"You know what this is right?"

"A photo."

"It's a sonogram photo."

"I know. I put it in there."

"We didn't have..." He looked at her.

"What?"

"We didn't have this last..."

When he looked at the photo and saw the date, he looked at her. "Are we?"

"Are we what?"

"Lily, are we....are we...are we having..."

Lily nodded. "Seriously?"

Lily nodded and her eyes welled up. "We're actually pregnant?"

"9 weeks."

"So, before Christmas you knew?"

"I had a feeling about Addy. I didn't want to destroy her thunder." He kissed her again...sitting in the same spot where he'd kissed her that first time. In the same spot where she'd fell in love with him all over again.

****

In August that year, in the midst of a rainstorm on the beach, Lily handed Emerson the only thing he'd always wanted, that he'd never been able to have. When Addy and Carter showed, Emerson smirked.

"Lily."

"Meet Faith Addison Cartwright," Emerson said as he brushed a tear away and put their baby girl in Addy's arms.

"I brought something for you," Addy said as Carter handed Emerson a bag.

"What's this," Emerson asked.

He slid a blanket out of the bag and smirked. Lily almost laughed. "One kiss and that blanket," Emerson joked.

"And I was all yours," Lily said as Emerson kissed her. The blanket that had been on the sofa in their condo that night that Emerson had shown up was now in his hands.

"That's where you two re-started time," Addy said. Lily hugged her and the parents started coming in little by little.

The barefoot billionaire became the best dad in the world, full of the best hugs, the most love, and had the two loves of his life in his arms. His dream woman, became his dream wife, and his dream wife made him become an amazing dad. The one that Faith could run to with every tear, every fear, and every happy moment. He loved his little family. Even when it gained two more babies, he never ever forgot how it all started, where it all started and why.

THE END